SPRINGTIDE
HARVEST

D1824595

J.D. MITCHELL

Published by J.D. Mitchell
www.jdmitchellwriter.com

Copyright © 2022 J.D. Mitchell

Book and cover design by the author

ISBN: 978-1-778-13022-9 (paperback)
ISBN: 978-1-778-13023-6 (e-book)

For my beloved Jenny, who wanted more juice.

ACKNOWLEDGEMENTS

It takes a village to write a novel, at least it did for me. I want to thank that community, my friends, for their support:

- ♥ My wife for reading endlessly;
- ♥ My siblings for the worlds we explored;
- ♥ My oldest friends, whose adventures formed this realm;
- ♥ Michael Santerre for the reassurance;
- ♥ Sue Cook and Lisa Kannegiesser Short for beta reading;
- ♥ Kat Howard for her editorial assistance;
- ♥ Jessica Gibson and Paula Wescott for proofreading;
- ♥ And all my friends from Write Around the Block for helping me down a long and winding road.

MAP OF FORNBRAD, LANESFORD, AND NEIGHBOURING LANDS

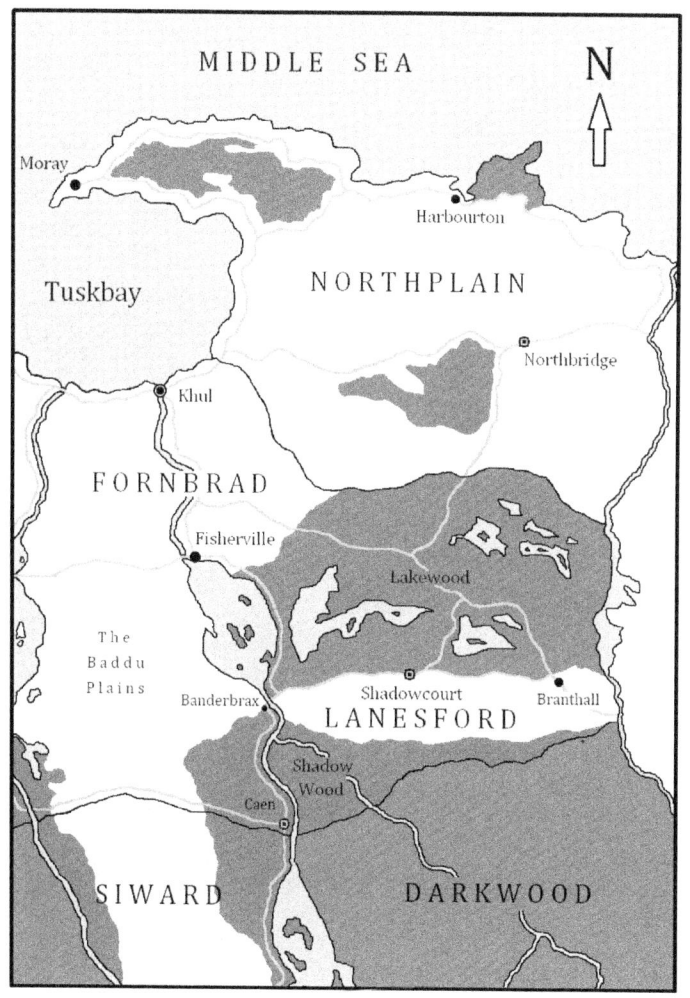

MIDDLE SEA

N

Moray

Harbourton

NORTHPLAIN

Tuskbay

Northbridge

Khul

FORNBRAD

Fisherville

Lakewood

The
Baddu
Plains

Banderbrax

Shadowcourt

Branthall

LANESFORD

Shadow
Wood

Caen

SIWARD

DARKWOOD

CONTENTS

April 1

Chapter I—Rake's Progress

Haskell fled the dockside tavern with the girl in tow. He led her, laughing, across the shadowy quay to an alcove in a stone-fronted warehouse. Her face was stained a ghostly blue in the light of an arcane lamppost, its dancing azure flame held within a twisted iron frame. She was beautiful, and her eyes sparkled with desire.

If only he could remember her name.

Gwen? Keila? He was so good with names but couldn't remember hers. "Admit it," he whispered. "You're a nymph crawled from the sea to tempt me." He stooped and brushed his lips along the slope of her neck.

She giggled and gazed at him greedily, lacing her delicate fingers over his bloody knuckles, cut against the bony face of a sailor in the tavern. Sailors didn't like tall Southron folk, even one born in the High City. The girl, though, didn't seem like a regular of such seedy dockside establishments. She had nursed her drink, not gulped it, and the weave of her dress was too fine; not as fine as Haskell's white tunic or short, oxblood surcoat, but neither was it commoner's rough-spun. No, she had to be a shopkeeper's daughter out for a bit of adventure.

He was happy to oblige.

"I... never—" she began. He drew her close and kissed her, grabbed a fistful of her hair, and kissed her throat. She moaned, her breath hot in his ear, and fumbled for his belt. He slid his hand up her skirt. Her eagerness was an elixir to him, a validation he could find nowhere else.

"Feckless scoundrel. I knew I would find you here," Master Slade said, his reedy voice dripping with venom.

Haskell sneered over his shoulder, his passion sinking like a man drowning at sea. The girl gasped and huddled against him.

Master Slade, bent by age, wore a mantle of dignity over his fine robes and a look of contempt on his sagging face. Behind him, the tidy rigging of moored ships glowed in the lamplight like the corded webs of titanic spiders. "Imbecile. I told you to work out those invoices by moonrise."

The girl ran. Haskell reached for her, but the silver pommel of Slade's cane rang off the wall in front of him. She vanished around the corner.

"Damn it, Master, she—"

"Was your true love? I suppose you left your coin purse in the tavern?"

Haskell clutched the cut purse-strings at his waist. He grinned. She was good but hadn't needed to rob him; he would have taken her anywhere, bought her anything just to have her. It didn't matter if her desire was hollow, that she gave it at all was enough.

Slade's cane hammered Haskell's jaw, the pain a flash of light and a vibratory thud. He went sprawling onto the cobbled street. Slade shook his cane in Haskell's face. "You bring only shame on your family, waste every opportunity—"

"Opportunistic thievery," Haskell muttered while fingering his jaw.

"What?" Slade growled.

"Usurers and moneylenders have nothing on you, *Master*. I delivered your message to Joshua, that was enough work for me." The memory was bitter: old Joshua's chin trembling with indignation as he crumpled Slade's message. In a fortnight, his ships would be auctioned to pay debts that had come due at just the wrong moment. Slade had arranged everything as neatly as his ledgers, and Haskell's father had bribed the right people. It was a brilliantly contemptible scheme.

Haskell looked out over the mirrored water of the bay. Khul, the High City, was overflowing with corrupt merchants and preening, backbiting nobles. The cheating, the gossip, the thievery cloaked as business; it was a game they happily played with other people's lives.

The thought of returning to his cramped office and hunching over the tiny desk in Slade's rat-infested warehouse, of enduring the incessantly dripping ceiling—each drip a steady measure of his wasted youth—was too much. Penning today's transactions would make the sordid business real; worse, it would make him indelibly complicit. He wouldn't do it. Not tonight. Maybe never again.

Slade looked skyward and sighed. "It's Joshua's fault—I can't be held responsible for the fool's lack of fiscal foresight. Have I taught you nothing? Gods know I've tried where your father failed."

"Father's nothing. My grandfather—"

"Your grandfather was a shiftless rake, like you."

"My grandfather was a hero. He broke the orcs. They wrote songs about him. You and father are cowards. Cheats." He pointed to the corner around which the girl had fled. "At least she had the courage to face her mark, not rob him via messenger."

Slade drove his cane into Haskell's chest, its silvered end

driving between his ribs, as if the grizzled shipwright was trying to pierce Haskell's heart. "I will beat sense into you, boy, or kill you trying."

Something splintered inside Haskell. Not in his head or chest—something lower. Deeper. A creeping fire filled him, its heat making him shake and filling his mouth with ferric rage. He looked up, slowly, along the haft of Slade's polished cane, past the wrinkled, calloused hands, and into the old man's hateful eyes. The iron heat only grew.

He swept Slade's cane aside, the implement clattering away into the night, and rose above his shrinking master. Haskell became a puppet of rage, his limbs jerked to violence by strings of loathing. In a half-crazed moment, he repaid years of Slade's brutality. He struck his old master without thought of consequence, only justice, and in a heady outpouring of hate, drove him to the water's edge.

And over the side.

* * *

Haskell ran uphill. He didn't know how he got there, only that he had left behind the squalor of the docks. He was surrounded by the stately homes of merchants and artisans: foothills of opulence below soaring granite mansions, each a pale mountain in the light of the waxing gibbous moon.

He stole into a cobbled backyard and glanced around, breathing hard and massaging his throbbing jaw. At least the shaking had stopped. The old bastard was probably alive. Probably. Part of him didn't care, but the City Guard would. They would be after him soon.

He crept to a shed abutting the house's back wall and gazed at a dark, second-storey window. It was high, but he could reach it. He had before. Its owner was a trader who had risen to prominence on the necks of better men and women: Haskell's father. Everyone would be asleep.

He clambered onto the shed, its mossy, slanted roof creaking under his weight. Reaching up, he blindly worked his stiletto between the windowsill and catch. He twisted the slim blade up and down, left and right, the window groaning as cold steel splintered old wood. A sharp crack echoed in the yard as the blade and latch broke.

The jolt caused his heel to splinter the weather-softened roof, and he tipped backward. Flailing for balance, he caught the frame with his fingertips, gripping the carved stone with his nails to stay upright. He steadied himself, looked at the fractured dagger, and swore. The stiletto had been a gift from his sister when he left to apprentice under Slade. She had been his only ally in the family after their mother died, the only one to treat him with anything but scorn. He set the broken dagger on the shed's roof. None of that mattered now.

He hauled himself up, held his taut body in place with one forearm, and pushed the window open with the other. He reached into the room and tumbled inside. His heel rattled the frame and his arm collided with a side table, knocking a heavy wood carving onto the floor with a bang. He grimaced but remained still.

Nothing stirred in the house.

He pulled himself up by the edge of a large mahogany desk. His father had stacked ledgers on the desktop, one slim volume open for review over morning mead. How many times had he faced the disapproving man over that desk? A hundred; a thousand? He rifled the desk drawers, taking in the study as he worked. Two wing-backed chairs faced the desk at a fastidious angle and the walls were lined with glass-fronted bookshelves, everything meticulously arranged to convey wealth and authority.

Only he couldn't find the bloody wealth.

"Where is it?" he hissed while rattling the last locked

drawer. It had to be inside. He growled and swept the stack of ledgers to the floor.

Haskell stalked to the wall, from which he took a long sword in a battered scabbard. He drew the weapon, pausing to admire its sharp, oiled blade in the pale moonlight. He ran his thumb over the cross-guard, its metal worn by his grandfather's hand, and admired the protective runes inscribed along the blade and the blood-red garnets in its pommel. Haskell, Son of Eskil the Younger, Son of Eskil Orc-breaker. A proud lineage, at least from the outside.

He reversed the sword and worked its tip into the locked drawer.

"I don't think grandfather would take kindly to you abusing his sword, though he would approve of your motive," his older sister chided from the doorway.

Haskell glanced up and frowned; though of all the household, he was glad it was Hilda. Her dark braid trailed down the front of a fine silk nightgown. Her face was hard, but her eyes sparkled with amusement, like she was silently laughing at a private joke. They undercut, very slightly, the cold precision she inherited from their father. She gripped a long dagger in her right hand and looked more than capable of using it.

"Where's the bastard keep his coin?" he demanded.

"Our *father* keeps his coin in that very drawer, but I will not have you ruin such fine furniture."

Hilda padded across the carpet and took Haskell's chin in her left hand, turning his face to examine his bruised jaw in the moonlight. At six feet, she was taller than most men, but Haskell had surpassed her years ago. She shook her head and pushed his chin aside. "Four years of apprenticeship to a worthy shipwright, yet you persist in your disobedience. Or was this another backroom brawl?"

Haskell scowled at her insight as much as her respect for

Slade. "Worthy? He teaches more about brutality than ships."

Hilda sighed. "The world is harder than your master's cane."

"I know that."

"You know nothing," she muttered. "Father—"

"Is a coward."

Hilda shook her head. "He is hard but sensible. You, however, bludgeon your way through life. The world will never match your naïve view of it, Haskell." She swept across the room and opened a bookcase. Running a finger along the spines, she removed a volume on noble houses and retrieved a small silver key hidden between its pages. She tossed the key to Haskell. "This is a mistake and the last time I help you."

He caught the key and scowled. "It's different for you—you're his favourite. You play his games. I…" He kicked a piece of chalk that had fallen on the floor; it skittered past the carving he had toppled. Fangs filled the oaken dragon's gaping jaws, its tongue curling up to lick its nose. Intricately carved knotted lines formed its scales, paint clinging to the recesses. Its raised surfaces were hard worn by the wind and waves of the briny sea.

Haskell had adored the heavy sculpture as a child, had run his little fingers over its details. He had imagined the prow it once adorned, the fierce raiders crowding the deck of its longship. He would sneak into his father's office, take down his grandfather's heavy sword, and dream of life outside the city, of winning renown fighting orcs and trolls. He had begged to be told tales of how his grandfather had ceased raiding to fight, of his battles and adventures, his highs and lows, but Haskell's father wouldn't spoil his boy with worthless words or wasted affection. His family wanted to bury their past. They were merchants now, not brigands. He heard those very words in his father's disdainful baritone.

He picked up the carving in both hands and set it on the open ledger, its weight crinkling the fine paper. He stooped and inserted the silver key into the locked drawer. It turned with a heavy, well-oiled click.

"You cannot stay in the city after this," Hilda said. "What life will you make for yourself?"

He lifted a sturdy leather pouch from the drawer, heavy with gold and silver that clinked softly inside. "I'll go to the borderlands with one of the caravans. To Branthall. I'll be out of Father's reach there and sign on with the Questers Guild."

Hilda scoffed. "As a mercenary? There is no glory left in the borderlands. The old wars are over, and the Questers Guild is a relic for drunks and failures."

Haskell rammed his grandfather's sword into its scabbard. "Then I should fit right in. I'll make my fortune honestly, fighting Darkwood monsters like grandfather did."

"You only know half his story. Grandfather could be cruel, especially to Father."

Haskell buckled on the sword and pouch. "You and Father wouldn't tell me."

"He fears you will become his father. You're certainly wilful enough."

Haskell put one leg through the open window and sat heavily on the sill. She didn't understand. How could she? They didn't want the same things. He didn't fit in her world.

"What will you do when you run out of coin?" she asked.

Haskell slapped his thighs and flashed her a cheerful smile. "I'll just keep the coin flowing."

Hilda laughed despite herself. "You're a fool, Haskell."

"Don't let Father miss me too much." He flashed an impish grin and slipped away.

"He will only miss his coin," she said.

Haskell jogged through deserted moonlit streets. He had

to get through the gates before word of his theft and assault spread. With one hand on his new pouch and the other steadying his sword, he was sure of only two things: the road would be long, and there was no going back.

April 2

Chapter II—Bodies in Motion

Haskell peered out of the roadside inn's bay window, its warped glass turning the tree-lined highway into a twisted caricature of stones and branches and sky. No doubt about it, a rider was approaching. Haskell heard hooves clopping over weathered cobbles laid by the slaves of a long dead empire. He had hurried over those same stones all night and day, chased by the spectre of a vengeful posse or messenger sent to raise a hue and cry against him.

The rider drew closer. Their armour gleamed in the light of the lowering sun.

Haskell downed his beer and gripped the worn old pack, bedroll, and supplies he had bought from the innkeeper. If he had to run, he would run. If he had to fight…

A line of people came behind the rider: a train of walkers, riders, wagons, and carriages travelling along the wide river swollen by winter melt and spring rain. A caravan so soon? What luck! They must have set out shortly after he did. But then, had they heard about him? He had bribed the gate guards to forget they had seen him, but they wouldn't stand up to any sort of questioning.

He rose, stooping to avoid the broad beams overhead, and turned to the bulbous-nosed innkeeper hunched over the counter. "You're in luck, a caravan just arrived."

"Bless th' gods. Are there rich merchants among 'em?" she said.

Haskell nearly choked. Of course there were; merchants of Khul setting out to ply their trade for the season. He was such an idiot. He cleared his throat and crossed to the bar, trying to force an air of calm over his rising panic. He looked down a hallway and through the open back door to a stand of bare poplars beyond the yard. "I think I'll go for a stroll, good lady," he said cheerfully.

The innkeeper let out a bronchial laugh. "Lady, he says. Have you decided if you'll be needin' a bed tonight, *my lord?*" she said with a toothless grin. "You'll be in fine comp'ny, I'm sure—rubbin' elbows in a big bed with a few rich merchants. Could be some profit in it for a bright young lad."

Haskell started down the hall, his blistered heels and toes chafing inside boots that felt full of blood. He had never walked so far in his life and wanted nothing more than to lay down on a nice, soft straw mattress; but discretion demanded otherwise. "Don't hold a spot on my account. The weather's fine enough to sleep outside."

"It'll be as cold as a devil's behind come nightfall, but suit yourself," she said doubtfully.

Haskell crossed the yard, the weathered brown cloak for which he had overpaid billowing behind as he made the stand of poplars. He drew up his patched, dark green hood and crouched behind an evergreen shrub, the tip of his scabbard digging a channel in the wet earth. A warrior in a suit of steel plate rode toward the inn atop a dappled white charger.

He looked absolutely regal; his brass-traced armour glowed in the failing light and a fine crimson cloak billowed from his shoulders. Haskell imagined himself in the warrior's place, only leading a fighting company against fearsome Darkwood monsters. He laid a hand on his pouch. Soon.

A youth slightly younger than Haskell cantered by astride a tall bay mare. He was dressed in a velvet tunic dyed a vibrant sapphire blue; his fitted, well-oiled boots shone in the sun and the fine gold chain about his shoulders clinked with every bounce of his steed. The mare was huge, at least fifteen hands (five feet) from hoof to withers. Struggling to keep up was a fat merchant bedecked in an embarrassment of gold, the metal jouncing and jostling conspicuously as he rode a smaller but spectacularly glossy black stallion.

All three passed in front of the inn. Haskell did not recognize any of them, though there was something naggingly familiar about the large merchant, who matched the youth. He suspected they were father and son.

Minutes later, Ethan, the innkeeper's lame, middle-aged son with a face covered in boils, came limping into the yard. He held the reins of the charger and stallion, which he began to cool down.

Haskell slipped through the trees to inspect the rest of the caravan. He might be able to travel with them after all. There was no shortage of merchants in the kingdom, and his father's circle were a chiefly seafaring lot, and not all of them knew Haskell, Eskil's shame. No, it was the caravan or nothing. While the land hereabout might be relatively safe, strolling alone through the Lakewood laden with treasure was a fine way to buy a shallow grave.

He broke from the trees with his head down and pack over one shoulder. Walking back along the road, he scanned the travellers' tired faces as they hurried to get a good spot close to the inn. The caravan was large—maybe one hundred people. He saw guards, traders, farmers, shepherds, messengers;

no one he recognized. His excitement grew.

He approached a messenger standing by a chestnut horse. The man wore the red and black livery of a noble and had well-oiled and turned-out gear. Haskell wished he had paid attention during heraldry lessons. "Ho, friend. What news from Khul? You set out, what, this morning?"

"As soon as the sun broke the horizon," the messenger said.

"All's quiet in the city?"

"As quiet as ever. A child was struck down and killed by a cart this morning."

"Ah, that's a shame. Anything happening around the docks? My sister lives that way, and I don't get into the city as much as I should."

The messenger shrugged. "Things are always a bit rough dockside, but I haven't heard anything unusual. Sorry I can't tell you more."

Haskell shut his eyes and sighed, a wave of relief washing away his tension and anxiety. Word of his crimes hadn't reached them.

"I'm sure she's fine, especially if she's as sturdy as you," the messenger said, mistaking Haskell's relief for worry.

"You're right, she can handle herself," Haskell said with a wry grin. "Your caravan's captain—he's the one I saw at the head of the line?"

"Yes, Captain Nedir. I saw him go into the inn, which is where I'm headed. Come along if you like. I'll take a bed as long as one's on offer—it's a long way to Siward."

Haskell clapped the messenger's arm. "You poor bastard. Let me buy you a beer."

It was getting smoky in the inn, which was packed with the wealthiest travellers. They were smoking, drinking, eating, and talking of trade and politics. Haskell kept his hood up just in case. He kept fidgeting with the hilt of his sword, which was in front of him on a corner table.

"So, you want to join up? Know how to use that long-sword?" Captain Nedir asked. Divested of armour and wearing a worn pair of hose and a belted, midnight-blue jacket, Nedir still struck an impressive figure. Much shorter than Haskell, he was broad-chested and strong-backed, his body moulded by the tools and deeds of a lifetime of soldiering. His face and hands were scarred from countless duels, and his brown eyes seemed to look right through Haskell.

Haskell became keenly aware of his inexperience, of how his battered sword had seen more combat. He routinely passed for a boyish man, could boast and carouse with the best of them, and gods knew he could hold his own in a fight, but not on a battlefield. He had the sudden urge to apologize, push the sword across the table, and leave. Eskil's sword belonged to a real warrior, not him. What did blood count for in the face of Nedir's poise and experience?

Haskell fought down his mad, fearful urges. "I had some lessons in Khul but learned more in its streets," he said with all the conviction he could muster. He raised his mug to display the recent scabs and old scars on his right hand.

Nedir's gaze briefly flitted to Haskell's hand and a wry grin crossed his lips.

Haskell sipped his beer and gazed at the patrons reflected in the warped windowpanes.

"What's your name, son?" Nedir asked.

This was it: if Nedir had heard of Haskell's crimes or he was recognized by someone in the room, it was over. He made to speak but choked on his drink, rising from his chair, and launching into a fit of wet coughs.

"Easy there," Nedir said, rising to slap him on the back.

Haskell felt ten years old. He sat down and pushed himself deeper into the corner. Clearing his throat and drinking more beer, he tried to ignore the curious looks and derisive laughs from the other patrons.

"Boy can't hold his spirits!" the fat, blue-velveted merchant bellowed from the opposite corner. His son craned his neck to gawk at Haskell. The youth's mirth was plain, but something else was in his expression. Was it recognition?

Haskell took a deep breath. He had to get it together; he was better than this. He straightened and tried to assume a carefree manner, chuckling at his own awkwardness. "I'm Haskell, Eskil's Son," he said with a cough.

Nedir's brows knit together. He scrutinized Haskell's sword: its garnet-encrusted pommel, worn guard, and the rune-inscribed throat of its scabbard. He cocked his head and regarded Haskell. "That would make you the Orc-breaker's great-grandson?"

"Grandson. I am son of Eskil, Eskil's son."

"Hm, I had you pegged as a thief fleeing the law with a stolen sword."

Haskell laughed a little too eagerly. His relief was overwhelming. Slade and Haskell's father were careful; they might even hush up Haskell's crimes to maintain respectability. His father was probably counting his blessings to be rid of his profligate son.

"Where are you headed?" Nedir said.

Haskell glanced up. "Hm? Oh, to Lanesford and Branthall. I want to become a Quester."

Nedir chuckled. "Young and foolhardy. There's no shortage of questers headed south to fight, even in these peaceable times. Our itinerary takes us through the Lakewood to Branthall. I'm surprised you didn't sign on with us in Khul."

Haskell shifted uncomfortably. "Yes, well, I thought it

would be more adventurous to set out alone. I thought better of it after a day's travel."

"Good. There are enough dangers on the road, even for a well-guarded caravan. You should join my company. We head to Shadowcourt from Branthall—you could see Old King Ferd."

"Thank you, but I want a company like my grandfather. To finish what he started, you could say."

"You want it all in one go, eh? Careful you don't get more than you can handle."

Haskell expected hard fights, dark dungeons, and trackless wilderness. What more could there be? "Did you fight in the Darkwood, Captain?"

"I did my time in that forest—it is aptly named."

Haskell frowned at Nedir's vague answer. "I can't wait. I've dreamt of fighting the old enemy since I was a boy. Khul's politics and double-dealing are too much for me."

"You'll find Lanesford a different place now, Haskell. It's a hard place full of hard people. There's little glory left in the borderlands."

"You sound like my sister."

"She sounds wise. Vagabonds and Guild-traitors dog my caravans now, not monsters of old. In that regard alone do I miss the war; the common purpose."

"Guild-traitors?"

"Those who have violated the tenets of the Questers Guild. Rogue Questers, you might call them. Or bandits. They fight for themselves and take what they want."

Haskell nodded. "I'm equal to the danger."

Nedir gave him a long look and smiled. "Have it your way, son. You will learn, as I did." He leaned back. "You can travel with us and eat with the other guards so long as you help mind the caravan, but I can't pay you."

Haskell nodded. The security of a caravan and food for the journey? It was more than he had hoped for.

Nedir signalled the innkeeper's son for another drink. "A word of advice, Haskell. Stay out of Branthall politics. There's more intrigue in that town than a weak king's court."

April 4

Chapter III—Mean Streets

Froba was hungry. *Really* hungry. She clutched her grumbling tummy through a tattered, two-seasons-too-small tunic, its left sleeve parted from the shoulder and frayed hem getting uncomfortably short. She sat on the trampled earth at the end of a narrow alley, hugged her scabby knees, and gazed listlessly at the mud-caked wattle-and-daub wall across from her.

The afternoon was wearing on and Branthall's shops were closing. She listened to the echoing footsteps of people walking down cobbled Main Street at the alley's far end. They were headed to the inn and Questers Guild outside Southgate. Froba's territory.

The long winter was over, and the ground was finally hardening. Scores of fighters, thieves, wizards, and mercenaries would soon campaign into the wilds. That required new arms and armour, mended gear, provisioning, and a host of other transactions: the business of war. More importantly, it meant new faces and easy marks.

Froba tossed a silver talent in the air and tucked it in her pouch. It had been a good day with lots of traffic and plenty of drunks; folk were in high spirits with summer around the corner. Early planting had started, and coin was flowing— right into her fingers. She needed adventurers like shepherds needed sheep, and Ferd would be after her for his share of the wool. If she didn't do enough fleecing, he would make her more than hungry.

A chorus of youthful shouts from the south side of town startled Froba, and she bumped the back of her head against the wall. She leaped to her feet and ducked down an alley, creeping toward the commotion. A bent old crone hurried in the other direction. Froba shimmed along a wall and peered around the corner.

A narrow side street sloped sharply downhill, past cramped shacks with fenced yards in which pigs snuffled and scrawny chickens pecked. Near the bottom, a gang of older youths savagely kicked a smaller boy. He managed to scrabble away, leaving one of his attackers holding a shred of brown tunic, and scrambled up the slope. His eyes and mouth were wide with terror. The jeering youths sent rocks and shouts of "greenskin" and "mullorc" after him.

Froba knew them, a gang of toughs from the Tannery, the lowest, filthiest part of town. She didn't know their victim. He wasn't human, not entirely; he was squat and had grey-green skin, wide-set hazel eyes, a small, flat nose, and a monstrously wide mouth with pitted, snake-like lips. A half-orc, more orc than boy by the look of him.

He shot past Froba, who stepped out to face the gang. "Hey, toads, this is Ferd's turf. Ye want him to drown ye in yer piss pot?"

The boys stopped but kept up their jeers and insults. The biggest stepped forward. Brent was his name. "We ain't scared o' Ferd," Brent sneered.

"Yeah? Why don't ye come up here an' say that?"

He took another step but hesitated.

"Yeah, thought so. Better get back to it or it'll be yer da's drownin' ye."

"At least we got folks. Go squat in yer alley an' cry yerself to sleep. Maybe Ferd'll come tuck ye in!" Brent said. The other boys mockingly blubbered and rubbed their eyes.

Froba spat, crossed her arms, and glared at them, maintaining a brave front despite their fiendishly accurate barbs.

"Watch yer back, ye sow," Brent said, kicking a fat pig for emphasis. It hobbled away squealing while Brent tramped after his cackling mates.

Froba knew he was full of shit, but she couldn't afford a big head. They were all getting bigger, and things didn't stay the same in Branthall for long. If Brent won a spot topside she could wind up in trouble. He was mean enough to pull it off, too.

She turned to regard the half-orc crouched behind a rain barrel and sniffling wetly. Why had she helped him? She'd never done so for others in a similar spot. Ferd didn't like his irregulars mixing or taking up with others. He preferred to pit them against one another, and gods help anyone who tried to go straight. No one could hide in Branthall. Not for long.

This one wasn't one of Ferd's. He looked too soft, like a lost pup. "Ye sure ye ain't no half-goblin? Half-orcs are supposed to be big an' tough. Yer all scrawny."

"I dunno—shut up," he said, wiping his nose and smearing blood across his cheek.

"Ye can always go back downhill if ye'd rather."

"No!"

"I don't know, maybe ye'll grow into it," she muttered, scratching her chin; a half-orc might come in handy. "What's yer name?"

"Orod."

She jabbed her chest with a filthy thumb. "I saved yer life, so ye work fer me now. Got it?"

Orod nodded unhappily.

She brushed past him. "Good. Now, c'mon." She could use someone to watch her back. He looked like a wimp, but it would be nice to have someone around for a change. Besides, she'd never had a friend.

* * *

Froba dragged Orod up Main Street's uneven cobbles, dodging sellers hawking charms and miracle cures, two disfigured mercenaries arguing the merits of spear length, and a spring lamb being led to slaughter. She pulled Orod aside three doors from the Market, causing him to splash barefoot through the gutter.

"Alright, ye gotta know the rules. Southgate's my spot. Town square's off limits 'cept for market days like today. Never work someone else's spot or ye'll get a knife in yer guts. Got it?"

"No," Orod whimpered.

"Gods, yer dumb. Where'd ye come from anyhow?"

Orod pointed over his shoulder. "Westhill. Me mum used to make an' mend." His eyes began to well.

Froba turned away and sighed. "Don't go blubberin' again. What'm I gonna do with ye?"

"Who's this milksop?" Ferd said. He stood over them, tall and lanky, like a malevolent scarecrow. Dark, oily hair dangled about his pox-scarred face. His cuirass was covered in black leather studded with steel in a repeating diamond pattern—hallmark of the Town Watch. He gazed contemptuously at Orod, one hand on his sheathed rondel dagger. "A gods-damned mullorc?"

"Th-this' Orod," Froba stuttered. "Them Tanners is getti—" Ferd grabbed her by the arm and pulled her up onto her toes, his fingers digging into her flesh.

"Tanners ain't me concern. Money's me concern," he said through clenched teeth. Orod fell back a step, but Ferd grabbed him by the shirt and pulled him forward onto one knee. "What d'ye mean takin' on this filth?"

"I need 'im to watch my back. Yer man Grig's a half-orc, ain't he?" Froba groaned.

Ferd knocked them together and threw Froba on top of Orod. "Don't talk 'bout things ye know nuthin' about."

She rolled over. Ferd had her money bag in his hands. "Hey!" she cried, reaching for it.

Ferd gave her a savage backhand, sending her back onto Orod, and tore open the bag. "A silver and six pennies? A halfwit with a hole in his purse'd turn up more in a week." He threw the pouch in her face. "There's two of ye now, so it'd better be a sovereign next week. I gave ye the sweetest plum, so make the most of it, or I'll slit yer mullorc's throat and see ye hang fer it."

"But I ain't never—"

Ferd thrust her down with the heel of his boot. "I've been soft on ye 'til now, and it shows. The first caravan'll be through any day. Work 'em or I work ye, get it?"

"Got it." Froba replied.

Ferd gave them each a glower. He sighed and looked down the street. "I dunno, maybe ye are too soft fer this work. Gods know I tried fer yer mum's sake. Maybe one or two o' them Tanners would take to it better."

Froba surged up and clutched Ferd's sleeve. "No, we'll get it—I promise!" She had to. Without Ferd's protection, she'd be as bad off as Orod. Every hungry brat would happily break her neck for a shot at Southgate. Forget living, the things she'd have to do to survive… She'd rather be dead.

Ferd looked at her and shrugged as if it was all out of his

hands. "Make it a sovereign and maybe I'll reconsider." He pulled free of her desperate grip and trudged toward the market, muttering and shaking his head.

Froba had never stolen a whole gold sovereign before. It was an impossible amount. A sovereign would feed her and Orod like kings for a month. More than a month. That sort of coin didn't disappear without a person noticing. She certainly wouldn't make it begging, cheating adventurers in alley games, or palming pennies off tables.

She rubbed her reddened arm and hauled blubbering Orod to his feet. What was she going to do with the idiot? Use him as a decoy, maybe? He was pitiful enough for that. She prodded him down the busy street, her mind a muddle of what-ifs and what-could-she-do's.

No one spared them a second glance.

Chapter IV—Perilous Paths

Haskell stepped off the highway and onto a rough and rutted dirt road. He meandered along the verge while chirping sparrows darted from tree to tree, flitting over the twitching ears of draft animals and between the carts and wagons ahead. He turned to watch the longer train of travellers carrying on down the paved highway, destined for Siward and Sheffield. Gavin, his messenger friend, waved to him from atop his brown courser. Haskell waved back.

He had done it; he was free, and his troubles far behind. He had met many people over the past two days and not one of them had recognized him, nor had word of his crimes reached them. Nothing could stop him now.

A small wagon packed high with bales of hay rumbled onto the eastern road in front of him. The teamster twisted in his seat to check that his cargo was secure. As he did, his grey draft mule, intent on a late morning snack of tender grass, veered toward Haskell on the verge. Its timing couldn't have been worse. The animal dragged its wagon out of the rutted track, causing the vehicle to angle over precipitously.

Haskell gasped, and a warning caught in his throat. The teamster cried out and lashed the beast to try to bring it in line. Travellers beside the wagon shouted, some pointing, some drawing away, while others lunged forward in a bravely misguided attempt to hold the wagon upright.

Haskell shot forward and slapped the mule across its thick, hairy lips, its protruding front teeth scraping his palm. The animal let out an annoyed bray but gave up on its snack. He shoved it back into line. The wagon pitched and swayed as it juddered back into the furrowed road. Sighs and a scattered cheer went up from those nearby; several travellers clapped Haskell on the back.

The teamster gestured for Haskell to hop in beside him. He was an older man, creased and hard; every mile he had travelled was worn into his face, and his back was bowed by long years of hard work. "Thank the gods you were standing there. Old Donner'll be the death o' me yet."

Haskell hopped in and rested his sword between his legs. "Thanks, I've never walked so far in my life. I'm going to need new boots at the end of the road."

"Where are you headed? The name's Corben, by the way."

"Haskell. I'm headed to Branthall."

"That makes two of us. From where do you hail? We don't grow 'em as big as you up north."

Haskell cleared his throat. Judging by his accent, Corben was from Northplain. Northerners gave Southron raiders roughly as much regard as High City sailors. Haskell picked at his scabbed knuckles. "My family are seafarers from over the mountains. They settled in Khul after the last war."

Corben took a swig from a metal flask and squinted at Haskell. "Oh, and who'd they fight for?"

Haskell drummed his fingers on the edge of the seat. "My

grandfather was a privateer who fought from Fornbrad to Si-ward. Eskil was his name."

Corben let out a dry cough of a laugh. "The Orc-breaker? I don't believe it."

"It's true—this is his sword." He half drew his blade, which Corben eyed suspiciously before making a doubtful grunt. "What of your folk?" Haskell said.

"From Northbridge."

"I lived for stories like The Siege of Northbridge as a child. I suppose I'll be living such stories soon enough."

Corben sniffed, though whether from amusement or deri-sion, Haskell couldn't say. "Nursed by my mother's sister throughout that long siege, I was. But that's a long way back now."

The ragged train of travellers passed deeper into the Lake-wood, the air sharp with the scent of pine needles and the earthy rot of overwintered leaves. The dry twigs of sleeping shrubs scraped the sides of the cart and pawed at Haskell's arms. As they entered a clearing, a pair of high-spirited cara-van guards named Bror and Torg, likely bored and seeking release, skipped up the line in their tartan trousers. They sang a jaunty tune in a throaty, impenetrable tongue, with spears over their shoulders and round wooden shields bumping their backs. Most laughed and egged them on with cheers and claps.

Haskell gave Torg a playful shove as he passed, the fellow twirling away with a grin and singing even louder as he carried on up the line. Haskell shook his head; how they had any en-ergy to caper, he couldn't fathom. He was dead tired after hours of trudging, even with his short wagon ride.

"Buffoons. They should have stayed in their filthy hovels," the large, sapphire-velveted merchant sneered from atop his stallion.

Haskell felt a twinge of ire. The arrogant prick. He would

be dead without the guards and porters around him, who had only laughter and song to ease their burdens. Men like him lived to steal others' joy, as if the emotion were a gem they could jealously hoard.

"Then who would guard your corpulent hide?" The words tumbled from Haskell's mouth, smooth and unbidden, filling the unhappy void left by the merchant.

Everyone in earshot laughed, except the merchant. He spluttered, his reddening jowls jiggling with rage. "Do you know who I am?"

The others' laughter filled Haskell with a warm sense of justice. It only eased his flow. "Another flabby ass whinnying just to be heard? I could smack you like I did old Donner here." He raised his palm to drive home his offer. The merchant grew apoplectic, which only broadened Haskell's smile.

"You insolent... such... the impertinence!" He spurred his horse, knocking aside his own porters. Someone made exaggerated brays and whinnies from behind, drawing the attention of those ahead. The merchant's son, restraining laughter, cantered after his father.

Haskell hopped out of the wagon and helped a porter to his feet. The porter smiled, cheerful despite his near trampling. Haskell smiled back; at least he was able to restore a bit of good humour in the merchant's wake.

A cry went up from ahead and the caravan ground to a halt. Haskell shuffled around a bend and stopped. Just past the clearing, the road ran through a mess of soupy ruts, a shallow stream, and up a rocky hill, its top awash in the red light of the westering sun.

Tired, sore, and hungry, no one contested the halt.

The weary company unpacked their bedrolls, blankets, and provisions wherever they thought best. With the woods pressing upon them, they formed larger, more animated groups around fewer fires. All but the merchant. He camped at the head of the column, and screened himself with porters and a thin cook, who was already rough-cutting vegetables into a large pot.

"Get that blasted canvas up, you toads—up, up!" he shouted at two blue-liveried footmen struggling with ropes and a heavy wooden post.

Haskell shouldered off his pack and joined Bror and Torg under a tall elm just off the path. "Who is that gasbag? I feel like I know him from somewhere."

Bror shrugged as he piled twigs for a fire.

"He's the Right Honourable Hambur from Branthall, head merchant 'round those parts, I'm told," a plump man said, extending his hand to Haskell. "M'name's Flint, a cook by trade." Flint was average height and above-average girth. Where some are overwhelmed by weight, Flint wore his like a well-fitted jacket. A mustard tunic was stretched around his belly, and he wore a grey wool cloak and forest green hood, the latter lowered to expose his balding head.

"Haskell," he replied, giving Flint's fleshy hand a firm shake.

"A pleasure, Haskell, a pleasure. My companions went on to Fisherville, and I'm lookin' to take up with some others. I was considerin' that Hambur—the man clearly has an appetite—but he's already got a cook. Besides, I suspect ye'll make fer more pleasant company."

"Gladly—sit, sit. I wonder, maybe you can turn our provisions into something a bit more enticing?" Haskell said with a wave of salted beef from his pack.

"Challenge accepted, young sir," Flint said with a wink. He dropped a bulging sack on the ground with a clatter.

Haskell gestured to the others. "This is Bror and Torg, our

entertainment for the trip—you might have caught their earlier performance."

"Happy to have you lot along," Flint said, digging in his bag.

Hambur, Haskell thought. The name was familiar. No one from his father's circle, but familiar, nonetheless. This was going to nag him.

Corben the Teamster joined them as they took their ease around a growing fire in the failing light. Flint, true to his promise, cooked a thick pottage of cured beef and root vegetables from their pooled provisions, plus a "secret ingredient" he kept in a small pine box in his pouch. The rich stew bubbled invitingly in a burnt orange ceramic pot, the aroma drawing envious glances from other groups in the darkening afternoon. At the front of the column, the merchant Hambur castigated his cook over the quality of his meal, startling several birds into flight.

Haskell drummed his fingers, took in the gloomy undergrowth, and chuckled, anxious to start a conversation. "My nursemaid used to frighten me with Lakewood monster stories as a child." He snatched up a switch and parroted her in a shrill voice. "Them woodland goblins'll come and 'et ye, boy, 'less ye mind yer manners!"

The others chuckled.

"Nah, no goblins up this way for a long time now," Corben said and spat into the brush.

"So o'tlander, you settlin'n Branthall, then?" Bror, the shorter of the two mercenaries, rattled at Haskell. Bror and Torg were rough-looking characters; both wore leather jerkins sewn with a lattice of nicked and dented iron rings. Bror's skin was like leather: oiled, scarred, and weather-beaten from hard fighting and harder living. This had only honed his sense of humour, judging by his perpetual smirk and mirthful eyes.

"... Yes," Haskell nodded tentatively, uncertain what Bror had said.

Bror jerked a thumb at his companion. "We be doin' th'same, Torg'an me. Th'coin flow like water down that'away, they say."

Torg nodded. He was six feet, silent, and imposing. He looked younger than Bror but with a touch of worldly sadness behind his neutral expression and watchful gaze, though the creases at the corners of his mouth and eyes implied a ready smile.

Haskell chuckled nervously at Bror's indecipherable chatter. "Shame these rivers aren't navigable, it would make an easier trip. How far would you say it is to Branthall, Corben?"

Torg deadpanned something in his thick language, throwing Bror into a fit of laughter.

Flint looked up while stirring the pot but said nothing.

"Seventy miles or thereabouts—maybe six days," Corben grunted.

Haskell tapped the ground with his switch. The awkwardness was too much. "Old Corben here lived through the Siege of Northbridge," he said conversationally.

Bror made an impressed noise, his exaggerated expression implying anything but.

"Why don't you tell us about your grandad, Haskell," Corben said.

"Aye, give'us a tale, lad," Bror cheered.

Haskell smiled and stood; that was more like it. "Okay, you're in for a treat." He cleared his throat and raised his hands. "Back when Corben was slightly less old than he is now—"

"Forget it, and fuck your grandad," Corben growled, though with a hint of a smile. He threw a stick at Haskell.

Haskell snickered and batted aside the missile. "Back in the dark times, when Corben was just a *babe*—thank you—the orcs ran rampant."

"Bloody orcs!" a man shouted through the trees. Apparently, Haskell had a wider audience.

"Yes, the orcs," he said a bit louder. "Huge, rapacious, green-skinned monsters, the orcs spilled in a green tide from the Darkwood to the Orkmounts, with ogres and giants striding among them like ships of war. Every kingdom felt the bite of their cruel black blades, even lands beyond the mountains all the way to the Horn of the Southron Sea, from where my people hail."

"God-damned pirates," a woman cried.

"Hear, hear," Corben said.

There was some laughter throughout the woods.

"Will you let me finish?" Haskell sighed, resuming his dramatic posture. "Woe to those who couldn't flee: the babes, the sickly, and women heavy with child—hacked to pieces and eaten alive! Those who fought met the same fate, the few who survived taken as slaves, though the living envied the dead.

"Lords set aside old feuds to form mighty hosts of horse and spear, shield and mail. Their colourful banners fluttered in the breeze like a silken rainbow, and their ranks were swollen by every man, woman, and child strong enough to bear arms. All in vain. Great battles were fought in wood and over field, but every victory was a loss and every loss a catastrophe. The monsters were too many and too fierce. Mail and shield were nothing to the horde and giants made a mockery of manor and castle. Only the stoutest strongholds held, and they became islands in a churning, monstrous sea.

"It wasn't until a mighty hero, Eskil Orc-breaker, arrived to turn the tide. He was always where the fighting was fiercest and the suffering most dire. He was taller than an orc and wore bright mail. They say his runic sword—this very sword,"

Haskell said, drawing his blade and holding it up to the firelight, "was blessed by the gods. No orc could stand before Eskil and live.

"Eskil's dragon-headed long ships, crowded with mailed fighters bristling with axes, spears, and shields, sailed south under crimson ensigns with black ram's head badges. They emptied the slave pits of Caen and shattered the Shadow Wood Hordes. That's where he faced the orcs' mightiest chieftain atop an ancient barrow. For an hour and a day Eskil's shining blade rang against the orc's jagged scimitar while their hosts battled around the ancient hill. Then, in the final hour, bleeding from a score of wounds, Eskil struck the mortal blow. He cleaved off the monster's head, and the burial mound on which they fought eagerly drank the orc's proud blood, like it had the ancient lord buried within."

"What happened then?" a young girl asked.

"Two and twenty years later, the orcs were broken and scattered. Many heroes were made in that time, and many died. Eskil, though: he lived. His fortune made, he sailed north to settle in Khul, seat of the king for whom he fought. Where I was born."

The woods filled with applause, and Haskell gave a bow.

"A penny fer the sword!" a man shouted, eliciting chuckles. Haskell waved him off and sat back down. Further down the road a minstrel took up a saucy tune on a recorder accompanied by a drum. The music floated through the trees, brightening the atmosphere.

"A fine story," Bror said, giving Haskell an appreciative jostle.

Haskell took a swig from his wineskin and proffered it to Bror. "I'm putting a party together to fight in Lanesford. I could use stout companions like you." Flint snatched the skin and took a long pull. After a contemplative pause, he passed it to Bror. "You could cook for my band, Flint. It'd be nice to have some hot food in the wilderness."

Flint frowned. "I think I'll try m'luck at somethin' a bit more usual, if ye take my meaning." He passed the skin to Corben.

"What're you about, then?" Corben asked Flint.

"Sixth generation cook," Flint volunteered around a mouthful of hard bread. "My family serves the finest houses in the realm."

Torg muttered something unintelligible, making Bror snigger. Torg handed Haskell a much lighter wineskin, which he raised. "Here's to a safe journey and fine new friends." Haskell swallowed a mouthful of sour wine and poured a stream onto the leafy ground. To placate the fickle gods.

Chapter V—Mercantile Interest

Hambur was drunk. He reached for a decanter of spiced wine on a nearby trunk in his tent; his folding chair creaked distressingly. Kerk, his trusty servant, but always too slow, rushed forward to pour more wine. Hambur stared at the red and gold patterns in the large Erdian carpet. He hated travelling by road. Everything hurt and he could feel another attack of gout coming on. Clerics and doctors? Nothing but grasping thieves. The Temple's potions, poultices, and cures could ruin a man, let alone their blasted healing spells.

His winter in Khul had been far too short, damn his devil of a wife. Two seasons in Branthall had been two seasons too many. There were no royal balls in Lanesford. No Merchant Hall dinners. No culture at all.

Hiam, Hambur's sixteen-year-old son, sighed. The insolent boy was lazing on a folding couch with his head in his hand, laying tarot cards on a trestle table. "This trip is tiresome, Father. Could a Questers Guild wizard not translocate us to Branthall?"

Hambur spluttered. Such a miracle of magic would run in

the thousands, if not tens of thousands. "A guild of thieves worse than the Temple. If I had my way, the wizards would be subject to us—we provide their precious compounds and materials. They would be nothing without us." He brushed at spilled wine on his surcoat.

Hiam squinted at his father. "Do you suppose that is where your tall friend is headed—to the Questers Guild?"

"The ruffian," Hambur growled. "How dare he ridicule me. I should have known Eskil would try to snatch up land in Lanesford. I bet he sent his son to curry favour with the King. The shark smells opportunity like blood in the water."

"I told you I recognized him at that inn. We could find out for certain—shall I invite him to dinner?"

"And have the brute skewer you with his monstrous sword? Your mother would never forgive me."

"I do not think there is any danger of that," Hiam said cheekily.

Hambur glared at the boy; what did he mean by that remark? He dragged Kerk down by the tunic. "Go see Nedir's man and ask about the young pirate. Someone must know something." Kerk nodded and beetled out of the tent.

Hiam flipped over more cards, gazing at them like a seer reading the future. "Perhaps we can strike a deal with Master Neyhün when we arrive. The old wizard has expensive tastes. We might leverage that to speed our journeys."

Hambur grunted and sipped wine; the boy was right on that score. He looked at Hiam's cards. The back depicted a serpentine black dragon constricting a broken tower under a star and crescent moon. Hiam laid a final card on a creamy gold and silver cloth. The first had an even-faced king sitting on a throne with a golden cup in his hand; the next a flat field and river below purple, dragon-circled mountains, a hand gripping a broken sapling in the foreground; the third a vagrant and his dog about to walk off a cliff; and the last a sad queen gazing at a gold coin in her lap, her throne intricately carved with lions, goats, and dragons.

"An odd court," Hiam muttered.

"Divining your future, boy?" Hambur sneered. Hiam was no magician, just a spoiled child in need of discipline. He would hire a tutor in Branthall. Yes, a nice draconian pedagogue to straighten out the boy.

"Let us hope not," Hiam said.

Hambur frowned. The future. He hadn't even broken ground at his manor, yet Eskil was already looking to undermine him. He turned as Kerk ducked through the tent flap. "Out with it, man."

"The register lists him as Haskell of Khul," Kerk said.

"We know that—what of his business?"

"It did not list his trade, Master. He is a traveller bound for the Branthall Questers Guild."

"I told you no self-respecting merchant would dress so shabbily or wear such a brutal sword," Hiam said.

Hambur sat back in his chair. "We'll reach Branthall soon enough, then I'll have the brigand. I smell Eskil's hand in this, the duplicitous old pirate. More drink, Kerk, I'm dry."

So, the boy thought he could saunter into Branthall to play the hero and win land from the king? Hambur fingered his gold chains, his eyes smouldering with hate.

The insolent boy knew nothing at all.

April 10

Chapter VI—Veneer

The rest of the trek passed with little incident beyond a broken wagon wheel and a brief scuffle between two travellers over a missing fish pie. Haskell was glad for his companions, gambling at night with upbeat but indecipherable Bror and Torg, and even happily enduring Flint's endless Tales of Culinary Triumph. But the closer they drew to Branthall, the more restless Haskell became. His long legs often carried him far ahead of the caravan, until the eerie quiet of the woods slowed his pace.

After nine days of wearying travel, he had finally made it. He hurried between freshly ploughed fields, Bror and Torg struggling to keep pace, and fell into the shadow of Branthall's tall stone walls. Most of the town's white lime render had fallen away; only small patches of grey-brown finish remained—lonely islands afloat in a rough sea of weathered stone. He gazed up at the two square gate towers soaring into the sky above. A dark tunnel ran through the prodigious gatehouse to a narrow street beyond, where he saw Nedir's horse being stabled.

After days of nothing but rolling hills, fortified camps, and sturdy cottages on small lakes and streams, Branthall looked impossibly huge, as if a titan had placed each cyclopean block in its massive walls.

Torg whistled at the sight.

"Now that's a'sight, for sure," Bror said.

"Toll's a silver," a poxy guard grunted. Haskell tossed him a coin, which he snatched from the air. Ferd, the guard, gave it a bite and took in Haskell's devil-may-care aspect. "I warrant ye'll be wanting the Tall Treeman off the Questers Guild. Southgate, end o' Main Street. Ask fer Luna if yer needin' company."

"Good eye, but that silver should be enough for my friends: these two, an old wagoner as taciturn as his grey mule, and a talkative cook in a mustard tunic. They'll be along presently."

Ferd glared at Haskell. He gave Bror and Torg a nasty look and spat on the ground. "We don't want no Siwarders 'round here, mate. Knife ye as soon as look at ye."

"Aye, maybe you'like," Bror replied cheerfully.

"You clearly haven't met many—" Haskell began.

"Make way! I am to enter Branthall before such ill-bred tramps," Hambur shouted from behind. He whipped his limping stallion to maintain its canter.

Haskell had had enough of the blustery merchant. Neither he, Bror, nor Torg moved aside. Hambur's horse checked and side-stepped with a snort, forcing him to work to keep it in line. "You again, eh? I know you now. Eskil trying to horn in on my territory? The whole of the Middle Sea not good enough for the pirate, so he sends his spawn to meddle in my affairs?"

Haskell ground his teeth. His palm itched for the hilt of his sword. He wanted to spit Hambur and rid the world of the churlish swine. "I'm my own man, you pig. My business is my own."

Hambur looked at Ferd. "You there, haul them out of my way."

Realization dawned on Haskell. He pointed at Hambur. "You're Amina of Khul's husband," he said with a chuckle. "She exiled you here after that load of adulterated spices was burned by the city. What was it—peppercorn with pawpaw seed? That must have been embarrassing and expensive." He stepped forward, hands on hips and chin in the air, daring Hambur to deny it.

Hambur's horse tossed its head and reared back with a squeal and a snort. "Hold fast, you blasted animal!" He jerked the reins to bring the horse in line. That was enough for the horse. It did a quick turn and toss, throwing Hambur off balance. He cried out, his pouches and gold chains jangling as he fell from the saddle into a heap of manure. Divested of its heavy load, the stallion trotted back down the road, whinnying as it went.

All of them, including Ferd and the tower guards high above, broke into gales of laughter.

"Villainy! Arrest them, arrest them!" Hambur cried, scrabbling on his back like an upended beetle.

Haskell gave Hambur a mocking bow and made for the gate, nodding to Ferd as he passed. "See you around, friend."

Ferd pocketed Haskell's silver and muttered. "Don't worry, *friend*. I'll see ye soon enough."

Haskell passed through the gate with Bror and Torg close behind. The guard, clearly moonlighting as a pimp, had tried to monstrously overcharge him, a silver talent being a labourer's daily wage. Khul had its fair share of corrupt guards, sure, but here and so soon? Haskell felt a pang of disappointment to have encountered one right out of the gate.

He emerged from the tunnel and was taken aback. Unlike

Khul's soaring houses of bright stone, Branthall was almost entirely wattle-and-daub. Its drab, progressively jettied buildings loomed over him like unfriendly giants, and while town and city both had narrow streets, Branthall seemed to have only one paved lane; its side streets were beaten earth with central gutters seeping with thick, reeking sludge—a far cry from Khul's ancient, tiled sewers.

"This town would burn to the ground if a dragon with a cold flew overhead," Haskell muttered. Bror and Torg chuckled. He greeted people in the street and in the Market Square, a few of whom returned his greeting, though more frowned and shook their heads, moving along or dumping chamber pots into the street. Haskell ignored them, noting instead the tailor and cobbler, blacksmith and armourer, grocer and baker: merchants whose services he would need very soon.

The town's stone defensive walls and towers were everywhere he looked, dwarfing everything below. Only the mighty stone keep rose higher, its massive southeast tower higher still, as did the many-columned, black marble Temple, its obelisk jabbing into the sky like a dark finger.

Following Main Street, they soon passed through a deep wooden arch and into a wide, half-circle cul-de-sac. Haskell took in iron-studded Southgate and two facing buildings. On his left was the Tall Treeman, which was aptly named. The main building had four narrow, irregular storeys stacked like a crooked trunk, and was flanked by two two-storey wings. One wing nearly met the town's outer wall, and the other connected to the arch back into town. The inn's door was bright green, and vivid green banners fluttered from its walls. A sign over the entrance depicted a cheerful, man-like tree with bright blue eyes and a long, leaf-tipped nose, its arms pumping as it strutted along a bright yellow road.

On his right sat the Questers Guild, which was quite different. A solid block of a building three storeys tall, it had many mullioned windows, white-washed walls, and a low front porch. A triangular shield bore the Guild's coat-of-arms: a black sword crossing a blood red axe on a cobalt blue field. Long banners dyed in the same three colours rippled from its bright walls.

Haskell let out a contented sigh. He was here at last. "Why don't you two check out the inn, while I—" Bror and Torg had already passed into the Treeman, its door swinging shut behind them. "—sign on with the Guild," he finished. He rolled his eyes, ducked under the Guild's low porch, and through its stately front door.

He emerged into a wide, cream-coloured foyer with dark wainscoting and exposed ceiling beams. The walls were festooned with trophies: black-fletched goblin arrows and thorny bows, dark orcish scimitars crossing pitted iron shields, a troll's head, giant red scorpion's tail, and the three snarling heads of a chimera. Best of all was the massive black dragon skull mounted over a double-wide doorway across the room. The skull's prodigious fangs rested on the floor, forming a grim covered walkway into the cavernous hall beyond.

"Amazing," he said with a broad smile. It was everything he imagined, and this was just the foyer. He lowered his hood to better see everything. Taking up a glass jar from a side table, he examined a cluster of fat, stubby worms with tick-like heads suspended in rust-coloured liquid. "So strange."

He set down the jar and crossed the creaky hardwood floor to the massive skull. Reaching up, he ran his fingertips gingerly along the dragon's dagger-like teeth. They nearly opened his skin despite his light touch. "How could anyone slay something so monstrous?"

"I see you've found our friend, Grimfyrrid," a smoky voice

said behind him.

"Ye gods!" Haskell cried with a start, lancing several fingers on the teeth. He whirled about. A tiny, ancient woman stood only a foot away, beaming up at him innocently with bright green eyes. He fell back a step, the floorboards creaking under him. She hadn't made a sound.

The old woman's face was like wrinkled hide, her chin bristled like a boar's back, and her head was framed by a mop of tight white curls. She was clad in dark leather armour, soft boots, and had a long, serpent-handled dagger in a gilded sheath in her belt. A platinum medallion bearing the Guild's device hung around her neck, and many brightly jeweled rings adorned her gnarled fingers.

"It is true," she said, gently nodding. "I am not the beauty I once was, but there's no need to gawk, my boy."

Haskell startled out of his reverie. "Apologies, grandma." He attempted an awkward bow, but his scabbard knocked one of the Grimfyrrid's pillar-like fangs, showering dust from above.

"Well, you're no ranger of the wilds, that's plain," the old woman tittered, reaching up to pinch his cheek with surprising firmness. She stepped back to regard him. "Let me see. A giant youth, shabbily garbed, with a long blade at his side, clomping around my foyer like an ogre raiding a pantry. Yes, a plain old fighter if ever there was one, but with Southron blood and a High City accent. If I had to wager—and I often do—I would say you are one of the Orc-breaker's kin. Or have I misread you?"

Haskell stood agape and rubbed his smarting cheek. Could this sorceress read minds? "Right on every count. I'm Haskell, son of Eskil, Eskil's Son, just arrived from Khul. Amazing. But you have me at a disadvantage, Madam. Who do I have the pleasure of addressing?"

"Oh-ho, an eloquent swordsman *and* the son of a son of a pirate," she said with a toothless grin. "You will prove interesting, won't you? Follow me." She spun on her heel and padded briskly across the foyer, beckoning him; her jeweled fingers scintillated in the sunlight slanting through the windows.

"But your name?" he said, untangling his scabbard from Grimfyrrid's teeth and clomping after her, drawn along by the glittering jewels on her hand.

Froba watched Haskell through the Guild's mullioned window. He was perfect: big and stupid with a nice, fat purse. She would try something different with this one. The old sob story wouldn't do. Not if she was going to get a whole gold piece out of him.

She walked back to the wooden arch where Orod sat waiting. He rose quickly and stumbled into a passerby. "Fuckin' half-breed," the man sneered. He shoved Orod down and wiped his hand on his jerkin as though the boy were contagious. The man entered the Treeman.

Froba stood over Orod and shook her head. At least he wasn't crying.

"W-what now?" he asked.

"I'll work the inn tonight. There'll be plenty o' newmeat from the caravan an' Griswold lets me run 'em drinks."

Orod stood and rubbed his elbow. "What about me?"

"I dunno? Hang 'round back."

"What if someone comes along?"

"Hide. Or see 'em off with some rocks. I can't hustle 'venturers *and* take care o' ye."

Orod nodded pitifully.

Him being such a milksop might work out in the end. A pitiful homeless girl looking out for a mullorc weakling was a good angle. She could use it to get in with the giant and help herself to a bit of his coin. He looked rich enough to maybe not even notice; she had heard the clink of his near-bursting pouch as he strolled along. Shit, the idiot was asking for it.

Besides, what choice did she have?

The old woman bustled through a door on one side of the foyer and up a steep staircase to the third floor. Haskell followed, hurrying down a crimson carpeted hall lined with dusty portraits. Stern, sober men regarded him from within the frames as he approached the panelled door through which the woman had passed.

On the other side was a room lined with shelves and tables packed with books, scrolls, treasures, trophies, and knick-knacks. A fire crackled in a hearth to one side, starkly lighting what more closely resembled a junk trader's stall than an office. Perhaps the old woman was a guild trader looking to offload some stock on an unwitting newcomer. He strode over a large carpet finely woven in black, red, and blue, its nap nearly worn bare from the boots of countless questers before him. The air was heavy with the cloying scent of pipe smoke.

The woman had perched on a mound of cushions piled in a high-backed chair, its back carved into a serpentine dragon that eyed Haskell over her snowy curls. She regarded him over a large mahogany desk that, unlike the cluttered room, bore only an inkwell, silver candlestick, thick tome, and plain box with an oblong metal device on top. He noted heavy shutters barring a window over a massive, reinforced chest behind her. The tidy desk reminded him of his father, as did the old woman's calculating gaze.

She lit a plain wooden pipe with the rectangular metal device, settled into her pillows, and took several long, deliberate draws on her pipe. Acrid smoke drifted from her mouth and nose. "I am Winifred the Fair, Guild Mistress—the first woman to be named and, I am happy to say, the longest-serving of all."

Haskell's eyes widened. This old woman was head of the Guild? He had expected a formidable captain, like Nedir, or an aged but splendid warrior, greying and regal, or even a powerful wizard, stern, learned and wise. But a shrunken old woman? He bowed and clicked his heels. "Hail, Guild Mistress."

Winifred smiled and gestured to a leather chair in front of her desk. It was hard and unyielding, a discomfort not improved by her instructions.

"To begin with, young man, a member must uphold the principles of the Questers Guild." Winifred proceeded to count them off with her gnarled digits.

"Firstly: always attempt to aid a fellow member in need.

"Secondly: never take, by any means, the rightful property of a fellow member.

"Thirdly: never inflict harm on a fellow member, physically or otherwise, directly or indirectly, through action or inaction.

"Fourthly: pay your Guild fee the first day of each month, or within a reasonable period thereafter, upon entering the vicinity of any Guildhall.

"Fifthly, and lastly: never extort the weak, engage in petty banditry, or comport yourself in a manner that would bring the Guild into disrepute.

"If you abide by these five rules," she said with a flourish of her outstretched fingers. "And remain in good standing, you will be entitled to aid, advice, guidance, training, a secure bank for your spoils, and discounted rates from the Guild's many affiliates."

Haskell's chair creaked as he leaned forward to contemplate the many qualified terms and conditional statements she had clearly, yet swiftly, related. This lecture felt like one of

Slade's lessons on the finer points of evading the law. Haskell didn't care for it.

"Naturally," she continued with a toothless smile. "Should you accept these terms, we require half a month's fee in advance. A mere ten pieces of silver, seeing as you are a new member in need of immediate advice, guidance and…" looking him up and down, "Outfitting."

Haskell sighed, coughing on the spicy smoke in the air. "Your terms seem fair, but tell me—what is the Guild's policy on freelance questers?"

She regarded him through smoke from her nostrils. "Oh, well, let us not speak of unpleasant things."

Haskell couldn't restrain a roguish smirk. Winifred was a steely woman who might give his father a run for his money. He was beginning to see why she rose to prominence. "Then I cheerfully accept your offer, though my acceptance is contingent on the Guild directing me to a suitable place where I and a small band of hirelings might seek our fortune."

"Of course, my lad, that is what the Guild is for," she said around her pipe stem. Opening the tome before her, its cover thudding on the desk's blotter, she took up a quill and scratched several lines three-quarters down the page. Rotating the tome, she extended it and the quill to Haskell. "Simply pay your silver and make your mark."

Haskell leaned forward to study the fresh entry, which read:

> Haskell of Khul hereby agrees to abide by the Terms and Conditions of the Questers Guild (the Guild), appended herein, which have been explained to him, and to remain a Member in Good Standing with the Guild, which will provide him with Questing Services as of this date,

so long as the Guild receives its Due of one (1) Gold Sovereign or ten (10) per cent of all Questerly Spoils each month, whichever is greater.

Signed at Branthall this Tenth Day of April: In the Twenty-First Year of the Reign of His Majesty King Ferd II of Lanesford.

Haskell reached into his pouch and scraped a single piece of gold across the desk with one finger. He took the quill and signed his name below the fresh entry. He noticed that many of the last entries had been struck out. "What happened to those—?"

"Excellent!" Winifred set a stack of ten silver on the desk, which Haskell took.

"Guild Mistress?" he said.

"Hmm?"

"Were those struck out in your book killed?"

She nodded. "Or worse."

"What's worse than dying?"

Winifred laughed long and hard, her jollity making Haskell fidget more than the hard leather chair. He didn't see what was so funny. She wiped her eyes, sighed, and gave him a strange, almost pitying look. "Oh, dear boy, there are many things worse than death. Far worse. I hope for your sake they never find you."

He frowned. Another question came to him. "Tell me, who slew the dragon whose skull rests downstairs? A mighty host, surely."

"No. One man, long ago. Brandt the Ironhanded he was called, founder of this Guild Chapter back when Branthall was just a fortified keep. You amuse me, Haskell, so I shall tell you the tale." She settled into her chair, stoked her pipe, and began to weave the story…

Chapter VII—Tale of the Black Wyrm

G rimfyrrid was a terrible black wyrm that hunted the length and breadth of Lanesford three hundred years ago. Its roar was like rolling thunder fit to wither the resolve of all who stood before it. Whenever Lanesford prospered, Grimfyrrid would appear, bringing death and famine. It would prey on cattle, devour crops, and lay villages low with foul poison strong enough to melt flesh and bone. Its terror would continue until the kingdom paid it a crippling tribute, only to start the cycle anew. The kingdom would rebuild and repopulate, growing stronger and richer; then Grimfyrrid would come again to feed on hope and prosperity.

"It was Brandt who, having pushed marauding orcs from the kingdom only a decade before, engineered the dragon's downfall. Weak King Ered IV was prepared to capitulate as soon as Grimfyrrid appeared, but Brandt would not have the avaricious wyrm destroy the stability he had fought to establish.

"Brandt met Grimfyrrid alone, traveling to its Darkwood

lair posing as the king's emissary. He arranged to leave it tribute in his newly constructed Guildhall, built where Branthall's stone keep now stands, though Brandt's hall was only sturdy oak then. He knew that the dragon, being faithlessly rapacious, would be unable to resist destroying his hall once it was paid. So, Brandt emptied his home, sent his folk away, and spent three days working in secret.

"With the sun setting on the third day, he signalled Grimfyrrid by lighting a beacon in his courtyard. Before long, the creature came cruising through the air, its long shadow advancing over the fields below, a terrifying black demon with wings as wide as Brandt's bailey wall. The dragon alighted on the palisade and the very ground shook with its roar of triumph.

"Brandt, unfazed by the display, bade Grimfyrrid to enter the hall through its wide carved doors to claim its due. The dragon, rightly suspicious and too proud to squeeze through a human's doors, no matter how wide, gleefully vomited its bile over the finely carved doorway, which smoked and ran like hot wax, exposing the grand hall to the open air. Grimfyrrid looked through the massive hole and demanded that Brandt bring out the two large chests it spied against the back wall.

"Brandt, bowing low, acknowledged the power and terror of the dragon, but claimed he lacked the keys, saying the keep belonged to the king, and that its inhabitants had fled. With many apologies, he cited his weak human stature and the vastness of the treasure as cause for his inability to drag them from the keep.

"Grimfyrrid would have consumed Brandt but, being vain, required a witness to its conquest: someone to spread word of its terrible power. So, compelled by greed and fearing no man, it passed through the breach it had made. The hall's hardwood floor groaned as the dragon filled the massive hall to the rafters. It seized a massive chest in each colossal talon, but as it stumped backwards, the hardwood floor shattered, dropping the greedy monster into a cellar bristling with pikes planted in the floor.

"Grimfyrrid shrieked and thrashed as the sharp steel plunged into its thighs and belly, shaking the hall with its throes. It spewed poison on the walls and ceiling, which began to crumble. But there were more than pikes in the cellar, for Brandt had also packed it with pitch, oil, and straw, into which he tossed a lit torch. The cellar erupted into a volcano of flame that consumed dragon and keep.

"But dragons are not so easily slain.

"Grimfyrrid burst from the flaming mound with a deafening roar. A dozen broken pikes protruded from its belly. Its hide was a patchwork of missing scales and scorched flesh. The dragon clambered from the flaming pit, ready to snap Brandt in two with its massive jaws. But the mighty hero held aloft his rune-etched sword, its cold metal glinting in the setting sun as he plunged the thrice-blessed blade through the dragon's throat and into its malicious brain. Grimfyrrid fell back, the burning ruin becoming its funeral pyre, though none mourned its passing.

"They say the fire burned all day and night, leaving only a pit of ash and Grimfyrrid's blackened bones, which now rest in this Guildhall.

"Lanesford took the black wyrm as its symbol that day, so we might never forget that the defeat of evil requires personal sacrifice, and that bargaining with the enemies of humanity brings only ruin."

Chapter VIII—Terms and Conditions

H askell sighed. "Astounding. I've never heard that one before. What became of Brandt—did he re-build his hall?"

"He did, and Brandt the Ironhanded went on to become King Brandt I, though it would ultimately be his undoing. But that is another story for another time. Let us return to the Guild's present business. Do you have a company with whom to adventure? The Guild can help you find companions for a modest fee. Many are in the wilderness hunting monstrous filth in wood and cave, but a few remain in town."

"Thank you, but I have already found some likely companions. I wish to lead my own expedition, and soon."

"You want to be your grandfather from the off, do you? Suit yourself." Winifred whipped a sheaf of parchment from the drawer in front of her and scratched several entries onto the prepared document. She lit a taper of crimson wax and dripped it carefully on the bottom of the parchment. Pressing a heavy metal stamp into the hot wax, she embossed it with the Guild's seal. She signed the document with a flourish and passed it to Haskell.

It read:

PERMIT OF QUESTING

WHEREAS the Enemies of Humankind make Continual and Unceasing War upon Humanity and its Rulers who, by the Grace of the GODS, have Rightful Dominion over the Human Realms betwixt the Middle Sea and Siwardian Mountains and the Barbarian Steppes and Deserts of Aldamen. And FORASMUCH as You have made Application unto Me for License to Arm, Furnish, and Equip Yourself and a Party of Worthy Adventurers, Henchmen and Hirelings in Warlike manner, against said Enemies of Humankind, I do accordingly Permit and Allow Haskell of Khul, the Quester, by Virtue of the Powers and Authorities vested in Me by the Guild of Questers and the Common Laws of the Human Realms, to War, Fight, Take, Kill, Suppress and Destroy the Enemies of Humankind, whether Aberrant, Bestial, Humanoid, Infernal, or Undead, or in any form Monstrous, in whatsoever Place you shall Encounter them; Their goods and treasures, to take and make Prize of.

And I do hereby Request all Vassals, Agents and Subjects of the Rulers of Humanity to permit said Quester with said Party, its vessels, vehicles and Prizes that they may have taken, freely and quietly to pass and repass, without giving or suffering Trouble or Hindrance. And this Permit is to continue in Force for Twelve Months next ensuing and not afterwards, so long as the Quester remains in Good Standing with the aforementioned Guild.

Given under my Hand and Seal at Branthall this Tenth Day of April: In the Twenty-First Year of the Reign of His Majesty King Ferd II of Lanesford.

Winifred, Guild mistress of Branthall.

"Magnificent!" Haskell said, rolling it up. She handed him a bone scroll case embossed with the Guild's seal; he tucked his permit inside and the case in his pack.

"Now, as for training—"

"I'm fine on that score. I trained in Khul and practiced on the road."

Winifred nodded slowly. "In the city *and* on the road? Well, then, I suppose you will have no trouble in the Darkwood." Haskell was happy to hear her agree. "I may have just the right spot for you," she said with an absent wag of her finger. She pulled a small book from a drawer and leafed through it, giving a particular page a tap. "Yes, this will do—a known labyrinth several hours from here. No map, sadly, but cleared successfully just over two years ago."

"Cleared? Why enter a place already swept of foes?" And treasure, he thought.

Winifred eyed him keenly. "Trust me, lad, when I tell you that Darkwood dungeons do not stay clear for long, so don't look disappointed. No, there are more than enough dangers in that evil wood." She was lost briefly in thought before coming back to herself. "I recommend you take no fewer than three Guild-members with you, though more would be better, and several mercenaries to round out your numbers. You can post a notice for a small fee or, if you are willing to wait a few weeks, one of our agents could find you suitable companions to interview. You will also need armour—the best you can afford—equipment and another weapon or two. You will find costs run up quickly, my boy."

"I do need armour, but my grandfather's sword is the only weapon I require. I'm confident that a few mercenaries and I can handle the creatures in a half-cleared crypt."

Winifred choked as she relit her pipe. "I see. It is your hide, not mine, so I will not try to dissuade you. I shall be very interested to hear a report should you return."

"And I will revel in the telling. I only hope it will be a tale worthy of Brandt the Ironhanded." He couldn't wait. He would buy the best armour, maybe a suit of shining plate like Nedir's, hire a few more companions, and make his fortune. It would be glorious.

"Have it your way, young one, but remember this: the deeper you go, the greater your peril—it is always thus below the earth. Now listen carefully. This is where you must go…"

Chapter IX—Ogre

C aptain Nedir raised his glass to his host. "This is very fine claret, Burgomaster Stieg."

"The best the South Coast has to offer. What the pirates let through, that is," Stieg replied. "If only you could guard the seaways as well as you do the forest roads, Captain!"

Nedir reclined in his deep leather chair and smiled. He savoured these quiet moments after a long, dangerous trek: sipping fine spirits offered by gracious hosts in comfortable parlours. He had dressed in his hose and belted jacket for the occasion but looked like a threadbare peasant next to his host.

Stieg wore a fashionable black tunic with paned sleeves, a vest embroidered with gold and silver dragons, fine black tights, and soft shoes with pointed toes. He had a large gold medallion around his shoulders that bore Branthall's device: the Wyrm of Lanesford coiled around a tower. Stieg's high forehead, aquiline nose, and strong jaw gave him a distinct appearance; coupled with his air of genial confidence, he was the type of person who commanded a room simply by entering it.

The parlour was large and richly furnished. Historical tapestries adorned the walls and expensive carpets the flagstone floor. The furniture was heavy and dark, much of it shipped across the Middle Sea at great expense. Stieg lived in one of the newer homes springing up in Branthall's north end, now called Hightown. Nedir gestured vaguely around the room. "You and Winifred have transformed Branthall in just a few years. I hardly recognize anything above the stables. Such grand houses."

"Thank you. We have worked very hard. Of course, it helps to have so many distinguished merchants, landlords, and craftspeople clamouring to live here. Was the road from Khul perilous?"

That made sense. Nedir had shepherded enough merchants and landowners to Branthall the last few years. "Not terribly. I never would have thought to pass through the Lakewood unmolested."

"Yes, times are changing. Farmsteads and hamlets have sprung up throughout the Lane. Winifred keeps the Darkwood goblins culled. We prosper once more."

"Settlers in the Lane? It feels like I was battling ogres there just yesterday."

Stieg laughed. "You are showing your age. It must be a decade since an ogre waded through our grasslands. You did your job too well."

Nedir nodded. Perhaps things were changing. Could Winifred and Stieg really turn things around with King Ferd? The goblins had destroyed so much in the last war. It was hard to believe that a bright, prosperous future could exist anywhere, especially here. He had only known war and its aftermath. With no enemy, men and women quickly turned on one another. Guildsfolk forsook their vows, soldiers became mercenaries, and commanders turned into bandit lords who spread as much woe as the old enemy. He ground his teeth. Images of his old, dead friends came back to him in flashes, one by one.

"Captain?" Stieg said gently.

Nedir snapped to and held out his glass for a servant to refill. The door burst open. Nedir dropped his goblet and sprang to his feet, whirling with a long dagger in his hand. How could he have been so lax, lulled by Branthall's new façade. Was this a plot of Stieg's? His mind shot back twenty years, to an assassin with dead blue eyes, missing front teeth, and wet incisors that resembled fangs. He had come to take Winifred's life, and Nedir's.

Hambur stopped short, his complexion ruddy and mouth working furiously as he looked from Nedir to Stieg. He had a dark stain on his left shoulder and brought the sharp tang of horse droppings into the room.

"Please sit, Captain," Stieg said without rising. He signalled another servant to begin cleaning up the spilled wine.

Nedir sheathed his dagger and switched to a chair beside Stieg, keeping his back to the wall. He shared a strained smile with the burgomaster while trying to slow his racing heart. It was safe. He lived, not the assassin, nor the would-be Guild Master behind the plot. Stieg was a good man. Things had changed—at least enough; the Guild was going dormant but ever watchful.

"I see you have returned from Khul, Hambur," Stieg said.

"I wish to lodge a grievance," Hambur growled.

"So soon? You have only just arrived. How is young Hiam?" Stieg said casually.

"My son? I was the one threatened by that rogue. Haskell's his name—Eskil's son, the ruddy snake," Hambur said.

Stieg looked to Nedir.

Nedir's smile faded. What had Haskell done now? The boy had made it his business to hassle Hambur on the road. Their petty battles to travel ahead of one another, trading barbs at every opportunity, their veiled threats and insults. If Haskell hadn't been so diligent in his work or good at keeping the help in high spirits with his stories and high jinks, Nedir would have taken him to task. Really, though, he enjoyed the boy's verve and had relished Hambur's discomfiture. "I know the boy. A bit of a fool but good company. I invited him to join me but he's intent on being a quester. He wants to chase glory like his grandfather."

"Yes, a cocksure youth. He made threats against me, openly ridiculed me, and just now tried to kill me," Hambur said.

That was too much. "Come now, Hambur—murder is it now?" Nedir said.

"A misunderstanding, I am sure," Stieg said.

"The scoundrel denied me entry to town and threw me from my horse—I could have been killed!"

Nedir shifted in his chair. That did sound plausible.

Stieg sighed. "Was the Watch present?"

"Of course, I called for him to be clapped in chains."

Stieg levelled a stony gaze at Hambur. "And did they?"

Hambur goggled at the burgomaster. "You will do nothing?"

"Captain Nedir had charge of the caravan and vouches for the boy, and the guards did not act. That settles matters, I would say."

"Nothing's settled," Hambur barked, stalking from the room.

Stieg drank deeply from his goblet. "I was mistaken, Captain. One ogre still stalks the Lane."

Chapter X—Seasoning

Haskell ambled across the cul-de-sac toward the Tall Treeman's chipped green door. His meeting with Winifred ran through his mind. Had he presented himself correctly? She wasn't at all what he'd expected. Rules and conditions didn't factor into his picture of the Questers Guild. It was the *Questers* Guild, after all. To quest after glory and gain by fighting orcs, goblins, and trolls was his calling, not adherence to a handful of legalistic dictates. This wasn't the High City; these were the borderlands, where bandits, barbarians, and bugbears roamed.

He ducked into the Treeman's long, smoky common room. It was furnished with large tables worn smooth from years of heavy use. The room was partitioned by a two-sided fireplace with a barroom in the back. A staircase on his left rose steeply to a railed landing overlooking the front room.

Seeing no sign of Bror and Torg, or anyone else for that matter, he strode to the back. His heavy footfalls were muffled by a generous layer of fragrant pine shavings spread over stained floorboards. He ducked through an arch to where the innkeeper was setting out long lines of pewter tankards on the bar. He was a brick of a man, all muscle and mutton chops around a broad nose and pointed chin.

"I suppose you just arrived and want a room?" he said.

Haskell flashed a strained smile; he couldn't take another gruff local. "Word travels fast. I just signed on with the Questers Guild, Master…"

The innkeeper grunted. "Griswold. Five talents a month for your own smaller room and board, if you'll have it."

Haskell was shocked; most inns charged four times as much for a private room and board. Guild discount, indeed. "I will, thank you. Say, did you see—"

"Simeon!" Griswold shouted, polishing another tankard.

Griswold's boy came out of the kitchen covered in flour. "C'mon, Sir," Simeon said, heading to the front.

Sir? Haskell could get used to this sort of treatment. He followed the boy through the common room and up the steep, creaky stairs. They went through an arch and down a narrow hall to the right. Simeon paused at a door halfway down and pushed it open. Haskell peered inside and understood why the rates were so reasonable: his smaller room was nothing but a closet with a tiny cot wedged between the walls, a washstand crammed beside the door, and a bedpan tucked under the cot.

He turned to his young guide, who was already slipping back through the arch to the landing. Haskell rolled his eyes. So be it; at least the price was right. He sighed and ducked into his closet. A commotion rose in the hallway as his pack hit the floor. He poked his head through the door only to be seized by a gang of scarred adventurers and grizzled hangers-on.

"There's th'wee boy!" Bror cried, pointing at Haskell from behind the throng. Torg had a massive grin on his face.

Haskell's attackers dragged him down the hall and onto the landing. Several burly men hoisted him into the air and carried him down the Treeman's treacherous stairs; Haskell's stomach dropped like he was cresting a waterfall in a barrel. They swayed dangerously down to the first floor and threw him onto a stool in a corner. His head glanced off the wall and shins knocked against the table as he fought to remain upright.

The adventurers called out for ale and Griswold obliged them; he emerged from the back with a fiendish grin and what looked like fifty sloshing tankards in his meaty fists and balanced on his broad forearms. Haskell was boxed in by an unruly crowd jostling and pounding his table. "Season the meat! Season the meat!" they shouted, shoving three tankards in front of him.

Haskell spied Bror and Torg in the background smashing their pewter tankards together. He glared at them and took up his own. He had no choice but to drink himself into oblivion.

April 11

Chapter XI—Bright Morning

Haskell struggled back to consciousness with a moan. He was sprawled naked over his sagging cot, his heels and knuckles resting on the floor. The sun streamed onto his face through the dirty window of his closet and made the air sweaty and close. Something heavy was lying across his abdomen. He shoved it, and it slid to the floor with a dull *thump*. Eyes closed against the offending light, he sat up with a groan and planted his feet on the floor. He rubbed his stinging eyes, worked his dry mouth, and looked blearily around the room.

Behind him, wedged between the cot and wall, was a bony, naked woman; a dark spill of hair covered her face. Luna, perhaps? She was alive but dead to the world. They must have had a good time last night because he didn't remember a thing. He lifted her onto the cot and covered her with a blanket.

He rose unsteadily and swayed to the washstand. Carefully pouring a pitcher of water into a cracked ceramic bowl, he splashed tepid water over his head and body. After a brief pause to steel himself, he hunted around the room for his clothes, retrieving his breeches from the corner, a boot from under the cot, his mysteriously stained tunic from the hall outside, and his other boot from under the woman's patched and faded blue dress.

Dressing carefully, and nearly falling over in the process, he belted on his sword, vomited in the bedpan, and started his day. Checking his belt pouch, he noted the absence of many coins, though not as many as he might otherwise. The gods were looking out for him.

Haskell emerged onto the landing overlooking the common room. It resembled a battlefield. He settled his stomach with a rind of stale bread from a table and leaned heavily against the rail. The previous night came back to him in vivid fragments as he surveyed the carnage below.

The night had started as one might expect, with ale downed in massive quantity and dangerous expediency, but then things became hazy. He recalled standing unsteadily on a table, presently overturned, while the unruly mob pelted him with… something. There was food at some point: wheat bread and watery fish stew. This prompted several grim memories of rough characters vomiting and urinating in various parts of the inn, while a raucous party raged on. There were men and women dancing, joyous cries, angry shouts, and a fight at some point.

Haskell remembered himself, Bror, and Torg huddled together over a table. He had promised them an ungodly sum to venture with him. He spotted the two mercenaries below, both lying unconscious in the fouled wood shavings. Simeon was sweeping up around their heads. Haskell clomped unsteadily down the steep, creaky stairs, stepped over a man face down on the floor, and nudged Bror roughly with his boot.

"What'in'tha name o'tha'gods!" Bror cried, his eyes tightly shut.

Haskell laughed, grimaced as pain shot through his head,

and hissed as he pressed a tender spot on his forehead. "A fine morning to you," he said through gritted teeth. "I came to make sure you weren't dead and were willing to join my party."

Bror raised his head off the floor, listening with closed eyes and a pained expression. He let his head sink into the filthy shavings. "Aye, y'scoundrel, on tha morrow. Nadda t'day." He threw one arm over his face to ward off the brutal daylight. Torg threw a handful of shavings at them both and rolled toward the wall.

Haskell left them to their hangovers, kneading his stiff shoulders and silently thanking the gods for a strong constitution. He followed a familiar voice to the bar in the back, where he found Flint speaking with another man.

"There's the young man his'self!" Flint said as he caught sight of Haskell.

"Easy, I'm still tender. These border types drink like they don't want to live," Haskell said.

"They're a rough breed, sure enough," Flint said a bit more quietly. "But here be a man what knows his manners. Zinzi, this's Haskell."

Zinzi rose and bowed. He had a fine, sharp-featured face with a touch of middle age, some grey at the temples, and a wrinkle here and there, but youth had not fully deserted him. His knee-length, burgundy tunic, once very fine, was worn and patched, but his tatty clothes didn't diminish his dignity. His clothing, what remained of it, was of the western realms beyond Bélon, a sizeable contingent of whom lived in Khul.

"Greetings, I am Zinzi, son of Zorin, from the land of Aldamen far to the west."

"Hail and well met, Zinzi, son of Zorin. I am Haskell, son of Eskil, recently from Khul. I haven't visited your lands but we're all brothers here, where humanity's enemies lurk."

"Well said. What, may I ask, does your family do in the High City?"

Haskell frowned and looked at the stained floorboards. Their business was theft, usury, and the worst kind of politics.

"I have been indelicate. Please, forget I asked," Zinzi said.

Haskell shook his head. "It's a fair question. My family are merchants, but I walk my own path now."

"Say no more. A parent's esteem is often hardest won. To business, then. Last fall, I came by strange paths to this town, where the early snows trapped me. I am out of funds and find myself in need. I am a valet by trade, speak several languages, and can serve in many capacities."

"A fine resume. No one in Branthall would employ you?"

It was Zinzi's turn to regard the floor. "Alas, no. These folk do not take kindly to those of my… geography."

Haskell thought of the poxy gate guard and could believe it. But why? From what he could remember from last night, Branthall drew adventurers from every kingdom this side of the Middle Sea. Surely Lanesforders were accustomed to outsiders by now. "Their loss. You seem a steady sort. I do need a secretary to organize my party. I'm terrible with budgets and figures. We're a small group, so you would double as my valet, if that suits you."

Zinzi nodded. "It would, indeed."

"And I've been ponderin' yer proposal too," Flint interjected, scratching his chin. "There don't presently seem to be much work about town for a cook, so I'd be willin' to follow you on a short engagement, if you'll have me."

"I would!" Haskell leaned in and whispered. "You're a fine cook—you're certain Griswold doesn't need you? Even on the road, your fare was finer." They shared a conspiratorial laugh as Griswold eyed them from behind the bar.

They set out the finer details of Flint and Zinzi's contracts, while working on the publican's inferior leftovers but superior ale.

Having eaten, and thankfully retained, his meal, Haskell picked his way through the common room. Simeon was scouring various forms of human ejecta from the stained floorboards. Haskell went into the courtyard and breathed in the crisp spring air. He bathed his face in the afternoon sun to the melodious cooing of a mourning dove.

The sound of children's laughter caught his attention, and he looked up to see an ugly boy and filthy girl, neither looking older than twelve, fighting with sticks in the alley beside the Treeman. He dimly recalled the girl fetching drinks for scraps last night, then remembered offering her a gold sovereign— an outrageous sum—to bear torches during his expedition. She had said something about her friend's dead mother being raped by orcs, but his memory was a blur.

He chuckled as the taller girl threw down the boy and mashed his face into the dirt. Still, he knew her grit wouldn't save her from the many unpleasant fates that lay in store, and the subdued boy did not look fierce enough to survive cruel streets. They were both just old enough to serve as pages. What struck him as odd was that, in a town like this, the Temple or guilds didn't take in strays. It made sense in large, uncaring Khul with gutters so low that a skulking orc could go overlooked. But here?

He wandered over and cleared his throat. "If I remember right, you agreed to be my torchbearer. I could be mistaken. I was very drunk."

The girl sprang up from the dirt and wiped a grimy sleeve across her dirty face. "Ye wasn't *that* drunk, mister. Me and Orod'll work fer gold." She elbowed her friend. The boy pulled himself up and nodded emphatically.

Haskell stared at Orod, who looked away shyly. Green-grey skin and snake lips? A half-orc, here? Branthall's people spat at Siwarders and shunned Aldamites, yet gave a half-orc free run of its streets? This was a strange town. "What's your name, lass?"

"Froba."

"Well, Froba, a promise is a promise." Haskell fished in his pouch and dropped a gleaming gold coin in her filthy palm. "Don't go running off with all that money, we head to the Darkwood in a few days." Orod brought up his wide palm, hesitated, and put both hands sheepishly behind his back. Haskell felt in his pouch, around penny and talent, and pulled out another gold sovereign. He dropped it in Orod's trembling palm.

The children gawped at the alien coins, then one another. Their shocked disbelief warmed Haskell's heart. They had probably assumed the promise of gold was a trick, like a dangled treat to bait a mongrel. He took a knee beside them. "Tell you what—you ragamuffins run along to the inn and tell Griswold I ordered you to help clean up, then get some stew. But for the love of the gods, wash up first. Children who don't wash turn into goblins, you know." He set them running with a push and watched until they flew through the inn's front door.

Maybe it had been a mistake. What would those two do with a whole sovereign each? But it had been worth it to see the look on their dirty faces. What was the point of wealth only to hoard it? Money was meant to be used, put to work, spread around. Gold and jewels did nothing piled in a treasury out of sight.

Still, what of the half-orc? Taking on the boy might be considered taboo. He wondered how that would play out with the Guild. He was sure Winifred had a policy on the matter; likely one with a host of conditions. He shook his head. Orod seemed human enough and hadn't chosen his parentage. Haskell could sympathize.

It was done, for better or worse. Besides, he was already employing Siwarders, a western foreigner, and was himself an outsider. Frankly, what did he have to lose?

Froba and Orod made for the inn. It had been a great night; Seasonings usually were. Froba's pouch was full of coin, many of them handed to her by Haskell, many more pilfered from his pouch. What a sap. He was making it too easy. Giving her and Orod a whole sovereign up front? Who did that?

She looked at Orod, who was fascinated by the gold coin, and slapped down his hand. "Put that away, ye nob. Ye want someone to take it off ye?"

She shoved open the Treeman's door and stepped inside, pulling Orod along behind her. The common room looked different in the day; the light didn't improve the atmosphere. Or the smell.

"Guuh," Orod groaned, covering his nose.

Simeon stopped sweeping and pointed at Orod. "What's that mullorc doin' in here?"

Froba jerked her thumb toward the door. "We're workin' fer that giant Southroner."

Simeon screwed up his face. "Daaad!"

"Oi, shut'it!" Bror cried, rising from the floor with wood chips in his hair.

Griswold bustled from the back. "What do you mean by bringing him in here, Froba?"

"Haskell's hirin' us. He said to clean up in here."

"Never mind that. My patrons won't take to a half-orc mooning about."

Zinzi stepped into the arch by the fireplace and gave Orod

a double-take. "There is room for him upstairs if Haskell has retained the boy. We have rented the larger apartments on the third floor."

Bror slumped at a table with his head in his hands. "Did th'lad hire th'whole town?"

"This fine fella is Bror. His big comrade, Torg, is on the floor just there," Flint said from behind Zinzi. "My word, an orc boy."

"Mullorc," Froba corrected.

"That is not a polite word," Zinzi said.

Froba looked at Zinzi. What a strange group. A sandie from the westlands, a fat northerner, and two drunken swits? What sort of party was Haskell putting together?

The footfalls and harsh voices of late risers sounded from above. Griswold shoved Froba and Orod toward Zinzi. "Out of sight, now. Give us an hour and then head up the back stairs to the third floor. Simeon, light us some sage."

Froba pulled Orod through the bar and kitchen and out onto the back stair. Apartments? The only shelter she had known was the floor of the Golden Cock, the tavern where her mother had lived, then its cellar after she died. They called it the Dragon Den. It was full of folk stretched out in filthy bunks, smoking black dragon from bamboo pipes until they wasted away. Haskell's place had to be better than that.

"Are y'sure about this?" Orod said.

"I ain't worried," she lied. She was used to stealing from questers, not working for one. What in the Nine Hells had she gotten herself into?

"B-but he's huge, and those others... they're scary."

"Who cares, we got gold in our pouches. *Gold!*"

"So?"

"So, Ferd only wants a sovereign. Everythin' else is gravy. We just gotta lay low and he'll never know how much we get.

Besides, all we gotta do is carry torches." She threw a pebble against the adjacent building. Everything would be fine.

"That's all?"

"Yep. If ye run into trouble, run away. I know ye can do that."

Orod hugged himself. "Ye'd run too if ye was bein' beat by them Tanners."

"No, I wouldn't. Bet on it." Froba was sick of his whining, of how his constant fretting made her own worries feel so much worse. She wished he would toughen up already.

She watched Luna going down on a warrior at the corner, all so she could get a fix of dragon's milk. More people drank the milk than smoked the resin. They said it all came from the seeds of flowers from the westlands, though some said they grew it in Siward. White dragon, black dragon, it was all expensive stuff, and Ferd's customers—townsfolk, adventurers, and streetwalkers—couldn't get enough of it. Like Luna, some would do anything to get it.

There were worse things than carrying torches into some dungeon.

"Can we go in now?" Orod asked.

She shoved him to the ground. "Last one in's a shit-eatin' dung-beast," she said, scrambling up the slimy wooden stairs. It was time to find out how rich outlanders lived.

April 12

Chapter XII—Temptation

The sky was overcast and a gathering wind whistled between the buildings, hustling townsfolk indoors. Haskell strutted briskly up Main Street, his scabbard swishing behind him. Zinzi followed a few paces behind, watching commoners gawk at the young giant like he was a godling out of myth. Haskell enjoyed the attention far too much. It made Zinzi uneasy.

Zinzi also felt conspicuous in his fine new, knee-length, burgundy tunic, hose the colour of fresh cream, and shoes of the softest leather; his scarf, replacing the one he had lost, was beautifully checkered in blue and gold. He did not enjoy drawing attention to himself in this town. But for Griswold's charity, he would not have weathered the long winter well. Thank the gods there were folk with some decency in Branthall.

He missed Aldamen. As soon as he had enough money, he would make for Khul and his own people. He would certainly find charity among them. For now, it was Haskell. Only, this quester business worried him.

They drew near a shop; its sheltered picture window displayed polished segments of steel armour laid on red velvet.

Haskell stooped under the awning and through the front door. Zinzi followed and was greeted by the smell of hot metal and fine oil. A solid block counter, nicked and worn, occupied the middle of the room. The walls were lined with shelves and cubbies stocked with steel chest pieces, back plates, greaves, helms, vambraces, mail hauberks, shields: everything a budding warrior could want, all within easy reach. A steep stair ran up the right-hand wall to the second floor.

Haskell grabbed a steel pauldron and turned it over in his hands, feeling the smooth, oiled metal.

"Ah, the young giant," a man said from a doorway at the back. He had wide eyes and a broad, toothy smile that reminded Zinzi of a crazed monkey. "I had a feeling your remarkable shadow would darken my doorway. I saw you pass the other day and said to myself, 'There goes a warrior of whom mellifluous bards will one day sing.'"

Zinzi doubted the armourer had thought anything so complimentary.

"Lunver's the name," the merchant said, entering the room. He shook Haskell's hand firmly and assessed the boy with a predatory gleam in his eye.

"Haskell, Eskil's Son, Orc-breaker's heir," he said proudly.

"Oh-ho? A proud lineage deserves fine armour. Leather, plate, or mail? We are working new steel from Khul."

Haskell looked from Lunver to Zinzi. "I'm told my grandfather wore a mail hauberk and carried a large round shield like my Siwardian companions. They say the Darkwood is rife with goblins, so I'd best armour myself against them."

Lunver nodded, eying Haskell's coin-glutted pouch with practiced furtiveness. "Darkwood goblins are quick and savage, true. Let's look at some real armour." He said with a wink, tossing Haskell's pauldron into a bin and drawing him along by the shoulder.

Zinzi followed them up the groaning staircase to an opulent showroom. The rafters were hung with vibrant red linen and the creaky floorboards were covered by a massive round carpet patterned with roses and thorns. A series of wooden dress forms clad in every conceivable form of armour were arrayed around the carpet. A table near the stairs held a line of dummy heads displaying iron caps, nasal helmets, crusader-like great helms, and knightly visored sallets and bascinets.

Lunver walked them past cracked pine dummies in thick, quilted gambesons and hard leather cuirasses with long bracers. "Our lowest grades of protection. Good against slashing and some piercing," he said with a dismissive wave. They passed a thick leather jerkin sewn with a series of small metal rings. "Somewhat better—longer and easy-wearing." Next, a long mail coat of overlapping steel scales. "Better still, but a good spear or bodkin would ruin your day."

He stopped at the next dress form, draped with a long, belted hauberk of mail. A long-hafted axe was tucked in the belt and a large, round shield was slung over its back. "Your grandfather would have worn something similar. Good, solid protection, and one of our most popular offerings. Excellent against enemy swords, darts, and spears. Not so versus a mace or morning star, which you will find in the Darkwood." He dragged Haskell away. "Now this is what I see on you. Good, versatile armour for a strong, fashionable man."

To Zinzi, it looked like a heavy crimson coat covered in clusters of flat steel rivets, slightly tapered at the waist, and belted over a black, diamond-padded gambeson with flared shoulders and long sleeves. Lunver lifted the skirt to show oblong plates riveted beneath. It was somewhat like the coat of plates worn by warriors in Zinzi's land, but inside-out.

"Brigandine. Overlapping steel riveted to durable canvass and a treated wool finish. Sturdier than mail—" Lunver pounded the chest for emphasis, "—yet nearly as flexible. You won't even know you're wearing it. Go ahead, feel that."

Zinzi checked the wool and steel. "A very practiced pitch. It must be popular, indeed. I note different thicknesses and grades of plate. Re-used?"

"Come now, Zinzi—" Haskell began.

Lunver glared at Zinzi. "You are a shrewd man. It has larger, thicker chest plates in front and high-quality off-cuts elsewhere. With such a fine valet in your employ, Haskell, you may opt for a rear-belted style for increased protection and a finer look."

Zinzi checked a slate chalked with prices. He was no armourer, but they seemed criminally inflated. So much for Guild discounts. "Is there nothing more economical? Master Haskell has much to purchase for his company."

Lunver ran a dry, calloused hand across his scraggly chin. "Perhaps. I do have several refitted suits."

Zinzi frowned. "I suppose their former owners retired in health and prosperity?"

Lunver puffed up. "No armour can guard against all evils. It would be sinful to waste good artifice."

"How much, Lunver?" Haskell asked with a gentle wave.

"One-hundred sovereigns. Trust me when I say every lass and lad will think you cock of the walk in such fine harness."

"Robbery," Zinzi said.

Haskell shook his head and put his arm around Lunver. "Friend, make it eighty for a complete suit and we've got a deal."

Haskell ducked out of the shop behind Zinzi. "We got a bargain!"

Zinzi was not listening, his attention on a shady character skulking in a doorway up the street. He was certain the rogue had been watching them but was now intently cleaning his fingernails with a small knife.

Haskell followed Zinzi's gaze and laughed. "Ho there, guard!" He strode toward the dark figure.

"Ho there, yerself," Ferd replied.

"I'm Haskell, Eskil's son. I didn't catch your name."

"Ferd."

"King Ferd!" Haskell cheered.

"Don't call me that," Ferd growled.

"Sorry, it's a fine thing to be named after one's king. Anyway, you steered me to some agreeable companionship the day before last. Maybe you know where she went?"

"The Gilded Cock over yonder, I warrant." Ferd gestured across the street, to a dark doorway flanked by canted bay windows; a cracked, wooden, tarnished gold rooster was perched over its door. Two skinny women in loose-fitting shifts were lounging out front. They threw Haskell lascivious looks.

"Zinzi, I'll be along presently," Haskell said absently. He looked totally enthralled.

"Do not forget—" Zinzi began, but Haskell was gone, lost to the two giggling sirens drawing him over the threshold. The pox-marked guard turned in the doorway, gave Zinzi a contemptuous bow, and rudely waved him off.

Zinzi hummed worriedly and started back to the inn. It struck him that he had never ventured off Main Street. Not that he was inclined. The unpaved side streets were full of trash and filthy children minded by dark windows and empty doorways. He thanked the gods again for blessing him with a patron, even if they had left most of Haskell's coin on the armourer's block.

"Copper for an auld 'venturer," someone said from his feet.

Zinzi regarded a palsied, used-up man sitting on the street;

his hair was white, beard matted, clothing torn, and hands and feet bound in dirty linen. The beggar had a broken sword and dinted, upturned helm at his feet. Zinzi fished out a penny and dropped it into the helm with a weighty clink.

"Thank-ee, foreigner, gods bless," the wretch said.

"The Guild does not take care of its own?"

The wretch snickered. "Not 'less a man has two pieces o' gold to rub together the first o' every month."

"What of the Temple? They must have a hospice for the infirm."

"Bah," the vagrant spat. "Temple keeps a man from starvin' or freezin', sure, just enough to ease their minds, but they don't help no man git on his feet agin. All them doctors tucked up snug in fine houses. Them priests with the healin' words o' a hundred gods but none to spare for him what's got no coin."

Zinzi frowned, having no answer beyond the clang of another penny in the wretch's helmet. "Gods be with you. May they bring you healing." He carried on down the cobbled street. Rain was coming and he had to get indoors.

* * *

The Gilded Cock was a picture in faded glory. Its dark, carved wooden trim and tables, generously graffitied, were dry and sticky from an age of smoke and open flame, as was the thoroughly blackened, embossed tin ceiling under which Branthall's elite once drank and debated.

Haskell sat on a backed bench ringed by laughing hangers-on. He had them eating out of the palm of his hand. Good, he needed more warriors. He signalled for another round and finished his story. "So, I gave the old bastard another jab and nudged him into the water for good measure." Roars of laughter and applause. The crowd's giddy admiration made him headier than the tavern's skunky beer.

A woman sidled up to him; she was dark-haired, shapely, and, best of all, eyed him with the kind of hunger he craved. "You're too much," she said in a rich contralto.

Haskell threw his arm around her and tipped back his flagon. "I figured you Lanesforders as a sour and untrustworthy lot, yet here we are."

Dirk, a mercenary sitting across from Haskell, laughed. "And I figured you as a jumped-up merchant—wait, ye are." The group laughed and tittered along. Dirk had a scarred face and a black pit where his left eye used to be. Luna, in the same threadbare dress that once graced Haskell's floor, had one hand on Dirk's thigh. Haskell didn't care.

Ferd sat beside them with a skinny girl on his lap and a glass of shriek, a clear, poisonous local liquor, in hand. "To questers! Without ye, I'd have naught but this face to make it in th'world." His companion showered his pimply cheeks with kisses.

Haskell saw Hambur's son stroll into the dank common room. He was accompanied by another affluent, well-groomed youth. Hiam shook off his fur-lined cloak and, seeing no servant, draped it over his velvet sleeve. Despite travelling together, Haskell and Hiam had not spoken.

"Slumming it, my lord?" the craggy bartender asked from behind the counter.

Hiam smirked; his companion, looking uneasy, reached for his arm. "Nonsense, Good Man. We have come to sample your local spirit, having heard of its potency."

The bartender gestured grandly to a semi-private cozy at the back. "Then proceed to my parlour and I will be with you forthwith!" The patrons laughed, but the tavern's mood had darkened at the intrusion.

Hiam inclined his head. "You are too kind."

The wealthy youths wandered to the back room; Hiam

gave Haskell's exposed, muscular chest a lingering glance, offering him a nod and a smile as he passed.

Ferd sized up the pair with a glance. He turned to a dark corner and jerked his head toward them. A lithe lad rose from the shadows and strolled to the back, his white shirt loose-fitting and leather breeches tightly laced. He entered the cozy and drew the curtain.

Haskell admired Ferd's cool manner. "Here's to fine new friends," he said, drinking and nuzzling his companion's ear; she smelled of cinnamon and rosewater. The room cheered and drank. Haskell didn't see too many fighting types aside from Dirk.

Winifred had said it might take a few weeks to find more warriors, but he didn't want to wait that long. He hoped to be on his way in three days. April the fifteenth: his eighteenth birthday. Lunver had said his armour would be ready by then. It was all too perfect, as if ordained by the gods.

"Tell me, are there any fighters here looking for a quest? The Guild Mistress tasked me with clearing a nearby hole that's rife with goblins. I hear they still blight your land."

"Tell us something we don't know," Dirk said.

"I see you've bled plenty," Haskell said.

"Bah, the fool dashed 'is eye out with 'is own mace," a woman blurted, prompting raucous laughter and a bread rind to be directed at Dirk's head.

Haskell stifled a laugh. Still, beggars couldn't be choosers. "Regrettable, Dirk, but are you interested?"

Dirk leaned forward. "I'll throw me lot in with ye, sonny, but I got terms. Two sovereigns a month. I sleep upstairs, so no need for room and board. Sound fair?"

It sounded criminal, but he was willing to play along. "Are you an archer? Some sort of specialist?"

Dirk scoffed and patted a mace dangling at his side. "No.

I have me mace an' me spear, which's more than enough, I promise ye."

Haskell sat back and drummed his fingers on the back of the bench. "A footman is worth *one* sovereign per month."

"Then split the difference. Thirty talents." Dirk took a swig of beer.

"He's seen some action," Haskell's companion whispered in his ear.

"Fifteen talents in advance—that's five more than you'd get for half a month's work—and twenty-five thereafter."

Dirk ran a hand over his scarred face. "Alright, deal."

Two mercenaries shooed patrons off a bench near Haskell and sat down. One was a chiselled woman with cropped hair and missing front teeth, the other a burly, bearded man with smiling eyes. Their jackets and hose were plain and frayed.

"I'm Trin, this is Rast," the woman said in a clipped tone. "We usually mind logging camps in the Lakewood but are after faster coin. Is there much in this venture?"

"The bloody merchants leave no gold for us," Rast boomed.

Haskell grinned. "Buckets of spoil, all for us. Hang the merchants!"

"Hear, hear!" Rast cried, as did many others.

"What are your terms?" Trin said.

"Fifteen silver now and twenty-five a month, plus room and board if you want it." Haskell said.

"Deal," Trin said, firmly shaking Haskell's hand.

"More than generous," Rast agreed, doing likewise.

Dirk scowled.

The woman beside Haskell squeezed his thigh and bit his earlobe. "I'm Ko. Room for one more?" Haskell flushed. This rainy morning was becoming a very fine afternoon.

Ferd sipped shriek and smiled darkly at another of Haskell's stupid jokes. He caught Dirk's good eye and motioned to Haskell with his chin. Dirk nodded back soberly.

Haskell was a perfect mark: a tall, young fool with plenty of coin to lose. He was amusing, sure, but going nowhere fast. Maybe in another life they could have been friends, but Ferd had a business to run. A man in his position couldn't afford friends.

Chapter XIII—The Dungeons of Argil

The party was snug in the den of Haskell's third-floor apartments. Orod pulled his blanket tighter as sheets of cold rain pelted the window. The rooms were fancy—way better than the leaky one-room shack he and his mum used to live in. The den alone was twice as big; its old carpet was ragged but nice, and the small fireplace on the outer wall made it cozy.

Around the fire was a turned pine couch piled with cushions, a few stools, and an old worn armchair behind him in which Froba sat. She braced her feet on his shoulders and shoved him forward.

"Cut it out," he said. She kneaded his back with her feet instead, which felt kind of nice.

Haskell and his lady were at opposite ends of the couch. He was massaging her feet while she mended Froba's tunic. Zinzi and Flint were playing Ur at a small table in the left corner. They were taking turns rolling four pyramid dice and moving smooth red and blue stones up and down a small, painted box-board. Past them was a curtained-off bedroom with a big truckle bed inside. A bed that was two beds? He had never seen a bed before, let alone two. He bet kings lived like this.

Orod worked his toes in the sandals Haskell had bought him and squeezed the gold coin in his draw-string pouch. A whole sovereign. With Haskell letting them live here and eat for free, it'd probably last his whole life. Well, maybe not his *whole* life.

"Orod, be a good lad and fetch us some water," Flint said.

He hopped up and went through a heavy curtain on the other side of the den. It was another room with four whole bunk beds and a counter with a pitcher and basins for washing. Bror and Torg were snoring away in the corner. Orod couldn't wait to try out his bed. Haskell was so rich. He filled a couple wood cups with water and went back into the den.

He wondered what would happen in a few days. Froba said they only had to hold torches, but his mum had told him never to go wandering anywhere, least of all in the woods. Nothing scared Froba, but the thought of monsters creeping through the trees and ready to snatch him up was terrifying.

"Where we goin', anyway?" he asked, handing water to Flint and Zinzi.

"To a dungeon the Guild found for your master," Zinzi said.

"A dungeon? We ain't done nuthin' wrong," Orod said.

Haskell laughed. "Not that kind of dungeon. This one holds enemies for us to slay and spoil to liberate."

Flint lunged at Orod with a screwed up face. "Things tha' would like to 'et up a young-un for dinner!"

Orod fell back a step, horrified. "I don't wanna be 'et by no troll! Me ma told me trolls grind stones with their teeth and eat little boys who don't do their chores."

Zinzi laughed. "As well they should, bless your mother's soul." He finished his move and passed the dice to Flint.

"Don't sound like no dungeon t'me. Why call it that?" Orod said.

"You've never heard the tale of Daegu and Hea?" Haskell asked.

"He don't know nuthin'" Froba said.

"Shut up, I know lots of stuff," Orod said.

Froba stuck out her tongue.

"I'll tell you," Haskell said, clearing his throat. "Once long ago, before the ancients—"

A rich and haunting contralto melody filled the den as Ko began to sing.

> Before Empire spread 'twixt mountain and sea,
> Warlords did clash and the lawless went free,
> as armies did war all but ceaselessly.
>
> In that dark time a foul tyrant did reign:
> Argil the Mad was the self-same lord's name;
> No evil unknown, resistant blame.
>
> Yet in those years lived a good man and true:
> Daegu the Doughty, all sin he eschewed,
> Loved more than Argil, who knew of it too.
>
> The mad lord, jealous, would not be forgot,
> And so Argil's vengeance 'ere would be sought.
> By his command Daegu's lover was caught.
>
> Pushed beyond reason and given no rest,
> Daegu raised his cudgel to bloody test;
> Before him did Argil's minions flee Death.
>
> Over hill and through dale Daegu did fly,

But his lover, Hea, he did not spy,
For Argil had fled with her by and by.

Level by level where none went before,
Daegu pursued them through dungeons of hor-
ror:
Through prisons of folk who lived nevermore.

He fought giants and goblins, devils and then,
Beasts that had been crossed with women and
men;
Gorgons and serpents and evil children.

He smote every creature that crossed his path,
Righteous was he, and in blood did he bath,
Yield he would not 'til his lover he clasped.

Daegu gives chase in the underground still,
Through every lost place, lest Hea be killed,
Until Daegu or Argil's blood is spilled.

Ko's voice trailed off. She snapped her thread and held up
Froba's tunic to assess her work. Orod stared at her agape. Ko
was so gifted and beautiful, like a noble lady.

"You've a beautiful voice, Ko," Flint said. Everyone
agreed.

"Bleh," Froba said. "Hea should'a gouged out Argil's eyes.
She could'a bit and scratched him, at least." Her tunic flopped
over her face.

Orod laughed. He still thought it was stupid to call a maze
or cave or whatever a dungeon. They couldn't all be Argil's
dungeons. Still, it was a good story, but sad. No one would
ever write a story about Orod. He didn't want to be anywhere

that could turn into a story like that.

"*I* think it's romantic," Ko said, crossing her arms.

Haskell was gazing at Ko. He probably thought her song was pretty romantic too.

April 14

Chapter XIV—Dressing Down

It was a Market Day, and the town square was crowded despite the chill air and overcast sky. Armoured adventurers mingled with townsfolk, from the filthiest vagrant to the wealthiest noble. The more industrious were busy. Buskers played at opposite corners; jugglers, contortionists and tumblers plied their craft in circles marked out by rope; food vendors were plentiful; and Branthall's vibrant cottage industry was on display at stalls and tables: jewelry, tools, stoneware, woodcrafts, eggs, religious icons, homebrew, candles, and charms.

Haskell and Ko, browsing arm-in-arm, drew envious glances from the crowd. Ko wore a fine green gown with a new silver eagle pendant on her breast, a red velvet toque on her head, and a red, fur-lined cloak. Haskell sported his crimson cuirass of riveted brigandine tightly belted over a plain, long-sleeved arming doublet. His vambraces and greaves were polished to a high sheen, and he had his sword and a new rondel dagger belted at his side. A green felt hat—peaked and folded in the latest fashion—completed his outfit. He knew they looked regal and cherished every jealous stare.

He hadn't seen so many people in one place since leaving Khul. It didn't surprise him; markets brought in folk from throughout the countryside, and executions were popular entertainment. Particularly the hanging of a Guild-traitor. He took in the wide, twenty-foot gallows erected between the keep and fountain. A gallery, its banister hung with flags and tricolours, was angled obliquely to the gallows so the judge and condemned could speak.

He saw Hambur and Hiam riding toward the gallery, bouncing along smartly in polished saddles, their gold chains jangling and furs billowing as they picked their way through the crowd. Hambur spotted Haskell and scowled.

Haskell laughed. "There's the Swinelord," he whispered to Ko, his gaze never leaving Hambur's. Ko giggled as she stared at the merchant. Hambur visibly trembled with rage. Hiam noted the exchange and, after giving Haskell and Ko a once-over, offered a courteous nod. Haskell returned the gesture. "Hiam's a decent sort. It's a shame he's that bastard's son."

The Council, Stieg and Winifred chief among them, assembled in the gallery. Soon after, a drum began a slow, steady beat from within the Keep. A thrill ran through the crowd; excited chatter and craning necks rippled from front to back. Children and indecorous companions were hoisted onto strong shoulders as a procession issued from the Gallows Gate. The condemned mounted the steep gallows stair to the dolorous drumbeat.

Watch Captain Owain, dark and severe, was first to mount the platform. His cloak billowed about a tight-waisted, black velvet brigandine cuirass. Next came a dark-haired young man in tatty tights and a stained shirt, his wrists bound before him. The hooded executioner hobbled onto the platform, followed by an axeman, who blocked the steep stair.

Stieg nodded to Owain, who stepped forward and unrolled

a parchment. "Let it be known that Béyn of Sepulchre, from the Kingdom of Bélon, is a common bandit and Questers Guild-traitor. Let his fate be a lesson to any who would walk his path, for they will be served in the same manner." He thrust the prisoner forward.

Béyn did not flinch from the crowd's taunts and jeers.

Stieg held up his hand for silence. "Béyn of Sepulchre, you have been found guilty of banditry in four kingdoms of the realm. You perpetrated wanton acts of violence in a campaign of terror, including the desecration of a sacred temple and the murder and mutilation of innocent men, women, and children. For these crimes, you are condemned to be hung by the neck until dead. How do you answer?"

Béyn spoke with a nasal Bélonese lilt. "Your laws exist so the rich may plunder their own people, laws written to justify the theft, exploitation, and murder of the poor. I have done nothing you do not perpetrate yourselves."

"That is not a denial," Stieg snapped.

Winifred's piercing voice, full of contempt, was blown in fits and starts by an intermittent wind. "Béyn of Sepulchre, the Questers Guild has five rules—rules simple enough for any child to abide." The crowd laughed and jeered. Haskell rolled his eyes. "You have broken all five in your short life, including taking the property of and inflicting harm upon your fellows, engaging in petty banditry, bringing the Guild into disrepute, and reneging on your Guild fees." The last item elicited much derision from the crowd, little of it directed at the condemned, who chuckled smugly. Winifred threw the crowd a sour look.

Stieg's voice carried over the noise. "Béyn of Sepulchre, you stand convicted of theft and murder, and will soon face Death. Do you have any last words for those you have so unjustly wronged?"

The crowd quieted.

Béyn regarded them with quiet contempt. "I may be destined for the Nine Hells, but this world is a hell you all richly deserve."

The crowd, fazed by his condemnation, exploded with shouts and catcalls. Haskell shook his head. Even if Béyn had paid the executioner, there would be no easy death now. The mob jostled and raged as the hangman shortened the rope. He tossed the noose over Béyn's head and tightened the knot at the back of his neck.

Béyn stepped onto the trapdoor without prompt and coolly, almost curiously, regarded the ferocious crowd.

The drummer beat a fast staccato.

Béyn met Haskell's gaze as the trapdoor opened, dropping him a scant four feet. The rope snapped taut, forcing his head forward as he struggled high above the roaring crowd. Those at the front pelted him with rocks and filth, expelling their pent-up hate and frustration.

It wasn't an easy death.

Ko turned away and pressed her hands against Haskell's chest. "Why did he do it?"

Haskell held her close and shook his head. "I don't know."

* * *

Captain Owain's office was tiny, its one narrow window admitting the noise and greasy food smells from the Market below. The room had a chest of papers, oaken desk worn from years of paperwork, and one splintery chair. It looked less like a council member's office than a cell.

Ferd grinned; then again, a cell's where a swit belonged.

"Don't smirk at me," Owain growled.

"Dunno what ye mean, Cap'n," Ferd replied, his expression slack.

Owain leaned over Ferd. "Why were you not at the hanging? I called out the Watch, which, it pains me to say, includes you."

"Had more pressin' business," Ferd said.

Owain ground his teeth. "There is no more pressing business. *Your* business is a stain on this town, and secondary to the oath you swore to protect Branthall."

Ferd gave Owain a momentary glare. "I haven't forgot no oaths, nor broken 'em."

"The crowd grew unruly. You were needed below, not out pimping on street corners."

"As ye say," Ferd deadpanned.

"I've been lenient with you, Ferd, but your connections will only carry you so far. Branthall will not become your brothel. Keep your whores and callboys off the streets."

"They ain't mine. We got certain understandin's, is all."

"You speak, they listen. That is enough."

"Ye'd rather our lads an' lasses be fightin' and carryin' on in the streets? They get mighty lusty after a bit o' slaughter, and ye know how it gets come winter."

"You disgust me. There are more discreet ways to handle these affairs."

Ferd laughed and scratched his craggy cheek. "Discreet's fer men like ye."

"What do you mean by that?"

"Just that street walkers and 'venturers are anythin' but discreet. That's me business. Yer's is in the Council Chamber." And the bedroom, the cheating bastard. Ferd wondered what Lunver the Armourer would think if he knew Owain was poking his saintly wife.

Owain shook a finger in Ferd's face. "Do not test me. I *will* put you in the stocks."

Ferd straightened and clicked his heels. "Aye, cap'n. I'll clean up the streets good an' proper."

Owain sat at his desk. "Good. I'm putting you on early

patrol. You're off the gate until I'm satisfied you've done your duty."

Ferd scowled. Fucking early patrol; what a prick. "I do more good at the gate."

"You'll do more good wherever I assign you. Now see to your duties in the Market."

Ferd left the room. He'd clean things up alright.

Nice and tidy.

Chapter XV—Ins and Outs

The Treeman's common room, thoroughly scrubbed and aired out, was crowded. The fireplace crackled and popped, warming patrons downing ale and devouring meat pies. A minstrel played a meandering instrumental on her goat-skinned doshpuluur, her long nails plucking its three strings and calloused fingers darting up and down the long neck crowned by a carved horse's head.

"Success in the Darkwood!" Haskell toasted.

Ko gasped and pulled down his wrist. The minstrel struck a sour note and stopped playing; several people hissed. Trin and Rast covered their faces.

Haskell frowned and set down his tankard. What had he done?

"Gar, newmeat, ye'll curse us all," a man behind Haskell said. He had half a nose and a cleft upper lip. "Prick yer thumb, put a drop into yer cup, and pour it out. Yo, lass, fetch this'un another," he said to Froba, who scuttled to the back.

Haskell looked to Bror and Torg, who shrugged. He pulled out his dagger, pricked his thumb, and squeezed a ruby drop into his ale. The scarred adventurer motioned for Haskell to get on with it. He tipped his drink into the wood shavings on the floor.

Froba rushed in and handed Haskell a fresh tankard.

"To the Worthy Dead," the adventurer said, raising his cup. Everyone in the room echoed him, Haskell included.

"Thank you," he said to the man, who grunted and turned back to his table.

Haskell regarded his companions. Zinzi was pensively sipping ale. Flint was busily dissecting his meat pie, sampling its components, frowning, and shaking his head. Bror and Torg chuckled to one another with amused bewilderment. Those two were always sharing a private joke. He worried they were accompanying him on a lark. Trin and Rast were drinking quietly. They looked embarrassed by Haskell's gaffe. What a fool he was.

He felt a sudden pang of uncertainty as his situation became very real. Tomorrow was the day. Everything was ready and nearly all his money was spent. No going back now.

A man entered the common room, blown in by a cold wind. Those near the entrance cried out for him to shut the door.

"Corben! Where have you been?" Haskell called too eagerly, drawing fresh looks of annoyance from the others.

The teamster weaved toward them between crowded tables. "At a room over the Gilded Cock. Closer to the stables." He plopped into a chair at their table and unscrewed his flask.

"I didn't see you there the other night," Haskell said.

"The company's a bit rough for me." Corben took a long swig from his flask.

"I've rented apartments upstairs. Plenty of room here, and Griswold has stables round back. You should join us."

"I did finish clawin' money out o' that tight-fisted armourer. I suppose I'm free for a run."

"I'll pay you a sovereign for this trip then see how things pan out."

"Fair 'nough," Corben grunted.

Haskell opened his pouch and counted out twenty silver talents. There was far more leather than coin in his pouch now. He felt uncertainty's bitter sting again. He handed the teamster the coins.

"Corben, this is Zinzi, my secretary and valet, and Trin and Rast, mercenaries from the Guild. Bror, Torg, and Flint you know. The girl beside you is Froba. She and Orod will bear torches on our expedition. Where is Orod, anyway?"

Froba forcefully shook her head. Haskell nodded and eyed the room again. He had gotten used to the boy these past few days, and nearly forgotten he was a half-orc, despite his startling appearance. The boy was something of a weakling. Haskell would try to toughen him up.

Rast elbowed Trin and raised his cup. "Here's to you savage Siwarders. Happy to have you on our side for a change." Trin laughed, as did most of the room.

"Here's t'you northern bastards," Bror returned with unusual clarity.

"What brings you east, foreigner?" Corben asked Zinzi.

"Yes, tell us about your homeland," Haskell said.

"Give us a story!" Rast cheered.

The minstrel ended her song and the room quieted. People turned to look at Zinzi. He took a drink and nodded. "In Aldamen, I served a wealthy merchant and tutored his young nephew. We were passing through the badlands on our way to your realm when our caravan was set upon by raiders. Our guards fought valiantly but the enemy was relentless. We caught only glimpses of the melee through the swirling dust but heard well the clash of steel and screams of our defenders.

"Seeing our fate, my charge and I rode hard through an

opening before we could be taken. The bandits pursued us into the badlands, but our steeds were fresh, and we eluded them. Of our journey through that parched land I will not speak, other than to say that it claimed the life of our mounts and my master's nephew."

"Incredible," Haskell breathed. "You must be strong and determined to have come through such an ordeal."

"Perhaps, though the gods were watching over me. Starving and mad with thirst, I emerged into your wilderness, where I found water to revive me, but I became lost in the woods."

"He must have strayed into the Elfwood," Corben said.

"No, he'd be dead," Trin said. "He found his way into Russenfield, or Umbria, maybe. What happened then?"

"I wandered for many days until, hungry to the point of death, I gave in to despair. That is when I was saved."

"By whom?" Flint asked.

"An elf princeling came upon me while scouring the wooded hills for his foes."

"No one's seen an elf for a hundred years," Haskell said.

"Aye, the elves withdrew to their haven long ago," Rast said.

"Why did the elf not slay you? No one who treads there lives," Corben said. Several patrons agreed.

Zinzi raised his hand. "The princeling took pity on me, wretched as I was. Of the path we took I am forbidden to speak. All I can say is that he brought me to your land and set me on a path to this place. Which way he went, I do not know."

Several people shook their heads and called the story false. Others were not so quick to dismiss it.

"I believe you, Zinzi," Ko said.

"Me too," Haskell said, raising his tankard. "Stick with me, Zinzi, and I'll send you home a rich man."

"Gods willing," Zinzi said.

They drank well into the night, but not too deeply or too late, it being the eve of their expedition. Haskell told them about his exploits in Khul. Rast fed them a tale about a giant troll, swearing to the gods that he saw the green-skinned monster striding through the trees like they were grass. Trin told them how she and Rast had saved some foresters from a pair of dire wolves as big as ponies. No one understood Bror and Torg, who grew more indecipherable as the night wore on, though that didn't stop anyone from laughing along.

* * *

Bror and Torg fled the heat and noise of the common room, strolling arm-in-arm up a side street. The night breeze was cool. Bright stars wheeled in the clear sky, heaven and earth marked by the stark black line of Branthall's fortified walls. Cresting a slope, they heard a clatter of metal ahead.

"Shh," a woman whispered.

"Shut it," a man growled.

Bror and Torg shrank against a wall with their hands on their long knives. They darted forward, hunched and silent, down a short, covered alley. Dim light illuminated a closed yard at the other end. With only a glance between them, they stole down the alley.

Haskell crept up behind them. He had seen them go out and, too excited to sleep, had followed. He edged forward, uncertain how best to announce his presence, but they saved him the trouble. They twisted about, their eyes hard and ready blades pale shards in the reflected half light. Haskell held up his hands and nodded questioningly ahead. Bror shrugged and Torg motioned for him to go back up the alley.

"Get a move on, Grig," the woman hissed.

"I'll move ye into the ground if ye don't shut yer mouth."

Haskell peered between Bror and Torg. Luna was hunched

over a candle lamp. She held out a sword to what looked like a storeroom with two narrow, reinforced doors. The sword had a distinctive twisted cross-guard set with turquoise, and its scabbard was heavily-embossed orange leather with a gold throat and tip. Haskell moved forward but Bror stopped him and shook his head. Haskell smirked, pushed past his friends, and sauntered into the yard. "Nice night for a walk, eh, Luna?"

Luna gasped and dropped the sword with a clatter. She turned and fell back a step. He could see her throat palpitate to the beat of her racing heart. "Haskell! What are you doing out so late?"

"Thought I'd take the air. Can I help? What's going on?"

A tall, muscular man stepped out of the storeroom. He had pale, greyish skin, deep red irises, sandy hair, and a line of little pits under his mouth. Another half-orc. Not startlingly different like Orod, more like a human who looked wrong. He wore a stiff leather jerkin and held a long-hafted wooden cudgel.

Behind him, Haskell could make out a few weapons, a suit of armour, and treasures on a table: rings, a pendant, and an ornate lockbox. The half-orc, Grig, closed over one of the narrow doors and moved toward Haskell. "This ain't yer concern, Southroner. Fuck off."

Haskell cocked his head toward Luna but looked into Grig's haunting red eyes. "Nothing Ferd should know about?"

Luna took Haskell's arm. "Let's go to the Cock."

The half-orc grinned, revealing jagged teeth. "Ye don't know nuthin' from nuthin', do ye, boy."

"I know you'd better drop that stick," Haskell said, putting his hand on his sword.

Bror came out of the alley and clapped Haskell on the shoulder. "There he is! Always pickin' up ladies in the strangest places, this one. Evenin' to you, lass," he said, nodding to

Luna. "C'mon, Haskell, time for bed." There was no negotiation: he tugged Haskell backward by his belt. Bror's compact frame disguised a surprising strength.

"We'll get that drink later," Luna said breathlessly, blocking the end of the alley.

Bror marched Haskell back to the street. Haskell didn't resist but was inwardly seething. He was their captain; who was paying whom?

Torg exited first, sheathing his knife. "Legitimate, that," he murmured in a thick Siwardian accent.

"What're you playin at?" Bror said, walking Haskell back down the hill.

"I know her. I wanted to say hello," Haskell said innocently.

Bror fixed Haskell with a steely gaze. "Lookin' for trouble, more like."

"What if I was? Questers don't shrink from danger or shirk their duty. That half-orc was up to something."

"Forget'it, lad. There'll be danger enough on th'morrow."

"Aye," Torg said.

Haskell sighed. They were probably right, but it galled him. He had been in Branthall only four days, yet everywhere he turned he saw corruption and intolerance. If he had wanted that he would have stayed in Khul. He couldn't accept it; wouldn't accept it. Not here. He would change things. Maybe not tonight, but some day. He would make everything right.

Dirk peered out of a deep doorway with his good eye. A sneer furrowed his scarred face. Haskell and them two swits. Who the fuck did they think they were, waltzing around Branthall like they owned the place? He watched his new comrades fade into the gloom.

Shit. Ferd wasn't going to like this. Not one bit.

April 15

Chapter XVI—Tithes and Dues

Haskell rose early and slipped from bed, taking care not to wake Ko lightly snoring beside him. He washed and dressed quickly, tiptoed out of the apartment, down the hall, and down the back steps. He drew his new fur-lined, midnight blue cloak and cowl tight against wet gusts of cold wind and made his way to Main Street.

He hustled along the deserted street to the wide plaza at the centre of town, past the dragon-spouted fountain, stocks and pillory, and tall stone Keep, its flags and pennants whipping in the wind. The Temple's broad columned portico stretched into the sky before him, its black marble obelisk drawing him to prayer in the grey dawn. Wide columns held up a triangular pediment adorned with chipped and broken relief sculptures. Its main figure was a muscular man wrestling two giant serpents. Haskell felt an odd kinship with the fellow, his own two serpents being his father and Slade; but those struggles were behind him now.

Ascending the Temple's steep steps, he went through a double row of columns and a broad, square doorway. He shook rain from his cloak in the vestibule and, after dropping a silver into the tithe box, strode down the nave's main aisle. The Temple was large, its many altars decked with fine cloth, silver receptacles, and ancient relics. The air was heavy with spicy incense and the melting wax of a thousand burning candles. The votives cast a warm, flickering light on a host of silent, motionless figures throughout the temple: animal-headed and many-armed gods, statuesque men and women, winged creatures; some carved crudely, some like beatific mortals turned to wood, gold, or stone.

He reached the rounded apse at the back and stood before a large altar. After lighting candles and a small mound of incense, he prayed.

He prayed for wealth.

He prayed for glory.

He prayed for the safety of his company.

Haskell concluded his exhortations by placing a small pile of talents on the altar cloth, one for each of his party.

"You seem devout," a woman said in a cultured, somewhat lilting, tone. She was taller than most, though not as tall as Haskell's sister. Her mousy hair brushed the shoulders of a white tabard, the space over her heart emblazoned with a black hammer and serpent on a chequered ground. She wore a long mail hauberk beneath, fine boots, and a belt of gold medallions.

"I give the gods their due. Haskell's my name. You have the aspect of a fighting priestess—does your order reside here?"

"No, my sect is from Bélon. We are missionaries spreading our faith through the realm. I am Yeoma of the Order of the Righteous Hammer, returned from the hills of Siward where we fought much evil. The Siwarders are stout folk, but uncouth. Too many venerate profane gods. Some even treat with dwarves, though they number fewer since we brought them enlightenment," she said with a chuckle. "You are from the north?"

Haskell found Yeoma's zeal off-putting. What did it matter which gods people worshipped? Was it not enough that they had faith and devotion? He wondered, a bit unfairly, if she had known the hanged Bélonese Guild-traitor. "I have two Si-warders in my party. They're trusty men. The gods they choose to venerate are none of my concern." Or yours, he thought.

She nodded and changed the subject. "I gather you are departing for the wilderness?"

"This morning, to the Darkwood."

She handed Haskell a palm-sized, stoppered clay pot. "God keep you. Use this salve to bind wounds and it will stave off disease. All that walks in those woods is our enemy."

"Thank you, this will help. Gods be with you." Haskell turned and left. Yeoma was striking and likely formidable in battle, but the further he strode from her, the more comfortable he felt.

Froba crouched behind a column as Haskell strutted away. She had no time for the Temple. It might be a more comfortable place than the Cock or the streets, but the priests and doctors were greedy. That seemed wrong. They were supposed to be holy and good but were as crooked as anybody. The sick and poor of Branthall were proof of that. But she had been curious what Haskell was up to, and now she wondered about this priestess.

She crept up the aisle, keeping to the shadows and careful not to slap the marble floor with her new sandals. She shuffled onto the plinth of a statue of a young woman clad in wet, clingy fabric. It was carved so perfectly she looked alive. The goddess was caught in ecstatic throes as a huge serpent coiled around her leg and torso. Froba grasped the snout of the snake and stood on her tiptoes to peek over an altar.

The priestess was gone.

Froba clicked her tongue in disappointment and slipped off the plinth. Turning back, she was confronted by a glimmering belt of golden medallions.

"I doubt the Goddess of Enlightenment would take kindly to little girls interrupting her rapture, nor the Serpent of Knowledge for having its nose squeezed," Yeoma said.

Froba gasped and darted around the priestess, her sandals slapping the smooth marble as she ran. She slid into the nave, heaved open the heavy front door, and rattled down the Temple's wide, marble steps and out into the rain. She paused in a doorway at the edge of the plaza to make sure she wasn't followed.

"Where've ye been?" Ferd said, shoving her into a dark corner. His pitted face and black, flinty eyes leered at her out of the gloom.

"Nowhere," she said petulantly.

Ferd punched her in the stomach, doubling her over. "Don't sass me, girl. Where'd ye get them new hose and shoes? Don't ye lie to me."

"Just some stupid 'venturer," she wheezed.

"So ye think ye can cut me out?" He threw her up against the wall and gave her a shake. "After I took ye in and kept yer stomach from meetin' yer spine? What's his name?"

"Ha… Haskell," she breathed, wet hair clinging to her face.

Ferd laughed cruelly. "Oh, this's too good. What's yer angle? Playin' the lost waif or sellin' yer cunny like yer whore o' a mum?"

"It ain't like that. He hired me proper!"

He jerked her violently by the tunic. "What could trash like ye do fer him?"

"I'm gonna carry torches an' stuff."

Ferd narrowed his eyes. "Stuff? He payin' ye to haul loot?" He held her throat against the wall and patted her down, coming up with her sovereign, which he brandished. "Ye are holdin' out on me."

"That's mine!" Froba croaked, swiping at the coin.

Ferd drove his knee into her stomach and threw her into the street. "That's fer cheatin' me," he growled, then kicked her in the groin. "An' that's fer bein' disrespectful."

Froba tasted iron with the primal pain.

He stooped over her. "Now. Ye'd better keep that coin flowin', missy, or I'll put ye out with tha other whores." He rose and gave the gold a toss before trotting off uptown.

Froba laid on her side, shivering on the cold doorstep and clutching her groin with both hands. Ragged breaths filled her abdomen with knives, and tears of pain and humiliation rolled off her cheek and nose.

It had been stupid to sass him like that. What had come over her? Maybe because the gold piece was the first thing she had ever been given. Not a penny or table scraps because someone felt bad for her: real money, honestly earned. Maybe that's why she had kept it so close, not in her stash at the inn. Stupid. But it was done.

She sat up with a groan and wiped away her tears. The party would be leaving for the dungeon soon. She had to get moving.

Chapter XVII—Adventure

The rain had stopped, birds were singing, and fresh, cottony clouds had become pink and purple batting in the sunrise. Haskell emerged from the Treeman in his scarlet brigandine, his fashionable hat replaced by a bright conical helm with cheek and nose guards. He rested a leather-gauntleted hand on his sword and regarded his party.

Bror and Torg lounged against Southgate in their iron-ringed coats and tartan trousers, looking a little too impressed by Haskell's armour. They had short axes in their belts and round shields slung on their backs. Trin and Rast were chatting with a townsman nearby. Both wore short-sleeved mail tunics and short swords. All four mercenaries had iron caps on their heads and long spears in their calloused hands.

Haskell smiled. Four fine warriors armed for battle and under his command. He knew in his heart that his grandfather would be proud.

Zinzi and Flint stood together, nervously chatting in woollen cloaks and hoods. Froba and Dirk sat in the back of Corben's wagon; Dirk's arms were crossed over his ill-kept scale mail. Corben sat in the driver's seat, his face shaded by a wide-brimmed hat. Orod sat beside him; he and Froba were freshly scrubbed and wearing their sturdy new sandals.

Corben's wagon was no longship, and the company no crew of hardened Southron warriors, but they were Haskell's. A captain at eighteen; his fantasy come true. He put his pack into the wagon. "What a fine band. And Froba and Orod—ragamuffins no more," he said, mussing Orod's hair.

The others laughed as Orod flattened his hair. The boy's wide, snake-like lips pulled into a frown. "I don' wanna be no goblin, do I?"

"Bein' a mullorc's bad enough," Dirk said.

Torg made a sharp but unintelligible rejoinder.

"Aye, he's a far'sight better'an you, one-eye," Bror said.

"Fuckin' swits," Dirk muttered.

Haskell frowned at the slur; these Lanesforders... "They're fine men, Dirk."

"Little gobos give ye much trouble down south, mate?" Dirk sneered at Bror.

"Nadda s'much as your mace, I hear," Bror said with a grin.

Haskell laughed, as did Trin and Rast, who rejoined the group.

"He's got you there, Dirk," Rast said.

Ko came outside and knotted a white embroidered kerchief around Haskell's neck. She put her arms around him. "For luck."

Haskell drew her tight and kissed her. Ko made him feel so powerful. So desirable. "I feel safer already."

Torg pumped one arm and muttered suggestively. Haskell looked at him askance. Better than Dirk's sourness, he supposed.

"You ruffians take care of him now," Ko said.

"Don'na you worry, lass," Bror replied.

Haskell led them through Southgate and down a low tunnel, accompanied by the flat echo of Donner's clopping hooves and the wagon's rumbling wheels. The passage was dark, damp, and smelled of mildewed clay. The raised portcullis at the end was backlit by the bright morning sky, making Haskell feel like he was passing through the stony guts of a great, flat-bellied serpent.

He exited the gate onto a path that wound down a hilly slope. The area was dotted with Judas-trees, their boughs and trunks heavy with clusters of pink, sweetly fragrant flowers. Worn gravestones filled the slope, marching away from the party in uneven rows. Many of the markers were badly eroded, the names of those buried beneath lost to time. An army of the departed lay in Branthall's shadow. Several crows alighted in the trees, glaring at Haskell between harsh caws.

Beyond the graveyard, far below, was a vast sea of dry, brown grass stretching to the horizon. Patches of green grass struggled through the husks of their forebears to drink the April sun.

Haskell rounded a high hill in the middle of the cemetery, behind which stood a massive oak, its thick boughs stretching to the sky as if celebrating spring's return. A squat cottage with a slanted thatch roof sheltered beneath the tree, as did a spindly man in a dirty white shift. He was planing a rough pine panel laid across two tall stumps. Six fresh coffins were stacked under a lean-to behind him.

The oak's branches creaked in a strong breeze, and the crooked man glanced up from his work. He regarded each of them with dark, measuring eyes as he shaved off another strip of pine. "Fine morning," he said with a gormless grin.

"It is," Haskell said awkwardly. No one else answered.

Haskell picked up his pace. How many questers had the undertaker buried in fresh boxes under stony markers? Where had they come from? What were their hopes and dreams? He led them through a wattle lichgate, hurried by the undertaker's dry cackle.

Further down, they left the path where it joined a highway; the road ran east through the Barbarian Plains to the coast, and west to the halls of Lanesford's Old King Ferd and the other kingdoms. Bror and Torg took the lead, lumbering down a steep embankment and along a rough track through the dry grasses of the Lane. Haskell and Zinzi strolled along after them, chatting about trade. Flint followed, going on at length to no one in particular about the merits of hot-water crust pastry. Corben's wagon bumped along behind him, while Trin and Rast brought up the rear.

They carried on through the damp fields for over an hour, until their feet and legs were soaked from the moist grass and their sodden cloaks pulled at their shoulders. They trudged up rises and down depressions, skirted boggy patches, and cut through wooded thickets. After crossing a high-banked stream, the wagon bumped over something in the grass and jolted to a halt.

"Shit," Corben said. He hopped to the ground and cleared away some weeds. The wagon had gotten hung up on a low stone foundation and charred wood.

Torg poked about with his spear, turning up several smooth, palm-sized, oval stones. "Goblins," he said, passing one to Bror.

"Out here?" Haskell scanned the landscape. It had been a pleasant walk and people said the Lane was clear. He hadn't anticipated any danger outside the Darkwood, not so close to town.

"Aye, likely." Bror tossed Haskell the stone.

It was a three-ounce stone with holes drilled through it. Three ragged, overlapping lines were engraved on its surface.

"What are these holes?"

Torg threw one hard and far. The bullet made a long, diminishing whistle.

"It's a scare tactic," Rast said. "A few goblin slingers in the brush start a panic, then come the spears. You're fine so long as you keep your head."

Haskell kicked at the debris in the grass. "They don't build out here, do they?"

Trin cleared her throat. "They did during the war and roamed the fields at night. I doubt this is goblin, though. They use mud brick. Besides, they keep to woodland caves these days."

"Do goblins talk?" Froba asked.

"A primitive language. Not difficult to learn, I'm told," Zinzi said.

"What do they 'et?" Orod asked nervously.

Flint jabbed Orod's tummy. "Any meat they can get."

Corben rose and wiped his hands on his jacket. "They eat vermin and anything else they get their claws on. Even each other. Help me get the wagon out. The axle and wheel look fine."

After freeing the wagon, they carried on. As morning wore on to afternoon, two tall hills rose from the grasslands ahead. Each was crowned with twisted, leafless trees. They were twin heralds of a steep, stony escarpment that ran into the distance on either hand. Drawing near, they saw a stream rushing down a steep, rocky pass between the hills, which rose above them like silent behemoths. A rough path switch-backed up the pass, over which the stream spilled. The climb wouldn't be easy.

Haskell grinned. "The Sentinel Hills. They guard our path to the Darkwood. We're nearly there."

* * *

Haskell stood in the wet leaf litter of a poplar grove on top of a flat, rocky hill a hundred yards beyond the treeline. He stared into a gaping rift in the ground as tall and wide as a man. The dungeon entrance. The grove was strewn with broken, soil-covered masonry blanketed by moss and brambles, as if the forest was trying to bury the past.

They had dropped a fallen birch into the entrance, its splintered top jutting out of the opening like a rungless ladder. A knotted rope ran down the angled trunk and into the earthy maw. Froba joined him at the edge. She had a sack of torches over her shoulder, each a tight bundle of long hickory bark with a pitch and linen core. She was squirming and had an arm across her stomach.

"Bumpy ride?" Haskell asked.

She just shrugged.

He shrugged back; if she had something to say, she would tell him. He eyed the breach like a hearty meal and clapped his gauntleted hands. "Flint and Corben will set up here while the rest of us look into this hole." He motioned to Bror and Torg. "Lead on, you two."

The two mercenaries were sitting on a fallen tree, grinning over a private joke. They grew businesslike and shared a side-long glance. Their wordless exchange must have been positive because they rose and joined Haskell. At least they were following his orders this morning. Torg went first, followed by Bror, both swearing in Siwardian as they walked backward down the slippery birch using the knotted rope.

Haskell climbed down after them. He let go of the rope halfway down, dropping into a dank, rectangular room, and landing in thick muck with a squelch. Roots covered the walls and hung from the ceiling of a roughly ten by fifteen-foot room. Torg's torch flared to life, bathing the space in hot orange light. The walls undulated with insects and writhing worms. Haskell felt like he had dropped into his own grave. Judging by his companion's faces, they felt the same way. He pushed down rising doubts. His grandfather wouldn't have feared this place; he must have endured dozens of such holes in the slave pits of Caen.

One wall held a low archway to a landing hewn from reddish mudrock. Torg already stood at the top, his torch held over a narrow staircase worming its way into darkness far below. The steps and its barrel-vaulted ceiling were coated with thick, glistening slime.

Zinzi clambered down the rope, a hard cudgel bumping against his thigh. He examined his mucky ankles. "I am glad I wore my old clothing."

Froba came next, followed by Orod.

"Gah, it's gross down here. Ye made us wash fer this?" Froba said.

"Aww, my feet is mucky," Orod complained.

Trin, Rast, and Dirk followed. The company packed the close, muddy chamber.

Haskell checked the torch-sacks slung over Froba and Orod's shoulders. He handed Torg's torch to Froba and lit another for Orod. They held the hot, bright flames away from their faces. "If there's trouble, keep back. Your job is to light our way, not be goblin food," he said with a wry smile. Neither looked reassured.

Haskell followed Bror and Torg through the arch with Froba between them. They passed down the stairs with the others close behind. Haskell steadied himself against the wall. "The Treeman's rickety stair has nothing... on this!" he said, one foot slipping on the slick stone.

The air grew colder as he descended, his skin gathering into gooseflesh and breath ejecting in short, vaporous jets. He gritted his teeth at the sound of their scuffling and scraping.

Anything could be waiting for them below.

He started counting steps to distract himself and, after several slippery minutes, set foot on level ground. "Seventy, by my count," he said, glancing at Froba. She looked at him expectantly.

They stood at the corner of a narrow L-shaped passage. Like the stairs, it had a dripping, barrel-vaulted ceiling a few feet taller than Haskell. A flat stone door with an iron rung stood several yards ahead. Bror and Torg were on his left at the other end of the hall. Their shields were raised, and spears poised to strike. Hardened fighters fully engaged.

While their leader prattled on about steps.

Haskell roiled with shame. The physical distance between him and the Siwarders might as well have been a gulf of experience. How could he lead this group through danger and death to success and riches? He growled away the pernicious thoughts. It was said that his grandfather killed his first man at sixteen and commanded scores of men at eighteen. This didn't even compare.

He drew his sword, its scrape echoing shrilly off the walls. "Dirk and Froba, listen at that door, everyone else with me."

The dungeon's reddish rock was darkly saturated, and its vaulted ceiling wept cold tears into a green, mouldy-smelling slurry on the floor. Droplets plinked and splatted onto his helmet and cloak as he crept up behind Bror and Torg. Just like in the alley last night; he prayed they would back him up this time.

The passage opened onto a rough-cut room that was broad and long. Orod's torch made shadows dance around the corners of five vaulted passages evenly spaced around its walls: two on the left, two on the right, and one on the other side. The one in the center of the opposite wall split into a "Y" further down. Those at the base of the left and right walls ran a good ten feet before turning sharply toward the top of the room, which is where the final two passages stood.

Haskell looked to Bror, whose face mirrored his own uncertainty. He spoke over his roiling insecurity. "Everyone pick a passage."

Trin and Rast went across the room. Bror and Torg right. Zinzi followed Haskell left.

Haskell's heart was in his throat; every clink, rasp, and splash echoed up, down, and around the passage. What in the hells would he find down here? What did a real goblin even look like? He sprang around the bend, sword out, and peered down a gloomy passage. It turned back to the room, the light of Orod's torch flickering at the end. He hurried down it with Zinzi close behind but hesitated at another stone door halfway down.

Should he open it? Get the others? His breath caught in his throat; he put a hand to his chest. The notion that everyone else had been seized by goblins overrode all other thoughts. He moved down the hall and around to the top of the chamber.

Everyone was there and came together in a tight knot in the middle of the room. Blazing torches lit faces as nervous as Haskell felt; everyone darted glances at passages occluded by shadow, their hot, fast breath crystalizing in the air.

"We didn't hear nuthin' at the door," Froba whispered. Her face was white in the warm torchlight. Dirk gave Haskell a confirmatory nod.

"The branches up top both dead end," Trin said.

"Aye, like the miners gave up mid-swing," Rast added.

Bror jerked his head to the right. "One door that'a'way."

"Ours too," Haskell said.

"Was there any m… monsters?" Orod stuttered.

"No, lad," Bror said with a half-smile.

"Can't say I like these tight spaces," Rast said, looking around. "I'll take a nice bit of forest any day."

Haskell felt like a mouse in the den of a hungry snake. He didn't like all this uncertain skulking. He needed something tangible, an enemy to overcome, not ghouls and phantoms conjured by his mind—enemies against which he had no defence.

"We'll try Bror's door," he said.

Froba swept her torch around the dripping room as the others shuffled down Bror's passage. She had heard questers talk about all manner of things below the earth: snakes fifty feet long; huge, wire-haired bugbears as silent as cats and that could crush a man's throat with one hand; mantis men that could snatch your head off in a flash. She held her hissing torch higher. Had something moved back at the stairs?

Dirk stood beside her, spear in hand. He gazed down the corridor and spat into the slime. "Move it. Lanesforders stick together," he said, nudging her after the others.

The party gathered around a stone door halfway down the hall. Rast burst through with a roar, followed by Orod and the rest. The rectangular chamber beyond, about the size of the one they had left, was full of rotten leaves, twigs, about a dozen rotted bed frames, and old bronze candelabras overturned in the muck. The others spread through the room, probing the wet trash for anything of value.

Rast kicked at a frame. "Who'd live down here?"

"Brigands?" Zinzi said.

"Goblins," Dirk said.

"In beds?" Haskell questioned.

Froba, toes numb from the icy slime, splashed to a large, round brazier in the middle of the room. Its three legs were entwined serpents that reared up to grip a wide, shallow bowl in their mouths. Its bronze was covered with fuzzy, mold-like turquoise deposits. She ran her hand over the rough, pitted surface. Who made it and why had it been left to rot?

"Goblins!" Rast shouted.

The sharp splish of running feet echoed from the doorway.

Froba whirled, her flaming torch scorching her cheek. She fumbled for her dagger. She'd never seen a real monster before. She wasn't ready. The mercenaries hedged the doorway with their spears. Haskell towered behind them, sword ready and face set, though she couldn't tell if it was with fear or determination.

Orod ran to her side and whimpered.

Zinzi stood in front of them, cudgel in hand.

Froba's heart raced, and her vision became strangely keen. She fixated on everyone's shadows—how they were stretched up the rough walls by the torches. She fought to steady her breath, which clouded the air before her.

It all happened so fast.

First nothing, then two, four, and more of the creatures rushed through the door. They were small but terrifying. Some leapt, some went on all fours. The goblins' skin was mottled, deep crimson into deeper burgundy, their eyes bright yellow with slitted pupils like a snake. They had spears with long, black bodkin ends and wore black, oily leather armour. They were frightening, yet alluring, like a tiger walking on its hind legs. It was as if some mad god had crossed a snake, a toad, and a human.

Two went down, pierced by spears as they crossed the threshold. A third skirted Torg's shaft and leapt onto Rast, the big man slipping and falling backwards. Froba blanched as the goblin landed behind him. Its yellow eyes met hers as it fell on its side. She had never seen eyes filled with such hate.

Then it was over.

The goblins that followed baulked, giving her companions all the opening they needed. Dirk ran one through with his spear, Bror and Torg cut down two more. Trin stabbed and hacked a goblin in the back with her sword, exposing its bony spine.

Haskell rounded on the goblin that was staring at Froba. She perceived a metallic flash and the creature's snarling visage going slack in slow time, its hate replaced by death's dull stare. Haskell's blade carried a line of beaded blood upward in an arc, the vital fluid glinting in the torchlight like the treasures he desperately sought. It was the most beautifully horrifying thing Froba had ever seen. She doubled over and vomited, her bruised stomach and pelvis contracting painfully.

"I ain't familiar with this breed," Bror said, helping Rast to his feet. "The ones down south are orc-green."

"The beggar sliced me proper," Rast said with a wince. A long gash on his forearm had made his right hand a bloody glove.

"Froba, your bag," Haskell called.

Froba wiped vomit from her mouth and splashed across the chamber. She loosened her sack's slipknot and drew out Yeoma's pot of poultice. Haskell opened it and scooped out a green-yellow paste that smelled of garlic and linseed. He smeared some on Rast's forearm and tightly bandaged it.

Trin wagged her finger in Rast's face. "If you die down here, you'll never hear the end of it."

"Not much in a fight, are they?" Haskell said. He looked giddy.

Bror made a warning hum over his shoulder from the doorway. "Don'na be quick to dismiss 'em. They're right deadly in a pack. An' there won'na be just these."

"What d'ye know, ye cowardly swit?" Dirk said.

Torg stepped forward with a growl.

Haskell stepped between them. "Goblins are enemy enough. Let's see if they're carrying anything."

Froba watched the others paw at the goblins' bloody corpses, flipping them over by their legs and arms like butchered animals. They probed the goblins' pouches and jerkins. She didn't know how to feel. They were the old enemy. Monsters of the Darkwood. Only, they were so small; smaller than her. They wore sad-looking armour and had tiny spears compared to their own. They were monstrous, with sharp claws, slits instead of a nose, wide snake lips, and needle-like teeth, but then, so was Orod. The only thing he had over them were his hazel eyes and human teeth. Is that what made him different from a goblin?

"Th'beggars be loaded," Bror said with a grin. He stood and showered irregularly pressed silver talents into Haskell's cupped hands. Froba saw that one side bore a regal, bearded profile crowned with laurels, the other a double-handled amphora.

"I've never seen this coin before. Looks old," Haskell said.

"Monsters are always stumbling on Old Empire stashes," Rast said.

Dirk sniffed. "Or pullin' coins off questers' corpses."

Haskell tipped the coins into his leather pouch. "Silver's silver. Grab that diseased bronze, too—it should still be worth something."

Froba watched them toss the corpses away from the door and followed them back to the first room, where they piled the decaying bronze. She pulled the linen sheet that she was using as a cloak tight around her. It was cold down here—she couldn't feel her fingers or toes.

Trin led them down the opposite corridor and put her ear to the stone door halfway around the passage. "I hear… clicking?" she said.

"Could be a trick," Bror said.

"Or gobos bangin' rocks together—get on with it," Dirk growled.

"By all means," Haskell said, gesturing to the door.

Dirk threw Haskell a dark look from his hollow socket; he shoved open the door and splashed into a large, square room. Haskell followed, and Froba watched him come face to face with the largest insect she had ever seen. Its triangular head, level with Haskell's, cocked to one side as it regarded him through black eyes that were emotionless orbs.

Froba bumped into the wall behind her and watched through the door, unable to move. Dirk thrust with his spear, but the beetle's front leg flashed out, catching him on the head. He lost his iron cap and went into a pile of rotted garbage. Haskell put his weight behind his sword tip, but the monster, so fast, sprang aside, dipping and weaving like a boxer. It hammered Haskell's chest, knocking him into a rotted strongbox that broke under him.

The others piled through the door as Haskell threw something into the insect's face, causing it to rear back. It rounded on the others, their spears glancing off its hard, arrowhead-shaped body. Its razor-sharp mandibles nearly snatched off Rast's hand. Trin drove at it with her spear, but it darted forward, forcing her back out of Froba's view. Trin let out a maddened scream.

Froba was paralyzed. She couldn't remember what she was supposed to do. Orod was standing by the door with his quivering torch held into the room, his eyes shut against the horror within.

She heard an angry shout. A sharp crack. A smack and yell, and a horrible shriek that froze her blood—worse than any barn owl or fox she had ever heard. Haskell charged off the floor with a bellow like the world was ending. The shrieking stopped. He stumbled back into view; his sword arm and chest were covered in thick, yellow slime. Trin backed into the doorway, sword out and breathing heavily. Her right cheek was a torn, bloody mess.

Froba took a tentative step forward, her mind slowly grinding back into action. Trin was hurt. Froba had the poultice. She pulled out the jar and held it up, her whole arm shaking, and tugged at Trin's mail shirt. Trin took the pot absently and gazed back into the room.

Inside, the others stood around the dead beetle on the floor. Bror and Torg's spears were covered in thick ichor that was spilling from the monster's sides and neck. Dirk had his mace in hand, a large bruise forming on the side of his face, and Rast was leaning on his spear.

Haskell used a rag to wipe the sticky fluid from his hands. "Gods, what a menace."

Froba looked at the room. It was like a garden, if vegetables were fungi and fruits were moulds. The crops were arranged around the room in rough patches: here a rotting goblin covered in green fungus, there a rat sprouting mushrooms. The room's gamey putrescence was overwhelming. Part of the right wall and floor had become a gaping, ragged hole taller than Froba.

Haskell went to the strongbox he had crushed, its wood sprouting black, fur-like fungus. A cache of pennies spilled from inside. He picked up a coin and tossed it to Trin. She scowled, grimacing as Zinzi pressed a poultice-smeared bandage against her ruined cheek. Rast wound another bandage around her head.

She threw the coin back to Haskell. "Copper, and not much. We earned more in the camps," she said, holding her cheek.

Rast looked at the wet garbage filling the room. "What a

mess. Old bronze and a few coins are a far cry from the riches you promised."

"The bug nearly ate me alive," Trin said.

Haskell looked around. "There's got to be more in here. Dirk, be a good man and gather up those pennies."

The others scattered throughout the room as Dirk scooped up hundreds of the slimy coins. He winked at Froba as a few handfuls made their way into his pouch. Froba brought her torch to the huge hole in the wall. A rough, egg-shaped tunnel burrowed through the rock and bent sharply to the right, out of sight. She wondered where it led but could only imagine a pit of giant beetles and huge, writhing worms with tooth-filled maws. She screamed, fumbling the torch as Trin clapped her on the shoulder.

"Careful you don't become a meal," Trin said, flashing a checkerboard smile.

Froba nodded and walked around the outside of the room. Rast was tearing at the putrescent goblin's pockets with the tip of his spear. Its leg rolled out of its socket like overcooked meat, exposing bone and black gunk that used to be flesh and blood. He gagged and fell away.

Across the room, Haskell checked a lidless chest filled with mouldy clothes. He wasn't looking half as confident as he tried to sound. Froba had assumed he knew what he was doing or had learned a thing or two at the Guild; watching him poke at the chest of garbage with his sword, she wasn't so sure.

At the back wall, beside a broken, overturned table, she noticed a strange mark on the floor. Someone had crudely carved a shallow, S-shaped snake into what looked like a large, wet paving stone. The symbol was stained algal green, which stood out against the darker floor slime. Had the broken table been in place and the floor clean, the stone would have been easy to miss. "I found somethin'," she cried.

Haskell brightened, hopped a patch of fungus, and crouched down where Froba pointed. "Oh-ho, what's this?" He drew his dagger and worked it into a seam, prying up the stone and getting his gauntleted fingers underneath. The others gathered around as he lifted it. Beneath was a hole flooded with black water. Something glowed deep inside.

"Magic," Torg said.

"Or a glowy worm to take off your hand," Dirk said.

Haskell scowled but didn't hesitate. He plunged his right gauntlet into the water and came up with a black pouch. It tore open in his hand, spilling bright, polished, cobalt blue and gold lapis-lazuli stones. He fumbled the oval and teardrop-shaped gems, some plopping into the water, which splashed Froba.

"Gah," she groaned, wiping black slime off her face. The others had a good chuckle at her expense. At least they had found some real treasure. Maybe enough to go topside. She didn't want to be in this icy hole anymore.

"Go on, fish out the rest," Rast said, all but slavering at the prospect of some real spoil.

Haskell went to work, and a pile of ornamental stones was joined by two stoppered, crystal vials filled with liquid. One was clear and ruby-coloured, the other cloudy and colourless. Both glowed with an inner light, like candles on a winter pine.

"Nice haul," Rast said, clapping Haskell's shoulder.

Haskell held up the glowing vials and grinned at Trin. "Good enough?"

"It'll do," she said, leaning on her spear. She looked pallid and tired.

Froba had no idea how long they had been down here, but it felt like forever. Her stomach hurt; her crotch hurt. She'd be lucky not to die of a fever after being in all this cold slime.

"Let's get outta this stinkin' hole while we're ahead," Dirk said, holding his bruised head.

"I'm with Dirk," Rast said. His bandaged forearm was oozing blood.

Haskell rose and tucked the vials in his pouch. "Fine. You, Trin, and Dirk wrestle that old bronze topside. We'll have a peek through that last door and follow right along."

Froba scooped the lapis lazuli into a small sack, palming a few for herself. Ferd would be after her for more money all too soon. Maybe there was an upside to all this danger after all.

Chapter XVIII—Ordeal

Orod watched Trin, Rast, and Dirk haul the bronze candelabras and big brazier up the slippery steps, grunting and swearing as they went. Haskell put his hand on Froba's shoulder. "You light their way, then stay here and keep watch. If anything comes down that hall, give a shout and run to us quick or upstairs if you can't get through."

Froba, wide-eyed and tight-lipped, nodded. Orod had never seen Froba scared, not really scared. Sure, he'd only known her a little over a week, but she stood up to the Tanners and acted like she belonged wherever she went. She sure looked scared now, though. He found that oddly comforting. If tough Froba was scared, maybe he wasn't such a coward after all.

"Orod, you come with us," Haskell said.

Orod's belly turned to ice. He was glad for the freezing slime and dripping ceiling, it helped hide that he'd wet himself. Haskell and Zinzi splashed down the passage after Bror and Torg, who stood at the stony door across from the stairs. Orod looked to Froba for reassurance, but she was lighting the way for the others.

"Go!" Haskell said.

Torg tugged the iron rung. The door opened more smoothly than the others, and he slipped and fell to the scummy floor. Bror leapt through the doorway with Haskell at his heels, the two nearly bumping into each other when Bror stopped short.

Orod saw a cramped, square room, its walls covered in green marble tiles so dark they were nearly black. He wandered in after Torg. The weird stone seemed to suck up light, making the small space gloomy. Two stone slabs (or were they doors?) stood side by side on the left wall. Neither had a rung or handle. Torg tapped one with his spear.

Zinzi came in last. He looked closely at a wall. His dark reflection leered back at him like a wraith. "I do not care for this place."

Orod had thought the muddy room at the top of the stairs had felt like a grave. This room felt more like a tomb. He shivered. "Can we go up now?"

Haskell sighed. He sounded relieved. "Yes, there's nothing here. Let's head up."

Zinzi made to leave but stopped.

"What's wrong?" Haskell said.

Zinzi turned. "The door is stuck."

The door they came through was closed and had no handle. Haskell pushed past Orod and Zinzi and gave the door a savage kick. It didn't even shiver. He hopped back on his smarting heel, glaring at the stone like he was going to hit it with his sword. He tried to wedge his fingers between the door and frame, but the gap was too narrow. He drew his dagger.

"I would'na do that, lad," Bror said.

Haskell turned. The look in his eyes scared Orod. "Why not?"

"Things don'na add up. Why's this room still have its tile,

and why'd tha door close over so quick and quiet? I'm no dun-geoneer but can tell we're in a pickle."

Haskell cleared his throat. "What do you suggest?"

"Maybe have a go at one o' them other doors. I don'na think this room wants us ta go back th'way we came."

Creeping dread filled Orod. What was going on? Bror was talking like the room was alive. He fought back tears.

Haskell frowned but nodded. He went to the leftmost slab and gave it a shove. It moved but resisted. He threw himself into it. Nothing. He growled and charged into the door, his helmet and pauldron rebounding with a clang. The door shivered in its frame, then the room shook violently, causing them to stumble about; it filled with a deafening grating noise.

Orod covered his ears, scorching himself with his torch. "The walls are moving!" he shrieked.

And they were.

The warriors threw themselves against the doors until the cold slabs had risen above the ceiling, leaving blank marble behind. Zinzi paced the room like a trapped animal. Haskell looked uncertainly from wall to wall.

"I'll die before this bloody tomb gets the better of me," he said.

"Poor choice o' words, lad," Bror said.

The room jolted to a halt, sending them into the walls and floor. The unbearable grinding echoed away into heavy silence. There were no exits. The bare marble drained the last of Orod's hope. He started to cry. He couldn't help it. He just wanted to go home. Why did his mum have to leave him? He hated her for leaving him, and he hated these big men for bringing him here to die. He didn't want to die.

"Search the walls," Haskell said, sheathing his sword.

Orod watched them run their hands over the streaked and

mottled tiles, probing any crack or depression with the desperation of drowning men. All but Orod, who stood stiffly in the middle of the room. He clutched the torch, shaking, his knuckles white. Sweat dripped from every pore on his body. The walls seemed to close in around him. Haskell was rich, he'd never gone hungry, never been kicked in the street. In Orod's mind, they were already dead, frozen corpses in this airless tomb. Ragged breaths puffed from his slack mouth and his vision narrowed.

He shouldn't have come here.

It wasn't fair.

He should be topside where it was warm.

Froba was brave. She should be here, not him.

"Here," Haskell called. He pointed to a catch concealed in a dark marbled whorl. He pressed it and the room shook, throwing him to the floor. He pounded the ground with his fist, but that didn't stop its implacable descent.

"Gods damn this place!" he shouted. It looked like *he* was going to cry.

Orod made a hysterical titter. He felt giddy. Crazy.

Haskell rose unsteadily from the floor. He arched his back and took a deep breath. He was cold and tired. His armour was so heavy, and his body a mess of aches and strains from his fights and wary loping. They had only just started.

He couldn't bring himself to look at his companions. What a fine captain he made. He imagined the Guild Mistress, perched on cushions in her dragon-crowned chair, laughing. Laughing at him with her glittering green eyes harder than the gems on her fingers. She had tried to warn him, but he hadn't listened. He fought back panicked rage as her words came back to him.

"Be ready. The further down we go, the greater our peril,"

he said over the grating din.

As if on cue, another grey stone slab rose from the floor. The room slammed to a halt as the portal came level. Torg put his ear to the door and said something in Siwardian.

"High-pitched voices, maybe goblins," Bror translated. "Whate'er they be, they heard us for sure."

"Well then," Haskell said, drawing his sword. "Let's introduce ourselves."

And with that, he kicked open the door.

* * *

Froba, crouched low and trembling, hugged the corner of the passage, one foot on the slimy stairs to the surface. Back in the sun and surrounded by tall stone walls, the idea of tramping into the wilderness had been exciting. Now, wet and shivering, she was just scared and alone. Clinging to her torch for warmth as much as light, she wondered if monsters could smell fear.

She was certain they could.

Froba was unsure how long it had been since the ear-shattering grinding had come from the door. She tried to remember what Haskell had said: keep watch, run, shout—but when and for what? She fought back fear and crept down the hall, pitch and smouldering hickory dripping from her torch to hiss into the ooze on the floor.

He had to be alive. She couldn't afford to lose him so soon. The treasure she had taken off him would only last so long. Then what?

The stone door loomed over her, its corroded iron rung level with her face. She had stifled a giggle when Torg fell in the muck. She wasn't giggling now. Could she even open the door? She reached for the pitted iron rung thicker than her trembling fingers.

The hallway exploded with that horrible grating noise and

the floor shook. She clutched her ears and made a fearful wail. Casting her torch into the muck, she made for the stairs, scraping her knuckles and stubbing her toes as she scrabbled up on all fours.

She didn't think of gold or Haskell or even the half-orc boy she was leaving behind. Plunged into darkness, all she could see was the bright hole to the surface in her mind, the rope dangling through it a cord to life and the world outside. She whimpered and struggled up the dark, slippery stairs, certain that goblins and trolls were grasping at her heels.

* * *

Time slowed as Haskell charged through the door after Bror and Torg. All his fear and uncertainty slipped away in a rush of adrenaline and purpose: fight or die. Four goblins visibly quailed as he rushed into the small room. The two rearmost hurled spears with fearful malice. Both shafts struck Bror's shield, one nearly gouging out his eye as it cartwheeled off his iron cap. The nearer two creatures drove forward with their weapons.

Haskell sprang around Bror. Black steel ripped along his armoured side; not that he felt it. He drove his blade into the goblin's throat, the tip glancing off hard bone and coming out the other side. Torg deflected the other's weapon with his shield and plunged his spear through its shrieking mouth, the long tip erupting out the base of its skull.

The two remaining goblins, spearless, and with their comrades' gory corpses thrown down, flashed dagger-like teeth and fled. They didn't make it far. Haskell cleaved the head from one and Bror drove his spear into the other's back. "Bloody gobos," he spat, yanking his spear out of the gasping creature. It stumbled and fell, and Bror finished it off.

Haskell wiped aspirated blood off his face, his confidence somewhat restored. Four more goblins to add to his tally; that brought them to an even ten. He, Bror, and Torg were well armed and heavily armoured, and they had Orod's torches and Zinzi to back them up. They would make it if they stayed together and went carefully. "If we keep this up, we'll find our way back."

"We'd best find it soon. There could be scores o' gobos down here," Bror said, eyeing the reinforced door.

The room was identical to the one they had left, but was unfaced, red mudrock like above, though much drier. A thick brown candle burned on a little square table surrounded by stools in a corner; a rack of goblin spears was against a nearby wall. Bror and Torg rifled the corpses, turning up more ancient silver.

Orod followed Zinzi into the guardroom, noting the man's disgust as he regarded the slaughtered goblins. Orod had looked away during the other fights, but forced himself to look this time, trying to be brave. The goblins were as short as him and, with their blood oozing into the cracks of the rough floor, he almost pitied them. These small, dead things were not like the monsters his mother had conjured to terrify him into obedience. The men had cut them down like weeds in a field. Why were people so afraid of them?

Were all monsters like this?

He thought of Zinzi's revulsion and looked at his own pale green hand, holding it up against the goblins' red skin. The people of Branthall were all sorts of colours from all sorts of realms, but none of them were red or green. What did that make him? Did Zinzi hate him as much as the goblins?

"Come, it does not do to dwell on the dead," Zinzi said, taking Orod by the shoulder.

Haskell shoved open the door, revealing a dark, cavernous

chamber. They fanned out through the arch and were greeted by rocky walls curving away into darkness. Orod raised his torch. The light barely illuminated the ceiling high above and didn't reach the far walls at all. Its warm light glinted off a broad puddle of water in what might be the middle of a huge round chamber. Rectangular stones were laid out in rows near the pool and a pile of rough wooden boards was stacked near the door, some of them hammered into long frames. What were the goblins up to?

"I wonder what they are building?" Zinzi said, echoing Haskell's thoughts.

"Naught that's good for us," Bror said.

Haskell took in the darkness around them. "How many torches do we have, Orod?"

"F-f-five," the boy stuttered.

Orod was being very brave. Haskell would treat him and Froba to something when they made it back to town. Maybe proper jackets and shoes—he worried about their health in all this cold slime. He hadn't imagined it would be so wet down here. He had thought of Khul's dusty catacombs stuffed with dry bones, not this hole. But the menacing darkness worried him more. "That won't last long if we light more. Gods know how long we'll be stuck down—" He saw a distant light off to his right.

A torchbearer led several goblins out of a corridor across the chamber. It stopped. The goblins' brows knotted with bewilderment. A larger one pushed past, and its face twisted with rage. It pointed at Haskell and barked several sharp commands. The torchbearer scuttled back down the corridor as the rest loped forward. Their ferocious whoops and howls echoed off walls lost in the darkness.

Haskell shook off his surprise. "Back to the door!" He fell back with the others, reaching the door as six goblins swept around them. Bror and Torg flanked Haskell with their large round shields. The goblins made dashing feints, looking for an opening.

Bror risked a glance at Haskell. "Get inside!"

Haskell set his jaw. "No, I'm with you."

Like a striking snake, the goblin leader shot under Haskell's sword and sank its teeth into his thigh. He screamed, pulled its lank hair, and tried to angle his long blade downward. Orod came through the doorway with a wail of mingled rage and fright. He rammed the flaming end of his torch into the goblin's face, driving it off with wild jabs between Haskell's legs.

The other goblins followed, forcing Bror and Torg to beat them back with their shields and slash wildly with their spears. A compact goblin leapt at Bror, only to meet the sole of his boot. Another leapt onto Torg's shield, dragging down his arm, its claws nearly opening his face. Orod ducked under Haskell and swung his torch wildly at one goblin, then another, the flame roaring as it cut through the dank air. He blistered the goblin captain's face, melting and curling its hair to embers.

"Get back!" Haskell shouted to Orod. He tried to right himself, but his savaged thigh exploded with pain.

Zinzi stepped into the doorway and bludgeoned a goblin with his cudgel.

"Orod!" Haskell lunged for the boy, but Orod's last swing propelled him into a stumbling half turn.

A warty goblin dashed forward and raked Orod with its dirty claws. The boy raised a hand to his neck. Blood welled through his fingers and his mouth worked silently. He crumpled beside the puddle, the torch rolling from his limp fingers. The goblin danced over him, taunting Haskell in the flickering light.

"You bloody—" Haskell cried, slashing out clumsily as

Torg dragged him into the guardroom. Zinzi yanked the door closed. The goblins scrabbled and pounded on the other side, forcing him to brace his foot against the wall. The door banged open and shut. "There is no lock!"

Bror added his weight to the rung, reducing the exchange to a judder. "I hate ta say I told you so, but…"

The goblins screamed their rage outside. Torg levelled his spear.

Haskell limped back and forth uncertainly, his mind working in circles. Orod was dead, they had to get out, but there was no way out, and Orod was dead. Dead because of him, and he would be too, they had to get out. He grabbed the goblin candle, their only source of light, off the table and lurched to the stone door at the back of the room. It opened smoothly, of course; the trick room's dark green marble glistened in the candlelight.

"Damn this labyrinth," he seethed.

There had to be a way. He turned around. There were the stools, the small table, four corpses, a backless rack of goblin spears, Torg, Zinzi, and Bror struggling to hold the door shut. He had an idea.

Lumbering to the rack, he swept the goblin spears to the floor. "Torg, haul the table in front of the stone door and toss the stools this way." He set the candle in the middle of the room and dragged the rack to the door, its stubby legs bucking over the rough stone floor. The door stopped jumping in its frame.

"What're they up to?" Bror said, adjusting his grip on the rung. A clanging blow sent a tremor through the door.

"They remembered their tools," Zinzi said.

"Good, that makes this easier." Haskell cut a length of rope from the coil on his pack and dragged the rack across the door. He bound its rung to the rack and heaped it with stools and goblin corpses.

They retreated to the marble room and laid the table on its side in the doorway. Bror and Torg stood in front, their shields overlapping and long, bloody spears set. Haskell stood behind, a goblin spear in one hand and his gory blade in the other. Zinzi had the candle. They were as ready as they could be, sheltering in the room that had doomed them to this fate.

Anxious moments passed. The door shuddered in its frame with each hammer blow. It fell askew as the first hinge gave way. The goblins caterwauled triumphantly.

Haskell had a sudden realization; he looked at Bror. "What happened to your bloody accent?"

Bror looked confused, then chuckled, his gaze never leaving the door. "Just a bit o' fun with you outlanders. Fun's over though."

"Southern bastard," Haskell said with a grin.

The door slipped and hung by a single hinge.

"Northern ponce," Bror replied.

The hinge gave out and the door fell outward as the monsters cut the rope. Six raging goblins surged through the rack. They came over corpses, stools, and one another in a mad rush for revenge.

Haskell hurled his spear, piercing the burned leader's belly, then the goblins were on them. Bror and Torg spit one each, but one slipped through. It thrust a spear between their shields, the long bodkin tip piercing Bror's leather coat. He fell back with a cry, clutching his side.

Haskell stabbed the grinning goblin in the arm, forcing it back with a howl. He hurled the table at the last three and slashed wildly with his bloody blade. The goblins scrambled for the doorway, slipping away as Haskell fell in congealed blood.

"To hell with you!" he shouted as the last goblin went

shrieking into the dark chamber.

Zinzi was stuffing rags under Bror's cuirass to staunch the blood. Bror looked unconscious. Had he struck his head when he fell? Torg slung his shield and he and Zinzi bore Bror between them.

Haskell rose from the slippery floor and rammed his sword into its scabbard. Froba had Yeoma's poultice, and she was lost far above. He hoped she had enough sense to go topside. Why had he left her alone? He growled at his ineptitude and cleared a path through the doorway. Grabbing Bror's spear, he limped into the chamber. There was no sign of the enemy, but Zinzi's candle was just a tiny circle of light in the darkness.

He hobbled forward. They couldn't go right—the goblins had fled that way—so he made for the shallow water, praying to every god he knew for another way. He stumbled on a charred broom head. No, a torch. Orod's torch.

"Hurry," Zinzi said, splashing through the puddle with the others.

A pool of Orod's blood had mingled with the cold water, but his body was gone. Along with their torches. He took up the half-burnt torch and peered into the darkness. He imagined the goblins parading Orod's corpse through cold, dark halls, jeering and pawing at him. Preparing for the feast. He shook his head. There was no time for mourning or self-recrimination. Later, if there was one.

He splashed after the others, who were passing through an archway in the far wall ahead. He followed and his heart lifted. In the dim candlelight was a stone staircase spiralling upward. Gods knew where it led, but it was something. They might yet escape.

* * *

Froba watched the rest of the party milling about beneath the poplars. Dirk, his head bandaged, sat on a tree stump drinking beer from a wooden cup. Corben sat in the wagon smoking a short pipe. Flint was stirring a small cauldron suspended over a fire. Rast helped Trin out of the fissure with his good arm. She shook her head. "It's no good, there's only stone behind that door."

"They're done for," Dirk said, standing.

"I don't like givin' up on them so easy," Corben said.

"Easy? Look at us," Trin said, gesturing to her face.

"Can you walk through stone?" Rast said.

"I say we leg it before the gobbos come lookin' fer us," Dirk said.

Froba couldn't argue with that, but it didn't seem right to leave them down there to die. "What about that hole in the wall?"

Trin shook her head. "I like my face right where it is. It took all of us to take down that beetle. Who knows what else is lurking down there?"

"C'mon, what're we gonna do when the sun goes down?" Dirk said.

Corben crossed his arms. "So we head back with the loot and leave 'em for dead? Don't seem right."

Dirk jabbed his chest with a dirty thumb. "I'm not dyin' so some foreigners can play quester. They knew the risks."

"The Guild rules say we can't abandon them without trying," Rast said.

"We tried—what else can we do?" Trin said.

Dirk threw his spear in the wagon. "I'll pay a bloody Guild fine if it means me skin."

"Look!" Flint said, pointing through the trees.

Froba went into a crouch. Four riders were approaching on horseback. Three wore plate armour, the fourth heavy indigo robes.

Trin and Dirk swore and readied their spears. Rast drew

his short sword, his other arm too stiff to wield a spear. Froba drew her dagger and scurried behind a tree.

One of the warriors cantered ahead of the others, his brown warhorse snorting with anticipation. His plate armour looked impenetrable. Froba couldn't even see his eyes through the lowered visor of his beaked helmet. The warrior levelled his lance at them. Its razor edge gleamed in a shaft of sunlight.

"Lay down your arms," he said.

* * *

The stairs were steep and long, and the party ascended with painful slowness. Heads down and exhausted, their armaments banged and scraped the walls as they corkscrewed upward. Haskell led them, his lungs, calves, and wounded thigh ablaze. He forced his feet up, over, and down; one stair, then the next. Every moment measured in suffering.

He didn't count the stairs.

Haskell pictured the silver Bror had showered into his hands. Twenty, maybe thirty talents; not even two sovereigns worth. They had the other treasure above, but with one of his band dead and another on the way, had it been worth it? Assuming they reached the surface alive.

His helmet clanged off something ahead and he stumbled back. He blearily regarded a dead end on a short landing at the top of the stairs. He was too exhausted to despair. He turned around and slid down the wall to the wet floor.

Torg and Zinzi, puffing and red-faced, bobbed up the stairs behind him. Bror was still unconscious between them. Neither spoke as they dropped to the floor. Had a horde of goblins charged up the stairs, none of them had the strength to raise a hand in their defence.

Haskell couldn't tell how long he sat senseless with exhaustion, but he eventually regained enough strength to retrieve his wineskin. His lower back and hips lodged a stiff complaint as he squeezed a stream of cool liquid down his parched throat.

He rolled his head left and right against the wall to take in his surroundings. There had to be a hidden door on the landing. The stair couldn't simply end here, could it? He wasn't so sure. Still, there was a chance.

He pulled himself up with a groan, his gauntlet scraping the wall as his injured thigh went into spasm. He hopped about, grimacing with pain as he scanned the rough walls.

Zinzi propped himself up on one arm. "Gods above, please show us a way."

As if in answer, Haskell's fingers depressed a plate near the base of the end wall, which began to grind into the floor. A stench like urine-soaked compost issued from beyond, hitting Haskell like a wave. He covered his face with Ko's handkerchief, its clean, cinnamon scent taking him back into her arms for one welcome moment. The wall slammed into the floor. The new archway let into the back corner of a room.

Haskell lit their last, half-burnt torch off Zinzi's stubby candle and held it through the portal. Beyond lay a large, square, low-ceilinged chamber with a broad pillar at its heart. It reminded him of a fine wine cellar under a high city mansion, only this cellar was heaped with rusted metal, leaves, bones, and stones.

A multitude of rats as big as sheep dogs scurried away from his torch. They had thick, black pelts and beady, red eyes. "I'll take rats over goblins," he said. Leaning in, he saw only one way out: a broken stone door on the left-hand wall.

"Am I dead yet? Gods, the stench," Bror said weakly.

"You look near enough. You know so much about goblins, but not enough to dodge their spears?" Haskell said, sweeping his torch around the room. The rats were getting curious.

Bror chuckled through gritted teeth. "Don'na make me

laugh, ye rascal. I figured you'd leave me for the rats, so I came to." Torg helped Bror up and handed him his spear.

Zinzi led them with the candle stub, picking his way through the chamber toward the broken door. Haskell used his torch to keep the growing pack of giant rats at bay. Bror was forced to poke a nosy rat with the butt of his spear, sending it scurrying. "I'm not'a corpse yet, you dastard."

The rats ended their pursuit about three-quarters of the way through the chamber. They gathered in a ragged line, standing on their hind legs and sniffing the air, darting about, but never any closer.

"This does not bode well," Zinzi said, looking from the rats to the stone door ahead. Its leading edge and bottom were gone, leaving a black, triangular void that light refused to penetrate. A series of chalk lines forming a crude eye were drawn on the stone in a shaky hand. The closer they drew, the colder the air became.

Haskell was unable to look away from the void. The glyph reminded him of the lines carved on the goblin bullet. It could only be a ward. Or a warning. "Can you fight, Bror?" he asked breathlessly.

Bror coughed and gripped his side. "Lad, I can hardly stand."

Haskell felt a fear he had never experienced. Not the aching fear of loneliness or rejection, or the trepidatious burn before a fight. This was lower, in his bowels, and higher, at the base of his skull. Cold. Primal. He fought to keep his bladder in check, his guts screaming at him to go back. Whatever was beyond that door was *wrong*.

He licked dry lips with a drier tongue and edged his foot closer. He felt like he was moving toward the edge of a cliff. Shame warred with fear as he held out the torch. He was their captain. Would his grandfather shrink in fear? He stared at the wards etched on the sword shaking in his hand, its blade painted with goblin blood. "Torg, s-s-stay here." If he was to die, he would die.

Now.

He ducked through the broken door and into a room beyond. It was just like the last—large, low-ceilinged, and square, with a broad column at its heart—but the walls and floor were clean. Black eldritch marble consumed his torchlight, and the thin, dry air caught in his lungs. There was nothing living here, only dust and whispers: urgent, unintelligible whispers. They filled his head, coming from everywhere and nowhere. He stumbled, his vision swirling as if he were drunk.

He swung his torch around, trying to focus his eyes. Another door, intact, lay dead ahead. A tall stone jar sat against the wall beside it. He turned. Blank walls, blank floor; his shadow beneath him—not a shadow, a sinister reflection. He looked to his right and saw past the column, an altar? Obsidian. Bronze, like before but unspoiled. And a presence. Malicious. Powerful.

Haskell stumbled around and leaned through the broken door. His companions looked pale and distant, yet close and vital, his double vision mingling like in a crazed mirror. "Voices, whispers," he said, the words raw in his throat.

"D-e-v-i-l-r-y," Zinzi sighed in slow time as if from the top of a long shaft. He wet his hand with water from a skin and flicked it across his eyes—a ward of his people. The droplets shone like sunlight, brighter than the pallid flame of his candle.

"Make for the far door," Haskell said. Was he whispering or shouting? He drew back into the room and pointed the way with his torch, knowing somehow that its wan light was greater protection than naked steel against the baleful shadow behind him. The whispers intensified. He prayed to every god of light for deliverance.

Zinzi ducked into the room, then Torg and Bror. They looked drained, corpse-like in the unearthly gloom. Haskell followed, holding his torch behind him for whatever meagre protection it might bring. They made for the door, always the door, that seemed so far off and the ground between so uneven. He was trapped in a living nightmare.

Zinzi stumbled headlong into the door. It juddered outward on dry hinges. He and Torg rushed through and vanished from sight. Haskell knew the thing behind him was moving, coalescing, stretching out fingers—it must have fingers. He sheathed his sword, pulled Bror the last few yards, and shoved him through the door.

Haskell glimpsed a feeble glimmer from the stone jar by the door. It was mounded with coins. He didn't pause, didn't think, just tossed the torch through the door, grasped the jar's curved handle in both hands, and pulled. Eyes tight against the lurking horror, he dragged the jar through the door and slipped, crashing to the ground. The jar broke at his feet.

Zinzi slammed the door.

Haskell gasped for air. The wide, dripping hallway felt like another world. It was as if he had clawed his way out of an ashen sea onto the shore of an island alive with colour—reddish mudrock, green slime, and harsh, leaping flame. The only sounds were their ragged breaths, the hiss of the torch, and the lonely splash of a distant drip. Torg helped Bror up against the wall. Both looked drawn, haunted. Zinzi backed away from the door, looking utterly spent.

Haskell looked at his feet. A trove of copper coins had spilled from the jar. He sat up with a groan and plucked a scroll case from the pile. Its dry and cracked red leather was embossed with an Ouroboros seal: a snake eating its own tail. He looked from its textured surface to the smooth stone door.

It too bore a crude, chalky eye. Was that the only thing holding back the shadow?

"We need to keep moving," he said.

Working quickly, every sack they had soon bulged with ancient copper. The bags dragged at their belts and beat their thighs, though Bror, too weak, carried none. The dripping corridor dead-ended at the edge of their torchlight, which was a blessing. Halfway down the hall they were already chafed, sweating, and sore from their treasures' weight. They couldn't keep this up for long.

They drew up to a pair of stone doors on the left wall. Haskell wrenched open the nearest, revealing a blank wall. Torg yanked open the other and was also greeted by stone.

Bror sagged against his spear. "Curse this hole and them tha' dug it."

Zinzi put his arm around Bror. "Its builders enjoy tricks— let us examine the end of this passage."

Haskell didn't have much hope but had fewer choices. He certainly wouldn't lead them back to that otherworldly chamber. He shuffled to the end of the corridor and craned his head. Voices were coming from behind the wall.

He set down his heavy sacks, removed his helmet, and put his ear to the rock. He felt a draft and heard two distinct voices. As he strained to make out their words, he noticed another catch on the wall beside him. He rested his forehead on the cold stone and sighed.

He was so tired, sore, and sweaty, yet chilled through. None of this had been right. Scratching at slimy rock like it was thin soil, only to harvest pennies and trinkets? He felt like a scavenger, not a quester. Where was the strong, proud foe for him to meet toe to toe; the hoarded treasure to take as spoil? Where was the glory?

Devils take glory.

He donned his helmet, tripped the catch, and whipped out his sword. The wall slowly descended; a vibrant white light spilled over from the other side. When the wall was halfway down, he vaulted it, landing jarringly in a perpendicular tunnel.

Righting himself, he sprang at two men on his left. Their shining plate armour was lit starkly from above. One held a shield and a longsword, poised and ready, the other a halberd levelled at Haskell's face.

He was prepared to die. Maybe then he'd find peace.

"Hold," the halberdier cried.

Haskell skidded to a halt in the slime.

The other warrior looked up a staircase on their left.

A third warrior descended and strode between their companions. They wore a white tabard over mail and a flat-topped great helm. A long-hafted war hammer in their hand gave off a dazzling white light. They drew off their helm, and mousy, sweat-flattened hair spilled about their face. Yeoma blew an errant hair out of her eye and shouldered her weapon. She smirked. "I have you at a disadvantage, Haskell."

Haskell fell against the wall, his helmet clanging off the stone.

"Let's get the hell out of here," he said.

Chapter XIX—Fireside

Haskell and Yeoma sat beside each other on stumps around a fire, its rising flames lighting the bare poplar branches above. Everyone was eating Flint's flavourful vegetable stew, thickened with bread and enriched by snared rabbits. They all drank pale beer from a firkin at the back of the wagon. The adventurers ate quickly, eager to sneak a second bowl before the small cauldron was empty. All but Torg and one of Yeoma's fighters, who drew first watch.

Flint was monopolizing Yeoma's other fighter, much to the priestess's amusement. "You have a fine cook, Haskell. You will start a trend with such a luxurious camp."

"Thank-ee, kind lady!" Flint said over the fire, never too far away to acknowledge a compliment. "We was lucky to catch a few rabbits for dinner, not that I was expecting comp'ny."

"Always expect company in the Darkwood, my good man. Though I must say, it is rarely so pleasant," Yeoma said.

"It would be finer if I had a proper oven…" Flint continued. Yeoma's fighter nodded away through the cook's aggressively thorough culinary chronicles.

Yeoma chuckled. "Not to be a poor guest, Haskell, but I was surprised to find three wounded mercenaries guarding a cook, a teamster, and a linkgirl. The Darkwood holds many dangers above as well as below. They were lucky we happened on them, not some hungry troll."

"Don't forget, we have a surly mule," Haskell said, making Yeoma laugh. "Though your point is well taken. I suppose I have been a bit careless. I don't suppose you'd help us clear this place?"

"No, my path leads elsewhere. Winifred says goblins are massing to the south. I fear yours are but the tip of the spear. I must confess that I am glad—my hand itches for my hammer when I am idle too long."

Haskell fought the urge to indulge in innuendo. "That is something we have in common. I hope to hire more spears to guard the camp after this haul, and maybe a few more to help clear the dungeon below."

Yeoma stared into her cup. "Yes, about that… common mercenaries are fine for guarding camps and rounding out numbers, but you won't find them very useful against more exotic adversaries. You need serious, Guild-trained fighters, and you would not go amiss with a wizard. You will find yourself in a situation best resolved by their arcane power."

Haskell frowned, though whether annoyed by Yeoma's advice or his own inexperience, he wasn't certain. After his desperate flailing below, he just wanted to drink, not dwell on his failures. Most of all, he didn't want to think about Orod. Were the goblins also feasting around a fire, not on rabbit but a tender half-orc boy? Or did they eat meat raw? He shook his head. "I'll look into it when I get back to town."

Yeoma gave Haskell an encouraging slap on the back. "You assembled a party and led a successful outing in less than a week, with only minor casualties. Few questers could boast of such a thing. Train hard, arm yourselves well, and you will win through."

"I will, and with this haul I might even stay solvent," he said sadly.

"You are amusing, Haskell, but do not count your gold until it is in the Guild Bank. Tell me, how many goblins did you slay?"

"Thirteen." Thirteen for one. Was that how it would be? A pitiless game of craps with their lives on the line? Haskell was sure he would survive. He was young, tall, and strong, with good armour and a famous sword. But the others?

"Come now, you're dry. Where is that girl with a refill?" Yeoma said.

Haskell glanced around the fire. He saw everyone but Froba and Dirk. Froba had taken the news of Orod's death quietly, almost matter-of-factly. She had just nodded and walked away.

"Let me refill your cup," Yeoma said.

Yeoma took their wooden mugs and went around the back of the wagon.

"His name was Orod," Froba said from deeper in the bed.

Yeoma squinted into the gloom, where Froba sat hugging her knees. "I beg your pardon?"

"One o' yer cause… cass-alties."

Yeoma dispensed foamy beer into a mug. "It is pronounced *casualties*, young one."

"He's dead, whatever ye call it."

"This Orod, he was your friend?"

Was he? Froba never had a friend, so she couldn't say. All she knew was that she was tired and lonely. Was that sadness? "He was dumb an' got killed."

"One should not speak ill of the dead. What is your

name?"

"Froba."

"Orod is with God now, Froba. There is comfort in that."

"Gods never did nuthin' fer me."

"Not true. For those who believe, the One True God offers boundless miracles." Yeoma looked skyward, her eyes filled with a light brighter than the fire behind her. "I have brought the sick back from the brink and healed the wounded. I have witnessed the greatest of my Order bring the dead back from the grave to live and breathe again. All through faith!"

Froba sneered. Preachers always gave with one hand and took with the other. "Fer enough gold, meybe."

Yeoma sipped her beer. "True, all things cost, even miracles. There are more people in need than we have the power to save, and few are the righteous who can channel the divine."

"Why don't ye heal the others if yer so holy?"

"Your companions? Their wounds are minor and have been treated. My power, unlike God's, is finite, and must only be used at need. It would be blasphemous to do otherwise."

"Whatever. Go drink an' hump like everyone else."

Yeoma splurted beer. "No, child," she coughed, "I will do no such thing."

"What's that?" Haskell said, limping over and sidling up to Yeoma.

"Nothing of consequence." Yeoma handed Haskell a cup and left.

Haskell looked to Froba, who shrugged. He looked at his feet. "I'm sorry we lost Orod. It wasn't supposed to be like this. We… He was brave. You too."

"He weren't brave, just stupid."

"I won't let that happen to you, Froba."

Froba sneered. As if Haskell could manage anything; he

didn't know any more than she did. He was just bigger and older. "*I* won't let that happen to me."

Haskell leaned against the wagon with a groan. He was pretty banged up. "I believe it. Of all my people, I worry least about you."

She glanced at his face dimly lit by the fire. What did he mean? She couldn't believe he felt anything for her. Her own mum hadn't done anything for her. No one had. Ferd always took more than he gave, and no Branthaller had given her anything for free.

Still, there was something strange about Haskell. He drank and humped and carried on like the rest, but he had paid her good, bought her new hose and shoes, and put her up in his fancy rooms. He hadn't even tried to make her do any sex stuff, just help around the Treeman. He hadn't paid much attention to her at all, really. That was the weirdest part. Why give her so much just to fetch and carry? He could have a hundred boys and girls for a gold piece.

"Haskell…" she began.

"Hmm?"

She rested her chin on her knees. "Nuthin'."

"Get some food and rest, Froba. Who knows what tomorrow will bring?" Haskell hobbled back and sat beside Yeoma's funny old wizard.

Froba knew they were trying to comfort her, but their words left her cold. She wanted to tell Haskell about Ferd and her troubled life. After all, these strong men and women seemed like her friends, but she couldn't bring herself to trust them.

"That's right, missy. Ye just keep yerself to yerself," Dirk said. He was leaning against a nearby tree. His missing eye was a shadowy crater in the gloom, his good eye glinted in the firelight. He shuffled to the end of the wagon and filled his cup.

"They ain't Lanesforders. Don't forget who kept ye after yer mum died. It weren't that jumped-up toddler."

"What're ye up to?" Froba said. She trusted Dirk less than Ferd, which was saying something. Ferd was hard, but she knew where she stood with him. Dirk, though…

"Never ye mind. Just stick by ol' Dirk from here on out. Lanesforders keep to their own. Remember that."

* * *

"Wizards live to weave magic," Neyhün said with a flourish of billowing, indigo sleeves and sloshing beer. "A marvellous thing, magic. I have practiced it all my life, yet never tire of the arcane."

Haskell was thrilled. His family wasn't so rich that they could afford a real wizard's services. "What's it like to do magic? I saw many tricks in the markets—flashes of flame and puffs of smoke, objects disappearing from the hand to reappear elsewhere. I imagine you can command more awesome power."

"Cheap charlatans and failed prestidigitators," Neyhün said. He jabbed a bony finger against his temple. "Men and women lacking the brains and resolve to master real magic. Precision is the thing. Each twitch of the finger, every tone of a phrase, the weight of material to seed the spell. Without precision a magician is nothing but a street performer."

"Yes, but what's it *like*?"

"Hmm," Neyhün said, draining his mug. "It is like… shaping reality with your fingertips, like calling up primal elemental forces through your veins. Where conjuring such power takes precision and concentration, manifesting that power is utter exhilaration, better than any sensation in this world."

"Amazing," Haskell breathed, trying to imagine the feeling. He fumbled in his pouch and brought out the two potions from the dungeon. "We found these hidden below. Do you know what they are?"

"Fine-looking potions in quality crystal. Would you like me to help you identify them?"

"Please!"

"It is a simple trick. Empty the mind and relax the body, focus inward, and wet the tongue with the fluid." Neyhün did so with the glowing ruby vial and smacked his lips. "A somewhat sour potion, clear in nature. It fills me with strength and vitality. Yes, this potion will heal wounds of the flesh. Go on, try yours."

Haskell took up the angular vial of glowing, colourless liquid and did as instructed. "It's sweet. I feel like I could stop a charging goblin with a word."

"You've got it, lad. That vial will give you power over creatures like in shape to us. It will not let you speak their tongue, but if they understand, and their will is weak, you can command them for a time."

"If only I spoke goblin, Orod might still be alive." He returned the potions to his belt pouch.

"Goblins are the least of your worries, my lad. There are more dangerous things on two legs, though perhaps few so numerous."

Haskell thought about the dark presence in that dry, horrible room. He shivered. "We encountered… something below. A nightmare I felt but couldn't see. And whispers. Terrible whispers in a room of black marble. We ran."

"Hmm, a wraith, perhaps, or some shade trapped between worlds. It is hard to say. You did well to flee. You are not equipped to face such terrors. The room sounds Late Empire, just before the Fall. You will sometimes find that strange marble below the earth. We in the Guild are attempting to classify it, as well as delineate between magical sources; but what am I saying? That is none of your concern."

"There was an eye chalked on the doors. I think the goblins made it. Was it a ward? Oh, and I found this," he said, holding out the Ouroboros scroll.

Neyhün flapped his hand dismissively. "Useless goblin superstition, no better than a peasant's. This, however…" He took the case, sniffed and felt its cracked leather. Popping it open, he tipped out a large, single-rolled scroll, which he partially opened. It was covered in flowing script, diagrams, and strange symbols. "This bears investigation."

He withdrew a leather mat from his pack and laid it across his lap. Lead weights dangled from either end and a small circle of green glass rested in its middle. He laid the scroll on the mat and the glass on the scroll. After a quick, intricate gesture, the lens rose six inches above the parchment.

Haskell's party applauded the magic.

"Make it dance!" Rast cheered.

"Gods," Haskell breathed, leaning closer. The glass distorted his view like the surface of a pond.

The lens panned back and forth over the mat. Neyhün made affirmative noises, like the wondrous magical scroll was some common broadsheet. He dismissed the lens with a wave, and it settled on the parchment. "Several basic spells. They are of no interest to me, but you might sell them to a lesser wizard."

A thrill ran through Haskell. "I would gladly add a wizard to my party! Do you know any looking for employment?"

Neyhün returned the scroll to its case and regarded Haskell. "You did survive the goblins and are clearly in need of assistance. I might have someone. His name is Grumzel, but he is presently engaged in my research. You could make this scroll his retainer when he becomes available."

Haskell took the proffered case. "Truly? I am in your debt, Master Neyhün. I will meet Grumzel at his convenience."

"You are welcome. Only, a word of warning. Potions may spoil and scrolls might be cursed. They might seem fair but only do you harm. Use the magic you find in this world, but do not stake your life on it. Magic is unpredictable by nature. It could save your life or be your undoing."

April 16

Chapter XX—Dreaming

Haskell did not sleep well. In his dream, Torg and Elsa, his sister, stood on a mountainous pile of crooked wattle-and-daub walls. "Does the family have business in Branthall?" he called from below.

"You don't know, brother? Torg and I are wedded. Help us build our wedding pyre. Or are you too sulky to help your kin?"

Someone tugged the hem of Haskell's tunic. It was Orod. He was whole again, scrubbed and clean. His hazel eyes were exuberant. He held up a flaming stub. "I counted the torches."

"I'm sorry," Haskell said inadequately.

"Don't worry, the fire will keep me warm."

Orod lit the pyre with the spent torch then vomited blood onto the dusty, black marble floor. He convulsed until he was a twitching pile of bloody flesh and linen.

The pyre became a raging inferno. The sky turned red and Orod's writhing corpse caught fire. "No, no, no," Haskell cried. He looked for water but found only cracked earth and dead trees waving in the still, hot air.

Dream logic told Haskell that he needed a potion to stop

the flames, but his pouch was gone. He took up his backpack, but it refused to open. He tore it apart, but it was full of dry, empty wineskins; he threw the pack into the dust.

Haskell paced helplessly. He pleaded with his sister for help, but she was now Yeoma, though Torg still held her hand atop the inferno. Their clothes blackened and burst into flame. A host of shrieks and wails filled the air, as if a thousand people were burning alive in the pyre.

"Come, brother, join us in blessed matrimony," Yeoma called over the cacophony of pain. The volcano of flame spit hot coals into the air. One landed on his forehead, setting it ablaze. He sat up and swatted his forehead. The rest of the party was breaking camp in the clearing above the dungeon. He had overslept.

The sun was shining through the trees, a bright patch lighting the ground where he had lain. He cast off his blanket but not the nightmare. Its horrible imagery still blanketed his mind. His thigh, tight and sore, sent a lance of pain into his groin. He clutched the wound and rested his head on his knee until the pain subsided.

Yeoma was saddling her horse across the clearing. She had been right, of course. About everything. He needed more followers. He looked at the wagonload of fuzzy, diseased bronze and sacks holding thousands of pennies. He hoped it would be enough. They had bled and Orod had died for that paltry treasure.

The nightmare's imagery began to fade, but not its foreboding. Were the gods trying to speak to him? So much rested on his shoulders now. He decided. They would return to Branthall. He would get them training and hire more spears. He tried it his way. Now he would do it the right way.

Chapter XXI—Money in the Hand

The Temple doctors were busy. A young woman in a white surplice tended Haskell's wounds. She washed his perforated thigh with fragrant sage water from a shallow silver bowl. Bror was lying on a table across from him, where a black-robed doctor stitched the wound in his side. Torg ran his fingers through Bror's sweaty hair as they clasped hands. Bror had been lucky. He'd lost a lot of blood, but the doctor found no punctured organs.

Rast sat on a nearby stool with an attendant sewing up his forearm. He was attributing his wound to a fearsome goblin as tall as him and twice as strong. Haskell must have missed that one. Trin, too; she was shaking her head, her cheek neatly stitched by proficient hands.

Haskell looked at his nurse. "It's funny that you wear white—you must be bloodier than me by day's end." She smiled and dried his puckered flesh with a cloth. The goblin's teeth had left deep holes in his thigh. The wound was as red and angry as the creature who made it. He hissed as she smeared a stinging, pungent substance over his thigh and bandaged it.

"Keep this wrapped, clean, and dry for three days," she said.

Haskell rose and pulled on his boot. He limped back and forth; the pain in his thigh was less bright. He looked out over the cool hall. At least a dozen tables bore corpses under white shrouds. Orod wasn't the only one to have died in the last few days. "I wish to hold a special service. Can you arrange it?"

"No need. The Reaping is tonight," she said.

"Reaping?"

"The other questers will guide you."

"Thank you," he said. But for what, he didn't know.

* * *

Zinzi stood at the low, battered counter in the bunkroom. He poured steaming water from a small iron cauldron into three ceramic basins. He set aside the cauldron and washed with a bar of white Erdite soap.

"Soap, hot water, room and board—what a blessin'," Flint said. He looked about furtively. "How'd you find it in the wood?"

"I thought my time had come in that labyrinth," Zinzi said.

"Glad I stayed topside," Corben said. Fit but saggy with age, his torso was covered in thick white hair.

"I didn't like gettin' caught out by that Yeoma. Thought I'd end up cookin' for a band of Guild-traitors," Flint said.

A far better fate than the one Zinzi had nearly met. That fearful shadow dogged his dreams. "Haskell pays well, but I did not expect to fight. I am reluctant to return."

"There might be bonuses once he finds his feet. I'm sure he'll take on more spears and a wizard," Corben said.

"I would feel safer with a wizard in the party, but I shall not venture below the earth a second time," Zinzi said. The goblins had been fierce. He had no wish to face them a second time. Raiders, elves, goblins, and shadows—he had had enough adventure for one lifetime.

Flint shook his head. "Maybe down in that hole, but there won't be no wizard sittin' in them woods. I'm goin' to keep lookin' fer more usual work, like I told Haskell at the start. I can put in a good word for you, Zinzi."

Zinzi nodded. His services were wasted on Haskell. He would try the few patrons newly arrived. Hopefully they were more disposed toward Aldamites.

They rinsed, spilling water on the floor.

"We've made a mess. I will clean up," Zinzi said.

"I'll get Orod t—" Flint started. "I keep forgetting he's gone."

Zinzi would never forget that desperate melee or the timid, monstrous-looking boy who had found courage at the wrong time. He cleared his throat. "If you will excuse me, I am due at the Guild."

* * *

Haskell sat in a high, hard chair in the Guild Bank. Zinzi was beside him with a chalk and slate in hand. Haskell watched through close-fitted iron bars as clerks sorted and weighed his treasure. Dressed in the Guild's red and black livery, the clerks worked at a long marble counter. They separated penny from talent, checking for counterfeits before adding them to a tray on a huge, bronze scale.

It was a nice setup for such a small town. Much more opulent than the disgusting office Slade had provided Haskell. But his clerking days were behind him now. He eyed a massive steel door behind the bars. It led to the Guild Vault, no doubt magically warded and sealed. Two watchmen flanked the entrance behind him, dressed in black brigandine and close-fitting helmets. They carried halberds and short swords. He didn't imagine theft was much of an issue here.

A clerk held a talent up to the bars. "These're ancient and cast in a quality mould. Good detail. I reckon they'd be, oh, fifteen-hundred years old."

Haskell nodded, impressed. "To think I had such history at my waist. Are they worth more?"

The clerk chuckled and shook his head as he tossed the coin into the tray. When all was counted, he balanced the scales, scratched out a note, and held it through the bars. Haskell leaned forward and took it.

It read:

> THE Questers Guild Bank of Branthall did Measure and Weigh, this Fourteenth Day of April: In the Twenty-First Year of the Reign of His Majesty King Ferd II of Lanesford, the following sums of Treasure:
>
> One hundred fourteen (114) Silver Talents weighing eleven pounds & eleven ounces
>
> One thousand seven hundred twelve (1,712) Copper Pennies weighing one hundred seventy-one pounds & three ounces
>
> Eleven (11) Lapis Lazuli Stones (Cut) weighing nine ounces
>
> One (1) Bronze Brazier (Diseased) weighing twenty pounds & seven ounces
>
> Three (3) Bronze Candelabras (Diseased) weighing twenty-six pounds & thirteen ounces
>
> Deposited by Haskell Son of Eskil the same day.
>
> The Value of the aforementioned Treasure being Truly Appraised and Duly Converted to:
>
> Sixty-nine (69) Sovereigns, including five

Sovereigns per Stone
    Thirteen (13) Talents, including two Talents
per pound of Bronze
    Twelve (12) Pennies

Less The Guild's Due:
    Six (6) Sovereigns
    Nineteen (19) Talents
    Five (5) Pennies

For a Total Yield of:
    Sixty-two (62) Sovereigns
    Fourteen (14) Talents
    Seven (7) Pennies

Sworn and Attested by [Illegible] the same day.

Haskell dropped his arm and gazed at the clerk. Less than seventy gold for two hundred pounds of loot? It wasn't right. He had spent over twice that since coming to town. They had sweated and bled for that spoil; Orod had died for it. Haskell squeezed his thigh, feeling the sharp, aching burn of his bandaged wound.

"Cash or note?" the clerk asked.

"Is this right?" Haskell said.

The porter scowled. "I signed it, didn't I?"

Zinzi took the note and chalked figures on his slate. "It seems accurate."

Haskell scowled. "It's just…"

Zinzi passed the note through the bars. "The coin, I think."

Haskell accepted a bag from the porter. He dropped a handful into his empty pouch and gave the rest to Zinzi. "I suppose it'll be enough for more spears. See that notices are posted: interviews at the Guildhall in three days. And pay our Temple debt."

"It will be done," Zinzi said, taking his leave.

Haskell handed the limp bag back through the bars. He wasn't sure he had enough to hire proper fighters, and gods knew how much the Guild charged for training. He sighed. Faith, he had to have faith.

Chapter XXII—Springtide Harvest

The sky was overcast and Branthall's streets utterly dark. It was a darkness for conjuring up the past, communing with spirits, or speaking of the evil that dwells in the world. The wide cul-de-sac outside the Guildhall was filled with silent figures, their faces sad, drawn, or defiant. They were the faces of men and women who had seen too much or lived too long. They did not speak as they huddled together in heavy cloaks. Each prepared for a journey from which their friends would never return.

Without word or signal, the shrouded host shuffled through Southgate, which stood open for them despite the early hour. A lone torchbearer led them. The tall defensive wall disappeared beyond the flickering light, devoured by the night. The host passed down the narrow tunnel, the sound of their scraping feet echoing off the clammy walls as they passed like shadows to the other side—issuing from the gate into the land of the dead.

Grave markers emerged from the darkness, though the host couldn't tell whether they moved to the markers or the markers to them. In the distance they saw a mist-shrouded hill. On it stood a man, his crooked face and grey shift lit by the hooded lantern in his hand.

They gathered on the hill around a score of deep, oblong holes in the turf, each ringed by damp soil with a long pine box across the top. Every coffin held a pale human body. The warm light on their faces could not disguise the fact that they were dead, each lacking the blush of life. Some were marred, the manner of their deaths obvious, while others seemed to slumber eternally.

Many of the living wept.

The crooked man was the first to speak. His words were shrill in the stillness, as if the air itself found speech abhorrent, each sentence commencing like a breaking pane of glass. Haskell stood among them, and the heaviness reminded him of the black marble chamber, though this place was peaceful, not full of horror.

"Since before Brandt built his wooden hall, those who fought the long war against the monstrous and unclean gathered at this place, for it seemed right to them. Here, beyond any god save Death, they came to honour the sacrifice of their brothers and sisters so they might never be forgotten. So it was and so it remains. We are here to recognize those who were first to fall this spring, reaped by Death to feed his brother War. Will any speak?"

A few did, most did not, their throats too thick or tongues clinging to their mouths. Those who spoke were brief, their words inadequate and unwelcome in the heaviness. They spoke of lives lived, things regretted, or vengeance to be had.

Haskell stepped up to a hole smaller than the rest, in which was laid a clay tablet inscribed with the names of the unrecovered dead. Stooping over the hole, he placed several objects inside. He turned to the others.

"These are for Orod, a boy who died before he could live.

As cold as it is here, it is colder underground where he fell. I came to fight this war, like my grandfather before me. So, before the living and the dead, I vow revenge against every last Darkwood goblin. Orod will not have died in vain."

He faded back into the group.

The crooked man, seeing that no others had words, spoke for them. "To fight this war is to be without and apart, but here we forge bonds stronger than those wrought by the womb, for it is the blood of experience that binds us."

The host bowed their heads, looking at their friends for the last time. "We remember our worthy dead," they said.

* * *

Froba watched the last mourner vanish through Southgate's iron-toothed maw. She had watched the silent, hooded questers climb the misty hill and seen the crooked man address them. A few spoke, Haskell, naturally, among them, but the heavy air made it hard to hear their words.

Now, with the hill deserted, she crept from her hiding place. Her heart was pounding as she came upon the coffins straddling their graves. She padded around the silent bodies to the lantern dangling from a pole. There, at the edge of the light, she found what she was looking for: a hole smaller than the rest.

She saw a tablet inside, not that she could read it. Haskell had put a fresh torch and flint and steel inside. She fished two silver talents from her pouch and laid them on the tablet. They said the dead had to pay the Boatman to cross the undying river. She didn't believe it but had to do something. Orod had died because of her.

"Ye was stupid—ye should never 'ave done fer Haskell and saved yer own skin instead," she said to the clay.

"It does little good to scold the dead," the crooked man said.

Froba startled and made to bolt but stopped. She hadn't done anything wrong, and she had as much right to be here as the others. "What good's fightin' an' dyin' anyway?"

"You of all people ask such a thing? Why do you not give up and die in the street?"

"There's no point in dyin'."

"And to live, sometimes we fight."

"Haskell's the fighter. Orod was just a kid. He shouldn't have been fightin' no goblins."

"And yet." He gestured to the tablet with a twisted right hand, as if it was all the proof she required.

Froba regarded him angrily. "Ye don't know nuthin'. Yer just in it for the coin, leechin' off folks like everyone else."

The crooked man laughed. "And what a vast estate I have acquired." He gestured grandly to the mist-shrouded yard. "No, child, I do not do this for material reward."

Froba looked at the grave goods at her feet. "Then ye must be grave robbin'."

"Never," he snapped. "My rewards come not from despoiling the dead."

"Then what's in it for ye?"

"Ah, now we come to it. I do *it*, as you so rudely put it, because it is my calling. My purpose. To serve is divine, young one, and doing is its own reward. What is *your* purpose?"

"I don't have no purpose. I'm just tryin' to get by like everyone else."

"We all have a purpose, little one. Only most do not know it. Most unfortunate are those who work against their purpose. They live fruitlessly, doing what they think they must while ignoring what they know they should do. These people, who may live freely and want for nothing, will never be satisfied. They are like wraiths living a half life. They serve their purpose in the end, albeit suffering a crueller fate than they might have, even if their purpose was to die. So, I ask again: what is your purpose?"

Froba thought for a while. "I just wanna live," she said, having no words to express what she felt inside.

The crooked man regarded her intently. "Go back to the living, girl. I suspect you will discover your purpose in the end, if you are willing to accept it."

Froba did as he suggested. At a run.

April 17

Chapter XXIII—One o' Them Days

F erd woke early. Grit was hissing against his window like dry rain, and his shabby room was lit by the greying dawn. His heavy straw mattress had sagged to the floor overnight, cocooning him in sheets. Try as he might, he couldn't get back to sleep.

He scratched his itchy cheeks, snarling as he scraped open a pimple. Wiping his bloody fingernail on his stained nightshirt, he struggled out of his pit of a mattress, rolled over the side, and fell onto the grimy floorboards; his knee knocked the bedpan, which sloshed onto his leg.

"Fer the love o' tha gods," he groaned.

He pulled himself up and padded to the washstand. Thankfully, the chambermaid had filled his water pitcher this time; not always a given. He balled up his nightshirt, threw it in the corner, and washed. Grabbing a silvered mirror, he assessed his craggy face, tilting the mirror to examine his slight chest, lanky arms, and narrow hips.

"Got it where it counts," he chuckled, waggling his dangling member. He glimpsed his dark, flinty eyes in the mirror and threw it on the nightstand.

He belted on his brigandine, sword, ragged cloak and hood, and set an iron cap on his head. He stared out his grimy window at the cobbled plaza below. A dust devil whirled dirt and garbage toward the keep looming over town. White pennants bearing Lanesford's black wyrm whipped in the wind, as did the town's flag and bright blue, black, and red banners, their colours muted by the earth-hazed air. Branthall. What a hole.

He sighed and passed into the hall, stepping over a shriek-soaked wretch face down on the floor, one linen-wrapped forearm propped up against the door.

"Morning, Gus!" Ferd said.

He lumbered down the hall and the staircase at its end, emerging into the Cock's damp, stale tavern. He wasn't surprised to be the only one up this early. The Cock's patrons were not, as a rule, early risers.

He raided the back pantry, turning up an apple and some stale bread, and filled a large mug with beer from a keg. Returning to the front, he slumped into a booth and breakfasted, listening to the wind whistle through the street as he ate his meagre fare.

Someone thumped down the staircase and into the pantry. Dirk joined Ferd with a foamy mug in his hand. The cyclops had a bandaged head and a sulky look on his face. Ferd chuckled. "Did baby have a fall?" he sang.

"Sit on a knife, ye poxy bastard. M'bleedin' head hurts."

"What've ye got?"

"The idiot pulled next to nuthin' outta that fuckin' hole. Froba and me lifted a fair chunk. The girl palmed a few stones right under his nose. She's got promise."

"Sure, if she gets her head outta her ass. If she lips me one more time, I'll throw her to the Tanners. Let 'em run Southgate, the hungry little pricks."

"Haskell don't know his ass from a goblin's hole. Ye should'a seen him. I almost felt bad for the sod. He's lookin' to hire more spears, and old Neyhün's settin' him up with a wizard. What a waste."

Ferd fixed Dirk with a stony glare. The turd was dancing around something important. "Why should I care?"

Dirk scratched at his scarred eye socket. "He an' them two swits saw Grig an' Luna at the stash."

Ferd frowned; what a useless tit. The last thing he needed were questers getting curious. "An' I bet ye just stood by, ye coward. What do I pay ye for?"

"What, I should'a laid into 'em? Woke the whole block and brought Owain down for a tour? Fuck off. I figured a few o' them might buy it in that dungeon. They nearly did, too, lucky sods."

Ferd leaned over the table and jabbed his finger into Dirk's chest. "That mace must'a dug out some o' yer brains. You do fer 'em next time. We can't have 'em blabbin'."

Dirk shoved Ferd's hand away. "We moved the stash, but I ain't no Guild-traitor. No murderer, neither. That's your line."

That was rich. Dirk was in it up to his neck, setting up questers like turkeys for a shoot. Fuck, things were going to get messy. "Yer in it plenty deep, me chum, so make double sure they get sorted in them woods. Tell Grig I wanna see 'im. Tonight."

Dirk drained his beer and slammed down his mug. "Fine. Now if ye'll 'scuse me, I gotta get me beauty sleep. Enjoy yer stroll."

"Bash out yer other eye."

Ferd rose and left the tavern. He stalked up the blustery street, drawing his hood against the gritty wind. Early patrol was bullshit. Gate duty was best, where he could fleece travellers and send horny adventurers to his street walkers. Devils take Owain. The swit had been fine with Ferd's business until now. Why the sudden change?

He wandered uptown, the lanes growing wider and dirt giving way to gravel that crunched underfoot. These new houses had straight, bright walls, clean windows, and slate roofs. Pink and purple snapdragons, white and lavender lilacs, and tulips of every colour bloomed in well-tended front beds and window boxes. They had been tenement rows when Ferd was a kid, not these genteel townhouses. They called it High-town now.

That's what had changed.

Stieg and Owain wanted to clean up this shit burg for a preening gaggle of wannabe lordlings. Half of them weren't even from Lanesford. Bloody outsiders would fill the Lane with farms and manor houses and bring in a whole new middling class. The gods-damned Third Estate. Devils take the lot. It made him pine for the war.

And now Haskell. This side hustle was going rotten. He was going to have to fix all of them. Froba too if she didn't wise up.

A red sun rose in the sky, turning the stinging grit into a blood rain. He pulled his hood tighter. "It's gonna be one o' them days," he grumbled.

* * *

Haskell hobbled across the Guild's foyer and touched Grimfyrrid's massive incisor for luck. He dragged himself up the stairs across the room, his body aching from labours in far less luxurious surroundings. At least he was alive. A fact he intended to prove to the doubting Winifred.

He limped down the third-floor hall to her heavy, wood-panelled door and raised his hand to knock.

"Come," she called from within.

Haskell put on a bright face and stepped into the room. "I have returned!"

Winifred stood over the chest under the window of her smoky office. She regarded Haskell over her shoulder. Gold light bathed one side of her face; the other side was shadowed. "My word, you survived." She slammed the chest closed. Its intricate, built-in lock clicked and whirled, disc within disc, as she clambered onto the cushions piled in her high-backed chair.

"I'm happy to disappoint," Haskell said as he approached the desk.

"I see you are not entirely unscathed."

"A goblin got too friendly, but I was lucky. One of my party died." He lowered himself into a hard, leather chair.

"A pity *you* were the one to live," a flabby voice said from behind.

Haskell leaned over to regard Hambur standing against a shelf behind the door. He leered at Haskell like a cat ready to pounce. What was he doing here? This wasn't his guild.

"Ah, fortune," Winifred said wistfully, drawing Haskell's attention. "The prime requisite for a successful quester. Skill and determination are key, yes, but they serve little if you stumble into a pit or contract a wasting disease from a pile of offal."

"Gods forbid," Haskell said.

"Get on with it," Hambur growled.

Haskell rose with a wince and turned with a scowl.

"In my own time," Winnifred snapped. "The Right Honourable Hambur has levelled a charge against you, Haskell."

Haskell leered at Hambur. The supercilious merchant was fiddling with the gold chains around his shoulders. A sudden, violent fantasy played out in Haskell's mind, one involving his dagger and Hambur's ample chins. "What charge could this pig bring against me?" He smiled as Hambur spluttered with outrage.

"He claims you degraded and threatened him and threw him from his horse. Do you deny it?"

"I do," Haskell said icily, lowering himself back into the chair. "But if he continues to insult me, I will not be held accountable for my actions."

"You will be held accountable, boy. Tell me, do you recall the Guild's third and fifth rules?" Haskell didn't. "Typical. In part, never inflict harm on a fellow member and never comport yourself in a manner that would bring the Guild into disrepute."

"Tell me this swine is not a Guild member?"

Hambur started forward. "How *dare* you!"

Winifred cut him off with a sharply raised hand. "I find your demeanour objectionable," she said with lowered eyes.

Haskell was uncertain to whom she was referring.

"Hambur sits on the Council of Branthall. While not a member of our guild, he is entitled to respect and consideration. That said, in this matter I have no authority. Haskell was not a Guild member when these alleged acts occurred. However—"

Hambur threw up his arms. "Outrageous!"

Winifred silenced him with a glower. "However," she continued. "I will consider it a strike against you, Haskell. If you further threaten Hambur I will eject you from the Guild. And should you be reckless enough to assault a council member… Well, you will find Branthall justice swift."

Hambur stamped his foot. "A warning? I demand satisfaction!"

"Any time you wish to test your steel against mine, I stand ready," Haskell said over his shoulder.

"There is no cause for trial by combat or ejection from my guild. Your so-called assault was an unfortunate mishap. I spoke with those present."

"This isn't over," Hambur said. He stomped from the room and slammed the door, his muffled rants audible as he stalked down the hall.

Winifred narrowed her eyes at Haskell. "Hambur is a blustery fool, but dangerous. I will not let you bring harm to my guild. Now, why are you here, other than to gloat over the fact that you live?"

Haskell opened and shut his mouth, wrongfooted by her incisiveness. "You said you wanted a report when I returned. Goblins are fortifying the dungeon, I thought you should know." He had no idea what they were doing in the dungeon, but it sounded plausible.

"Goblins are like rats—both infest this world. All we can do is cull them, as you are doing."

Cull them like cattle? The goblins had been ferocious, but not like he had imagined. They had spears, armour, candles, furniture. He had thought monsters only sought to take and destroy, not build. "Why not eradicate them? I'm sure if we all banded together, we could—"

Winifred crossed her thin arms and shook her head. "You sound like Brandt the Ironhanded. Like him, you are too naïve for your own good. I will tell you the tale of his ending one day, for it is instructive."

Haskell frowned and entwined his strong arms. "I'm no fool. I've risen to the challenge and learned my lessons."

"Boy, if you carry on as you have, I promise you one thing—this spring will be your last."

April 18

Chapter XXIV—Meeting of Minds

I t was sunny but cool, and Southgate was full of rosy-cheeked revellers in bright outfits. It was the Feast of Saint Ulbricht, a holy man with the distinction of having been devoured by trolls in the Lakewood. His death kicked off a week of revelry, a time to celebrate life and renewal.

A time for Branthall to milk questers of their spoils.

People danced to the beat of a spirited drummer, the sprightly drone of a chanter, and a tambourine. Vendors were everywhere. The courtyard was filled with the savoury smell of roast mutton and game birds, steamed dumplings, and baked and fried breads. Every kind of alcohol was being hawked in the streets.

Froba sat at a small, round table set up outside the Tree-man. She would normally be working the crowd, picking pockets, playing the lost waif, and grifting newmeat; but with a full purse and a healthy stash upstairs, she could afford to sit back and relax.

She watched Haskell and Ko dance in the street. They wove in a figure eight, kicked up their knees, and spun while gazing lustily at each other. They were good, even with

Haskell's limp. Their smooth, skillful movements and fine clothes were attracting stares, both appreciative and jealous. Haskell and Ko were eating it up.

Trin was dancing too, with a circle of women decked out in flowers. Rast was with a group of wallflowers under the Guild's porch, talking animatedly and glancing shyly at the dancers.

They could all have it. Froba was happy right where she was.

"Cheer up, lass. It's a beautiful mornin' and you're alive," Bror said across the table.

Froba scowled and nibbled her pigeon-on-a-stick. She watched Torg weave something out of two strips of soft leather. "What's that?"

"Sling," he said. He made a final knot and held up a woven, palm-sized pocket with a twisted leather thong on either end. One side ended in a loop, the other a knot. He leaned forward and tied it around her head with a bow on top.

Froba frowned but fell into a smile. She pulled the sling off her head, put her fist in the pocket, and pulled the cords tight. Torg showed her how to fit the loop over her finger, whirl it, and release the knotted end.

Bror set a small satchel of goblin bullets on the table. "You can kill at two hundred feet with that. Or keep birds an' squirrels outta your garden."

"Thanks," she said. The unfamiliar word didn't come easily to her lips, and their gift made her suspicious. "Why're ye so nice to me?"

"Aww," Bror said, giving her cheek a pinch. "A little waif like you? Who could resist?"

Froba pushed his hand away. "It's 'cause Orod died, isn't it?" Bror and Torg shared a look. Was it guilt? "How'd he die? Haskell won't tell me the truth."

"He died fendin' off a goblin—a big one. Saved Haskell a world o' pain, only he went out too far. An' they got 'im."

"Stupid. He was supposed to watch my back, not get himself killed. I should'a left him in the street."

Bror looked at her sternly. "I think you know how that'd have turned out. Orod took Haskell's coin an' did his duty. That was his choice, not your doin'."

"You didn't know him none. He just did what he was told."

"Aye, *he* did just that. And then some."

Froba whipped her leg with the sling straps. "Who ever heard o' a cowardly mullorc?"

"Never ran afoul of an orc, but I reckon they take all kinds, same as us."

Torg rocked off his stool and shooed Froba out of her chair. "Practice, practice," he said, giving her rear a gentle kick for good measure.

"Aye, have a go at some targets at the Guild. That'll brighten you up," Bror said.

Froba circled the yard, keeping to the fringes to avoid the revelers. She stole along behind Rast and the other wallflowers to the Guild's main entrance. She didn't feel like practicing.

She went inside and toured the foyer. It was filled with trophies she'd seen through the windows a hundred times before. She got a better look at the ones against the outside wall, but they weren't very interesting. Everything was dusty, old, and worthless. Except the dragon skull. It was massive; she couldn't even reach its front teeth, just its long, column-like fangs. Standing before it, she could imagine the dragon swallowing her whole. She shivered and moved along.

Creeping up the steep stairs, she ran her fingers along the dark, polished wood panels and worn weave of the crimson runner. She pretended the stairs were a bloody waterfall cascading down a hellish, otherworldly rock face, and leapt onto the exposed wood beside the fall. Inching upward, her shoulders scraping the bevelled panels, she traversed the phantasmal terrain. On reaching the top, she vaulted onto the landing and turned to shake her fist at an imagined nemesis. "I defy yer bloody waterfall, demon!" she whisper-shouted.

"Are you bringing demons into my hall, defiant one?" an old woman said behind her.

Froba whirled and was confronted by an ancient, white-haired woman in dark leather armour. She had a wrinkled hand on the hilt of a sheathed serpent-handled dagger. Winifred, the Guild Mistress. Ferd had warned her about the old woman. Tricky, he had said. Considering Ferd, that meant something. "I'm just playin', not callin' no demons."

Winifred cackled, showing her purple gums. "Well, you're clearly no wizard. A thief perhaps?"

"I ain't stole nuthin'," Froba said, hands on her hips. She felt the coin-purse and dagger hidden at the small of her back.

"Well then, a rich old woman like me has nothing to fear," Winifred said with a gleam in her eye. "Follow me, child."

Winifred led Froba past portraits of old men frowning at one another across the hall, past her office, in which Froba spied an endless array of knick-knacks, to a cozy parlour at the end of the corridor. The room was furnished with armchairs, side tables with boxes of tobacco, and silver trays of port, brandy, and whiskey in crystal decanters. There were several shelves of books and even more knick-knacks.

Winifred took Froba to a window overlooking a courtyard bustling with activity. Warriors sparred with wooden weapons in a wide ring below. A group of burly men and women lifted heavy objects near the outer wall. Lithe runners raced around the perimeter, and a few nimbly circled blindfolded men wielding wooden staves.

So, Froba wasn't the only one disinterested in partying. She wondered if they had lost friends, too.

"Do you know what they are doing, young one?"

"Duh, practicin'," Froba said.

"Yes, they are adventurers being trained by the Guild."

"The Guild, so what?"

Winifred twisted Froba's ear. "So, mind your manners."

"Ow! What'cha do that for?" Froba drew away.

"Training. Are you tired of living on the street?"

"I ain't livin' on no street. I work fer Haskell."

"Polishing guttersnipes, is he?"

"Better 'an Ferd, anyway," Froba sneered. Damn, she had let that slip. Tricky old bat.

"Yes, you've crossed that bitter fellow, haven't you? On what business?"

"None o' *yer* business," Froba said.

Winifred laughed. "You're definitely one of his. You're a bright girl, but I have a thing or two to teach you." She dangled a small coin purse between her fingers.

Froba felt the small of her back. "That's mine!" She snatched the purse from Winifred and counted the coins inside.

Winifred laughed. "I like you, child. Sit, and let us speak of your future." She gestured to a high-backed armchair.

Froba looked from the cozy chair to the old woman's bright eyes glinting, with what, she didn't know.

"Alright, old lady, but keep yer hands to yerself," Froba said, clambering into the chair.

* * *

Hambur paced the flagstones of a damp, narrow stone room. The shabby table, rough chairs, and tatty reed mat offered no comfort. Not that he intended to linger. The keep was a dull place for duller functionaries. When he did come, it was to the richly-appointed Council Chambers, not this dank cell. Nevertheless, his purpose demanded discretion.

The door creaked open and Ferd sauntered in. He was dressed in black, ill-kept brigandine. Hambur couldn't hide his disgust. "It is about time."

Ferd threw himself into a chair, put his booted feet on the table, and folded his arms over his chest. He regarded Hambur with deep set, obsidian eyes. "Yer one to talk—I was about to come lookin' fer ye."

Hambur tossed a small bag of gold on the table. "Perhaps you would rather conduct business with someone else."

Ferd snatched the bag and made to rise. "Ye know, I think yer right."

Hambur stepped in front of the door. "Hold on now! I came here in good faith."

Ferd sniggered. "Nuthin' respectable goes on down here. Meybe ye should find another line o' business."

"Now see here—"

Ferd cut off Hambur with a sharply raised hand. "What's eatin' ye?"

Hambur paced the room. Problems. Setbacks. That's what was eating him. "The goods were not as valuable as hoped. The market is glutted." Eskil and his lot were to blame; blocking his shipments at the docks, forcing him to send goods overland or sell them at a tenth their price.

Ferd emptied the pouch onto the table and counted the gold. "So squeeze more money outta that tight wife o' yers."

"My wife," Hambur grumbled. What sort of woman would cut her husband's income over one mishap? Adulterated spices—what rot; he had tasted them, and they had passed. He only did what every other merchant was doing. Hambur slapped the table, jumbling Ferd's neatly stacked gold. "Now see here, I need materials for my manor and outlay for my tenants—"

"Stop, I'm tearin' up," Ferd said.

Hambur had no time for games. His tenants would arrive soon to build his manor and work the land. "When can you gather another shipment?"

"This ain't no game. Comin' by used goods is a tricky business. Force it an' we'll both be doin' the gallows dance."

Hambur waved his hands. "No details, just make it happen. I need rings, amulets, wands, artifacts—anything that will fetch a decent price in Khul. No more weapons and armour." Excuses, always excuses, just like at the docks. He needed results, not prevarication.

"Oh, sure, I'll get right on it." Ferd slid the gold off the table and into his pouch.

Hambur toyed with his gold chains. "I have another matter to discuss."

Ferd sighed and retrieved a short knife from in his boot. He started cleaning his nails. "Yer boy do some mischief that needs covering up? Some pretty boy on tha side spilling daddy's secrets?"

"Wha—how…" Ferd knew too much, the meddler.

"I know yer business better than ye, ye hog. Now speak plain, I got business topside."

"You're as insolent as him."

"So ye've got a problem with some fella, eh? What's he done that I should care about?"

"He threatened and assaulted me. I want satisfaction. Winifred, gods damn her, made me wait days to see her only to refuse to act."

Ferd stopped cleaning his nails. "A Guild boy, eh? Dangerous satisfyin' yerself on one o' them. The boy who saw ye off yer horse?"

"I want him ruined. I want the cur wallowing in the streets as an example to any who would challenge their betters." And to keep Eskil from undermining Hambur's ambitions, but Ferd didn't need to know that.

Ferd sized up Hambur like a slab of meat. "I know 'im. Easy mark. Sure, I've got something ye can use. Somethin' real juicy."

Hambur leaned on the table, unable to suppress a smile. "Tell me."

"Oh, I will, but I'll lose money on this, so yer gonna do me a favour."

Hambur scowled. "I have already done you enough favours. Our arrangement stands."

"See, that's the thing. We're in this business deep, and it's mighty dirty work. People've been askin' questions. If someone were to come fer me, I'd spread the filth around. Count on it."

"You wouldn't dare," Hambur hissed.

Ferd grinned. "Dare nuthin', that's just tha way o' this wicked world."

Hambur paced and fidgeted with his chains. He didn't like the sound of this. "What do you propose?"

"I need more pull in town. Couldn't manage it m'self before, but with ye in town we could swing it. If I'm, say, Watch Captain, I could arrange things neat-like, business-wise and for our troublesome friend."

"Oh, consider it done," Hambur mocked. "Even I can't oust Owain from his position. Not without cause."

"No problem," Ferd soothed. "I'll do for the good captain. All ye need to do is bluster—I know ye can do that—and see that yer friends do the same. A dirty trick or two, and I wind up where I ought'ta be."

Hambur settled in an unsteady chair. Doors would swing

open with the Watch Captain in his pocket. There was profit in this.

"Deal?" Ferd said.

Hambur grinned. "I think we are in accord. Captain."

April 19

Chapter XXV—Cockfight

The back room of the Gilded Cock smelled like a chicken coop. It was filled with a chaotic crowd of scoundrels and gamblers gathered around a cockpit, some hunched low, others craned high; all were heaping a raucous stew of derision and adulation onto a pair of fighting cocks. The birds growled and cawed, locked necks like a pair of wrestlers, and tore at each other with beak and spur.

Haskell's bird was winning. It had torn its bigger opponent bloody. Feathers, blood, and dung littered the pit. "Come on, you beauty!" he cried, smirking at his betting partner across the ring. He had goaded her into five-to-one odds on the lighter bird, which had looked fighting fit and spoiling for a scrap. None too soon: he hadn't done well at dice and the cards hadn't treated him any better.

He needed this. The Guild's damnable taxes and fees were too high. He couldn't afford to train himself let alone the others. This was the only way he could win enough money to train properly and hire the right people. This was his only chance to do things right.

The bigger cock got its beak into the smaller's chest and

tore out a patch of feathers. Haskell's bird fluttered back only to be gouged by its enemy's spurs. His cock flew out of the ring. "No, no!" Haskell shouted with a handful of other losers, one of whom kicked the wounded bird. A fight broke out between him and its handler. A new ring formed around them with quick bets being made.

Haskell was tempted to join but had no idea how much he had lost so far. He'd definitely run out if he kept going. Damn, he nearly made it that time.

"Pay up, foreigner," his creditor said with a grin.

Haskell slapped five sovereigns into her palm. "Buy a poor man a drink?"

She chuckled and winked but went to watch the fight.

Haskell slunk over to Ko's side table, sat, and put his arm around her. "That was bracing," he said.

Trin and Rast sat across from them. Trin signalled a serving girl. "You've got a real talent for losing money, Haskell," she said.

Haskell waved her off. "You're one to talk."

Ko leaned into Haskell and hugged herself. "I don't know how you can watch that sort of thing. It's barbaric."

"We need to keep our blood up to face the horrors of the wood," Rast said. He scratched his bushy beard. "Speaking of monsters, have I told you about the strangest creature I ever saw?"

"Here we go," Trin said, taking a tankard of beer from the serving girl.

"Was it bigger than the troll?" Haskell said, but Rast wasn't to be denied.

"T'was in the Lakewood, not a league from these very walls. I was watching over a camp and had just put up my spear to take a piss when this cock, bold as you like, struts out of a hedge laced with nightshade. Only it wasn't all bird. It went on two legs and had a cock's head, but with a red beak full of teeth. The black feathers on its neck were raised like a pinecone. Below that it had the body of a jet-black snake and blood red legs."

"Horrible," Ko said.

"Sounds like a cockatrice, a monster out of myth," Haskell said.

"Truly!" Rast said. "It was as big as a hog, had wings like a bat, and a barbed tail in all the colours of a rainbow. It looked this way and that, scanning the wood with eyes as black as night. A black tongue flicked in and out of its beak, and its tail whipped to and fro like a cat ready to pounce.

"I thought for sure I was dead. But a pheasant started from its hollow. The monster leapt at it like a shaft from a bow, hissing a death rattle that haunts me to this day. The monster's icy breath struck the pheasant dead—not only that—by the time its prey hit the ground you'd swear it'd been lying three days in the sun. As soon as the beast laid into the worm-ridden meat, I grabbed my spear and ran mighty quick, let me tell you."

Ko shivered. "How you can face—" She looked up and gasped.

A man in heavy boots marched to their table. He was bald and had a hard, angular face like an edged weapon, which bore the nicks and scars of long campaigning. He wore a moss green coat of finely embroidered linen and had his hand on the hilt of a broadsword; his prodigious bicep stretched the fabric of his sleeve. His cloak was a black-furred animal skin with a purple sheen; its surface shimmered, distorting the air around him like a mirage over black sand.

"Ye moved on quick, woman," he said.

The milling crowd turned toward them.

Haskell looked from Ko to the warrior. "I didn't catch

your name, friend."

"Join us for a drink, Quin," Rast said.

"Shut it, forester," Quin snapped.

"You said you were heading south, that you might not return," Ko said.

"I said I *might* be gone a year, and ye said ye'd wait."

Titters and murmurs ran through the crowd. Haskell saw money changing hands. He had played this game before, many times in many dockside dives. He found Ferd's bookie in the crowd and nodded. The odds were ten-to-one. Haskell placed his pouch on the table and nodded back.

All or nothing, this was a game he had never lost.

"Stove 'is head in, Quin!" a man shouted from the back.

Haskell stood, towering over Quin. "Come now—Quin, is it? We're all brothers and sisters in arms," he said.

Quin looked at Haskell like he was a dung pile in the street. "Who're ye, newmeat?"

"Alright, Quin," Trin said, rising from her chair.

Haskell waved her down with a gentle shake of his head. He knew what he was doing. "Haskell, Eskil's Son. You might have heard of my grandfather."

Quin laughed. "The Oath-breaker?" The crowd sighed and groaned at the slight.

What had Quin meant by that? "That's Orc-breaker, little man," Haskell said.

"Ye shouldn't trust every bard's tale, sonny. A longer line o' faithless pirates ye'll never see."

The precision of Quin's insult didn't register in Haskell's mind, only heady indignation. He swung at Quin's smirking jaw, wanting to smash the liar's mouth, but Quin had played this game before, and played it well. His fist hammered Haskell's belly like a giant-hurled boulder. Haskell doubled over. Quin grabbed him by the collar and threw him forward, propelling him through the laughing crowd. Haskell fell to the floor and retched.

Ko banged the table and stood. "Stop it, Quin!"

Quin bridled at the sound of her voice but did not turn. He stepped toward Haskell, but Trin and Rast came between them. "You made your point, Quin," Rast said.

Trin put her hand on her sword and spat sideways. "We need him alive, Quin. Don't make us involve the Guild." The spectators booed while jostling for a better view. More money changed hands. Haskell rose on one knee. It was all his cramping stomach would allow. He squinted up at Quin between gasping breaths. Stupid. He let the bastard get in his head.

"Break it up," Ferd said, pushing Trin and Rast aside.

Quin started forward but it was only a feint. He grinned at Trin and Rast, daring them to react. The crowd whooped and hollered for more.

"Everyone out or it's the stocks for the lot of ye," Ferd shouted.

Quin strode casually around Ferd. He stepped over Haskell on his way to the door.

"Damn… liar," Haskell said between gasps.

"Ask around," Quin said. "You can keep the faithless whore." He strode from the room, followed by a train of chattering onlookers.

Rast helped Haskell up. Ko hugged him.

"Quin's a bully—don't listen to him," she said.

Haskell was gnawed by doubt. His father refused to tell him everything, and his sister and Slade said he didn't know his grandfather. But they just wanted to hide that Eskil had been a pirate before he was a hero.

A faithless pirate, Quin had said.

"It isn't true," Haskell said, more to himself than anyone else.

Ferd laughed and clapped him on the back. "Truth's a funny thing, boy. It depends on where ye stand."

* * *

The back room had emptied. Ferd sat on a barrel by the door, drinking shriek out of a dirty glass. He would have let Quin beat Haskell to a bloody ruin, but people would want to know why he hadn't stopped it. He already had enough trouble with Owain. Not that it mattered much. The fool had wagered on himself and lost; he was in hock up to his eyeballs to Ferd. It was perfect—utter poetry. He broke into a bout of laughter.

Grig slunk through the door as Ferd wiped away a tear. "What's so funny?" Grig said.

Ferd wiped his nose with a snotty rag. "Yer ugly face, is what."

"Fuck yer mother," Grig sneered.

"By all means." The bitch: she could rot.

"Fuck you, too, longpig. Dirk said yer lookin' fer me?"

"Yeah. Got a special job for ye."

Grig drew close. "Another quester?" The mullorc's red eyes made Ferd's skin crawl. He was a monster through-and-through, no matter how human he looked.

Ferd nodded. There was one every year; some piece of newmeat looking to make a name, strutting around like they were cock of the walk. Haskell was going to be trouble. He could smell it as plain as the chicken shit on the floor.

"What'd ye have in mind?" Grig said with relish.

Ferd looked at several fighting cocks lying limp and lifeless near the back wall. He knew what to do with troublesome cocks. "Lots o' dangers out in them woods. One of 'em could happen across a certain dolt and his merry little band."

Grig licked his jagged teeth. "Aye, that could happen. I know just the right dangers, too."

"I thought ye might. Dirk'll tell ye when and where. Grab

everything. I don't wanna see their stinkin' faces in town again."

Chapter XXVI—Underbelly

Haskell fled the Treeman in his fur-lined hood and cloak. He heard a sharp laugh as he crossed the cul-de-sac. He didn't look, just hurried down the alley beside the Guild. Everyone was talking about his fight with Quin over Ko. He held his abdomen, still sore from Quin's powerful blow. Haskell had always been a winner when it came to fights, women, and money. Now…

He emerged in a squalid lane in a part of town to which he'd never been. He took a long pull of bitter wine from his skin and wandered aimlessly, his mind churning. Everywhere he went, conversation stopped. His friends' smiles had become forced. Gawkers whispered to one another and tried to hide mocking grins. Gods, let them forget; let some other salacious gossip catch their interest. He quickened his pace and drank deeply, the wine sour in his stomach. He wanted to hide, to numb his humiliation.

This damned town. He was trying to play the Guild's game, but they wouldn't let him. Everyone had their hands in his coin purse. Winifred and the Guild were worse than lords and bankers. This couldn't be what Brandt wanted for his town. It stank like an open sewer.

He stopped mid-stride. It really stank.

The tenements on this street were cracked and crooked. Refuse was everywhere and sewage seeped downhill. Low-ertown, they called it. He held his breath against the gamey reek of excrement and spoiled vegetables. He made a quick exit down a narrow alley that had become a tunnel, one tall building settling into the other like a drunk leaning on a sober man. Several large rats scurried under a back step as he skirted a garbage pile. Or was it a person? On the other side was a neighbourhood of squat, drab homes with small, fenced yards in which chickens pecked and pigs nosed.

He tried to head up but, lost in a warren of lanes and alleys, ended up further down. Haskell found himself in a long open area into which all the town's muck and detritus drained. A scummy, red-brown mire of pollution lapped against the town's cliff-like defensive wall. He raised Ko's kerchief to his mouth.

Even in the populous High City he had never entered such a malodorous slum. Trash was heaped everywhere, in which a host of filthy children played like rats. A row of tenements faced the sewage pond. Several older boys, as dirty as the doorstep on which they sat, were perched near Haskell. They were passing around an earthenware jug.

"Oi, that's a right giant!" one of the urchins shouted.

A gaggle of foul-smelling children crowded him with out-stretched hands. They were tiny, ill-fed creatures. Haskell held his belt pouch, squeezing the scant coinage inside.

"Get out of it!" a lanky lad cried, kicking away the cloud of children. He looked up at Haskell. "Here fer a piss?"

Haskell frowned. "Piss?"

"Ye daft?" the boy said, turning to his sniggering chums. He pointed to a huge wooden tub two doors down.

Haskell nodded. Of course, the tanners, dyers, and butchers would be as low and far away from the rest of town as possible. Khul had streams that drained into the bay and fresh ocean breezes. Not here. The stink would be unbearable in summer.

"Oi, Flora, fetch a penny, ye tart!" the boy shouted, startling a little girl. She was maybe five years old and wore a dirty sack dress. She had been staring at the top of the outer wall far above. Flora bolted over the gang-infested doorstep, the boys mercilessly pinching her and pulling her matted hair as she struggled through.

"Get on with it, outlander," the tanner boy said.

Haskell strode to the tub, unlaced his breeches, and released a heavy stream through a crusty skin floating on top.

The boys applauded. "Nicely done!"

Haskell re-laced his breeches. Flora scurried up and held out a penny. Her grubby hands barely rose past Haskell's knee. The boy snatched the coin and gave her a cuff, sending her into the dirt. Haskell hauled him off the ground by the tunic.

The tanner boy sneered. "Like 'er? Just this copper an' she's yers."

Haskell's vision tunnelled and swam. He hurled the boy into his comrades on the step, the lot going down in a heap. He drew his sword with a rasp and stalked forward. Flora rushed in front of him with her hands raised. He glowered at the gang, who spat and shouted at him like a pack of goblins.

Haskell took the penny from the dirt and stalked in the other direction. He took a long drink of wine. A sickness was growing in his belly, and it wasn't from the drink or lake of sewage beside him.

Chapter XXVII—Mercantile House

Hambur's house was impressive. It had four rooms on two levels and an excellent kitchen and cellar. Zinzi would even have his own bed. He sat at a table that was not ostentatiously large, only comfortably so. Hambur was at its head with Hiam and Kerk on his right, Flint and Zinzi his left, and the footmen, maid, and scullion further down.

A large, realistic painting hung over the fireplace. It depicted a younger Hambur with more hair and less belly, hand in hand with his steely-eyed wife. Both wore silks and furs and were standing in front of a grandiose curtained bed. A very small Hiam sat at their feet.

"You have a very fine household, Sir," Zinzi said.

"How very good of you to say so," Hambur replied.

Zinzi's guilt was overshadowed by relief; here was a house he could properly serve. Haskell did not require a secretary and cook; he needed more warriors. Flint certainly felt the same. Zinzi sipped a fine, spicy wine. "I might be prejudiced, but I am certain you will find Flint's fare most agreeable."

Hiam munched a spiced and brandied apple slice. "I am

more than impressed by these delectable beginnings."

"Talent wasted on that brigand. I would be happy to employ you more suitably," Hambur said as he licked his fingers.

"Haskell possesses creditable traits, though tact and wisdom are not among them, as with most youths," Zinzi said.

"You are too charitable, though not where this fine fare is concerned," Hambur said.

The shorter footman went around the table filling glasses while the scullion set them each a small, blue ceramic plate. It bore steaming roast chicken in white sauce over a bed of bread, snow peas, and thinly sliced radishes. Hambur and Hiam each received a breast, thighs for Kerk and Zinzi, and wings and drumsticks for the footmen. Flint had outdone himself. Everyone breathed in the luscious scents of garlic, rosemary, pepper, and thyme.

Hambur's eyes widened. "An aroma fit for the gods!"

"Ye are too kind, Sir," Flint replied.

"I seldom agree with my father, but on this we are of an accord," Hiam said.

"You are a credit to your profession," Zinzi said, raising his wine to the blushing cook.

They all tucked in, muttering their delight as they sliced and devoured meat with their knives. "You should invite the Burgomaster to dinner, Master," Kerk said.

Hambur nodded with a full mouth. "Tell me, Zinzi, have you seen enough? Better than that flea-ridden inn, eh?"

"Certainly, but I will always think fondly of the Treeman, for it kept me through dark times. One should always be thankful for the gifts the gods provide."

"Hear, hear," Hiam toasted.

"Your proposed duties are agreeable?" Kerk asked.

Zinzi nodded. "It will be good to have challenging work again. I look forward to tutoring Hiam, and your manor has many logistical considerations to which I am happy to turn my mind." From what he had glimpsed, the manor's planned construction was a disorganized mess doomed to failure. Zinzi was no builder, but he could oversee and organize the work, accounts, and supplies. After all, being in the Lane with a small community around him was far better than returning to the Darkwood. He shook off the image of blood welling between Orod's fingers.

"I am happy to have rescued you," Hambur said, shaking his glass for more wine.

Zinzi cleared his throat. "My friends are uncouth but have many fine qualities."

"Perhaps I should save them all from that young pirate," Hambur chuckled.

Hiam held out his glass for the scullion to fill. "I must compliment you on your new retainers, father—skilled and wise."

Zinzi gave Hiam a modest nod. They would need to hire mercenaries for the manor's defence, but he didn't want to entice the others away from Haskell.

Hambur leaned toward Zinzi. "Just be sure to beat some respect into my boy. He has far too much cheek."

Zinzi gave Hambur a neutral smile. "It will take several days to conclude my business with Haskell. A week, at most." He worried about breaking the news to Haskell; despite his bravado, he was a sensitive young man. Zinzi sipped his wine, praying that everything would turn out for the best. For everyone.

April 20

Chapter XXVIII—The Help

Froba tiptoed across the Cock's common room toward the table at which Ferd dozed; his arms were crossed, and he was in his favourite armchair. She heard the publican rummaging in the pantry behind the bar. She would just leave a sovereign on the table and go. Wait, how would he know it was from her?

"Where's me money," he asked, eyes still closed.

"Shit," she said.

"Shit, nuthin'—money now."

She put a gold piece on the table, careful to keep her distance. Ferd regarded it briefly, then shut his eyes again. "Where's the mullorc?"

"He died," she muttered.

Ferd chuckled. "Serves 'im right fer takin' up with ye."

Froba bit her lip and stared at her feet. He wasn't wrong. She thought about mentioning Winifred but kept quiet. It was better he didn't know.

Ferd took the coin off the table. "Something's come up. Stick by Dirk from here on out. Leave Haskell to Haskell, ye get me?"

"But—"

Ferd fixed her with a glare. Froba closed her mouth. He hadn't even moved, but she knew better than to keep talking.

"Get what ye can outta the turd then cut 'im loose. Stick by Dirk, no matter what goes down. Clear?"

Froba nodded.

"I'm givin' Southgate to them Tanners—"

Froba gasped. Brent would make a mess of Southgate. He'd definitely come after her. "But they'll—"

"Open yer trap again and I'll give *ye* to 'em. They'll run Southgate how they like so long as they pay up. If they don't, I'll tan *their* hides."

"What about me?"

"Dirk thinks ye got some talent, so ye'll run with him for a while. Find another sap and milk 'em proper. Now beat it."

Froba walked away in a daze. Free of Ferd? She had dreamed of it for so long. Now that it was here, she was terrified. She felt oddly betrayed. Working for Ferd meant something in Branthall. Who the hell was Dirk? Just Ferd's lackey. What did that make her? She felt sick to her stomach. This was worse than any thrashing Ferd had given her, and he hadn't touched her at all. She wiped away a stubborn tear and wandered out of the Cock.

* * *

Haskell sat in the cavernous Guildhall. Zinzi was beside him, scratching at a long sheaf of parchment with a quill. The hall was mostly empty and gloomy despite the afternoon light. He had displayed his Questing Permit, longsword, potions, and spell scroll on the table as proof of his viability. Sadly, they had not been necessary.

Zinzi's neatly scribed roster bore the names of a long line of mercenaries and beggars: men and women with more vim than usefulness, but no real fighters. Nearly all were desperate for paid work; half hadn't even been sober. For a town full of adventurers, they were proving hard to retain, though he harboured doubts about his own desirability.

He owed Ferd so much money that he had to take out a loan at a ruinous rate of interest. Coupled with his sordid run-in with Quin, he worried he wouldn't be able to find any real help at all. He finished a mug of mead and waved down Betty, the hall's dour waitress. "How many have we seen, Zinzi?"

"An even score." Zinzi sighed and rubbed his temples.

"It's been a rather grim harvest, hasn't it?" Haskell looked over his shoulder at Bror, Torg, Trin, Rast, and Dirk. It looked like Bror was describing a fighting move: he rose from his seat, slapped his palm against one shoulder, and banged his fist on the table. The others snatched up their sloshing tankards and laughed. He hadn't realized how lucky he had been to find such a dependable crew right off. Someone cleared their throat, drawing Haskell's attention.

A lad stood at their table. He was probably a few years younger than Haskell and had wavy locks and a toothy grin. He was wearing bright green wizard's robes that would fit a man half again his size, complete with a pointy hat. It was a style worn well before Haskell was born. He looked ridiculous.

"Name?" Zinzi asked.

"Ladomas the Thaumaturge!" he said with raised hands and twinkling fingers.

Zinzi regarded Haskell with disbelief.

"So, you weave magic?" Haskell said.

"I am the finest wielder of the arcane this side of Khul," he announced, striking what he likely thought was a dramatic pose.

"What magicks can you produce?" Zinzi said.

"Observe," he cried, throwing up his arms.

Haskell was dazzled by a bright flash and loud bang. A

cloud of smoke appeared over the table, out of which a shower of sparks rained. Everyone in the hall turned, the dramatic display only highlighting the pregnant silence. Ladomas kept his arms in the air. His grin grew more strained by the second.

Haskell clapped out of politeness. "Well, thank you."

"I come cheap," Ladomas persisted with a wink.

"I am sure you do," Zinzi said.

"Well, then—goodbye!" The floor around Ladomas erupted into a pillar of green smoke.

Haskell leaned around the cresting cloud; he saw a billow of green robes slip through the door. "What a strange fellow."

A pudgy man in a fine grey tunic and stylishly pointed shoes stepped up to the table, coughing and waving away green smoke. "The boy used too much saltpetre," he said.

"Your name?" Zinzi asked.

He gave Zinzi a peevish look. "Grumzel of Sheffield."

Haskell sat forward. "Greetings, Grumzel. Zinzi, this is Neyhün's man."

"Vocation?" Zinzi said neutrally.

"Prestidigitator."

"I trust you can wield more powerful magic than young Ladomas?" Zinzi said.

"Certainly," the man sniffed.

"Zinzi, there's no need for questions—Neyhün recommended him. Please, Grumzel, have a seat," Haskell said.

The wizard scraped a chair across the floor and sat.

"What, precisely, is a prestidigitator?" Zinzi asked.

Grumzel gave him a sour look and addressed Haskell. "I studied under the venerable Wizard Winklesmith of Sheffield, assisting in his magical research and maintenance of his arcane library."

"Amazing," Haskell said. A wizard of distinction, clearly.

Haskell couldn't believe his luck.

"Indeed," Grumzel said.

"What are your specific qualifications?" Zinzi said.

"I am fluent in the languages of elves, dwarves, orcs, and goblins, and can weave several spells. For example, I may suss out magical auras or make one fall into a deep slumber."

"Such power will be useful, eh?" Haskell said, elbowing Zinzi. He couldn't wait to see real magic in action.

"Truly, but if I join your band, I must be well protected. Channeling the arcane is tiresome and I cannot be interrupted while doing so. I must also be permitted to recuperate after using my most potent formulas."

"Somewhat limited," Zinzi muttered.

Haskell frowned at Zinzi. It was unlike him to be so impolite. "I'm certain you are more than qualified, Grumzel. Master Neyhün mentioned you were conducting research—are you finished?"

"I am afraid not. I will likely be engaged until month's end, but I saw your notice and thought I ought to inquire. Frankly, Master Neyhün insisted I do so."

"Inconvenient," Zinzi said, noting the delay.

Haskell waved him off. "No matter, Neyhün mentioned as much when we spoke in the woods. Could you—*ah*—give us a demonstration?"

Grumzel glanced around the hall. "Here? Well, I suppose it would do no harm."

He rose and took up a solid stance. Murmuring, he traced an intricate pattern in the air with his fingers. His words echoed in Haskell's mind, and his steady, intricate movements were fascinating. Grumzel's left hand moved downward. He tossed a spray of fine yellow sand into the air with the other, his left palm halting as the arcing grains reached their parabola. The incantation ended with a shout. The lines he had woven became a faint golden web, in which the grains of sand seemed to catch for just an instant.

Haskell grew intensely tired, sleepier than he had ever felt in his life. His muscles relaxed, his chair seeming more comfortable than the coziest mattress. He wanted to slump back and let beautiful, rejuvenating sleep take him. He had worked hard. He deserved it.

Someone was lightly slapping Haskell's face. He drew himself back to consciousness from the depths of an exquisite slumber. Blinking, he found himself slouched in his seat with his head hanging over the back. He sat up and looked around.

Zinzi slept peacefully on the table beside him, his face resting on the roster. Several warriors were asleep across the hall, as were Haskell's party, except Dirk, who gawped at the wizard with his one good eye. Betty was also awake, the mug in her hand dribbling mead onto the floor.

Haskell shook his head to clear away the cobwebs. He extended the spell scroll to Grumzel.

"You're hired," he yawned.

April 21

Chapter XXIX—Misnomer

Thief was a misnomer, at least in the present context. The so-called thief, or burglar, was really a scout: the eyes and ears of a party. The one to whom wizards and warriors turned when the door would not open, the opposition was too strong, or the path suspiciously clear. The "thief" found another way. A way that, admittedly, required certain skills.

Winifred sat cross-legged in her favourite parlour chair. She took a pull on her long wooden pipe, rolling the warm, savoury smoke around her mouth as she watched Froba through the window. The girl was a natural.

Half-starved and small for her age, she was still able to haul herself onto the tiled roof across the courtyard and clamber up the octagonal wizards' tower jutting into the early morning sky.

She could see why Ferd had taken a shine to the girl.

* * *

Froba gazed up the sheer face of the angular stone tower, its conical roof stark against the cloudy sky. The ground floor climb had been easy. The stones were large and rough, their mortar deeply set, and the windows firmly shuttered. The tower, though, was tightly laid, had small windows, and an overhanging roof.

Winifred had been a pain the past couple days, drilling her hard and quick with the back of her hand. Still, she was a better teacher than Ferd and more attentive than Haskell. Not that she trusted the old bitch. But she liked the training. It kept her mind off things, like when she was going to talk to Dirk and what the hells was going on.

She grabbed the sill of the lowest window and clambered up its frame, clinging to the carved stone as she reached for a gap in the stonework overhead.

"Get down from there!" an elderly man howled from inside. He was sitting on a wooden privy bench, his robes hiked over knobby knees. He had twisted around to scowl up at her. "Have you no manners?"

Froba scrambled up the wall like a frightened squirrel. She grabbed a fluttering banner, scurried up the vibrant blue material, and passed hand over hand along its horizontal iron crossbar. Swinging over, she hooked her leg in the tower's highest window and, thighs and abdominal muscles straining, hauled herself up to straddle the cold stone sill. Panting, she looked down.

The old man leaned out his window and shook his fist. "I will transmute you into a… toad, you… monkey!"

Froba stuck out her tongue.

Someone hauled her inside by the ruff of her tunic. A pudgy, unfamiliar wizard in fine grey, gold-trimmed robes glowered at her. "What are you doing?" he said.

They were in a small, book-lined cell with a stout looking door. He leaned out the window but kept hold of her tunic. "Good morning, Master Neyhün—I did not realize you had translocated back so soon!" He rounded on Froba. "Only wizards are permitted in the Tower. Who do you think you are?"

"Leave off, ye puffed-up bookworm. I'm guild trainin'," she said, trying to pull away.

He squinted at her. "More like burgling."

"Tha guild mistress' trainin' me proper," she said, pulling away. He let go and she went sprawling onto the floor.

"Master Neyhün ought to be Guild Master, not a doddering old assassin. This Guild is a stain; look at this so-called library." He gestured at the tomes, manuscripts, and folios around them. There were at least a hundred volumes. Froba had only ever seen one book in her life. She couldn't even read the notices posted in the Market.

She climbed back to her feet. "Looks like a lot o' books to me."

"You are as unschooled as you are common. Why am I bandying words with you? Go out the way you came!" He sat at a stone counter and took up a mortar and pestle.

Froba looked at her mended outfit. Common? Sure, it was plain, but they weren't rags. Stupid wizard. She scowled at him and went to the window. A suede wineskin hung on the wall. She drew the skin's cord over her shoulder and climbed out the window.

Reaching up, she clung to a gap in the roof's overhanging boards. After a brief dangle, she pulled herself up its red clay tiles. She sat on the edge and looked out over Branthall's massive south wall.

The fields of the Lane were growing greener. She pictured the stream cascading down the Sentinel Hills, and the leafy Darkwood clearing where a dank hole led to a deep dungeon. What would they find down there next time? Would everyone come back alive?

She thought of Orod and tried to imagine him battering

goblins with his torch, but she couldn't. He had been such a little wimp. She wondered what Winifred would have made of him, had he lived. She probably wouldn't have given him a second glance.

Froba wondered if she'd really be free of Ferd. Everywhere she turned he had been there with his hand out. She couldn't see that changing. At least she had a good stash now. She thought about the pretty blue and gold stones she had lifted last time. She hadn't really felt bad about it, it was her job, but she didn't want to do it again.

Maybe it didn't matter. Maybe Winifred would straighten out Ferd for her. Make it so she was part of Haskell's crew, not Ferd's. Something inside her didn't think so. That's not how Branthall worked.

She sighed and drew around the wineskin. Pulling the cork, she smelled a sweet, yeasty alcohol and took a drink. It was a dry wine with a sharp alcoholic bite and a hint of honey. It washed her dry throat, quenching her thirst and warming her belly. She kicked her sandaled feet and watched the questers begin to train below. Froba, mistress of all she surveyed.

Chapter XXX—The Night Before

C orben and Torg were stretched out in their bunks, bellies full and contentedly drunk. Rast and Flint were kicked back on the turned pine couch, regaling one another with tales of woodland skirmishes and gastronomic triumphs, though neither really listened to the other. Bror, listening to no one, absently scratched the tender scar on his side. He prodded the fire with a poker, its charred wood glowing with inner heat. Trin sat on a stool in the corner, sharpening a spear with quick, practiced strokes while Froba looked on, awkwardly running her dagger across a whetstone. Trin's face was healing, but the ugly scab on her cheek would leave a prominent scar.

Zinzi scratched entries into a ledger at the den's small table. Things were getting dire for Haskell. "If you will forgive my saying so, I have never seen coin spent so quickly. Ten sovereigns for healing and funerary rites; twenty for repairs; and six for stabling, re-provisioning, and laundry. Plus your gambling losses and incidentals."

Haskell, shirtless, was slouched in a well-worn armchair with Ko across his lap. They were sharing wine out of his skin.

"That's why I hired you, good, sensible Zinzi. Just tell me when I'm out of coin." Haskell squeezed ruby liquid into Ko's giggling mouth. Some dribbled down her breasts and the silver eagle pendant he had bought her, both exposed by a low-cut shift.

The pendant had cost five sovereigns.

Zinzi sighed, thankful everyone had been advanced their wages. He snapped his ledger closed and set it aside. "Then I must inform you that the party is out of funds. Moreover, you are only paid up with Griswold to the end of April, and you owe Ferd ten sovereigns, eleven talents." It had been foolish of the boy to gamble his money and borrow more. It didn't matter that they hadn't interviewed any decent fighters, Haskell couldn't afford them.

"No matter. We'll be off to the woods as soon as Grumzel is ready," Haskell said. Ko sucked his neck and bit his chin.

Zinzi shook his head. "You cannot afford to wait. Grumzel's research could be delayed, or he might fall ill. Ferd also charges a ruinous rate of interest. You must pay him back before month's end or fall deeper into debt."

Haskell made to speak but Zinzi pressed on. "Consider that you might net nothing on your next outing. There is little time for a third." Assuming everyone survived, he did not say. Zinzi was glad to be leaving but hadn't found the right moment to tell Haskell.

"Good, I didn't want to kick around town anyway. I've got it all figured—we don't have enough people to guard camp, so you and Flint stay here. Corben can wait for us on the Sentinel Hills so he can spot danger before it gets close."

"Hear, hear," Rast cheered. Trin grunted. Bror continued staring into the flames.

Zinzi said nothing. He and Flint would have to tell Haskell soon, but they didn't want to disappoint him. At least they had a few more days. Hopefully his outing was a success. It would lessen the blow.

Haskell ran his fingers up Ko's thigh. "Then it's settled. We'll strike out tomorrow and return with plenty of coin. Not just that, but gems and jewels." Ko punctuated each sparkling word with a moan; she latched her lips onto his as if to suck the very treasures from his mouth.

Haskell rose and threw Ko over his shoulder. "Onward, brave Ko, to the cavern of delight!" She shrieked and kicked exaggeratedly. Haskell tossed her on the bed and pulled the heavy curtain closed. The others tried to ignore the muffled squeals, giggles, and thumps from within.

Flint rose, red faced, and awkwardly worked his hands. "I need to rise early to arrange the supplies, so…" He retired to the bunkroom.

Zinzi sat in the vacated armchair and folded his hands over his belly. He would never have to face the Darkwood's foul inhabitants again. It was for the best; his advice was wasted on Haskell. It would be good for the boy to see his own mis-spending in black and white.

Yes, his leaving was for the best.

April 22

Chapter XXXI—Waylaid

I t was a fine morning to range into the Lane. The wind was cool on their faces and the sun was full in the sky. Birds flitted through the grass, chirping happily. The company was laughing and in high spirits. Dirk was the only one not enjoying himself, but that was normal.

Froba stuck by Corben all morning. Dirk kept throwing her strange looks, like he had something to say. She'd hear it when they got to the dungeon. She wanted to enjoy her freedom a little longer.

They made the Sentinels in good time and were soon at the summit. She climbed back into the wagon as Donner lapped the cool Darkwood stream. The others had crossed into the trees ahead, though Dirk was hanging back. She avoided his gaze.

Corben gave Donner a slap on the rump; the mule answered with an indignant bray. The wagon bumped and jolted over the rocky terrain, the teamster guiding them around the worst ground with clicks and flicks of his lash. He would set up camp and wait with Donner like Haskell had planned.

"Corben?" Froba asked.

"Hm?"

"Why'd ye come here?"

"Whaddya mean?"

"*Here*, on this trip, with Haskell."

"The loot we hauled back last time ought to be answer enough. I'm gonna buy another mule with the coin I've saved."

Froba fended off a low-hanging branch as they entered the woods. "But ye could've gone anywhere with yer mule cart—yer rich."

Corben chuckled. "*Rich*, she says. Why'd I come? Haskell did me a good turn on the road to Branthall, and I guess I felt like a bit o' adventure before I get too old."

Froba nodded as they jostled along. She guessed that made sense, though she wouldn't risk the Darkwood if she had a choice.

They veered right along the wooded ridge. The stream's babbling faded as they drew closer to the slope to the dungeon. She glanced up. Several tall, dog-legged creatures with huge swords loped from the trees ahead. Something flashed down from the ridge. Someone fell.

Froba stood. "Loo—"

A powerful tug nearly dislocated her shoulder as she was wrenched from the wagon. Ground became sky and she heard more than felt her head hit something hard. She tried to stand but pitched onto the ground, clinging to the moist vegetation as the woods spun around her. Breathing heavily, she waited for her vision to steady before clambering to her feet. She tried to focus on the wagon. Someone was wrestling with Donner's reins. Corben was lying on the ground.

Clashes and shouts came from ahead as the others battled under the trees. Where was Dirk? What had he been trying to tell her? He couldn't be in on this. She didn't know what to do.

She was on her own.

The hyena-man—Torg had called them quori—towered over Haskell despite its prodigious stoop; he parried a powerful downward swing, its sword notching his. The quori wore a thick, boiled leather cuirass and bracers and had a furry, reddish-brown face with black, beady eyes and a short, black snout. It let out a high-pitched, ululating laugh, exposing long, wolf-like teeth.

He threw off the quori's sword. It hopped back, evading his counter-slash. Bouncing lightly on padded hind legs, the monster lowered its guard and beckoned him with a black-furred hand, taunting him.

Haskell glanced left and right. The others were struggling, each fighting a private duel below the leafless trees. He wouldn't let it end like this.

He darted forward, slashing at the creature's leg. It parried easily, swirled its longer blade around his, and knocked his sword from his hand. Haskell growled and charged in, drawing his dagger. He grasped the creature's belt and rammed the top of his helmet into its laughing snout. The quori gurgle-yelped and reared back, its teeth and lower jaw smashed and bleeding. He jerked it forward by its belt and plunged his blade into its muscled throat. It gurgled, spitting blood, and slipped to its knees.

Haskell scrambled for his sword and whirled around. Bror was kneeling on a quori and hacking its face to bloody ruin with his axe. Torg, several yards away, was struck on the arm by a morning star. He managed to deflect the same quori's sword with his spear, but its blade slid up the shaft and clanged off his steel cap. He fell sideways.

Haskell dashed forward. The quori turned, regarding him

with one good eye, the other blinded by a long scar down its face. Its greying snout curled contemptuously and it loosed a hyena laugh.

It countered Haskell's wild slash and brought its morning star down on his shoulder. One long spike passed through a metal plate but was stopped by his quilted gambeson. Another nearly punctured his neck. The quori stepped in and shouldered Haskell to the ground. He flipped over and kicked out but misjudged the creature's height; his foot passed between its long dog legs. It kicked his wrist, forcing the sword from his hand. He scrabbled backward as it stabbed at him.

Bror roared a guttural cry and charged with levelled spear. Haskell clutched his dagger and tried to rise, but the quori was fast. It dropped its morning star and warded off Bror's spear with the flat of its sword. Stepping in to grab Bror's wrist, it spun him into Haskell, knocking them both to the ground. It kicked Bror in the back as he tried to rise, pushing Haskell back down.

The quori pointed its sword at Haskell's throat and grinned disturbingly. "Yoo a no good claan-boss, hooman, but will be good slave."

Haskell gritted his teeth. The battle was over. He had lost.

Bror rocked off Haskell and onto his knees, breathing hard. The three remaining quori dragged over Torg, Trin, and Rast, resting their clawed hyena feet on them like hunters showing off game. His friends were in bad shape but breathing. He didn't see Dirk. A fourth quori with a huge bow ambled through the woods in the distance. It waved and let out a triumphant cackle; the others responded with a torrent of laughs.

Had Dirk abandoned them? Was he dead? How could they have lost, all six of them fully armed and ready? He had believed that, together, they could handle anything. If only they had Grumzel's magic they…

Magic.

Haskell slipped off a gauntlet and worked his fingers into his belt pouch. He felt around bandages to the crystal vials within. His fingers brushed angular edges; that was the one. Neyhün had warned him not to stake his life on magic, but he had no choice. He withdrew the glowing, colourless vial and popped it open.

The laughing grey-snout caught the movement and saw the vial in Haskell's hand. Wide-eyed and snarling, it raised its sword to pierce Haskell's throat.

Froba stood and stumbled, her head and vision clearing. Grig. Grig was their attacker. He was wrestling Donner to get the wagon around, whooping gleefully at the melee raging deeper in the woods. Why was he here? This couldn't be a job for Ferd. Breaking thumbs and collecting debts was one thing, but this?

She growled and loaded her sling, set it whirling, and sent the bullet at Grig's head. The stone went wide, twittering like a bird darting through the branches.

Grig shot her a baleful glare. "Ye little sow!" He let go of Donner and loped at her. She fumbled for another stone, but he closed the distance and lifted her by the tunic. She dropped her sling to grip his clammy wrist. "Ye know what I do to strays like ye?" he said, licking his jagged teeth.

Froba spat in his face.

Grig flung her to the ground with a roar. She landed hard, knocking the wind from her lungs. He stood over her and raised his long, wooden cudgel.

"Put that down!" Dirk said, hauling down Grig's arm.

Grig shoved him back. "Hands off, slime!"

Froba squirmed back on her elbows, struggling to breathe.

What were they doing?

Dirk pointed toward the others. "It's over, them outlanders are quori meat now. Did the teamster see ye?"

Froba looked at Corben. Donner was standing over him, teeth bared and ears back.

"He didn't see shit, but this one had a go at me," Grig said, menacing Froba.

Dirk glared at her with his good eye. He opened his mouth, but Haskell's voice rang through the trees like a shockwave.

Haskell downed the potion as the quori drove its sword at his throat. The sweet fluid filled him with a warm confidence. "Stop!" he shouted. His vision blurred. The command, imbued with the potion's magic, filled the ears of his enemies. He watched the grey-snout blink as if struck by a wave of confusion. It shook its head and regarded its companions, who gawped at one another and the humans at their feet.

Had it worked?

"This is all a misunderstanding. Let's not fight but help each other as the gods intended," Haskell said.

The leader straightened and sheathed its sword. It extended a clawed hand and pulled Haskell to his feet. The quori yapped to its men, some of whom chirped and nodded. "Grig did lie-trick us? Is bad to fight yoo?" it said tentatively.

Grig? Where had he heard that name before? No time for that now. Haskell clapped it on the bicep. It was so tall and strong. "Of course! But all's forgiven. Come, let's see to our friends."

He stooped over unconscious Torg. His arm looked bad; it was purple and bulging around the wound. Luckily, his helmet had taken the sword blow.

Rast was semi-conscious, his eyes and nose bruised and swollen, and his bushy beard full of blood and mucous. He didn't seem in danger of death. Trin, though, was in bad shape. A black and white fletched arrow had pierced her chain shirt and right breast. Pinkish blood bubbled from her mouth with each laboured breath.

"Fucking dogs… got me good," she gurgled with a bloody grin.

Haskell drew the ruby vial from his pouch and grasped the shaft with his other hand. He paused to steel himself and mouthed a silent prayer.

"Do it," she burbled.

He tore the arrow from her chest.

Trin screamed, lurching up with a coughing gurgle. Haskell took the back of her head and poured half the potion down her throat. She rocked forward with a hoarse cry and vomited bloody phlegm. Overcome by a series of wracking coughs, she clutched her chest and took long, gasping breaths. "I'm… healed," she breathed, massaging her chest through her armour.

There was no time to marvel at the magic.

Haskell stood and accepted his sword from the quori-boss. He swooned, suddenly light-headed. This magic was heady stuff. He removed his dented helmet and scanned the woods. Dirk waved at him in the distance. Froba was with him and the wagon just behind. "Please, help us," Haskell said to the grey-snout.

A quori took up Torg and Bror supported Trin, who was weak and still coughing up blood. The unlikely allies went to their friends. Froba was holding her head but looked okay. Dirk was unwounded; he eyed the quori suspiciously.

"What happened, Dirk?" Haskell asked.

"I saw off a quori that jumped Froba and the teamster. She's alright, but the old man's in a bad way," Dirk said.

Haskell stooped over Corben, who was very pale. The side

of his head was a mat of blood and mangled flesh. Blood trickled from his nose. Haskell gave him the last of the potion. He watched with sick fascination as Corben's flesh scabbed and skull popped back into place. His colour improved. Days of healing in as many seconds.

Haskell stood and felt another wave of dizziness. The potion's magic was ebbing, at least he imagined so. He uncorked his wineskin and took a mouthful, then another. He had to send the quori away before they regained their senses. What if the creatures chased them into the Lane? The party was exhausted and beaten. They wouldn't stand a chance.

He had an idea.

Haskell smiled at the grey-snout. "You're a good clan-boss. There's a dungeon under that hill. It'd be good if your clan hunted the goblins inside. Good slaves."

The quori grinned, exposing its red tongue and sharp, glistening teeth. "Alright, hooman." It gave Haskell a playful punch and led its companions to the stream.

The party took Torg from a quori and laid him and Corben in the wagon. Rast and Trin sat in the front. Haskell led Donner towards the water. He watched the quori reach the base of the ridge. They ducked through a rocky opening from which the stream issued; their boss turned and waved. Haskell waved back. He'd have to explore that route. If they returned.

The walk back to town was long, slow, and painful. No one spoke, giving Haskell plenty of time to think about how foolish he was. If only he hadn't pissed away his money. If only he had found worthy fighters at the Guild. If only. He thought about the questions he should have asked the grey-snout: where they were camped, what they knew about the dungeon, what valuables they had and could they share them? Instead, he was trudging back to town with nothing. Less than nothing.

He was an utter failure.

He ground his teeth and shut his eyes. It would take weeks for everyone to recover. The healing draught had been a godsend, but it only sped the process. He could see that by Trin and Rast's weak swaying in the lurching wagon behind him. Haskell didn't have any money to pay the doctors to heal Torg. They would have to rely on the last of Yeoma's poultice and trust to the gods.

Even if everyone was ready in time, April was nearly over, and he had no money for room and board. They would have to live like tramps in the wild. Most of all, he dreaded facing the people. Their mockery over losing to Quin had been bad enough. They would never let him live this down.

Thoughts of this kind dogged him all the way to town. They struggled up the embankment and out of the Lane. Haskell crossed through the lichgate and wound through the trees and grave markers up the cemetery path. A cry went up from the tower as they approached. He led the wagon up the slope to Southgate. After chocking its wheels, he sank to the ground, his legs and lungs on fire. He looked out over the fields below and punched the ground. What was he going to do?

"Haskell?" a stern voice said from behind.

Haskell raised a gauntleted hand. "A moment, please."

"Haskell of Khul," the man said with deliberate evenness.

Haskell looked over his shoulder. Watch Captain Owain, armed and armoured, his dark hair and crimson cape blowing in the breeze, glared down at him. His silver medallion depicted a stylized eye over a crossed sword and spear. Four guards in chain shirts and black and white tabards stood behind him, their long spears low and ready.

Haskell pulled his unwilling body into a stance. "I am."

"You are under arrest," Owain said.

Haskell looked to his companions, who were as confused as him. Dirk whispered something to Froba. This was unbelievable. What could he have done? It couldn't be for Hambur, not now, or that little gang leader in Lowertown. No, they wouldn't have gone to the Watch. "On what charge?"

Owain shook his head. "Not a charge. A conviction."

* * *

Haskell just wanted to sit down. To be left alone. Every muscle ached, a condition not improved by his stint in a damp cell. His battered sword and blood-spattered armour were on the Council Chamber's dark, polished table, the armaments reflected in its surface. Winifred stood beside him, Hambur across the table, and Watch Captain Owain at the end. Burgomaster Stieg sat in a high-backed seat at the head of the table. Two halberdiers blocked the chamber's dragon-carved doors.

Stieg handed a rolled parchment to a nearby page and frowned at Haskell. "This is very serious, young man. You assaulted a respectable merchant and shipwright—the master in whose charge you were placed by your family."

The page delivered the red-sealed document to Haskell. It was an Attestation of his crimes in Khul. How, and why, did it come here? Were his father and Slade so vindictive that they would pursue him all the way to Branthall, in another kingdom? Clearly, they were. "I merely paid him back in kind."

"You beat and nearly drowned a respectable elder. Unforgiveable. You are fortunate Master Slade was not drowned or we would be having this discussion at the gallows."

Haskell ground his teeth. To think anyone would speak kindly of that crooked old devil. "*Master* Slade is a tyrant and a cheat. You wouldn't speak so reverently of the man if you knew him."

"I do know the man!" Stieg said, slapping the table.

Haskell jumped.

Hambur leered at Haskell. "He also stole a princely sum from his father and his grandsire's legendary sword. This churl is an outlaw who fled justice. He should be put to death."

Haskell threw the Attestation on the table beside his sword. "I only took what was mine. The weapon and money are my birthright. My father is no more a warrior than I am a clerk. He had the blade collecting dust on a wall."

Winifred cleared her throat. "With respect to my learned colleague, neither act is a capitol offence. Haskell has been banished from Khul. Justice has been served."

"He fled justice—that makes him an outlaw," Hambur seethed.

"One would think you had been rolled into a river, Hambur," Winifred said.

"The ruffian cast me from my horse. I could have been killed!"

"Enough of your bickering," Stieg said. "Haskell is no outlaw but is guilty and unrepentant."

"But not profligate," Winifred said. "He serves king and country within my guild. He has slain many goblins and just returned from the Darkwood, where he overcame a band of quori. To impede him goes against the principles for which Branthall stands."

Hambur scoffed. "He is a drunk who swans about with prostitutes and thieves. Is such behaviour becoming of a quester?"

Haskell planted his hands on the table. "I don't answer to you." He wanted to draw his sword and strike Hambur dead.

"You will answer to this council, or you will hang," Stieg said firmly.

Hambur grinned and fingered his chains. "I am also owed two hundred-fifty sovereigns for translocation of the Attestation by guild wizards."

Haskell started. Hambur had acquired the evidence against him? The bastard. How did he even know? Haskell's hand edged toward his sword. To think the Guild had a hand in bringing this evidence against him. Utter betrayal. His finger twitched against the jeweled pommel of his sword.

Winifred dug her fingers into Haskell's arm and drew him upright. "Burgomaster, if you will permit—"

Stieg's gavel banged like a thunderclap. "Haskell, son of Eskil, you brutally assaulted your elderly master, stole from your father, and have shown no contrition. Quite the opposite. But for your service to the Questers Guild, I would banish you from Branthall to live penniless in the wild. As it is, you are fined twice what you stole—half for Branthall and half for your father, whose sword shall be returned. You will also reimburse The Right Honourable Hambur his two hundred-fifty sovereigns. Lastly, you shall be taken from this place and pilloried in the Market the day after tomorrow."

Haskell's jaw went slack. Did he say twice the amount? And pay Hambur? He had only pennies to his name. "I was waylaid in the Darkwood and have little but my sword and armour."

"Then the gods have also judged you by inflicting such misfortune."

"With respect, Burgomaster, this is a crippling penalty," Winifred said.

"It is fitting for such wanton acts aggravated by his flight and shameful betrayal."

Haskell raised his hands in supplication. "Please, I'll lose everything. My company is all I have."

"My judgement stands. You shall be gaoled in the Tower until the Questers Guild sells your assets. You shall then submit to Winifred's direction, serving as she sees fit. The Guild shall withhold two-thirds of your spoils until your debts are discharged. That, if nothing else, should compel you to conduct yourself more wholesomely. A record of your punishment will be sent to Khul." Stieg's gavel cracked with finality.

Captain Owain signalled two spearmen, who took Haskell by the arms. They marched him, dumbstruck, from the chamber. Hambur flushed with delight.

"Satisfaction," he rumbled.

April 23

Chapter XXXII—Prisons

The morning was cool, windy and dry, turning Branthall into a maelstrom of dust and grit. Ferd sat at a table in the Cock's back room, listening to the wind howl outside. Dirk and Froba sat across from him. Grig sat nearby, throwing Froba dark, seething looks, like she was a lost kitten he would happily drown.

"Ye three cocked up royal," Ferd said, looking at each in turn.

"Ain't my fault," Grig sneered. "I got them quori all lined up. Them outlanders were dog meat."

"They was supposed to hit 'em *after* we raided that dungeon, ye prick," Dirk said.

"They wanted 'em as slaves, not goblin meat. Besides, it was that potion that fucked the plan, not the quori," Grig said.

Dirk sat back. "How was I supposed to know the bastard had a potion like that?"

"It's yer job to know!" Ferd snapped. "And what about ye?" he said to Froba.

She looked up dumbly.

"She was with the old man," Dirk said.

"Little bitch nearly took my head off with that sling," Grig said.

"He threw me on my head. What was I supposed to do, thank 'im?" Froba said sullenly.

Grig shot up and threw over his chair. "The little sow was in my way!"

Ferd buried his dagger in the tabletop. He had had enough of these bumblers. "I don't care who did what or fuck-all. We're all in the shit now, me lovelies."

Grig kicked his chair and stalked back and forth.

Ferd pointed at him. "I'll skin ye alive and hang yer useless hide from the Tower if ye don't keep yer head." He glared at Dirk and Froba. "Did Haskell get anything out o' them bewitched quori?"

"Nuthin' I know about," Dirk grumbled.

"I could fill a scroll from here to Erd with what ye don't know," Ferd said.

"Haskell don't know nuthin'," Froba said, avoiding Ferd's glower.

He didn't like how she'd been carrying on these last weeks. She'd been too sure of herself. He was certain she was holding something back.

"I say the giant prick has an accident in gaol," Grig said.

"Owain's got him in the Market Cells watched by his own guards. We can't get to him," Ferd said.

"What's it matter? The kid's played out. I say we find more newmeat to milk. Where's Luna? She should be here," Dirk said.

"She can hang for all I care," Ferd growled.

"Watch yer mouth. She's one of us," Dirk snapped.

Ferd sat back and crossed his arms. What a sap. They were all a bunch of useless tits. It was a damn good thing he suckered Hambur into ruining the boy. It had been a great play to leverage Hambur against Owain, but he hadn't expected the boy to walk out of the Darkwood alive.

He caught Froba eyeballing him. That little bitch was up to something, all right. He'd have it out of her, but first. He slid a small jar of white liquid across the table. "That Haskell's a sucker fer the dragon if ever I saw one. Next time he so much as stubs a toe, ye give him this for the pain, got it?" Froba nodded and stared at the bottle. "He ain't got nuthin' now, so ye two just make sure it stays that way. Keep the blighter down and get 'im in the Den. He'll fit right in."

* * *

The morning grit had turned to evening rain, making Haskell's cell chilly and damp. He had pulled his weathered, brown cloak and patched, green hood tight against the cold. He missed his furs but was thankful for what he had. The guards had let him keep his dagger; it was his only weapon now. They probably wagered on whether he would use it to end his shame. He wondered what odds Ferd's bookie would give him.

Ko stood in the claustrophobic hall outside, her wet, fur-lined cloak tight about her shoulders. The earthy scent of fresh rain clung to her from outside. Haskell eyed the silver eagle necklace on her breast; its bright metal glowed dully in the cell's rushlight. He wondered how much it would fetch at market.

Ko pulled her cloak tight, hiding the cool silver and her warm flesh. "It's not fair. You deserve better for all you've done," she said.

Haskell crossed his arms. "Stieg doesn't think so."

"That awful Council. You only took what was yours."

Haskell gazed at the moss growing on the rough stonework under his window. "Will you be there tomorrow?"

Ko withdrew into the shadows. "I—"

"I don't want you there," Haskell said without turning. "You shouldn't be shamed alongside me." He knew she would abandon him. Why stick by a disgraced quester with nothing to his name? He couldn't offer her any kind of life now.

Ko gripped the necklace under her cloak. "I… I've got to go."

Haskell listened to the patter of her feet as she fled. He threw himself onto his cot and rubbed his eyes, listening to fat raindrops pelt the walls outside. He heard someone shuffle down the hall and nervously clear their throat. "Hello, Flint. I hope you've brought good news."

"Oh. Well now, this is awkward," Flint stammered.

Haskell sighed and dropped his arms on his chest.

Flint stood in the doorway, wringing a sodden hat in his meaty hands. "I hate to be leavin' an' all, but I said from the start I was lookin' for usual sort of work. It's dangerous in them woods, an' I'll have a proper kitchen now."

Haskell closed his eyes and wished for a gallon of wine. "Where?"

"Well, that's the thing, it's a bit delicate—"

"Don't say it."

"—it's that merchant, Hambur. His cook up and quit and his chamberlain, Kerk—a fine fella—offered good terms. He's buyin' out my contract and puttin' it toward your debt."

Haskell stared at the heavy wooden beams above. Was everyone going to leave him? Of course they would. Could he blame them? Yes, he did. He would have stuck by every one of them had their roles been reversed. Definitely. No question.

"Sorry, Mr. Haskell, but April is up and gone, or near enough, an' I've naught to do just sittin' around the Treeman."

"Do what you must."

Flint came in and set a small basket beside the cot. "Griswold let me do up some pies for ye."

Haskell peeked under the covering napkin. The scent of spiced meat greeted him from a small mound of golden pastries. "This only makes me miss you more."

Flint smiled. "Maybe I can sneak a few pies out o' Hambur's back door."

"Don't endanger yourself on my account. Wilderness monsters have nothing on him. I'd make the Darkwood my roof before living under his." Gods, he might have to do just that.

"Things'll turn out, you'll see," Flint said, backing into the hall. He gave Haskell a half-hearted wave and left.

The gaoler poked his head through the door and eyed Haskell's basket. "Shall I fetch anythin' before lockin' up yer lordship?" he said with a rotten smile.

Haskell snatched a pie and bit the tender pastry in half, moaning as he tasted its rich, flavourful filling. He peeked at the gaoler gazing greedily at the pie.

"If you want a few of these, bring me a gallon of wine."

April 24

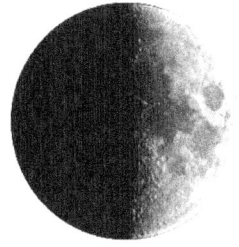

Chapter XXXIII—Satisfaction

Winifred ran her quill across a name on the register, killing another warrior with a stroke. Hambur strolled across the worn carpet in her office. He leaned over the back of the chair in front of her, looking positively euphoric. She sighed. "What is it?"

"Come, Winifred, be of good cheer—the day is lovely and our futures bright."

"You are uncharacteristically cheerful. Have you managed to ruin the prospects of another young warrior, or are you still flush from Haskell's disgrace?"

Hambur chuckled. "I am done with that boy. Justice has been served. I come before you with an opportunity."

Winifred took her pipe from within her cushions and relit it. She sat back and drew several thoughtful puffs. "You speak, of course, about your settlement in the Lane."

Hambur sat in the chair. "Indeed. I need mercenaries to defend my humble manor. This is one of the services offered by your guild, yes?"

"Certainly," Winifred puffed. She drew out a leatherbound volume. "How many spears do you require?"

"Oh, eight or ten. I would be happy to buy out the contracts of Haskell's retainers. You could put it toward the lad's debt."

Winifred chuckled smoke. "Very thoughtful."

Hambur put a hand on his chest. "I am not heartless."

"I will extend your offer to them and find others. I can have a list drawn up in a few days."

Hambur laced his fingers over his belly. "Very fine. My tenants will arrive soon. I mean to set out as soon as possible." He noticed Haskell's sword lying on the desk. "My word, is this the pirate's sword?" He leaned forward and grabbed its hilt. Winifred snatched the scabbard as Hambur sat back, drawing the blade. He turned it over, examining its runes in the sunlight slanting through the window. "I do not know what the fuss is about, it looks common enough. The cross guard is worn and grip all frayed. Disgraceful."

Winifred raised an eyebrow. "Do you specialize in legendary blades?"

Hambur tossed the sword on the desk. "No, of course not—what a ridiculous suggestion. I sell arms and armour on consignment now and again but am merely a dabbler."

Winifred drew on her pipe. A strange response. Hambur was hiding something, but his pathetic games did not interest her. "Yes, I believe adulterated spices are your specialty."

Hambur threw her a dark look and rose.

It was preposterous that King Ferd had made Hambur a baronet; the greedy old fool was handing out land to any oaf with a bag of gold. But would the clods be able to hold it? "Do you seek mercenaries with any particular background or specialization?" she asked.

Hambur threw up his hands on his way to the door. "I leave the matter in your capable hands. Whoever you choose will suit me, I am sure."

"Indeed." Winifred blew out a stream of smoke.

She knew precisely who to send.

* * *

Naturally, it had to be sunny. Haskell had prayed for a dreary morning and a small crowd, but it wasn't to be. A gaggle of gawkers had already gathered near the gallows. He put his neck and wrists into the pillory's grooved wood. Owain swung the hinged top into place with a rusty squeal. The wood was swollen from the rain, its surface cold and slimy against Haskell's skin. He was so tall that he had to half-squat; his lower back and thighs cramped almost immediately.

Owain locked the two halves together. "Your two-hour sentence begins now." He hung a painted board around Haskell's neck. He couldn't see the sign but knew what it said: "Haskell, son of Eskil of Khul. Stole from his father and assaulted his elderly master."

The jeering was started by a small group of drunks leaning on one another near the fountain. This prompted others to point and laugh. People began to leer and whisper, the crowd growing while Haskell awaited the inevitable. The inevitable came as Hambur's two blue-liveried footmen bearing a large basket between them, their faces turned away from the stench inside. They dropped the basket on the ground. The mound of offal and spoilage was black, yellow, and brown with no hint of colour to indicate what it had once been.

Hambur stood front and centre, his eyes alive with delight. Haskell had never seen such a smugly satisfied man. That was the worst punishment of all. A fiddler struck up a saucy tune and capered once around Haskell. The merchant was going to heap as much embarrassment on Haskell as money could buy. He closed his eyes, but the image of his taunters' sunlit faces lurked behind his eyelids.

He didn't think he could live through the next two hours.

How long had it been: two minutes? Four? One?

The crowd took up the proffered ammunition with gusto. A drummer and piper joined the fiddler in the accompaniment of Haskell's shame. They added flourishes to each wet splatter, every dull thud and slimy smack of spoiled tubers, rotten eggs, bloody entrails, and clods of dung. Furnished with such abundance, the crowd circled Haskell until he was a living, breathing thing of garbage. He was driven to insensibility by the unrelenting assault of jeers, cheers, music, and filth.

Something hard struck the tip of his left thumb, numbing it down to the hand. Another cracked off the pillory. Haskell gritted his teeth but didn't cry out. He refused to give Hambur the satisfaction.

"Soft items only!" Owain barked, but a hard stone cracked off Haskell's forehead, causing him to go limp. "Enough!" Owain shouted. Two guardsmen pushed off townsfolk intent on making parting shots.

Owain unlocked the pillory and Haskell collapsed in a heap. Bror and Zinzi approached from the back of the crowd. "Take him, justice has been served," Owain said. He pointed out a bucket beside the fountain.

They doused Haskell where he lay and took the sign off his neck, turned him over, and doused him some more. Haskell tried to rise but only flopped over like a clubbed fish. They wrapped him in a blanket and carried him away.

Bror spotted Dirk outside the Cock. He had one arm around Luna, who hugged him around the middle and gazed languidly at the Temple.

"Lend us a hand," Bror grunted.

Dirk scoffed and polished a wrinkly apple on his leggings. "Not me concern."

Bror spit on Dirk's boot as they struggled by.

Dirk laughed. He tried to feed his apple to Luna, but she

had nodded off, lost to the world in a dragon-haze.

Chapter XXXIV—Rite of Passage

Froba whirled her sling over her head and let the bullet fly. It twittered down range, smashing the training yard wall with a sharp smack. She had missed the target by a good two feet. Thirty feet was tough, and the target wasn't even moving. Not like Grig's head had been.

Working with Darkwood monsters was bad. Hanging bad. She hated that they had made her a part of it. When would it end? Maybe it didn't matter. Ferd said only three things came out of the Keep: taxes, rich bastards, and broken men.

She supposed it was up to Haskell now. If he was strong enough to stay off the dragon things could go back to normal. But then, what would Ferd do next? He wouldn't stop there. What could she do?

She sent another stone downrange. The bullet thwacked off the target's stand.

She had watched Haskell's punishment from a distance and felt embarrassed but didn't know why. She had seen scores of people flogged, branded, or put in the stocks; people with their tongues cut out or hands cut off. Most had come from the streets; a couple had even worked for Ferd. She pitied them, sure, but had never felt a twinge of shame before. Had the others felt the same? Dirk sure didn't, but that was Dirk. Bror and Zinzi had been there. Not the others, though. What made them so different?

She sent another stone flying—through the hoop this time, but still too close to the frame. She had to center it. Get things in line.

She hoped Ferd was wrong about broken people. She could understand why Haskell was always looking for a fight: it was simple. Make a stand; live or die. The dungeon was scary but at least it was honest. Winifred was teaching her to sneak and steal, but to fight for humanity. What did Ferd ever teach her? To be afraid? To fleece outlanders? No Lanesforder had given her anything for free. Everything cost in Branthall. That much she knew for sure.

* * *

Night had fallen and Froba woke with a start. She was doubled up in the den's armchair. Had she cried out in her sleep? In her dream, Ferd was stabbing her in the belly with a knife, its blade glowing with a dull red heat. She had tried to fend him off, but her arms wouldn't move fast enough. He had plunged the knife into her, over and over, its blade filling her insides with roiling fire while her flesh sizzled and burned.

Her belly throbbed at the memory, and she pressed her forehead against her knees. The skin of honey wine she drank last night had been a mistake. Maybe it had been Griswold's watery fish pottage.

She rubbed her face where the rough weave of the chair's grimy fabric had left an impression. Still more comfortable than Ferd's place. Which is where she'd end up if Haskell didn't come around. She doubled up as fresh pain filled her insides, like someone was squeezing her guts.

"Gods," she squeaked.

Froba shivered. The fire had died to a few embers. She slipped out of the chair, staggering a little as her belly did a flip and pulled into a tight ball. She had never felt anything like this before. That frightened her.

She hobbled to the hearth and added kindling, slipping to her knees to blow on the embers. The kindling took and she added a small log. Sitting on her haunches, she took a deep breath and scratched her thigh. Her finger came back wet and sticky. She pulled up her shift and was confronted by a crimson mess between her thighs. Her heart began to pound. She went back to the chair. The cushion bore a dark, accusatory stain.

What was happening?

What would she do when the others woke up?

What would they say?

She couldn't burn the cushion or throw it away. Wash it. She had to wash it.

She stumbled about uncertainly for a few seconds then stole into the next room. Bror and Torg snored away in the corner. She tip-toed to a long counter bearing several jugs and basins. Reaching up, she grabbed a heavy ceramic jug and filled a bowl with water. Some splashed on the floor. One of the slumbering forms snorted and rolled over. Froba set down the jug and crept from the room.

She brought the sloshing bowl and soiled cushion to the fireside and scrubbed the stain with a cloth. The water turned pink when she rinsed it. She felt a rush and blood dripped to the floor beneath her.

She sobbed.

"Piss," a soft voice said behind her.

Froba leaned over the cushion to hide what she was doing.

Ko stood with one hand on the back of the armchair. She

was nude but for a scarf around her shoulders. The warm light of the crackling fire accentuated the curves of her body. Her long, dark hair spilled around her shoulders.

"Use piss, then water," she said.

Froba couldn't read Ko's face. Was it disgust, condemnation? She looked away and tried to cut off her tears, but only succeeded in releasing a choking sob.

"Roll up that cloth and wedge it between your legs," Ko said.

Froba did as instructed then got her own bedpan. Ko handed her a fresh cloth. She wrapped herself in a knitted wool blanket and pulled up a chair. "Dab, don't scrub. Keep going until it comes clean."

Froba cleaned the cushion then herself, guided by Ko. With the last traces erased, Froba propped the cushion up to dry by the fire. She scooted to the foot of Ko's chair and wrapped herself in the edges of the blanket. Ko ran her fingers through Froba's hair.

"Am I a-cursed?" Froba asked.

"Some say so. You're a woman now."

"They can have it."

Ko smiled. "It's not all bad."

"I ain't gonna die o' the pox like my mum or have no baby."

Ko rapped the top of Froba's head. "Respect your ancestors—they guide you." She continued more softly. "I remember your mother. Gods, she must have been little older than you when she died. She seemed like a woman to me then, but I was only a child."

"Do ye know who my 'da is?" Froba asked.

"No. She wasn't a very careful girl."

"Ye ain't too careful with Haskell."

"You don't—no, how could you?" Ko said to herself. "Before you lay with a man, go see an old midwife—the older the better. The temple sells potions but they're expensive. Your mother didn't bother and had, well…"

"Me," Froba said unhappily. She looked at the fire and frowned. "Why did ye stick by him?"

"Haskell? He's fun and full of life, or he was. He'll spring back. He's just had some bad luck."

"It's no life I'd want, whorin' about with 'venturers."

"I'm no streetwalker."

"What's the difference?"

"You went into the woods with Haskell, didn't you?"

"So?"

"Wasn't it exciting? Surrounded by dangerous warriors and fighting for your life? I bet you've got a taste for it now."

Froba screwed up her face. The only thing she had a taste for was good food, dry wine, and a warm place to sleep. The dungeon was frightening. Fighting Grig had been terrifying. Hustling on the streets was worse.

"It's no different for me, only the creatures I face are hulking men who thirst for my affection. And the treasure! It's all just a game, you know. I could play the good daughter and marry some boring shopkeeper, but where's the adventure in that?" Ko mussed Froba's hair. "We all have our strengths. I'm not a fierce warrior like Trin or a skulking little goblin like you."

"Still sounds like a whore to me," Froba muttered.

"Better than a filthy goblin," Ko sneered, though not unkindly.

April 25

Chapter XXXV—Gifts

Haskell held his throbbing, bandaged forehead. It was sad that his most prominent scar would be from a punishment, not a battle. He propped up his pillow and sat against the headboard—a luxury he would soon be without. Zinzi sat on a stool beside the bed.

"What's the damage, Zinzi?"

"You are fortunate to have such a thick skull, my friend."

Haskell chuckled, but that brought fresh pain. "My assets?"

"We obtained good value for your armour and equipment. You are fortunate in that regard."

"Fortunate? You'll forgive me if I disagree."

"You will soon recover. A patron or another party could furnish you with a weapon and simple armour. It could be much worse."

Haskell sank against his pillow and closed his right hand. It had been three days since he held his sword. He would never find its match—it was so much more than a weapon. "No, I—"

"There is more."

Haskell looked at Zinzi. What more could there be? He had nothing left to lose.

"Hambur has purchased our contracts—everyone but Bror, Torg, and Froba, who do not wish to serve him. The money was put toward your debts."

Haskell looked at the wall. "Even you?"

"Yes, I will serve as his steward."

Haskell said nothing. He had known this would happen after Flint left. His going encouraged the others to leave, like guests from a dull party.

"I will tutor young Hiam and oversee the building of Hambur's manor in the Lane."

"I rely on your wisdom more."

Zinzi smiled. "Untrue. You are too old and willful for my lessons."

"Who will nag me when money runs short?" Haskell said with a smirk.

"Bror will be equal to the task, perhaps with more success." Zinzi laid a hand on Haskell's shoulder. "Work hard, keep faith in your heart, and things will turn around."

Haskell nodded. His head hurt and he was getting sleepy. Zinzi looked at him with sympathy. Or was it pity? Haskell rummaged in the bed for the medicine Froba had given him. He found the bottle and took a mouthful, grimacing at its bitterness but craving it all the same.

Zinzi took and examined the bottle. The liquid was milky with a fine black sediment. "What is this?"

"A potion Froba gave me. It's bitter medicine, but I'll soon be floating off on a cloud." He found himself wanting to be on that cloud more and more. It was a better retreat than a seaside holiday in July.

Zinzi sniffed the contents. "Milk of the poppy. I believe the locals call it dragon's milk. Do not drink too much,

Haskell. It is a potent medicine."

Haskell gave Zinzi the cork and settled into his pillow with a yawn. "That's what Froba said. She's a good girl."

Zinzi corked the bottle and set it aside.

"Yes. A good girl."

* * *

Froba entered Winifred's parlour. It was lit by a small lamp. A small pine box was on the chair in which Froba had sat during their first meeting.

"What is it?" she asked.

"A gift, child," Winifred said.

Froba didn't trust the old woman's wrinkled smile. "Why ye giftin' me?"

"Distrustful as ever. Go on, open it."

Froba eyed Winifred as she removed the box's lid. Inside was a shaped breastplate of boiled, red-black leather. She lifted out a cuirass inscribed with subtle patterns. It had a skirt of soft, iron-tipped leather strips. Matching greaves and bracers sat in the bottom of the box. The oiled hide filled the room with a spicy musk. "Why armour?"

"You are a quester now. A quester needs armour."

Froba ran her hand over the smooth leather. It was beautiful. "What's it gonna cost me?"

"Very little. Seek your fortune, with Haskell or whomever you choose, and tell me what you see and hear."

That smile again, Froba didn't trust it. "That's it?"

"That is all. You have promise, child, but more importantly, you live when you should be dead many times over. Fortune smiles on you and Haskell. That interests me."

"I just come off the street and Haskell's broke. How're we lucky?"

"Lucky where it counts, but do not let that go to your head. Fortune favours the prepared more than the bold. If Haskell had heeded my counsel, he would be better off. My counsel to you now is to put on your armour."

Froba drew on the cuirass. Its moulded pauldrons sat awkwardly on her shoulders, the sides gapped, and its skirt straps drummed against her shins.

Winifred laughed. "Well, he was taller than you." She slid out of her chair and tightened the armour's straps. Froba grunted as Winifred tugged her roughly this way and that. "You'll want a gambeson under this, but your tunic will serve for tonight." She stepped back and chuckled. "Well, you'll grow into it."

"Quit laughin'." Froba pulled at the tight armour. She grabbed the greaves from the box and put them on.

"This will protect you against many weapons, but a footpad does not charge into battle like a witless warrior. You must keep back, wait for an opening, and exploit it. You, little one, will turn the tide of battle with a well-timed stone or thrust of that dagger you think hidden.

Froba felt the blade sheathed at the small of her back. Winifred sniggered. "Subtlety, girl. Subtlety and misdirection are your closest allies. Now go; stalk the streets in your armour and grow accustomed to its weight."

* * *

Froba skulked through streets lit by the half moon above. Her cuirass chafed her neck and its skirt clacked against her greaves with every step. That wouldn't do. Fishing some pilfered string out of her pouch, she tied the offending strips together, took a few unobstructed steps, and smiled.

Shrill voices echoed from the adjacent street.

She crept forward and peeked around the corner. Ko was being hassled by a gaggle of young girls. They wore bright dresses cheaply dyed, and their hair was braided under linen wimples adorned with spring flowers prettier than they. They were the kind of desperate, grasping people she avoided at the Cock.

"There she goes, Mistress of the Sire-Thief, Beater of Old Men," the tallest viper said.

"I'm surprised he didn't take that pretty silver necklace to pay 'is fines," said another.

Ko glowered at them but didn't stop. "You're a jealous kettle of vultures. I'd be ashamed to keep company with such sloppy tarts."

"Shame, she says. Is that why your man's not on your arm?" another shot back.

"Our men are real fighters, not some rake ashamed to show his face," the tallest said.

Ko laughed. "Real fighters? Your pack of vagrants would have been whipped through the street like the dogs they are." She flounced down the street.

The gaggle fumed and hurled dirt and garbage her way.

Froba sneered. She took out her sling, loaded it with a clod of dirt, and sent it into the back of the tallest woman's head. The viper went down, cursing and crying for the Watch.

Froba sniggered and ran down the alley. She doubled back to the Guild and lurked across from the Treeman, its doorstep lit by a large carriage lamp. Ko strode toward the inn, wiping away tears. Never let them see you cry: it was a lesson Froba learned even before she could talk. Ko swept into the inn. Froba crept to the window by the door. The Treeman wasn't crowded, not like the Cock would be at this hour. The towns-folk here would be in bed and most questers were in the wilderness. Only street-walkers and sneaks like Froba were out at this hour.

Ko sat at a shadowy table and gave herself over to grief. Froba frowned. Ko, so beautiful, could have any warrior she wanted. Why not find another if she was unhappy? Ko had only been with Haskell a few weeks, after all. Froba didn't understand.

"This ain't yer turf," a boy said.

Froba turned, dagger in hand. Brent and three Tanners had formed a ring around her. They were brandishing knives and heavy sticks. She had let her guard down. Some thief. "Wrong, ye turd. I'm a quester now, not one o' Ferd's bootlicks. Go drown in yer shit pond down yonder hill."

"Look what she's wearin', Brent," the smallest boy said.

Brent sneered. "So what? Dress up a whore an' she's still a whore."

The Tanners advanced.

Brent was bigger than her, but her armour would probably turn his ballock knife. She took up a low stance that Winifred had taught her, arm back and dagger low. "Watch yer tongue or ye'll lose it," she said.

"Oooh," the Tanners moaned sarcastically.

Brent stepped toward her with a wicked grin.

The inn's door flew open. Griswold stepped out and brandished a stout club. "I told you lot to clear out. Get lost or I'll set the questers on you."

"Ooh, big man with a big stick," Brent said.

Froba took the opening. She shoved aside the smallest Tanner, ducked past Griswold, and hurried through the inn. She flew out the back door and ran down the alley, scaled a nearby house, and vaulted onto a dark, second-storey balcony. Peering through the balusters, she watched the Tanners come around the alley. They spread out and looked for her.

Brent crouched behind the stairs. "Go find the bitch. We got a score to settle."

The others headed her way. One went left, back to Main Street, another scurried down the alley, while the last, the smallest, went right under her. She watched him creep toward a dead end.

She could end him. It'd be easy, and one less Tanner to worry about. He was shorter and probably weaker than her. She could sneak up on him, cover his mouth, and stick him in the neck like Winifred had taught her.

No. She couldn't kill this kid, not even if his gang wanted her dead. She'd never killed anyone, not even a goblin, and the little snot reminded her of Orod. If she hadn't saved Orod, he might've ended up a part of their gang. Shit. What was Ferd thinking by giving Southgate to the Tanners?

Froba climbed up the balcony and to the building's flat roof. She could see most of Branthall up here. The keep's high tower soared over thatched and shingled roofs bright in the moonlight. She went house to house toward Hightown. Bare earth streets gave way to gravel as she hopped between roofs, some so close she could straddle them. Hightown's fine homes made her wonder how Flint and Zinzi were doing. She was gripped by a sudden and unfamiliar loneliness.

She had the barest memory of her mother; Ferd was the only guardian she had known. Hunger and exposure had been her only companions until now. She felt the absence of Trin's calmness, Rast's dumb stories, Corben's grumbling, and Zinzi's even temper. She even missed Flint's endless chatter. The sense of loss was new and unwelcome.

She wandered across the roof, hopped down to its neighbour, and froze. Ferd was crouched a short distance away, his foot resting on a decorative rail along the building's front. He turned and looked her up and down. "Where'd ye get that getup?"

Froba swallowed. "Guild Mistress's trainin' me."

Ferd sniggered. "Yer funeral."

Froba's mouth went slack. That wasn't the response she expected. "Ye ain't mad?"

He gazed back across the street. "Ye took in the old bitch? Didn't expect that."

The implied praise made Froba a roiling cauldron of fear, joy, and guilt. The frothing emotion manifested as a choked sob; she tried to pass it off as a cough.

"Quiet," he whispered.

Her mind was a muddle. Ferd's cruelty and derision were the only constants in her life. She was always at fault—never quick or devious enough, always forced to hustle and scrounge to pay him off. He had never said a kind word to her. Never.

"Ye did good landin' Winifred. That makes ye a player."

Froba bit her cheek. Praise? What was this?

Ferd looked at her soberly. "There ain't no friends in this game—just winners and losers. That Haskell's a loser. Ye know it."

"Yeah," she said uncertainly. Haskell wasn't bright, and maybe he was a loser, but she didn't hate him.

"I don't know what scam the old lady's got ye runnin', but we stick to the plan. If Haskell and them swits find out ye've been scammin' 'em, they'll turn on ye before ye can spit."

"But them Tanners—"

"Forget 'em. Or knife 'em, I don't care. Just remember, if I go down it all comes out, and ye know what Guild-traitors get in this town."

She pictured the bandit dangling from the gallows. It was easy to imagine Bror and Torg looking up at her with sad disappointment, Haskell and Ko turning their backs. She didn't want that.

"It don't need to come to that," Ferd said. "If I know what they know, I can keep yer pals outta my business and ye in their good graces. Everybody wins."

"But Haskell, he's—"

"Forget 'im. Dirk's gonna set 'im up real nice. Ye did yer part, and no harm done. It's not like we're slittin' his throat. It's the others ye gotta watch now."

"Yeah, but—"

"Shh." Ferd crouched down and motioned her closer.

She stooped down but stayed out of reach and looked through a window across the street. A dark-haired man was on top of a woman in a fancy bed. Their thrusting, sweat-soaked bodies glistened in the moonlight. She heard their grunts, saw the woman's fingers dig into his clenching buttocks. She saw the man's upturned face.

"Ain't that Owain?" she whispered.

"Aye, an' he's in a right pretty place."

"They're humpin', so what?"

Ferd winked at her with an unbecoming smile.

"Yeah, only that ain't his wife."

* * *

Haskell woke suddenly from a deep, dreamless sleep. His bed-clothes were soaked with sweat, but his head was clear. He knew who had betrayed him.

Ko slept beside him. Faithful Ko. He hadn't expected her to stand by him, nor the others. Maybe he could turn things around, but the odds—the whole town—were against him. Damn his slow wits. Why hadn't it come to him sooner? The fear and confusion after the battle, the exhaustion, his arrest and punishment; all of it had driven the name from his mind.

Grig.

He rose and swept into the den, padding to the window by the fireplace. He looked out over the buildings along Bran-thall's defensive wall, and at the bright half moon above. Grig. He'd barely heard that name in the alley, and only in passing. The half-orc and his cache. Grig and Luna.

It made sense; she would line up a mark and Grig would

take them down. The armour, that distinctive sword, the trinkets in the storeroom. It could have been his sword in Luna's hand that night. It would have been but for that potion.

"Grig did lie-trick us?" The quori had said.

Grig and Luna.

He would sort them out. Both of them.

April 26

Chapter XXXVI—Confrontation

Y ou there—move that wagon, damn your eyes!" Hambur shouted from astride his black stallion.

Corben, reclining in the driver's seat and wrapped in a cloak, was sipping strong liquor from a metal flask. He gestured at himself questioningly.

"Yes, you, you drunken lout! Move!"

Corben threw the insistent merchant a dark look, tucked away his flask, and gave the reins a lash. He clicked at his mules. "On, Donner, on, Harriet." The wagon rattled to the edge of the courtyard, and away from a party of labourers hauling supplies.

"Ho, Corben! A fine enterprise is it not?" Rast called, bustling over from the Gilded Cock.

Corben saw two skinny waifs lurking at the corner. He drew the wagon to a stop. "Finer than what Haskell can pay."

"Aye, poor lad."

Corben nodded at Hambur, who was dressing down the porters. "Still, he's a damn sight better than this one. I hope he falls and breaks his neck."

Trin approached from an alley. She threw a wink behind

her and belted on her sword. Her chain shirt had been mended and she was already looking fighting fit. "Nothing like a good rut before setting out."

"Say, Trin," Rast began sheepishly. "I don't suppose you'd spare a silver for a man in need?" He glanced at the girls on the corner. They were already chatting up other customers.

Trin leaned back against the wagon. "They're overcharging you, but you're an ugly brute. If you drank less, you could screw more."

Rast glowered at her and recounted his pennies. "Corben, could you—" A silver talent glanced off his chest and he fumbled his change.

"Make sure you get full service for that," Corben said, scratching the large, itchy scab under his blood-stained hat. The wound had healed quickly, and his head was finally clear. He thanked the gods again for that potion.

"Gods bless!" Rast said, beetling to the corner.

Trin eyed Corben. "He'll never learn if you spoil him."

"Ehn, we could all be dead tomorrow. Let him have some fun."

Trin spat through her teeth. "Getting paid to sit on cottars and laze about the Lane? Sounds like a fine summer."

"I wouldn't settle the land hereabouts for any money," Corben said. "Maybe them monsters stick to the woods an' maybe they don't. Wouldn't stake my life on it."

"You there, get that wagon over here!" Hambur shouted from across the square.

Trin gave Corben a wide, exasperated stare.

"Back we go," he sighed.

* * *

Haskell felt stronger but his spirit was thin. He had waited for the common room to clear before venturing downstairs. Conversations still stopped around him, but people didn't laugh and gossip anymore, they just turned their backs or looked away. He couldn't decide which was worse.

He leaned beside the window and gulped cheap wine from a clay jug. His head hurt. He could take more dragon's milk, but he'd run out soon and couldn't afford more.

Bror joined him at the window.

"I can't abide this idleness. I want to be out there again," Haskell said.

"You will. When do you meet Winifred?" Bror said.

"This morning." He took another mouthful of wine. He was already late. No sword, no armour, no money. No hope. What could she offer? The Guild took more than it gave.

A fluffy column of goats and sheep ambled through the Main Street arch, their bleating a rolling shrillness that echoed around Southgate. "I think we're being invaded," Haskell chuckled. His face fell.

Hambur cantered through astride his stallion.

"I want to gut that swine."

Bror clapped him on the back. "Lookin' to trade up for a noose?"

Haskell scowled.

Zinzi rode by on a champagne mare with a dark brown mane. He wore a new, burnt orange, fur-lined cloak. Hiam rode beside him looking as fine and fashionable as ever. Haskell felt a jealous pang. He hadn't ridden in months and had left all his fine clothes in Khul. He looked away, working his jaw.

Carts and wagons bearing timber, ploughs, manure, barrels, and other supplies followed. Corben drove by with his wagon hitched to Donner and a new sorrel mule. A ragged bunch of mercenaries came after, Trin and Rast among them. They looked happy and carefree. Rast spotted Haskell in the window and waved.

Haskell nodded back.

"They were fine companions," Bror said.

"They'll be sorry they took up with that windbag."

"He's a bastard, but you do love windin' him up."

"I'd love to wind him up by his neck."

Bror sighed. "Lad, you need to learn to let things lie."

Haskell shook his head. If only Bror knew. Later, he had other business now. He took a deep breath. "Time to go."

"Good luck, lad."

Haskell went out and across the cul-de-sac, looking at the Guild's rippling banners and bright coat of arms before ducking under the porch. He went through the foyer, giving Grimfyrrid's right incisor a pat as he walked into the empty Guildhall. Just one more minute, then he'd go.

He stood at a nearby window. A spiteful pang ran up his spine and settled in his cheeks. Torg was sparring with Quin in the practice yard.

Was Quin stealing Bror and Torg away? Or had they gone to him? How had Torg healed so quickly? Did Quin pay for Temple magic? How could they not tell him?

Something shrank inside Haskell. Doubt assailed him in his father's scornful baritone: he was a failure, an embarrassment, nothing like his older sister—so confident and clever. He closed his eyes. Slade and his father's reach had proved longer than he thought possible, extended by Hambur's gleeful vindictiveness. He steadied himself against the window frame.

"Pining away? I see punishment has dampened your spirits," Winifred said.

Haskell ground his teeth. "That pleases you?"

"That depends. Are you chastened and ready to continue from where you left off?"

"Where I… ?" Haskell turned. "I was left robbed and

beaten on your doorstep—and what a welcome I received! Arrested, judged, fined, shamed. The Guild has done nothing for me."

Winifred's eyes narrowed. "Is that what you think? The Guild did not assault your master. Its agents did not steal from your father. Nor did it run recklessly into danger against all sense and counsel. No, that was your doing. But for my intervention you might have been hanged as an outlaw."

Haskell took off his pouch and shook it out, his last pennies clattering to the floor. "Will these cover my dues? Dress me in armour? Will the Guild aid me or leave me in the street?" He threw his pouch at her feet.

"You are distraught, so I will forgive your vulgar display," she said coolly. "Guild rules one and three you seem to know, yet conveniently forget the fifth even as you break it. Collect your pennies, boy. You will need them."

"Why? No one can win in this den of thieves."

"This den of thieves has kept the realm safe for hundreds of years and will continue to do so long after you are dead."

"Safe? Why then was I ambushed? It was your people who arranged it. Your defenders of the realm who tried to sell me to quori and steal my goods."

Winifred eyed him doubtfully. "Lanesforders treating with Darkwood filth? Such a thing hasn't happened in the Guild's long history."

"The quori who ambushed us used a name—a name I couldn't place until last night. Grig, a half-orc from your town in league with a whore pimped out by one of your guards."

Winifred cocked her head. "Can anyone support your claim?"

"Is my word not enough?"

"Your word is worth less than it was. Tell no one of this and leave the matter to me. You have other business to attend to."

Haskell shook his head. "What could be more important to the Guild?"

"The Right Honourable Hambur requires guards for his manor."

A choke caught in Haskell's throat. "No, never—not for that pig."

Winifred stepped over Haskell's pennies and drew close. She glared up at him with cold, dangerous eyes. "You are in my charge. If you would rather rot in the Tower, we shall happily oblige."

Haskell's heart was fit to explode and his eyes to rupture. "I have been punished already," he seethed.

Winifred gripped her dagger's serpentine hilt. "Not enough to humble you, boy. You have failed to learn the most valuable lesson."

"Educate me."

"You are not unique. You have no destiny and are not chosen by the gods. You, Haskell, Eskil's Son, are no better than a thousand other petulant sons and daughters fleeing the life they were given. So, yes—Hambur. You will learn patience, boy, and I will educate you."

Haskell turned and shut his eyes. "He can't have agreed."

"He already has."

It wasn't possible. He wouldn't bow and scrape to him. "I won't—"

"You will make your way to his manor and aid in its defence. Your former secretary, a far better man than you, oversees its construction."

Haskell tried to grip the hilt of his absent sword. His situation would be laughable if it weren't so cruel.

Winifred huffed. "So like your grandfather. Selfish and arrogant."

"What do you know?" he sneered.

"I spared you the truth when we first met."

Not this. Not now.

"Eskil was a traitorous man who pillaged Lanesford every bit as much as the orcs he fought. The orcs feared him like jackals fear lions fighting over the same carcass."

"No," Haskell managed.

"They say he was always where the fighting was fiercest and the suffering most dire. Indeed. He freed Fisherville, yes, and took their goods for his own. He emptied the slave pits of Caen into the holds of his ships. He shattered the Shadow Wood orcs only to hoard their plunder."

Haskell stared at the cobbles outside, unwilling to listen but unable to stop.

"What did the Orc-breaker do once his fortune was made? Left his men to die in a pointless battle while he sailed away with their share. No one sings Eskil Oath-breaker's tale only because so few live who remember it. All that remains is his elegantly crafted lie."

Haskell's jaw trembled. He wanted to vomit. His father's refusal to tell him Eskil's tales. The things unsaid in the family. Slade and Hilda's words. Their wealth. He couldn't deny it. Not anymore.

His life was built on lies.

Winifred started toward the door then turned. "Should you ever be ready, Hambur awaits." She turned on her heel and strode from the hall.

Haskell's burgeoning shame collapsed inward. His vision reeled and breath caught in his chest. He kicked over a chair, screamed at the ceiling, and fell to his knees. He balled his fists in his eyes. He would not cry. He would not.

Failed clerk and adventurer, son of a crooked merchant, the son of a duplicitous pirate? He wanted to run his dagger through his heart. Only, there was no need; he had enemies enough to indulge him.

He gathered his pennies from the floor and looked out the window. Torg was gone. Everything and everyone were gone. No, he still had one thing left.

Revenge.

* * *

Haskell dragged Luna into the closed yard, the scene of her deceit. He thrust her into the storeroom doors.

"In the mood for something rough?" she said with a tremulous waver.

"Talk," he said.

She shrugged coyly. "We can talk at the Cock—"

He slammed his fist into a half door. "I'm not playing games, Luna." The door rebounded; the storeroom was empty.

Luna squirmed in his grip. "Haskell, you're hurting me."

He leaned in. "You set me up."

She looked away. "What are you talking about?"

"Grig's Darkwood cronies fouled up—they left me alive. Did you clear this room for my party? It would have been a good score."

"No—"

"No, he cleared it himself, or just you?"

"I can't…"

Haskell jerked her up by the arm; her shoulder popped. "They took everything from me, Luna. I've got nothing left to lose."

"He'll kill me," she whimpered.

Haskell ground his teeth. "Who?"

"Grig!"

It took a second for her surprise to register. Haskell threw himself sideways. Something hammered his shoulder. He backed into the yard's rear wall and stumbled into a crouch. Grig's cudgel chipped the stone where his head had been. He kicked Haskell in the chest.

Haskell grabbed his dagger and slashed at Grig's calf, but the half-orc fell back toward the alley. Haskell pulled himself up the wall.

Grig's eyes were crazed. He levelled his cudgel at Haskell. "Ye still got somethin' to lose, sonny-boy, and I mean to take it."

Damn Stieg for taking his sword, and damn Bror for stopping him the other night. They could have ended all of this before it began. Haskell grimaced at the tight pain in his chest and back. "A fair fight too much for—"

Grig shot in, flicking his club at Haskell's face. Haskell came in too, slashing up and away. Grig's cudgel missed Haskell's right cheek, while Haskell's dagger went through the half-orc's lip and nose.

Grig fell back holding his slashed face. His cudgel caught Haskell on the ear. Haskell stumbled and saw stars. He drove Grig into the alley with wild stabs, one catching the half-orc's wrist. The cudgel fell from his grip.

Grig ran.

Haskell lumbered after him but stumbled into a woman in the street. He rose and gave chase. Each footfall jarred his smarting back and shoulder and his mashed ear throbbed. Grig sped down the lane and ducked into an alley. Haskell couldn't keep up and limped to a stop. Grig was gone. Had they been somewhere decent, the Watch might have gotten him, but not here. There was no justice in Branthall.

He had failed. Again. He knew Winifred wouldn't act. She would prevaricate, the Watch would throw up their hands, and Grig would get away. Worse, it was only a matter of time before Bror and Torg left him for Quin. Then what? He was no leader, no quester. He had nothing to his name, not even a name.

He drank the last of the dragon's milk and broke the bottle on the ground. Forget it. Forget everything, at least for a little while. He would get thoroughly drunk and knew where. A penny went far at the Cock. And why not? Things couldn't get any worse.

Chapter XXXVII—Settled

A misty drizzle fell in the Lane. It soaked the people pushing carts and wagons up a grassy rise that was quickly churning into glutinous mud. Zinzi led his mare to a pine grove straddling a creek below the slope. The creek was fed by a quick-flowing stream spilling down the low rise. He wondered if it was the same water that spilled down the Sentinel Hills. He shivered and pulled his cloak tighter.

"Confounded muck," Hambur said, clinging to his stumbling stallion.

"You did not need to join us, Sir. I wish you had stayed in town until I had made things more comfortable here," Zinzi said.

"Hear, hear," Hiam said, bringing his mare to Zinzi's side. The boy looked more miserable than his father if that was possible. He sensed that Hiam might be somewhat of a challenge.

"Nonsense, I must be present at the ground-breaking—it is my duty as lord of the land," Hambur said, followed by a noisy sneeze.

Zinzi raised his eyebrows—as a newly minted baronet,

Hambur was a far cry from nobility. He smiled as Corben rumbled by, grumbling incoherently as Donner and Harriet lumbered up the slope. A load of bundled sticks rattled in his wagon.

"Steady on, Corben, it's only the first day," Rast said, pushing the wagon from behind.

Zinzi was glad for their company. He could rely on his friends to pull their weight and keep them safe. They had braved harsher trials than the building of a manor in the Lane. Still, he worried about the quori they had told him about. Hyena-men taller than Haskell and twice as fierce? He eyed the other mercenaries milling about; he didn't know these men and women.

He urged his horse out of the pine grove and up a clean section of hill. Trin stood at the crest, water dripping from her hood as she scanned the horizon. He saw nothing but grassy hillocks and the occasional tree rising from the half-dead field. Still, the Darkwood's memory loomed like a predator crouched in the grass.

"Those quori are out there somewhere," Trin said. "Maybe we should have stuck by Haskell. Now that we're here, I don't know."

Corben's wagon trundled by with Rast just behind. "We have ten spears and a host of cottars—we'll be fine," Rast said.

Zinzi was not convinced.

"It'll get dark tonight under all this cloud," Trin said.

Corben tossed a bundle of sticks to the ground from the wagon. "I told you I don't trust those beasts to keep to them woods."

"We shall raise some simple fortifications," Zinzi said. Gazing out beyond the horizon, he couldn't shake a growing sense of dread.

* * *

Froba sat with Bror and Torg in the Treeman's common room. She was curled up on a chair beside the fire. They weren't alone. Quin sat across from them with two of his companions, Lera and Sai. Where Lera was broad, strong, fair-haired, and missing an ear, Sai was tall, reedy, dark-haired, and had both of his. Surprising, given his profession.

"Did you hear? Your man Haskell had a go at a half-orc not an hour ago," Sai said, fiddling with a bandolier of lock-picks and thieves' tools.

Froba perked up. That wasn't the plan. Ferd had told them to lay low and keep Haskell down, not start a fight in the street. What was Grig up to?

"Is the lad alright?" Bror asked.

"Grig or your man?" Lera said, sipping ale.

Froba chewed her lip. This was bad.

Bror stood. "Where's the villain?"

"Keep your seat, your friend's fine. More or less," Quin said with a chuckle. "Grig got through Southgate. Won't see the creep around any time soon, I'd wager."

Froba frowned. This wasn't good; or maybe it was. It could change things for Haskell. Maybe she could get Ferd to shift everything onto Grig.

"Grig'll head to Siward if he's smart," Lera said.

"Where's Haskell?" Torg said.

"Enough about him—we're here to talk to you lot," Quin said gruffly. He was a hard man with a tough reputation. His companions got full share of the spoils, Guild training or no, but they also tended to not live very long.

Lera scratched the rough patch where her ear used to be. "You three managed to survive two outings under that son of a pirate. A lot of us lost a pretty penny betting against you. I can't believe he brought a cook and a valet into the Dark-wood," she laughed.

"Ridiculous," Sai sniffed, tinkering with a probe.

Bror resumed his seat. "You wouldn't question it if you'd tasted Flint's fare."

"At least he had five good spears," Quin said.

Sai grinned. "I doubt he'll find anyone to follow him now."

"Was he paying you fair? Sounds like you two were doing heavy work," Quin said.

Bror ignored a steely look from Torg. "We'll hash it out. Haskell's a bit hasty but a good fighter. He and me were the only two to best a quori, and he saved my skin that first time out."

"After risking it," Sai muttered.

"Ye can't trust the Oath-breaker's kin. He'll sell ye out just like his grandad, mark me," Quin said.

"Never trust a Southroner," Sai said.

Bror threw the thief a sour look. "That's rich comin' from an Umbrian thug."

Lera laughed. "Hey, we're not all as bad as him."

Quin laid his palms on the table. "Look, I'll come right to it—the boy's no good but you two seem decent. Winifred's put us on to some Guild-traitors holed up to the southwest. They're worth a hundred sovereigns a head, but there's a couple wizards with 'em. A sneaky little girl and a couple southern bastards might come in handy."

Torg uttered a sharp southern rejoinder.

"Share a fire with a Lanesforder and couple'a Umbrian cutthroats? Pass," Bror said. Two men across the room laughed.

Froba agreed. She didn't like Quin's manner, plus she heard he had been hunting trolls, and now Guild-traitors? Dangerous work. More dangerous than goblins and quori, that was for sure. Like Bror and Torg, she'd rather hash things out with Haskell. If they stuck together, they might just work everything out.

Chapter XXXVIII—Gutter

Haskell raised his head from the sticky tabletop and knocked over the jug; the shriek was gone. He didn't remember drinking that. Someone was playing a spirited tune on a stringed instrument, the music tinny and unreal in his ears. He wasn't sure when Ko had left. They had danced and carried on, there had been hot, sticky fumbling in the back room, and then she had wanted to go home. Going home meant facing tomorrow.

"Fuck tomorrow," he said, lurching up from the table. He staggered through the crowd. Someone's face loomed into his tunnelled, swirling vision.

"Whoa, steady on!" the man said, directing him in a stumble to the bar.

Haskell struck it, belched, and snickered. He reached into his pouch, fumbled for the coins inside, and poked at the pennies in his hand. "Wha—"

"Say again, my lord?" the publican said with a mocking hand to his ear.

"—five coppers?" Haskell said.

The barman leaned over to gawp at the dull coins in

Haskell's hand. "Such riches," he said grandly, eliciting laughs from the room.

Haskell regarded his blurry neighbours and chuckled along. He hadn't heard the joke. A hard tap on his shoulder drew him back to the counter. He focused on a tall glass of shriek. Pennies tumbled from his hand as he took the glass.

"Y'r health," he toasted, raising the cup with an unsteady hand. He brought the stinging liquor to his chapped lips but was yanked back. Someone dragged him away; someone incredibly strong.

"C'mon ye souse," they said.

Haskell tried to focus on his escort. "Wh—"

"Out ye go," the unsteady shadow said with a heave. The tavern filled with laughter.

Haskell's head struck the door frame as he blundered out into cold rain; he slipped on wet cobbles and fell into the street. There he laid, in the dark, barely registering the muffled laughter and voices inside. He squinted at the shadowy buildings leaning over him and the heavy clouds drenching his face in rain.

He dragged himself through the gutter and into a doorway. His head was spinning. He rested it against the wall and listened to the rain batter the rooftops. It was some time before he noticed someone crouched beside him, their face obscured by a dripping hood.

"Well now, ain't ye a sad sight," Dirk said with a chuckle. "Hard thing, seein' a quester so low."

Haskell only half-registered Dirk's words. His neck was stiff, and his chest and back were sore despite the shriek. He threw up on the doorstep and himself. "It hurts, Dirk."

"Don't worry, ol' Dirk has some medicine."

"I haven't got anything left."

"Questers stick together, right?" Dirk said kindly.

Haskell nearly cried. Maybe he did, but that could've been the rain. He knew Ko would leave next. Bror and Torg would have already taken up with Quin. What was Haskell? Nothing.

At least he had Dirk, who had what Haskell needed.

April 27

Chapter XXXIX—Den

Froba hurried down a narrow dirt lane to a door behind the Cock. Haskell hadn't come home last night, meaning he could only be in one place. If he wasn't already dead. The door was propped open; steep stone steps descended into smoke and gloom. The Dragon Den.

She went in.

The Cock's cellars had a dirt floor, and the air was filled with dense, sweetly cloying smoke. Small lamps hung from low rafters, though their feeble light barely penetrated the miasma. The first cellar was like any other: full of jars and barrels of pickled and preserved food, wine, and beer, and a healthy collection of shriek jugs. The cellar in back, connected by a low arch, was a much different place. It was crammed with bunks only a couple feet apart. It's where Ferd's crew could sleep when the weather was bad, and where his patrons dozed away their lives.

She hunted among the bunks, craning high and dipping low to search faces through the smoke. There were so many; more than she remembered there being. Men and women from all walks of life, reclining on mats and flattened pillows, their clothes loosened and eyes glazed. Some were here on a lark, others because they had no choice, though the line between them grew shorter each day.

She found Haskell at the back. His arm was in the aisle, and he was oblivious to the dead rat a foot from his head. His filthy shirt, long past white, was open, and his unkempt hair was plastered to his head. His tall boots were off and caked in what she hoped was mud. His oxblood surcoat, crusted with filth, was balled up beside him.

"Have the pixies come to mock me?" he said, trying to touch her face with dirty fingers. His eyes were bloodshot.

Froba pulled away and waved at the air. "Yer stink'd wither a pixie. What've ye been doin', rollin' in the gutter?"

"How the mighty have fallen," Haskell chuckled.

"Yer mighty good at getting' yerself in trouble."

"You sound like Bror."

"Skint are ye?"

Haskell nodded. "Dirk's been helping me. There's nothing up there for me now."

Froba shook her head. "Ye got better friends down the street, gods know why."

"You're a good girl, Froba."

She felt a guilty twinge. Seeing Haskell like this was painful. That surprised her. She gave him the milk, sure, but figured he'd pull through—he always had. Besides, she'd just been doing what she had been told. This wasn't her fault. Why had she even come? Ferd would kill her if she helped Haskell.

She stood and nudged him with her toe. "Come on, ye lummox, ye don't wanna waste away down here, do ye?"

He lifted his head and looked at her outfit. "You got new armour—it looks good. Did I buy that for you?"

She sighed and did a slow turn. Gods below, why did she come here? For Ko? Bror and Torg? Herself? She swore and stamped her foot in the dirt. Ferd was going to kill her.

She crouched and brought Haskell around with a slap. "Hey, lummox. Winifred gave it to me. C'mon, ye can talk to her 'bout it."

"Hmm, Winifred? Watch out for her, Froba."

Froba tisked and rose with her hands on her hips. He was coming out of it, but she still couldn't get through to him. "Fine, ye just lay there. I'll get someone ye might listen to." She went back along the row and through the archway.

A hand clapped over her mouth, and she was held tightly around the arms. She kicked back and they both went into the wall.

"Oh-ho, she's a fighter," Brent said in her ear, which he licked. "I'm gonna have fun with ye, girl."

She tried to mash his face with the back of her head, but only managed to brain herself on the rock wall.

"Get her feet, Alix," Brent cried.

A boy grabbed her ankles, and they carried her, kicking and fighting, to the steep stone stairs. The Tanners were so big and strong, but her writhing was slowing them down.

"Quit squirmin', ye tart," Brent shouted.

She wriggled out of Brent's grip. Her back struck the steps, her armour softening the blow. "Fuck ye!" she cried, spitting up at Brent and heaving against Alix, who clung to her legs.

Brent went down on one knee, fist raised to hammer her face. Haskell grabbed him from behind and whirled him into the wall. Brent drew his knife, but Haskell kneed him in the gut. He wrapped his hand around Brent's and forced the knife to the boy's throat.

"Little goblins should stick to the woods," Haskell said with a sick grin.

Brent struggled as the knife gouged his neck. His eyes began to water, and his ripped leggings turned dark with urine.

The briny reek competed with the cloying smoke filling the cellar.

Haskell spun Brent around and wrenched his arm back and up, the boy's shoulder dislocating with a meaty pop. Brent went into the dirt with a snivelling whimper. Haskell cut Brent's belt and took the boy's pouch and knife. He turned on Alix, who screeched and ran upstairs.

Froba sprawled down the steps. "Haskell," she squeaked.

Haskell slouched back to the Den. "Go home, Froba."

Froba pulled herself up. She would go home alright, but not without him. Her conscience wouldn't let her.

April 28

Chapter XL—Hard Lessons

The curtain to Haskell's room flew aside, flooding the room with harsh daylight. Ko shrieked. Haskell fumbled for his dagger slung over the bedpost but knocked it to the floor. He felt so heavy. Torg pulled him naked out of bed and shoved him into the washstand with a clatter.

"Mornin'!" Bror beamed from the doorway.

"You bastards scared me out of my skin," Ko said, bashing Torg with a pillow.

Haskell worked his sharp, aching shoulder and deeply bruised chest; the pain had returned a hundredfold. The last thing he remembered was Ko dragging him out of the Den, the two of them staggering back to the inn as she tried to hold him upright. He also recalled leering faces and vicious laughter. "What do you two want?"

Torg muttered harshly.

"Aye, no fight at all," Bror said.

"What are you playing at?" Haskell said.

"I could ask ye the same. Are ye done stewin' in that vat o' self-pity? Gods, it's pungent in here."

Haskell sat on the bed and ran his dirty fingernails through his sweaty hair. It was getting long, but that was the least of his worries. He had come to a decision. "I'm quitting this damn town."

Ko wrapped her arms around him. "You can't!"

Haskell rested his head in his hands. "I've lost everything. I don't know, maybe I can catch up to Captain Nedir. He only has a few weeks on me. Gods, it feels like a year."

"But... don't you love me?" Ko murmured.

He did. She was everything he could want: clever, beautiful, fun. But he didn't deserve her. "You're better off without me."

Torg scoffed and paced to the wall and back.

Ko rested her head on Haskell's neck, her hot, silent tears running down his back.

"You've got three people willin' to stand by you. Four if you count Froba, and you should. You know the Guild Mistress's trainin' her?"

Winifred took on Froba? What was her angle? There was always an angle. Was it to get to him? "It's all lies. Everything. My grandfather was a kin-slaying pirate—"

"An' mine was hanged for rustlin' cattle," Bror interjected.

"This place, it takes and takes," Haskell said.

"Same all over."

"The people here are more loathsome than goblins."

"You think it's any better out there?" Bror said, motioning about vaguely.

Haskell shook his head. Bror couldn't understand. "It's all rigged. I can't win."

Bror held out his knife hilt-first. "Then end it."

"Bror," Ko sighed.

Haskell drew back.

"You're down, you get back up, or waste away in the street.

Now or later, it's the same in the end. What's it gonna be?"

"What if I did stay, what then? Without a penny to my name; no armour, no reputation, no sword. I'm no leader and barely a fighter. You should join up with Quin—I know about you and him."

Torg rolled his eyes. "Bloody hells."

Bror sniffed. "That joyless bastard? Not on your life. So you're a jumped-up clerk who bit off more than he could chew? So what? The important thing is that you came through when things got tough. See, I recall a lad tha' stood up before hardened guild fighters one misty night not so long ago. He talked o' riddin' the realm o' a menace threatenin' all free folk. He was a starry-eyed fool, but full o' hope, all the same. The kind o' young'un that can get world-weary folk to think there can be a better world."

That Haskell was dead: trampled by a loutish merchant and left to die in a dirty burg. "I can't change the world, Bror."

"Forget the world. All you gotta do right now is stand up."

Haskell sighed. "You make it sound easy."

Bror laughed. He had a mischievous gleam in his eye. "Far from it."

* * *

Haskell circled a small, hard guild-trainer in the yard; both were shirtless and held polished wooden swords. Haskell's opponent was five feet tall and well into middle age, but broad and muscled like one of the Temple's marble gods—though his chiselled form bore many old scars. Haskell was sweating despite the cool morning air, and his arms and torso were covered in welts.

"Come on, ye brute," Lang goaded, his front teeth missing.

Haskell directed his stick at Lang's face only to have it knocked aside. Lang dashed left and buckled Haskell's knee with a wicked blow. Haskell made a wild swipe as he fell but missed. He crashed to the ground, scraping his elbow and chest. "Enough," he cried, rolling onto his back.

Lang leaned over him with a disappointed glare. "Ye think orcs and trolls'll say 'fair enough' when ye throw in the towel? This ain't no game." He prodded Haskell's belly with his stick.

Haskell drew in his limbs to ward off more blows. "Leave off, Lang."

"Bah, I've seen yer type afore—princelings that swan into town and think they're cock-o'-the-walk. Know what happens to 'em? They go off merrily into them woods and end up in some goblin's pot. I bet some o' that coin ye lucked into was once in some princeling's pocket. Think on that."

Haskell sat up. "Don't lecture me like some witless kid. I've seen action."

Lang cracked the top of Haskell's head. "Back alleys and whorehouses, and it shows. All ye lordlings are too tall, brash, and rich fer yer own good. Ye get just far enough in life to think ye know it all, then find yerself in a tight spot. Around here, that tight spot'll be yer last."

"I'm no blueblood," Haskell said, rubbing his head. Everything ached and his throat was dry. He wanted wine and craved dragon's milk.

Lang rapped Haskell's knuckles. "All I see is a petulant rich boy used to gettin' his own way. Why'd ye choose this life?"

Haskell snatched Lang's practice sword and narrowed his eyes. "You think I was going to be my father's pawn—fatten his fleet so he could cheat the world? I'd rather be a highwayman. More honest." He pushed away Lang's sword.

"The wastrel has some fire after all. Where was that fire when ye were fightin' me?"

Haskell scowled, clambered to his feet, and grabbed a towel.

Lang looked at Bror and Torg sparring with other mercenaries across the yard. "Ye didn't tell me why ye came here. Runnin' from yer father ain't no kind o' answer."

"I came to make a name for myself, to follow in my grandfather's footsteps before I knew what he was."

"And now yer stuck. Cry me a river. Names don't make themselves, boy, and everyone's got an oath-breaker in their line. Now why did I beat ye?"

"You're too fast." Or he was too slow. He wasn't sure when he had last eaten.

"Wrong," Lang barked, making Haskell twitch. "I beat ye because yer a brawler. Ye may have won some dockside fights up in that fancy city, but I bet ye never crossed paths with a canny dwarf or tall troll. Yer gutter tactics won't count for nuthin' 'gainst them. The dwarf fights dirtier and the troll is bigger."

Haskell frowned, reminded of the slippery goblins and powerful quori, and how he had struggled against both.

"I beat ye because you fight like a brainless ogre—all brawn and low cunnin'. I fought yer type and I won." Lang waved at Branthall's outer wall. "Out there ye'll face beasts, goblins, giants, vermin—all manner o' things in all manner o' forms, some with no form at all. Tell me, stripling, how do ye fight them?"

Haskell looked at the ground. "I don't know."

"Good," Lang said cheerfully. "Now yer ready to learn, so let's fight for real."

Haskell's stomach grumbled. He opened his mouth to protest but snapped it shut at Lang's warning glare. It was going to be a long morning.

* * *

Froba crept across a small, carpeted room toward the back of a huge, green armchair. She heard warriors shouting outside yet stepped lightly, probing for creaky floorboards. The old woman was here somewhere. The room was dark with its heavy curtains pulled tight; a candle on a sideboard was her only light.

She drew two long pieces of metal from under her leather bracer and crept to a lockbox on a small table beside the chair. She eased her tools into the box's lock and felt several levers inside. The lock was complex, not like the ones she had already mastered. Still, no harm in trying.

She applied pressure with her tension bar, put her pick to the back of the lock, and zipped it out. The tumbler didn't budge. Froba bit her lip and probed each lever, applying pressure until each clicked into place. The last gave way and the lock snapped open.

Froba grinned. She slipped her tools under her cuff and opened the lid. A step-cut, octagonal ruby was nestled in black velvet inside. The stone's facets glowed, enticing her to caress its smooth surface. She licked her lips and reached for the gem. A curved pin sprang from the box with a metallic *ka-chung*, striking out like a mechanical viper. Its tip pierced her palm. She swore and shook her hand.

"You're dead, little one," Winifred said.

Froba dashed around the chair; only embroidered cushions sat within. She turned about, furiously seeking the old woman. She moved to the window and threw open the heavy curtains. Blinding sunlight streamed into the room.

Bror and Torg were attacking Haskell in the sunny courtyard below. Bare-chested, they fought with practice weapons, Haskell warding off their blows with a long wooden sword. A small, old trainer with salt and pepper hair circled them, lashing exposed limbs with a wooden stick. Lang the guild-trainer.

Something struck Froba on the back of the head, ramming her forehead into the window frame. She whirled around but

Winifred wasn't there. A heavy book lay at her feet. She looked to the bookcase, but Winifred wasn't there either. "Where in tha hells is ye?" she said, rubbing her head.

"You were doing so well—I was truly impressed—then you had to muck it up."

Froba followed Winifred's voice back to the large green chair, where the venerable guild mistress reclined once more, her leathery cheek resting against her jeweled fist.

"No fair—I looked there!"

"I did not hear you approach the box, and you handled the lock well."

"Ye could'a told me 'bout the trap," Froba grumbled.

"True, but hard lessons are the best learned. Did we learn anything?"

"Not to trust ye none." Froba sucked her oozing hand.

Winifred chuckled. "A valuable lesson."

Froba opened her mouth, but her belly turned to fire. Sweat beaded her body. "Ye poisoned me, ye witch," she croaked.

"Don't be so dramatic. You will live."

Liquid fire filled Froba's bowels, and she doubled over. She stumbled to the door, fumbled with its handle, and hobbled down the hall.

"Don't soil my carpets!" Winifred called. She spun the box on the side table. The ruby was gone.

Winifred bristled at the loss. It was a valuable stone, and she had been confident the girl would not pick the lock. She wiped the brass needle clean, pressed the mechanism back into place, and settled into the chair. She smiled despite herself.

"Good girl."

Chapter XLI—Negotiations

Haskell dumped a bucket of cold water over his head and down his naked, sweat-soaked body. He passed the bucket to Bror and Torg, who refilled it from a covered well and did likewise. They toweled off at the back of the practice yard and let the late morning sun dry their sore bodies.

Haskell looked at his companions. Both were shorter, Bror more so, but each stronger than he. They had scars up and down their muscled bodies, a tale of hard-fought lives written in bites, stabs, tears, and gouges. Haskell, by comparison, had mostly knicks and pale scars from childhood accidents and barroom brawls. And disgrace. He felt the rough scab on his forehead and looked at the Guildhall entrance down the yard. "Lunch in the hall today. I'm starving."

Torg nodded to Bror, who scowled but nodded back. "Now that you're on your feet again, we need to talk. That's t'say, if we stick by you, we want a share o' the spoil. As partners, not just hirelings, you understand."

Haskell nodded. It was fair, even if a thousand times more than they presently earned, but academic until there were spoils to divide. He snapped Bror with his wet towel and smiled for the first time in days. "You're lucky I'm desperate."

Torg seized Haskell and ground his knuckles into Haskell's scalp. Bror repaid Haskell with several wet lashes. Their horse-play was interrupted by a splash of water. Frozen mid-grapple, they gawped at naked, dripping Froba, glowering unhappily with a bucket over her head.

Haskell averted his eyes. "Gods, Froba!"

"Ye never seen no girl afore?" she said.

Bror and Torg laughed and shook their heads.

"That Winifred's a bitch," she said.

Froba followed the others into the Guildhall. Bror and Torg dumped their armour on the floor and sat at a table with Haskell.

"What's for lunch?" Bror said.

A frumpy server plonked a wide tin platter and three slosh-ing mugs on the table and wiped her hands on a dirty apron. The platter was heaped with bread rolls, hard cheese, pickles, and carrots.

"Betty, you're a goddess," Haskell said, tearing into a fresh roll.

Betty rolled her eyes and walked across the hall.

Bror took up a carrot and waved it about limply before taking a bite. "I canna wait for the next harvest. Still, better 'an we ate as lads, eh, Torg?"

Torg, with a look of pure innocence, fellated a long, thick carrot, its blunt tip poking suggestively against the inside of his cheek. Bror choked on bits of carrot and Haskell snorted mead.

Froba climbed onto a chair and leaned across the table, seizing a mug in both hands. Sitting cross-legged, she drank deeply, smacking her lips before gulping more honey wine. It was good stuff. She'd have to refill the skin she took off that blowhard wizard in the tower.

"Winifred's mistreating you, Froba?" Haskell said.

"Stupid cow poisoned me," she grumbled.

"Poison?" Torg said.

"She tricked me," Froba said around a mouthful of bread.

Haskell grabbed a hunk of cheddar. "She's a tricky one. Winifred the Fair—it's a good thing she had her looks when she was younger."

"No, she was plain," Lang said, snatching the cheese from Haskell's fingers.

Haskell frowned. "But she's Winifred the *Fair*."

Lang wheezed, which turned out to be his laugh. "As fair as a banker's scale. I've known Winifred since th' old days, so ye take my word for it. We just called her that to wind her up." Betty swept by to hand Lang a mug of mead and dropped another on the table.

Haskell sucked spilled honey wine off the back of his hand. "I should have guessed that."

"Remember that next time ye deal with her." Lang knocked his mug against Haskell's. "To Winifred th' Fair, as crooked as they come, but good people all th'same."

They raised their mugs and drank, though Froba didn't join. She didn't feel like toasting her poisoner.

Lang laughed at her. "Ye remind me of her, lass. Life's hard, but ye need to laugh at it, and yerself, now and again. Winifred learned that. Eventually. That advice goes double for ye." Lang cuffed Haskell upside the head and strode across the hall.

Haskell smoothed his shaggy hair. "Here's to Lang the Bastard, small but wise. Good people." They laughed and drank to that. "Thanks for hiring the curmudgeon—he really put me through my paces."

"I knew some good, hard knocks'd snap you out of your funk. Just wait until tomorrow—you won't be thanking me then," Bror said, throwing Froba a knowing look.

Froba looked away and buried her face in her mug. She hadn't given Bror her whole stash, that would've been stupid, but there was no hiding the lapis lazuli stones. She was sure Bror had guessed from where the gold and silver had come. Honestly, she'd done Haskell a favour—he'd have pissed away the loot in one of Ferd's dens if she hadn't palmed it. That made them even in her books.

Haskell grew glum again. "Maybe, but I don't have armour or a sword, how am I going to fight? With one of Lang's sticks?"

That gave Froba an idea. It was crazy. Stupid, really; but it made a kind of sense. Better yet, it felt right. Like Winifred said: when the others were stumped, the thief found a way. She grinned.

Haskell eyed her suspiciously. "What's so funny?"

"Best ye don't know." She took a long drink of wine.

Haskell frowned but said nothing.

Bror drummed the table and leaned on his elbows. "So, what's next?"

Haskell sighed and slouched in his chair, working his neck and shoulder. "Winifred's assigned me to Hambur's manor. She says I need to learn my lesson."

"Not that swine," Bror said.

"Yes, but I'll be answering to Zinzi. I'm not looking forward to it."

"There you go—they'll have weapons and armour at the manor. Munitions-grade stuff, probably, but it's something," Bror said.

Froba liked the thought of seeing their friends again. She wondered what they'd think of her new armour.

Torg spoke in Siwardian and gestured south.

"Aye, we'd be close, true enough." Bror said. "The manor's not too far from the dungeon. We could steal away easy enough."

Haskell leaned back, still working his shoulder. "I wouldn't want Zinzi to get in trouble."

"Knowing our Zinzi, he might just send us on our merry little way. Why not go find out?" Bror said.

Torg nodded his agreement.

Froba waved her mug at Betty. "I'm comin' too but give me a couple days."

"Are you sure? It'll just be us this time," Haskell said.

Froba grinned. "Yeah, s'long as I get a full share."

Grumzel shuffled toward them through the hall. "Ah, there you are, Haskell."

Froba nearly started off her chair. The tower wizard?

Grumzel glared at her. "You have not been taken in by this imp, have you, Haskell?"

"Come now, Grumzel, this is Froba, the Guild Mistress's protégé," Haskell said.

Grumzel looked like he had swallowed a rot grub. "Yes, well, I have completed my research and may join your party. Such as it is."

"Kind o' you," Bror said.

Torg muttered something.

"Who was shamed?" Grumzel asked Torg.

Bror and Torg shared a look of surprise.

Grumzel looked amused. "I've been locked in the tower for weeks. Master Neyhün insisted I venture forth, 'there being no substitute for experience in the field.'"

Haskell rose and took Grumzel's hand. "I'm glad you're here. I must admit, I nearly forgot with… everything. Never mind, it's good to have you."

Froba scowled and gulped wine. Hopefully the stuck-up wizard wouldn't get in the way. As far as anyone was concerned, Grig and Luna had sold them out, not her, Ferd, or Dirk. They'd probably never see the half-orc again anyway, not if he was smart; and if he did show his face, she'd crack it open with a bullet.

April 29

Chapter XLII—Ego

Froba set the ruby on the leather tome on Winifred's desk. The gem's facets glinted in the smoky light from the fire. She leaned this way and that, admiring its shimmer and shadowy depths. The old woman would know who it was from and what it was for.

If she'd learned anything in Branthall, it was that justice was erratic and made-to-order. Let it work for her and Haskell for a change. Everything cost in Branthall, and they had paid their dues.

She took what she needed and left.

April 30

Chapter XLIII—Consequences

Zinzi cantered through the settlement. The rain had stopped, the ground had hardened in the sunshine, and the post and wattle shells of four cottages sprouted from the hilltop. Cottars were weaving more panels out of sticks, washing laundry in the stream, and digging out the manor's foundations further east.

He pictured the whitewashed walls of future cottages aglow in morning light, their thatched roofs dry and clean. A blacksmith would come to make and mend, followed by a wainwright and a cooper. The families would grow and their farms would spread. The manor would prosper.

A pack of young children chased one another through the grass. They prodded Hambur's black stallion with sticks as they ran by.

"Confound it, man—control your spawn," Hambur bellowed, returning from his morning ride. His rides were a time for Zinzi to ensure an orderly workday, but this one had been short.

"Ye three, git back t'work!" a man shouted, scattering the children. He caught the youngest and whipped the boy with his own stick. "Sorry, Sir."

"Beat them more regularly. Gods, but these peasants are infuriating," Hambur said.

"I find them rather invigorating," Hiam said.

"You would."

Hiam smirked. "At least he addressed you properly."

"I am more concerned about the fields getting tilled. These hovels are taking too long to build." He pointed at a random tenant. "You there, how long until the fields are done?"

"Ye said ye wanted these cottages built first," the farmer replied.

Hambur growled. "Forget what I said and do as I say, man. Get the plows and start on those fields. We need barley, beetroots, beans, turnips, cabbage, carrots, tomatoes." He emphasized each word with a slap of his palm.

"As you say," the farmer grumbled, walking away. "Tellin' me when ta plant, the…"

Zinzi walked his horse to them. Hambur's meddling was putting them behind schedule; planting should have already started but Hambur kept meddling in Zinzi's plans. "Back so soon, Sir?"

"Father's stallion became spooked upstream. He's being very ornery today," Hiam said with a smirk.

Zinzi didn't doubt it. He looked northward along the path to Branthall. He would need to invent more distractions for his master.

An old tinker crested the hill in front of a rattling handcart pushed by Haskell. The elderly man took off his hat, wiped his sweaty brow, and shook Haskell's hand. Several tenants wandered over to browse the tinker's wares. Zinzi smiled to see Haskell again.

Haskell caught sight of them and wandered over. He was wearing his frayed, brown cloak and faded, forest green hood.

His surcoat and laced shirt had been washed but bore faint stains. His breeches were weathered, and his tall boots caked in muck. He had a drawn, haunted look that made Zinzi frown. Without pack, armour, or sword, he did not look himself.

Hambur brought his horse around, blocking Haskell's advance. "What is the meaning of this trespass?" he said.

Zinzi braced himself for Haskell's retort but none came; he did not flinch or look up, simply retrieved a note from his pouch and held it up.

Hambur snatched it and chortled. "So, Winifred has sent you to do some real work, eh? I think we have something suitable for you, don't we Zinzi?"

Zinzi looked at Haskell, who looked away. "Yes, he could take charge—"

"Nonsense, we have daub to muck—he has two hands, doesn't he?" Hambur said.

"Yes, but—" Zinzi began.

"But nothing, he works for me now!"

"I just want to serve," Haskell said dejectedly.

"That's the spirit! Move it, you pirate—off to the stream with the other commoners."

Hambur brought his horse around and drove Haskell to a group of settlers mixing mud, grass, and dung to clad the cottages. Hiam looked at Zinzi with a pained expression. Hambur trotted his horse back triumphantly, his sortie complete. Haskell stripped to the waist and was soon elbow-deep in a large, muck-filled tub.

"This is turning out to be a fine day after all," Hambur said.

Hiam turned to his father. "I am weary of these fields, Father. Let us return to town for the May Day celebrations. Zinzi will see to things here while we enjoy some well-earned comfort."

"A fine suggestion," Zinzi said. He needed to organize work parties. A delivery of stone would soon arrive, and they needed the manor's foundations dug to the builder's specifications.

"What?" Hambur said absently, still gawking at Haskell. His horse skittered to the left as a child toddled toward him. "Confound it! Collect your things, Hiam. We're leaving."

Hiam grinned. "As you say, Father."

"I will see to things here," Zinzi said.

"Make sure the pirate is properly rebuked," Hambur said with a leer, then made for the tent. "Kerk!"

Zinzi dismounted and handed his reins to a footman. He strolled to where Haskell was toiling. The boy was already covered in sludge; he looked thoroughly rebuked to Zinzi. "It is good to see you, Haskell."

Haskell scowled and threw more dung into the tub with a wet slap. "Is this to be my fate? Two sovereigns a month for hard labour, one for the Guild and one for my debts? It'll take me three hundred years to pay it all back."

"What of the others?" Zinzi said.

"The others," Haskell sighed, sitting on his haunches. "We need spoil, Zinzi."

Zinzi looked downstream. The Darkwood was not far off, but then, it would be a misuse of Hambur's resources. Still, a case could be made. "We might be able to work out something. Hambur is fickle, and see—" he gestured to Hiam and Hambur riding north with Kerk. "He has departed thanks to young Hiam and the camp's discomforts. Now, what about the others?"

"They should be along in a couple days. I didn't want them to see…" Haskell hung his head.

"Yes, understandable." Zinzi noticed the other muckers and washers enjoying the drama; the entire settlement was gawking. Zinzi turned about and clapped his hands. "Back to work, all of you!"

He put his hand on Haskell's shoulder. "Clean up and come along. I think we can find more suitable work for you."

Hambur wouldn't like it, but Zinzi needed someone to take charge of the mercenaries and oversee their defence. He had been considering Trin for the post, but decorum dictated that Haskell be granted the position. He was a Quester after all.

* * *

Grig crouched lower as a group of farmers moved oxen to the fields. The quori knelt in the dry grass beside him, its red-gray fur and leather cuirass camouflaged it well. There were a good forty cottars, plus some porters and waggoners. He counted ten spears and Haskell.

He picked at his scabbed lip. The fuckwit had ruined everything. No newmeat had ever survived the quori. He snarled. That bitch Luna blew it. He should have done for her a long time ago.

The quori boss growled and gripped the hilt of its two-handed sword. It glared at Haskell through its good eye. Their goblin companion stood. It peered through the narrow slit of the chitin visor shielding its eyes from the sun. The quori pulled it down by the hem of its black chainmail. "Stay low," it said in guttural orcish, their common tongue.

The goblin slapped away the quori's hand. "Don't touch me, toad!"

"Quiet," Grig said. "How many men can you manage, goblin?"

"Enough," it said.

"Goblins are useless—not even good slaves," the quori rumbled.

The goblin captain menaced the quori with a long, oily

blade. "You cannot do this without my kind, yet you call us useless, you slime?"

"By the shit-faced gods of pestilence, quiet down. We'll all get a piece. Go gather your men," Grig said.

"The boss-boy is mine," the quori said.

"We will feast on their bones for years to come," the goblin said.

"Sure, fill your boots," Grig said. It didn't matter who killed who—he would get revenge. And soon.

* * *

Hambur passed through his townhouse's door, tracking dry mud into the tiled foyer. "I have been knee-deep in filthy peasants for too long," he griped, tossing his outerwear at Kerk.

"You do make such a mess, father," Hiam said, picking his way around the mud.

Kerk peeked around the cloak and jacket heaped over his outstretched arms. "It is nice to be home, Master Hiam."

"Never mind the boy—brandy, in my sitting room." Hambur plodded down the wood-panelled hall.

"Best hop to it," Hiam said, handing his cloak and gloves to Kerk.

Hambur went into the sitting room, where he perched on a chair. He fought against his belly to reach his boots. Where was that other footman? Hiam leaned in the doorway. "Help me off with these, boy."

Hiam visibly balked. "I'll fetch someone."

"Disobedient... child," Hambur groaned as he released a foot from its sweaty prison. He threw it into the doorway. "You aren't too old to turn over my knee."

"To have Zinzi turn me over his knee, I think you mean. I will be certain to tell him when we return." Hiam dodged Hambur's second boot. Kerk clutched a silver tray laden with crystal as he evaded the errant footwear.

Hambur sighed and tried to catch his breath. Zinzi wasn't the sort of tyrant Hiam needed—too soft—but the man was damned efficient. Hambur settled into his favourite armchair. He gestured with both hands to Kerk, who hurried forward to pour him a large glass. Hambur gulped down the smooth, restorative brandy—its burn welcome in the chilly air. "Close that damn window, would you?"

"Flint wishes to know what you would like for dinner, Master," Kerk said, shutting the window.

"Gods, I need proper food. I must have dropped a stone in two days. Pork for dinner and eggs and rashers for breakfast," Hambur said.

"I think I shall retire," Hiam said.

Hambur scowled. When the boy "retired," it was to slum it in town. The fool was going to get robbed, or worse. "Stay out of that blasted den of thieves. You are a man of breeding. Cavorting with gamblers and prostitutes..."

"Perish the thought," Hiam said, withdrawing into the hallway.

Kerk followed him out and shut the door.

Hambur slouched in his chair with his glass on his stomach. It was good to be home.

"I wouldn't be surprised if they poisoned that brandy," Ferd said.

Hambur rocked out of his chair with surprising agility, glass still in hand. "Where the devil did you come from?"

Ferd was casually examining a bauble on the desk. "Here an' there."

"Get out of my house, or I shall summon—"

"The Watch?" Ferd grinned.

Blasted imp. What did he want now? Although, maybe… "You have another shipment? The peasants rob me blind with bread alone. Timber. Plows. It is endless." Hambur ran his hand over his bald, sweaty head.

"Nope, the last consignment fell through."

Hambur downed his brandy. He could not afford more excuses. "Then get another."

"Not so easy. See, that Haskell was the last consignment."

Hambur waved his hands. He exchanged his glass for the decanter. "I do not wish to hear it—that is your affair, I merely—"

"Yeah, and I *merely*. Merely don't count fer nuthing' to the hangman. Treason's treason."

Treason? Nothing he had done amounted to a capitol offence. He merely—only—passed on goods; where they came from was not his concern. Ferd was a Watchman. Doing business with a Watchman was inherently reputable. Ferd's hard, ebony gaze seemed to bore right through Hambur. He drank from the decanter. "What do you intend?"

"Time's up fer Owain. Ye'll hear about it soon enough—old Lunver's positively frothin' at the mouth. Now's yer time. Get yer friends together and make sure me name's put forward as replacement."

Hambur nodded. "Easy as that?"

"Easy as that," Ferd repeated. "Then ye and me can work on getting' ourselves paid fer our trouble."

Hambur growled appreciatively. That part sounded just fine.

May 1

Chapter XLIV—May Day

Haskell mopped his brow with a linen handkerchief. It was hot in the airless tent with the sun beating down outside. He was restless despite having so much to do. He sat back, laid his pen in the ledger on the folding table, and worked his shoulder and chest. Neither had fully healed. He took up a ceramic cup and sipped very passable wine. He wanted it to be dragon's milk.

He rose and tugged at his bulky, brown canvas vest: a jack of plate, or poor-man's brigandine, that had thin iron plates sewn inside. He crossed the bright carpet, stood in the mouth of the tent, and rested his hand on the hilt of a very battered short sword.

They had moved the tent between the cottages, which were spanned with low barriers of felled pines. A wattle gate in the north barricade let out onto the path to town. He wouldn't have considered raising defences in the Lane two weeks ago, but hard experience had taught him caution.

Zinzi was with a group of tenant farmers near the fields. He was directing them, leading them. Zinzi was a more certain leader than Haskell, who had so much to learn. He was grateful, really. Zinzi had put him in charge of general defence, though Haskell had left the finer details to Trin and Rast, who knew more about such things. His job was mostly paperwork. He supposed that made him a very sad marshal. Haskell, Oath-breaker's Issue, Pauper Marshal, and Clerk to the Steward of the Swinelord of Lanesford.

He chuckled grimly.

"Would you look at this sad sight," Bror said, walking through the gate. "Do you call that mess armour?"

"Disgraceful," Torg said with a smile.

Haskell grinned. "At least I match you now."

Bror crossed the yard and peeked in the tent. "You're livin' the high life out here. Where's his eminence's servant? I need a fanning."

"Oh, that duty falls to me," Haskell joked.

Rast leaned on his spear nearby. "You should've been with us in the Shadow Wood two summers back. *That* was heat. So hot the treetops burst into flame! The camp wizard said it was a devil summoned from the land of fire by the weather, if you believe that." Rast scratched his beard. "Maybe that's why they call them hot spells."

"Pull the other one," Bror said.

"I thought it was a good story," Froba said, joining them. She was actually smiling.

"Look at the little warrior out of myth—did you find that armour at the Temple?" Trin said, pulling at Froba's studded skirt straps.

"When did you lot get here?" Haskell said.

Froba pointed to a wagonload of stone being dragged uphill by a team of oxen. Good, they could start laying the manor's foundations. Corben had already brought around his wagon to help distribute the stone. With the fields fired and tilled, cottages built, and foundations mostly dug, Zinzi had made fine progress. That meant Haskell could lead their Dark-wood patrol tomorrow or the day after.

Grumzel bustled up, out of breath. "I told you to wait for me! Some companions you make."

The others ignored the wizard.

Haskell motioned them into the tent. Bror and Torg claimed Hiam's folding couch. "Better than rotting away in a dragon den, eh?" Bror said, running his hands over the fine fabric.

Haskell craved the sweet, oily substance, the want like an itch in his veins. He had a bamboo pipe in his pack, but there was no black dragon in camp; a sad fact he'd discovered yesterday. "I thought you'd spend May Day in Branthall," he said.

"Let them have Branthall, but I figured you'd have a proper bonfire built by now—when's the party?" Bror said.

"We're making it a half day. There's still too much to do," Haskell said.

Grumzel sat behind the desk and sniffed Haskell's wine; he glanced around the tent. "Where did the little thief go? Girl, fetch us some water!"

"I'll get it," Haskell said, taking up a glass and pitcher from a stand.

"Nonsense, you are captain of this company," Grumzel said.

Haskell gritted his teeth. "Zinzi has put me in charge of general defence."

"That should be *my* job," Trin said from the doorway. "It's just like you to swan in and take my post."

Bror winked at Trin. "She's got you there, lad. The nerve."

Haskell handed Grumzel his water. "You'll have it, Trin. Zinzi only gave me the post out of pity."

Torg said something saucily in Siwardian.

"Aye, the lad's notion of defence is a cook and a valet around a Darkwood fire," Bror said.

"I've got enough on my shoulders without you on my back," Haskell said.

The others made noises of mock sympathy.

"Uncouth rabble," Grumzel muttered. "When can we venture forth, Haskell? I am curious to see this dungeon of yours—its strange marble and the creatures within."

"Tomorrow or the day after," Haskell said.

"Spoil after all? I thought there might be," Bror said.

Froba came into the tent with a long, leather-wrapped object in her arms. She handed it to Haskell, who looked at her quizzically. Judging by Bror's and Torg's grins, they were in on the surprise.

"It's a present," Froba said.

He pulled open the leather wrappings to find a longsword within. It had a simple crimson belt and scabbard embossed with a ram's head, his family crest, and plain steel fittings. The hilt had a rounded pommel and a straight crossbar. "It's beautiful," he said, drawing the blade.

It was inscribed with runes. Familiar ones.

This was no copy; it was his grandfather's blade. "How?"

"I told ye not to ask," Froba said.

He stooped and pulled her into a crushing hug. She fought him at first, maybe thinking it was a prank, but settled into it. When he released her, she looked like she might cry. It struck him that she might never have been hugged, never thanked. "Thank you, Froba. I don't know how you managed it but thank you."

He unbuckled his short sword, tied on the new one, and drew it. The fittings felt different, but right. It wasn't worn and frayed by his grandfather's hand—it was his and would serve him on whatever path he chose.

Grumzel came around the desk. "Is that the Orc-breaker's sword? It is a magical blade."

"I knew it was famous, but magic?" Haskell said.

"Oh, yes, quite renowned, but see…" Grumzel clapped his hands, the sound echoing like they were in a small stone room rather than a canvas tent; he moved his palms outward over the blade, which began to glow a faint blue.

Haskell held it up, awestruck. The others clapped.

"Give us some fireworks next!" Rast said.

Grumzel scowled at them.

"You'll put it to use soon enough," Bror said. "Maybe we can accidentally take a few of Hambur's mercenaries into the Darkwood, too."

"Sorry, count us out," Rast said, tugging his beard.

"Yeah, and while you're away I'll change all the locks," Trin said with a smirk.

Work stopped at noon so the celebrations could begin. People washed and decked the cottages and themselves in greenery. They wore carnations, tulips, and lilacs as crowns or pinned to their breasts. The settlers drank and danced to a fife and a drum, weaving arm in arm in long serpentine chains or holding hands and dancing in circles.

A Lanesford girl was named May Queen and duly discharged her office by waving a smouldering wand of braided cedar and holly over a procession of cattle. They built a massive bonfire to the south and slaughtered a bullock; the smell of its roasting flesh filled the air. Everyone feasted well.

Day passed into night. The bright moon was waxing gibbous in the sky, though the bonfire cast a brighter swathe of light. Haskell had dodged a few of the tenants' daughters all day; he suspected they were engaged in a conspiracy to steal kisses. It made him miss Ko, but he knew she wasn't one to rough it in the Lane.

He spent the evening drinking, bowling, and playing darts with his friends. A few couples still danced, but things were winding down. He had to admit it: things weren't so bad, especially since Hambur had left. He hoped the bastard had found something to distract him in town, at least until he could get to the Darkwood and back. He could pay his debts and buy his freedom if they scored a proper load of spoil. He couldn't wait to get his life back.

Haskell drank more of Hambur's wine and listened to birds twitter in the cool night air. Bror stood and tossed away a bone. "Alright, let's turn in. Where do we sleep?"

Haskell frowned. Birds twittering at night? He heard several hard cracks from behind and a wet thud and groan beside him. A familiar black and white feathered shaft was protruding from Bror's belly.

Bror looked at the shaft like it was ale spilled down his shirt. "Quori?" he said, shocked. Torg leaped up and pulled Bror toward the barricade.

The music stopped. A dancer dropped to the ground as more twitters shot through the crowd. People stood and looked about, their confused shouts becoming frightened screams. High-pitched screeches came from the dark field beyond the fire.

"Goblins!" Froba shouted, pointing south; she was crouched in the grass away from the fire. Panic took the crowd. People and sheep fled in every direction, sowing confusion.

Haskell moved away from the fire. Dozens of screaming goblins were crossing the field toward them, gleefully slinging stones into the panicked mass. This would become a slaughter if he didn't act. "To arms, to the barricade!" he shouted.

Rast and Trin took up the cry as people fled around the

cottages and scrambled over the barricade. Haskell vaulted the stacked pines and drew his sword. He hunted for his helmet and drew it on.

Several mercenaries joined Trin and Rast at the south wall, along with a dozen tenants armed with axes, daggers, and swords. A few had short bows. He saw more mercenaries gathering beside the tent. Torg left Bror with Corben and Zinzi in the northwest cottage. Others fled north into the darkness.

Too few—there were too few left. No one had expected an attack so soon. Goblins hadn't been in the Lane for years. "Come on!" he shouted to the others as he joined the line.

The goblins were small, half-lit figures slinking through the grass, the firelight reflected in their eyes like advancing predators. There were so many. They slung a final whistling salvo. Stones clanged off helmets and sent a settler into the dirt. One dented Haskell's jacket, staggering him.

The goblins charged. A shrieking tide of scarlet flesh, yellow eyes, and dark leather leapt up the barricade. The defenders screamed their defiance; they hacked, stabbed, and impaled the creatures, but there were too many. Goblins surged over the wall, turning the forward line into a broiling melee. Everything became a seething mass of limbs and bodies, mail and leather, and flashing weapons. Shouts. Screams. Clashes and the sudden, ferric tang of blood.

Haskell waded in. He stabbed a goblin in the thigh, kicked another off a settler, opened a hissing creature's throat with a swipe of his sword, and rammed his blade into the armpit of another. A spear swung backward, its haft catching Haskell on the arm.

A goblin disembowelled a man with its sword. Haskell kicked it against a handcart and Rast gutted it with his spear. Torg threw himself at the goblins, heedless of danger, with a long dagger in one hand and an axe in the other. His ring mail turned a goblin spear as he split open a goblin's head. They could beat them, if only—

Shrieks drew Haskell's attention to the left. He stumbled back and turned. Goblins were mounting the east barricade with slings in their hands. The monsters were endless. Grumzel rushed forward with two mercenaries. "I'll hold this flank!" he cried.

A goblin spear thrust into Haskell's belly, its iron tip catching in his jacket, nearly winding him. He staggered, wrenched the spear free, and hacked the goblin to the ground. A line of flame erupted along the east wall, but more screaming came from his right. He stole a glance and his stomach fell. Two quori towered over a group of men and women, their huge swords rising and falling in crimson arcs.

Haskell lurched toward them. He punched a goblin, hopped the tent's guide wires, and charged. The quori-boss pointed at Haskell and screeched a challenge. Their swords met with a mighty clash. They wrestled with naked steel, pushing and pulling, their blades angling, tips seeking as they circled each other on ground littered with the dead and dying.

Froba fell back as the goblins crashed into the barricade. She whirled her sling overhead, waiting for an opening. A cottar went down, pierced by two goblin swords. Trin stabbed with her spear, mechanically, again and again, like she was hoeing a field. Haskell stepped in, slashing and stabbing with his massive sword.

Rast ran one through but lost his spear. Two goblins leapt on him; he threw them off with a roar and stabbed them with his dagger. A goblin stumbled behind him and raised its sword. Froba let fly—her bullet shot into its skull, dropping it like a rag doll.

She readied another stone, remembering to breathe.

More goblins hopped onto the east barricade, but Grumzel blocked her shot. He flung open a scroll in his right hand, the parchment fluttering in an invisible wind, and wove quick signs with his left. The scroll's runes and formulae glowed like blue fire. He drew a cascading arc of liquid flame out of the parchment and flung it onto the barricade; it clung to wood, armour, and flesh, setting everything alight. The goblins blistered and flung themselves screeching to the ground.

Screams from behind snapped her out of her reverie. She turned. Two massive quori with blades as long as her were butchering men and women. She set her sling whirling and put a stone into one of the huge creatures. It went back against the wall and slid down. Haskell locked swords with the grey-snouted quori and drew it off into single combat. She reloaded.

Then she saw him: Grig. Of course he was here—a ghoul feeding on the wounded and the dead. He crept up on a man, slit his throat, and cut away his victim's purse.

This was her chance to make things right; to secure a better future for herself and her friends. She sent a bullet at Grig, but it went low, skipped off the ground, and hammered his left side. He twisted into the pine wall. Looking over, he caught sight of her and snarled. He vaulted the barricade before she could fire again.

She rushed through the gate and came around the northwest cottage. Grig was gone. She heard a splash in the pines below, their tops lit by flickering flames. She crept halfway down the slope and peered into the darkness, but it was no good; deep, jittery shadows obscured everything but the reflective creek. "I know yer down there!" she shouted, her sling singing overhead.

"Wrong," Grig said from behind.

Froba turned as he stabbed her with a long knife. The blade stuck in her cuirass below her collar bone. She stumbled back and he kicked her in the chest. Froba sailed out and down, landing on her left shoulder and tumbling into the icy stream. Her left elbow struck a rock, numbing her forearm.

She shot up and was spluttering and wiping her eyes when Grig barreled into her. She went back onto the stony shore and Grig was on her, his fingers around her throat and thumbs crushing her windpipe. His bloodshot eyes were wide and jagged teeth gritted in a rictus of murderous glee. She felt her eyes bulge and face swell. She kicked under the cold water, but her sandals only dug trenches in the streambed. She clawed at his scabbed face, but his arms were too long, so she dug her nails into his hands. He didn't register the pain.

"You want it, little sow?" he growled.

Froba arched her back, her hip grinding into Grig's erection, and threw her good hand under the cold water. She reached under her cuirass and grasped the dagger at the small of her back. She brought the blade out of the water and plunged it into Grig's thigh.

He howled and stood while clutching his leg. Froba clung to the hilt as it slid from his flesh. She pushed herself up and drove the sharp metal into his groin. Grig gasped and clasped his ruined manhood. He stumbled back through the water. Froba followed, choking, her vision full of black spots. She stumbled to her knees. Eyes, neck, heart, liver, groin—Winifred's training flashed through her mind. Her bullet had torn open Grig's leather jerkin; with a hoarse shriek, she drove her dagger through it and into his left side.

Grig pushed her head, slipped, and fell onto the bank with her dagger in his side. He cried out pitifully, his face pale and sweaty as he gasped through blueing lips. He scraped weakly at the mud and stones, his struggles lit by the fires above.

Froba staggered up and stood over him, her body heaving with each wheezing breath; water dripped from her sodden clothes and off her fingers into the creek. "Ye got nuthin' t'say now, huh?" she croaked.

He did not. For Grig heard nothing and breathed no more.

Haskell gripped his sword in both hands as the quori's blade slid down his. He angled his blade at its grinning face, but the quori pressed forward, levering the edge of its sword at Haskell's neck. He stepped right and withdrew, the quori's blade slashing his arm. Lang had drilled him hard, but he was no match for the quori.

It cackled and tracked Haskell's every move with its sword. "Yoo still a bad claan-boss," it goaded.

The battle raged in every direction. It would all be over in minutes. There was no one to help him, no potion to save him. "We're no longer friends?" he said, stepping back and glancing furtively at the ground. Circling, he backed himself into the northwest corner, where cottage met barricade. This was it, he had nowhere to go. The quori grinned and leaned in to finish him off.

Haskell sprang forward with a one-handed thrust, his blade shooting forward with dramatically increased reach. The quori jerked back and parried, tripping on a corpse of its own making. Where Haskell had maneuvered it.

He barrelled into the quori, and they both went down. He smashed its face with his pommel, rose, and reversed his blade. He stabbed down furiously; his sword squeaked to a halt in the quori's armour, the tip piercing its belly. The quori screamed and swiped upward, ringing Haskell's helmet. He fell sideways. It hacked Haskell's side and back as it rose, keeping him off balance. His armour buckled but held.

The creature, dripping blood and clutching its belly,

stabbed as Haskell spun in a wild swing. The force of Haskell's attack drove the tip of its sword through the armour over his heart. The quori's sword and grinning, severed head fell into the dirt. Haskell fell forward. Blood dripped into the dust through his perforated armour. The wound was deep, but not deep enough. It had taken everything, but he had won.

Was it enough? He was in a hellscape bathed in orange light and wreathed in black smoke, out of which shrieking, impish goblins leapt. The dead littered the ground. The tent had collapsed and caught fire. The southeast cottage was a column of smoke and flame, dancing and twisting like a fiery ifrit urging them to greater violence.

It took all his will, but he drew himself upright. He stumbled south, where the hard pack was churned into a black morass. Everywhere, men, women, and goblins wrestled or lay dead on the ground.

Three huge goblins mounted the barricade, their cruel grins lit by fire. The largest wore black chainmail and had a glimmering, jewelled medallion around its neck. It came down from the log and caved in a cottar's head with its spiked mace. One of its guards rushed at Trin's back as she wrenched her bloody sword out of a goblin on the ground.

Haskell went forward and tried to raise his sword, but his blood-slicked arm burned, its muscles torn and used up. Froba staggered in front of him and stabbed the guard in the side, but her dagger caught in its leather armour. It threw her into Trin, and they both went down.

Haskell lumbered ahead, but too slowly. He slashed the goblin's neck as its morning star hammered Froba's back. He bowled the goblin over. It fell where Torg was wrestling the goblin captain. Haskell rammed his blade through the captain's snarling face, pinning its head to the log barricade.

Trin hauled Rast out of a pile of bodies beside Haskell. She shook and shouted at the pale, bloody man, but he didn't stir. A twittering stone rang Haskell's helmet. He fell against the barricade. His helmet tumbled onto goblin corpses piled on the other side.

That was it; his strength was gone.

He gripped the trunk's rough, sticky bark and took long, ragged breaths. A hot breeze tousled his sweaty hair. A stone embedded in the wood near his hand, another ricocheted up into the air. A cohort of goblins had gathered to the southeast to pepper the survivors with stones. A few cottars with bows fired arrows at them over the barricade, but they were outnumbered.

Haskell prayed. Not to any particular god, he simply looked into the smoke-filled sky and asked for deliverance.

He was answered by a bright star in the distance. It was a shooting star, one that flew over the field beyond the bonfire. It was held aloft by a warrior in white. She led others on swift horses as they smashed into the goblins.

Salvation had come.

May 2

Chapter XLV—The Living and the Dead

It was gloomy in the catacombs. Froba was on her back, the flat stone slab strangely warm through her armour. She stared at a vaulted ceiling hewn from rough, black stone. It reminded her of the dungeon. Bones filled the niches around her.

I'm dead, she thought.

"What do you know 'bout it?" Orod said.

Froba turned her head. Orod was beside her.

"I was wonderin' when ye'd show up," she said.

"Wasn't easy. It's cold underground."

"Is that where I'm at?" she asked.

"Why'd you abandon me?"

"Quit moanin'. Orod th'Complainer, even after yer dead."

"It's your fault."

Froba looked back at the vaulted ceiling. "Don't matter seein' as I'm dead too."

Orod held a blood-crusted gold piece in her face. "This ain't mine. I never wanted it." He jammed the coin into her mouth; she tasted its metallic tang and choked. Orod was suddenly on her with both hands over her mouth, his knees digging into her chest.

She tried to raise her arms, but they were numb; she clumsily batted his wrists. Orod's crazed eyes were red, not hazel, and his grimace was filled with jagged teeth. Like Grig's. She tried to buck him off but was so weak. Why couldn't she beat him? He was pathetic. He started making a high-pitched wail, his eyes flashing. They were yellow. A goblin's eyes.

Filled with hate.

Froba retched and gasped for air with her face in the dead grass. A woman was singing in a high, clear voice. She felt warm hands on her naked back and let out a wheezy groan as shards of glass crawled under her skin; slowly, painfully. She buried her face in the ground and screamed.

"I am filled with His fire!" Yeoma shouted, pressing her palms into Froba's shattered back. "Heal her, Lord, in Your name. Let her be cleansed and live anew!"

Haskell sat with his back against the south barricade, surrounded by goblin dead. He watched as Froba's bones knit together under her flesh. He had witnessed the miracle of the healing potion, how it had brought Trin and Corben back from the brink, but its liquid had not contained Yeoma's zealous fervor.

Yeoma stood, a look of ecstasy on her face. She took up her silvered hammer and kissed it. "By my hand are the bones of the righteous remade and the wicked broken." She turned, looking through Haskell like she was blind. "Are you ready to receive His light?"

Haskell pressed the wound over his heart and nodded.

* * *

They had won, but the cost was high. Thirty casualties: eighteen killed, twelve wounded, seven grievously. He hadn't been able to walk without tripping on corpses. They raked the southeast cottage into a pyre and dug a pit for their dead. Wolves howled nearby, drawn by viscera steaming in the cool night air. The settlement was ringed with glowing, predatory eyes for a second time. With the goblins thrown into the field, the wolves didn't lack for fodder.

Haskell sat in the wagon beside Corben. Froba had her head in Haskell's lap. He absently stroked her matted hair with one hand and held the goblin captain's medallion in the other. They had found Lanesford sovereigns in the quori's satchels and more ancient silver in the goblins' pouches. Grig's corpse had yielded all kinds of treasure.

The wagon was part of a convoy bound for Branthall. Yeoma and Zinzi led them. The cart ahead bore corpses stacked like wood: cottars and mercenaries laid open by sword and spear; their faces split, bodies broken, and limbs hewn away. It was especially hard to look at Rast's sallow face. His cold lips would never tell another tall tale. He tried not to listen to Trin's quiet sobs behind him.

Bror, his belly healed, put his arm around Trin. "Rast was a good man, I'm sorry he's gone. You've still got us. Cold comfort, I know." Trin laughed despite her grief.

They reached Branthall as the sun rose into a joyous sky. As they snaked up the graveyard path, Haskell looked at the Keep's tower rearing above the town's formidable walls. It was a bastion that had withstood hundreds of years of war. What were his struggles compared to that?

The wagon rumbled through Southgate and Corben guided them alongside the Guild's porch; the other carts and wagons carried on up the street. The survivors clustered in the middle of the cul-de-sac. Zinzi, still on his horse, looked at them uncertainly. Yeoma, her cloak and tabard torn and bloody, spoke to him from her horse. Haskell knew her advice would be sound.

He hopped out of the wagon and retrieved a much-abused wheelbarrow from the porch. Torg and Trin threw in sacks of spoil, the bulging leather settling with a clink and jangle. Haskell untied a rope from the back of the wagon and ran it through an iron ring under the porch. He hoisted Grig's corpse like an angler's trophy. Guild-traitors netted one-hundred sovereigns a head. What was a treacherous half-orc worth?

Trin ran her hand over her close-cropped hair. "Two years Rast and me fought together, but nothing like that. Skirmishes, even an ogre once, but not like that. Goblins and quori fighting together? They were looking for us, Haskell. That was revenge."

Haskell nodded but had nothing to say. He looked away from the treasure to the Guild's bright banners. Blood for coin, his and others'. He couldn't help but think he might be ahead after this. It didn't bring him comfort.

"There they are!" a man shouted.

Haskell went for his sword. Townsfolk surged from the Treeman. "Three cheers for the defenders!" someone said, prompting a chorus of hurrahs. The crowd clustered around them. Several seized Haskell and hoisted him into the air, blood-crusted armour and all. He flailed for balance as he was tossed and jostled to shouts of his own name. He tried to get them to put him down. They didn't hear or didn't listen.

Lang, his sturdy, aging body bare, watched through the window as the throng bore Haskell into town. "Our young giant has won back the mob."

Winifred, sprawled naked on her rumpled covers, smoked and admired the view. "The fool thinks he is Brandt reborn. He has witless daring and dangerous charm."

"Ye give him too much credit. He's not as sly as you," Lang said over his shoulder.

Winifred sent a large smoke ring into the air. "Don't be so sure. I don't need some stripling stirring things up. Not now. Besides, I told you it would end this way."

"You also told me the boy would not return from his first adventure, yet here we are."

"There's no accounting for luck."

Lang looked at people clustered in prayer before Yeoma. "Yeoma's noticed the boy. Maybe her god protects him."

Winifred sniffed. "Tell me you haven't been taken in by that zealot. Her one god is but one of many, none of whom care for humanity. That is our duty."

"Her religion's dangerous—more so with Bélon eyin' the Rus."

Winifred grunted. "I keep sending her to contested parts of the Darkwood, but she stubbornly survives."

"I'd feel guilty, but she does enjoy her work."

Winifred toyed with the bedsheets. "What about Owain. Is it true he's been carrying on with Lunver's wife?"

Lang laughed. "Yeah. Don't blame 'im, she's a right pretty lady."

"Someone went to a lot of trouble to discredit him. The mob has taken to it with gusto."

Lang gazed at her sidelong. "Uh-huh, an' I hear Ferd had a hand in it. He's more devious than ye credit him."

Winifred growled thin smoke. "Leave him to me."

Lang looked back out the window. "I have done, an' look what's come of it."

"Sacrifices will be made."

Lang nodded and looked at the people milling around Southgate. "I don't know, the mood's different. Maybe it'll take this time."

"It will end as it always does—in war, death, and strife. It has been so since before the Empire and the long years since. But we will endure."

Lang chuckled mirthlessly. "No matter the cost?"

"No matter the cost."

Lang grinned cruelly. "So says Winifred, fairest she in all the kingdoms wide."

"I have other fine qualities. Now get back in this bed you made, or have you lost your legendary vitality?"

Lang narrowed his eyes at her. "Ye smoke too much and it shows, ye ugly old thing."

She grinned around her pipe stem. "Aye, but I've got it where it counts."

Chapter XLVI—Loyalty

Haskell, rested, bathed, and his money in the Guild Bank, sat in Winifred's office. He gave her an account of the attack. She listened intently, puffing away on her pipe, and nodding now and again. The only emotion she showed was a slightly raised eyebrow over Grig's presence.

"The half-orc was go-between for goblins and quori? That is troubling," she said.

"He must have had co-conspirators. Who did he sell to? Where did the stolen goods go?"

"None have been found, but Branthall is a center of trade. Things come and go every day, into the countryside, the Steppes, other kingdoms. We will continue to investigate, of course, but I suspect you have eliminated their primary agent. That particular well has run dry—and your Guildmates will be safer for it. You should be proud."

Haskell knew this would happen. He wasn't disappointed, just tired. He shook his head.

"There is one more matter," Winifred said. "Hambur has lobbied to receive a portion of your spoils. He argues that you were under contract to him, and that his tenants and mercenaries did most of the fighting."

Haskell drummed his fingers on the arm of his chair. "Funny, I didn't see him during the battle."

"Nevertheless, he did suffer losses, as did his tenants, who stand to benefit from his reimbursement." Haskell opened his mouth to speak but she cut him off. "I will ensure that his share is modest, and that the survivors are compensated directly."

Haskell chuckled mirthlessly. What a world.

"You have been exceedingly fortunate, you know," she said.

"Do tell."

"You came here encumbered by coin and misplaced pride and have courted disaster at every turn. You should be dead."

"I've endured enough barbs already, Winifred."

"Your manner says otherwise."

Haskell bit his tongue. He had survived bitter trials and saved many lives. How much would he need to achieve for her to recognize him? Or to lose? "Can a person not change the course of their life?"

"They can, but there is no deeper meaning in that. They are not fulfilling some plan or special burden thrust upon them. The moment they see themselves as singular they are lost. They have started down a path to ruin, for them and all around them."

"Even kings?"

Winifred stoked her pipe. "Especially kings. You have bludgeoned your way through life, Haskell, but will one day meet a barrier too large even for you."

Gods, she sounded like his sister. He was no skulker, no backbiting merchant who wheedled the enemy—he met challenges head-on. Honestly. Rightly.

"I never did tell you about King Brandt's ending, did I?" she said.

"No."

"Then I shall. He was a popular man—too popular for his own good. Brave and goodly, he was also too brash and trusting. King Ered did not long survive his weak response to Grimfyrrid's predations. His counsellors murdered him, but their timing was poor. Before they could install a puppet, the people clamoured for Brandt to be king.

"Brandt needed little prompting to take the throne, and he was a great king. He cleared the Lane, expanded and fortified his borders, and earned the respect of the other kings. Lanesford prospered like never before, its grain, lumber, and wool was sought after. Farm, pasture, and mill sprang up throughout the kingdom.

"Then the barbarians invaded from the east. Brandt raised an army and met them. As always, he led from the front with his cohort. Only, secret deals had been struck, and the life of a good king was forfeited to the greed of evil men. Ered's councillors had designs on all the realms and wanted the wealth and power Brandt had wrought.

"With the battle nearly won, Brandt met Atraxus the Barbarian Lord in single combat, which is when Brandt's cohort withdrew, save a loyal but insufficient few. With his friends slain around him, Brandt fell to despair and Atraxus' sword. But the conniving councillors proved short-sighted yet again. The barbarians rallied around their triumphant king and won the field.

"Lanesford was overrun, its farms and mills razed, livestock stolen, and people slaughtered or enslaved. Forced back to ancient strongholds, our people fought a long and bitter war to drive the enemy out. So it has been for hundreds of years. Barbarians, orcs, and goblins are not our oldest enemies, that distinction falls on humanity itself.

"It has taken generations to claw our way back from the horror of the last war. Unless we are careful, the cycle will begin again. It is a delicate balance—one that requires sacrifice."

"Like Brandt and his hall," Haskell said.

"The hall was an easy sacrifice to make. Places can be rebuilt. What Brandt could not sacrifice was his foolish pride or misplaced faith in others. Some sacrifices require a piece of ourselves."

Haskell rose from his chair and started to leave. "I have lost my home, family, and legacy."

"Those are nothing. What more are you prepared to lose?"

Haskell paused in the doorway. "My life, if it comes to it."

Winifred glared at him over her pipe.

"Boy, dying is the easiest thing of all."

* * *

Froba started awake. She had been afraid to sleep, the memory of her nightmare still fresh. That wasn't why she had woken this time. Ferd sat on the end of her Temple cot. She settled back on her pillows.

Her room was long and narrow and hung with religious tapestries. An open window let in a cool breeze. The cot beside her held a body covered by a sheet, she wasn't sure whose. She fished a sovereign out of her pouch and flipped it to Ferd.

He caught it but tossed it face-up on her coverlet. "Told ye that cow'd be the death o' ye."

She looked from King Ferd's minted visage on the blanket to her Ferd's scarred face. He had changed. Ferd was acting more like a big brother—she imagined, never having had one. It was confusing and made her feel an odd sense of guilt.

"Why ye actin' so weird?" she said.

"Yer a mouthy little bitch, so I guess yer fine. I told ye

before—yer a player now, so play. I saw Grig strung up at the Guild. What went on out there?"

"He… nearly throttled me, only I knifed 'im."

Ferd laughed. "Grig always liked 'em young, the worm. Ye did for him?"

She nodded.

"No one got to 'im before ye?"

Froba shook her head. "Haskell don't know nuthin'—ye can lay off him now." Stupid. She shouldn't have said it like that. She was tired.

Ferd mussed her hair. "Little assassin, yer a keeper."

Froba's stomach churned at the praise. She didn't know how to take all this warmth and affection. "Shut up."

"Ye gonna be up and about tomorrow?"

Froba nodded. "Yeah, why?"

"Oh, I got a spot o' business lined up, only I need ye to keep that old Winifred busy. Can ye handle it?"

Froba chewed her lip. So that's why he was here. "I dunno, she's tricky, but I can go see her. When?"

"First thing tomorrow. I got things planned—just keep her in the Guild."

Dirk came in and went to the cot beside hers. He hesitated before pulling back the cover. Luna lay beneath. She was washed, her hair brushed, and hands laid on her breast. She looked almost beautiful, nothing like the sad creature she had been in the end. Froba wondered when the dragon had gotten her. Dirk took off his hood and gazed at her tenderly. Was he crying?

"Where'd ye find her?" he asked without looking over.

"Some slob found her in an alley near the Den. Rats had been at 'er," Ferd said.

Dirk covered his face with his hood. He was crying. What the hells was going on with everyone? Ferd being nice, Dirk sobbing like a little baby. He'd gone around with Luna some-times, but this?

"How'd she die?" she asked.

"Dunno. Dragon probably done her in," Ferd said.

"Did ye do it?" Dirk croaked.

Froba frowned—did who do what?

"What?" Ferd said coldly.

Dirk looked at Luna. "Did ye off her to save yer hide?"

Ferd sprang up and grabbed Dirk's frayed tunic in both hands. "Say that again an' I'll do *ye*, ye slime. The bitch did herself in—not me, not nobody else. She was a dragon whore ye paid to suck yer filthy cock, so don't go soft on me now, me chum." He threw Dirk off and stalked to the doorway, turning and flashing Froba a smile. "Ye did good, kid."

He slipped into the hall.

Froba shivered. She looked at the gold in her lap. The old Ferd would have beaten her to take it; this new Ferd had thrown it away like it was nothing. She tucked the sovereign in her pouch and pulled the blanket up to her nose. Dirk snuf-fled and coughed nearby.

If she was doing so good, why did everything feel so wrong?

* * *

Dirk entered his room over the Cock, a metal bed-warmer and rushlight in hand. He was exhausted. Ferd had been on him to move fresh goods from the Keep to Hambur's wagons. The blue hog hadn't shut up the whole time. Why Ferd took up with that bloody merchant was beyond him. He closed the door and jumped. "Gods!"

Winifred was perched on his footboard. The faint light of his rushes barely illuminated her craggy face. The coal of her pipe glowed as she drew on it, the crinkle of burning tobacco loud in the quiet room.

"Guild Mistress—ye scared me near to death."

"Indeed." Winifred exhaled a cloud of smoke, the vapour creeping throughout the room.

"T'what do I owe th'honor?" he said.

"Business," she replied.

"Happy to do a job fer ye." What did she want with him? Nothing good, he was sure.

"I have questions about this Darkwood business," she said.

"The boy's dungeon?" he said innocently. Did she know what Ferd was up to?

Winifred narrowed her eyes. "Grig."

"The half-orc? He was in on that goblin business in the Lane, wasn't he?"

Winifred smiled and puffed smoke from her nostrils. "Half the truth, as we both know."

"Not sure I know what ye mean," Dirk said nervously. He went to the bedside, keeping the old woman out of his blind spot. He set the pan and rush light on the trunk with a trembling hand. What was the bitch on to? He wasn't going to hang—not for Ferd, not for anybody.

"Who else was involved?" she asked over her shoulder.

Dirk straightened and put his hands on his hips, easing his right hand over the hilt of his dagger. He checked Winifred's faint reflection in the window. "Just ol' Luna, but she's out o' the picture," he said, a frog catching in his throat. He was sure Ferd had poisoned her.

Winifred sighed. "No one else?"

Dirk half-turned and slowly drew his dagger. "What—" his next word was an incoherent gurgle. Winifred's serpent-handled dagger had severed his neck from jugular to larynx in a neat, curving line. She hadn't even turned around. Blood jetted onto the wall and door. He grabbed his neck and tottered into the wall, sliding onto his rear.

Winifred stood and slid her dagger back into its sheath. She drew on her pipe, filling the room with smoke. She stared dispassionately at Dirk as he tried to mouth a curse. His vision began to tunnel. She crouched and leaned forward.

The room went dark.

Whether due to unconsciousness or the rushlight going out, he would never know.

May 3

Chapter XLVII—Lair

Froba pushed open the heavy panelled door and peeked into Winifred's gloomy office. The fire had burned low, and the window's heavy shutter was drawn and barred. She crept over the worn carpet and around the desk. The spicy scent of tobacco was overwhelming.

Winifred's chair was carved with scales and its hand rests were dragon claws. The very top—the dragon itself—glared down at her through eyes of darkest garnet. The pile of cushions—blue, red, and black with gold and silver embellishments—looked as ancient as Winifred and as threadbare as the carpet.

She climbed onto the chair, wincing at the stabbing pain in her back. What good was healing if it left you all weak and sore? She looked at a thick tome open on the desk. Paragraphs were scrawled down its pages. She couldn't read the spidery handwriting but knew that each was a quester agreeing to abide by the rules of the Guild. Froba put her finger on one of the most recent entries, where she had scrawled her "X" in black ink. Several others had joined in the days since. She wondered which signature was Haskell's.

Some entries had been crossed out with heavy, deliberate strokes. She paged back through the tome, the number of questers struck from the record increasing as she went. Four pages back, the dead began to outnumber the living; at six pages, the living were hedged in by the dead.

"The cost is high in an endless war," Winifred said from the doorway. She was drinking from a battered tin cup.

"But we've won. That's what people say."

"People are fools, especially those in my guild. They quest only for death."

Froba frowned, confused. "I wanted to ask ye 'bout Ferd."

"You're a quester now. You needn't worry about him."

"Yeah, well, he don't know that. An' that business in the woods with Grig, Ferd's man—"

"The boy's affairs do not concern me," Winifred snapped. Had she meant Ferd or Haskell? Winifred crossed the room and stepped onto a stool along the wall. Reaching up on her tiptoes, she took a beaten gold medallion from its shelf. She stepped down and wandered to the desk while examining the treasure. She tossed it at Froba. "Do you know what this is?"

Froba caught it and sat heavily on the cushions. She turned the medallion over in her hands. Its gold had been beaten into knotted lines framing a smooth drop-shaped ruby. It was rough work—old. "Is it magic?"

"An important question. It is the famed Amulet of Ailbhe. Men sought it for centuries, chasing rumour and scouring crypts for any trace. Hundreds quested for what you hold in your hands. Many died in the process."

"Who found it?"

Winifred stood beside her, cup in hand. "I had that honour."

"What's it do?"

"Nothing."

"What ya mean, nuthin'? It's gotta be magic. Why else would all them 'venturers die fer it?"

"I told you—because they are fools."

"That's stupid." The medallion looked less impressive now, an old trinket to melt down and its smooth stone recut.

"As I said."

"Why be Guild Mistress if ye don't like 'venturers?"

"We all serve our purpose."

"But without us, all them monsters would burn th'kingdoms."

"True. If not goblins, then orcs, if not orcs, ogres and trolls, or troglodytes, barbarians, or dwarves. And when we are through with them, we fight each other."

"It's gotta end sometime."

"It never ends, child."

Froba tossed the amulet onto the book of corpses. A Guild footman knocked and stepped into the office. He looked nervous.

"Word just arrived, Guild Mistress. The Council is sitting without you."

Winifred narrowed her eyes at Froba. It was like she could read minds. "Do you know anything about this?"

"No," she said, looking away. She hadn't done anything wrong, just talk. That didn't make her feel any less guilty.

* * *

"Keep up!" Winifred snapped as they bustled up Main Street, the old woman's tight white curls bouncing and medallion buffeting her chest. She and Froba pushed their way through a large and boisterous crowd that seemed to block the street with deliberate timing.

"How can someone so old move so quick?" Froba wheezed. Her left lung felt full of needles.

"One must be quick to make it in Branthall."

Gus the Beggar seized Winifred's shoulders in his linen-wrapped hands, his boozy breath wafting over her. "Spare a sovereign fer one o' yer auld boys?"

Winifred kneed him in the groin and pitched him into the gutter. "Ferd," she growled.

They passed into the Market, forced to weave between dancers and drunks to reach the Keep. A small knot of rabid-looking men and women were in front of the gate, all shouting.

"The Lane for Lanesford, Swits for the South!"

"Out with Owain!"

Winifred drew herself up and eyed the Keep like she was about to throw it down. "He's outdone himself this time. Follow me and keep quiet."

Froba followed, looking up at the soaring tower as they passed through iron-studded doors. Two guards came to attention with a scrape of halberds. Froba and Winifred crossed the Keep's inner courtyard and hurried up a narrow, winding stair. They bustled along a heavy stone balustrade along a gallery over the main hall and up another treacherous, corkscrewing stair. Even this far in, they could hear the mob chanting outside.

Froba was nearly doubled over by the time they reached a set of heavy oak doors. Twin dragons were carved on them; their long, serpentine bodies looped in and out to heads that roared at one another across the astragal bar. Their front claws gripped the base of long, iron door handles, one of which turned, and the door was thrown open.

Captain Owain swept from the room, nearly colliding with Winifred. His crimson cloak swept around him as he jolted to a halt. Owain and Winifred exchanged the briefest of glances, hers a squint, his a glower, before he strode down the hall. Winifred crossed the threshold and glared around the Council

Chamber, her eyes emerald fire. Hambur stepped back and clutched his gold chains.

Stieg turned in his high seat. "You are late, Winifred."

"I just received word and was waylaid in the street," Winifred threw Hambur a look that would wither steel. She sat beside Griswold, who whispered in her ear.

Froba stepped inside but stayed by the door. Ferd stood across the room. He had a Cheshire grin on his face and a silver medallion on his shabby black cuirass. Winifred scowled at him, which only broadened his smile.

"I see Owain has been replaced without my counsel," Winifred said.

"Owain admitted his guilt and stepped down willingly. Over half the Council backed Ferd to replace him."

Froba chewed her lip. Ferd had done it. She didn't think he would pull it off. Ferd was Ferd, not some highborn lordling. He didn't fit in fancy chambers like this.

The Council filed out, though Ferd lingered by the door. He waggled his eyebrows at Froba. She didn't care for this new Ferd at all.

Winifred sat back and took a long breath. "This is a mistake, Stieg."

"Perhaps, but Ferd knows the people, particularly the questers and lower sorts. That could prove useful if he's properly guided."

"He is unfit. I thought I had made that clear," Winifred said.

Stieg rose. "Unfit or unwanted?" Winifred didn't answer. "We shall see," he said, leaving the chamber.

Froba watched Winifred sitting at the big, empty table. For the first time she looked small. She rose and shuffled to the wide doorway.

Ferd lounged against the jamb with a look of triumph in

his obsidian eyes.

"Mother," he said.

Winifred fixed him with her emerald glare.

"Son," she replied coldly.

Chapter XLVIII—The End

Haskell ducked out of the Guild Bank, under the porch, and stepped into a light sun shower. He tucked the bank receipt and a handful of coins into his pouch. His companions' shares left him with precious little, and the Guild put two-thirds of that toward his fines. A sizeable chunk had also gone to pay his debt to Ferd. The rest was for living and healing expenses. That left a few talents for him and Ko.

He ran a hand through his shaggy hair. He would need Zinzi's advice on how to budget. There had to be savings somewhere.

He crossed the cul-de-sac. Some townsfolk patted him on the back and called him a hero. They offered to buy him drinks, but he politely declined. His head was full of costs and figures that did nothing for his darkening mood. He stood in front of Southgate and looked at the Treeman's chipped green door.

He had a mad craving for black dragon's numbing smoke. He glanced up Main Street and listened to the inn's sign swaying in the breeze. He had enough for one ball of resin. He was so sore and tired, his right arm ached and his back and chest burned.

He bit his cheek and went into the Treeman. His friends were crammed around a table near the front of the room. Flint, Zinzi, and Hiam were there as well.

"I see Hambur finally drove you out," Haskell said.

"The man of the hour," Hiam cheered.

"There's the rascal," Bror said, his arm around Torg. They raised their tankards. Corben nodded gruffly, though Haskell detected a faint smile at the corners of his lips. Trin, dressed in cobalt blue brigandine, flashed her checkerboard smile. Froba smirked and dusted off a stool at the end of the table.

Ko wrapped an arm around Haskell and pressed a mug into his hand. "Welcome back, lover."

"I made you a special dish!" Flint announced to the room.

Haskell frowned. "What's the occasion?"

Zinzi stood. "Happiest of belated birthdays, Haskell."

The common room filled with many happy birthdays and many more disparaging remarks about his age. Flint drew a cloth off an ornate pie, its corners in the likeness of cottages and the middle diagonally bisected. One side was red-glazed with a ram's head of crispy bacon, the other golden with a bacon sword. There was much adulation from the crowd.

Haskell chafed his hands. "What's inside?"

"Mutton in the middle and pheasant in the cottages, all spiced with the courage of its defenders—the secret of which I'll take to my grave!"

Hiam raised his tankard. "Here's to your victor—"

"Shh—no!" Haskell interjected.

Hiam lowered his tankard and regarded the steely-eyed adventurers around him. "Ah… to what then shall we toast?"

Haskell sighed and raised his drink, looking at the empty places set for Rast, Orod, and many others throughout the room. "To fine friends and the worthy dead."

His sentiments were repeated by all.

"I am certain a bard will weave you a song after hearing of your deeds," Hiam said.

Grumzel crossed his arms. "We would have been overrun without my magicks."

"And half the settlement would still be standin'," Bror said to everyone's amusement.

"It was fabulous magic, Grumzel. I only wish I had a better view," Haskell said; Grumzel waggled his head happily and drank. "Dish us up some of that, Flint," Haskell said, sitting down with Ko.

He looked at the cheerful band of misfits around the table and thought about his lost family, legacy, and pride. He found he no longer cared. A cold hand that had been squeezing his heart loosened its grip just a little. He grinned at Froba, who was eating a corner of pastry.

Haskell banged the table. "Wait, everyone—Froba hasn't been seasoned!"

People moaned and murmured disapprovingly. Tables were bludgeoned by calloused fists and the smoky air filled with cries for more ale. Haskell caught Froba before she could bolt and shoved a tankard into her hand. Trin motioned for her to drink. Drink she did, as did they all.

Like there was no tomorrow.

EPILOGUE

I t was cold underground and nighttime was the hardest.
At least, he thought of it as night. It was impossible to
tell time without the sky.

Orod lay on the floor of the hut he had slaved to build,
huddled with his tormentors under a giant rat's pelt. He was
glad to be sheltered from the drafty chamber, even if goblins
stank like warm meat.

Like them, Orod could see in the dark. He watched the
cool blue heat of their breath eject from mottled red, orange,
and green mouths and faces. Night underground was a bright
painting on a midnight blue canvas. He called it Darksight. It
was a secret he had kept from Froba, from his mother, even.
It was something just for him. Above ground. Down here he
was just another worker struggling against the cold and the
dark.

He ran his fingers over the ragged, tender scars across his
neck. After the battle, he had awakened on a bed of moss in a
stone room lit by a golden lamp. The goblin shaman had put
a cold, mucky poultice on his burning throat, wrapped it, and
prayed over him for what felt like days. It had given him time
to think about why the others hadn't come for him. Were they
killed, lost in the dungeon, or did they think him dead? Did
they even care?

He didn't think Froba would leave him. She saved him

from the Tanners, after all. But he was stuck underground, and she probably had all kinds of treasure now. They all probably thought of him as a useless mullorc, anyway, one who was probably eaten by goblins. Would he risk his life in their place?

These thoughts had gone around and around in his head until he didn't know what to believe. Then the goblin warriors had come, and he had no time to think. They whipped him down endless stone corridors and up stairways back to the start—the huge circular chamber in which he had fallen. Where they put him to work.

"Day" underground was any sort of light, a precious thing. The goblins worshiped it—praying together when the communal brazier was lit and blessing each torch and candle. Light meant warmth and colour, clear sight, and reading each other's faces. It was celebrated more than the summer above. Still, like the world above, light meant work; and the goblins worked him hard.

For days he laid wooden duckboards and platforms on stone footings. He raised frames of sticks, spanned them with bones—human, goblin, and what else, he couldn't tell—and packed them with fleshy mushroom paste to form walls. It was hard, long work and the goblins were brutal, but the work kept him warm.

The goblins whipped, beat, and cursed him until they had built a little hamlet in the chamber. Its lanes were duckboards, the homes squat, round mushroom huts, and its fields were dirt mounds in the central pool. The trickle that fed the pool was their stream, the clay jugs it filled were their fountains. They even had livestock: rats, grubs, and beetles. It was theirs but, in a way, also his. He had worked beside them and built everything with his own hands.

Then the big goblin lord with the jeweled amulet and dark

mail had come. His bodyguards were huge, and his gang bristled with weapons. The lord addressed Orod's band, who seemed hesitant. Orod couldn't understand their words, but it seemed like the lord was shaming them—that language was universal.

His guards beat and derided the men until they relented. Some of the women took up the lord's cause and berated their mates, while others bared their teeth, pulled their braided hair, and waved snot-nosed infants in front of fathers. The men went all the same. Few returned.

Those who did were horribly wounded. Orod helped bind their stumps, set their broken bones, and cover their pierced flesh with the same poultice that had saved his life. He found himself feeling sorry for them, his captors.

After that, the goblins didn't curse or beat him quite so much. He knew he should hate them but found himself wanting to help them. Life was so strange. Lost from the world above, made a slave, and working for the creatures his mother had used to scare him into obedience, Orod felt something like belonging.

It was a new experience.

ABOUT THE AUTHOR

J.D. Mitchell is a Canadian writer of speculative fiction. His stories are informed by his historical studies and transient upbringing. The latter, while terribly angst-inducing, exposed him to a rich tapestry of people and places, as did his varied service industry jobs and a sixteen-year stint in the Public Service of Canada (but who's counting?). He lives in Ottawa, Canada with his wife and two wonderful goldfish.

Please consider leaving a review online or
sharing your thoughts via social media.

Thanks for your kind support!

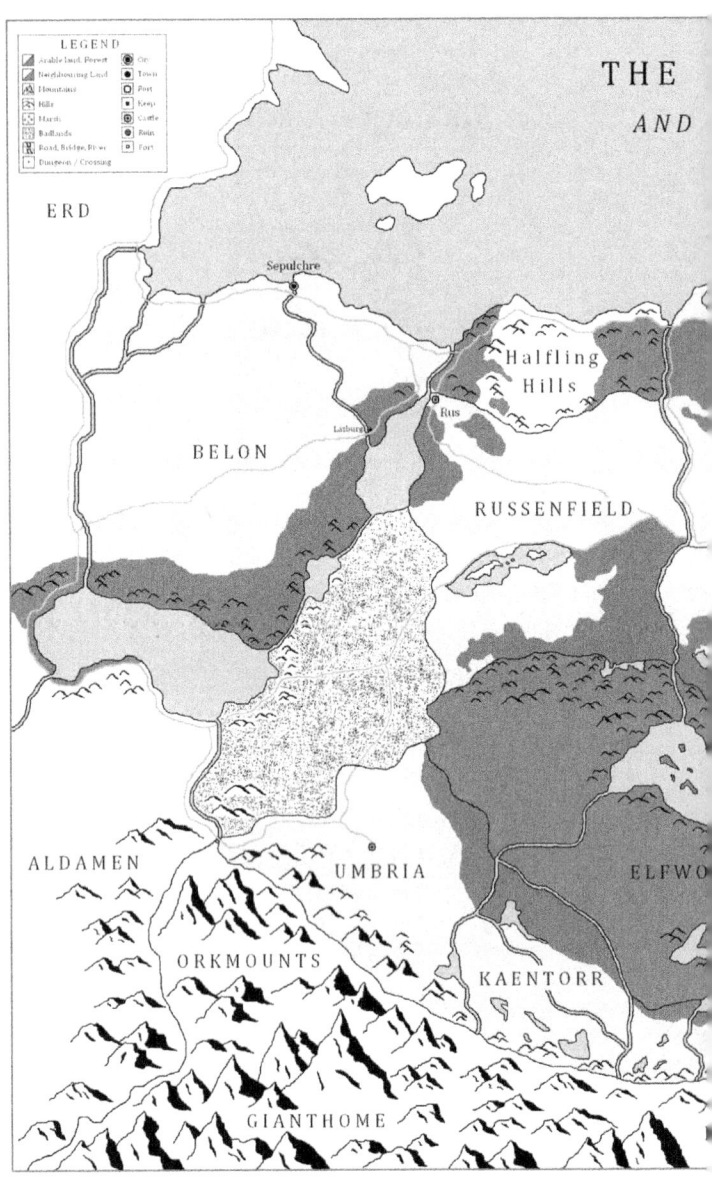

Printed in Great Britain
by Amazon

18216768R00241